Celia still couldn't make herself accept that Ty was here, in Corvallis. The man she'd once made the disastrous mistake of trusting. Arriving any minute.

You simply have to make it through this one meeting, Celia, and then he'll go away. With stern concentration, she tried to relax muscles that insisted on growing more and more rigid with dread—

There he was.

She forgot how to breathe.

He was striding down the sidewalk toward her, looking up, probably searching for the sign that said *Jana's*.

She'd anticipated that he'd look handsome. But "handsome" was something you might say about a male model in a magazine ad; it was too stiff and flat an adjective for Ty Porter. He had the kind of appeal that pulled your gaze to him, then wouldn't let you look away.

He stopped at Jana's entrance and scanned the tables. She knew the moment he spotted her because she could literally *hear* it, like a bell ringing.

He threaded his way over, looked down at her, and smiled. It was a subdued smile, but it had the same thousand-volt impact of the smiles he'd once given her in a high school ceramics classroom and then years later in Las Vegas.

Praise for Becky Wade

Books by Becky Wade

My Stubborn Heart

THE PORTER FAMILY NOVELS

Undeniably Yours
Meant to Be Mine
A Love Like Ours
Her One and Only

A BRADFORD SISTERS ROMANCE

True to You

MEANT TO BE MINE

BECKY WADE

BETHANYHOUSE
a division of Baker Publishing Group
Minneapolis, Minnesota

© 2014 by Rebecca Wade

Published by Bethany House Publishers
11400 Hampshire Avenue South
Bloomington, Minnesota 55438
www.bethanyhouse.com

Bethany House Publishers is a division of
Baker Publishing Group, Grand Rapids, Michigan

Printed in the United States of America

ISBN 978-0-7642-3089-9

Cover design by Jennifer Parker
Cover photography by Mike Habermann Photography, LLC

17 18 19 20 21 22 23   7 6 5 4 3 2 1

CHAPTER
ONE

Will you marry me?"

Celia glanced up at Ty and found him gazing down at her. His gorgeous blue eyes regarded her as if she were the most desirable woman on the planet.

"What did you just say to me?" She had to speak louder than usual to be heard above the happy din of the Las Vegas casino.

"Do you want to marry me?"

"Ty Porter, that's not funny."

"Who said I was kidding?"

"Me. I'm saying it." Their romance had only begun four days ago. Granted, they'd been the four best days of Celia's life. Because of him, she'd spent her daylight hours in a haze of bliss. She'd spent her nights thinking about him, staring up at her hotel room ceiling with eyes as round as Ping-Pong balls, too excited to sleep.

"Your turn, miss." One of the dealers at the craps

table pushed two dice toward Celia with his slim stick, bent at a ninety-degree angle at the end.

"Feeling lucky?" Ty asked.

"Yes." Ty liked her—*her!*—which made her the luckiest girl in Vegas. Their good fortune during the past two hours at the craps table hardly compared.

Celia picked up the dice and gave them a shake. The group of players gathered around the table focused their attention on her. Some called out encouragement.

"If you roll a seven," Ty said, "I vote we get married."

"You're incorrigible."

"If you roll a seven, sweet one, I'll take it as a sign. We'll get hitched tonight, and you'll be stuck with me for life." He placed all his chips on the pass line.

"Ty!"

"I've just proposed to this little lady here," he announced to the table. "If she rolls a seven, we're going to make it official."

The players hooted and hollered.

"He's just joking," Celia informed them.

Their excitement drowned out her rationality. Several players raised glasses. Others added additional chips to their bets. All heartily approved of Ty's plan. Apparently the decision to hang a lifetime commitment on the roll of two dice made perfect sense to sloshed tourists in Vegas.

Celia tossed the dice. They flew to the opposite end of the oblong table, bounced off the bumper, and skittered to a stop. A 3 and a 4.

Seven.

The table broke into an uproar.

Celia stood amid the clamor. The sight of the dice, an

unmistakable three and an unmistakable four, branded into her brain.

The dealers reached forward to dole out chips to all the players.

"You just doubled my money," Ty drawled. "Thank you kindly, Mrs. Porter."

"I'm not Mrs. Porter." Teasing tinged her voice. She didn't want to be too hard on him, not when the notion of his wanting to marry her was so outrageously flattering.

"Determined to wait until after the ceremony?" He tipped the dealer and requested a tray so he could pack up his chips. "You coming?"

"Definitely." She didn't want to tell him this, at the risk of seeming pathetic, but she'd follow him anywhere. They said their good-byes and headed toward the cashier.

"Looks like they're eager to start in on the wedding night!" one of the players called after them.

A chorus of guffaws.

"Here's to the honeymoon!"

"Congratulations on your marriage!"

"They actually think"—Celia turned and waved to their well-wishers—"we're going to get married."

"That's 'cause we are."

Once they'd cashed in their chips, they made their way to the taxi line outside the front entrance. Cool December air scented with car exhaust enveloped them. Ty held Celia's jacket for her while she shrugged into it, then wrapped his arms around her for extra warmth. He stood behind her, his front to her back, as they shuffled forward in line.

Celia checked her watch. One thirty. Any other city would have been dark and shuttered at this hour. Here, lights blazed, slot machines jangled, and people clogged the sidewalks. An older couple in sweats and fanny packs stood in front of them. A group of twenty-year-olds dressed like Kardashians stood behind them.

Celia had never felt more distanced from her regular life. Nor a greater sense of surrealism. Nor happier, thanks to him.

Ty Porter, the high school crush she'd never outgrown.

During childhood and adolescence, her father's job had relocated their family to a new city every few years. She could remember how furious she'd been at the age of fourteen when she'd been forced to move, yet again, the summer before her ninth-grade year. They'd settled in Plano, Texas. The address of their unimaginative house in their dull subdivision had dictated that she'd attend Plano East Senior High.

Celia had decided to hate it. She'd managed to stay that course until the moment when Ty Porter had taken the seat next to her in Introduction to Ceramics.

She could recall exactly how he'd looked that day: a tall, well-built sophomore with golden-brown hair and dancing blue eyes. His appearance had been good enough. But then he'd gazed at her as if he really *saw* her. He'd cracked jokes under his breath. He'd asked her advice on his coil pot.

Within two weeks, every hope and dream she'd ever had about the opposite sex had coalesced into a devoted and long-lasting infatuation with him.

"You cold?" He tightened his arms around her.

"Not a bit."

He rested his chin on the top of her head. They inched forward.

Ty'd been incredibly sweet to her during their high school years. He'd always gone out of his way to flirt with her and to make an unpretty teenager feel very pretty indeed. Despite her prayers, though, their friendship had never led to anything more serious than *Mrs. Celia Porter* doodled through her spiral-bound notebooks. Oh, he'd dated plenty. But he'd always chosen beautiful, outgoing girls his age or older. Girls Celia had envied with every drop of teenaged emotion she'd possessed.

After his graduation, Ty had enlisted in the Marines and moved away. Celia had slunk around in a cloud of despair over him that whole summer.

A year later she herself had graduated and moved to Oregon for college. Two and a half years ago she'd completed her degree and taken a job as a restaurant sous chef.

All told, she hadn't seen Ty for seven and a half years. But when her high school friend Lacey had called and informed her that Ty would be competing in bull riding in the National Finals Rodeo in Las Vegas, his name had hit her like a lightning bolt. The passage of time and distance had not squelched her affection for Ty Porter.

Celia had convinced Lacey to meet her in Vegas for a girls' weekend and bought tickets for them both to the rodeo.

She and Ty reached the front of the line. A taxi pulled up and a casino employee held open its door as they climbed into the backseat.

Ty leaned toward the driver. "We're going to get married—"

"No!" Celia burst out laughing. "We are *not* getting married."

"We want the corniest wedding chapel around. Nothing classy, you understand? Just pure Vegas—like the kind you see in movies. Do you know a place like that?"

Their driver nodded, and the cab slid into traffic.

Looking pleased with himself, Ty leaned back and extended his arm across the top of the seat.

Celia turned her upper body to face him. "You're crazy."

"Yeah," he admitted, grinning unrepentantly.

"You're joking about this wedding."

"Try me."

This kind of thing—taking a bet to the limit, following through on a dare—was not out of character for the Ty she'd known in high school. "You really want to drive to a Las Vegas wedding chapel?"

"I really do." He pushed her jacket sleeve up and trailed tiny kisses along her forearm. "You rolled a seven. Your fate is sealed."

Celia smiled, drunk on pleasurable sensation, drunk on the joy of looking at him. It was possible that Ty, however, was just plain drunk. How many drinks had he had? Hard to recall. She'd been too wrapped up in mooning over him to pay attention. Except for this wedding nonsense, he didn't *seem* drunk.

"You're adorable," he murmured into her arm, then reclined against the seat.

They stared deeply at each other.

Dark and light from the passing hotels of the strip played over his face. He had a smile that flat-out demanded a girl smile back. Eyes a shade of blue so light and bright that it stole your breath. Sandy brown hair, always a little mussed, cut by someone who knew exactly what kind of damage they were wrecking on the hearts of females everywhere.

Tonight he wore a white T-shirt under a rugged brown blazer-style jacket. He'd stuffed the front of his T-shirt into his jeans above a leather belt that didn't showcase any of the many rodeo buckles she knew he'd won.

"I can't get enough of you," he said.

In response, she tried to look sassy and chiding instead of just lovelorn.

"I can't," he insisted.

Celia had enjoyed a few pleasing dating relationships in her time. But she'd never had anyone she liked half this much say these kinds of things to her.

"You've gotten under my skin, Celia. I don't see how I'm going to go on without you." His brows lowered. "How come you're smiling? Don't you have any pity?"

"Yes, Ty. I have plenty of pity. I'm just not convinced that you deserve any."

He closed the distance between them and kissed her. "You have this way," he whispered, "of hitting me right in the heart."

Her fluttering breaths mixed with his. "I feel the same way about you."

His smell, like the Piney Woods of Texas, wrapped around her and further fogged her brain. During her years there, she hadn't really liked the state of Texas all that much. Yet—irrationally—she adored Ty, whose accent oozed Texas, who smelled like Texas, and who wore square-toed alligator cowboy boots.

"I'm crazy about you," he said.

"I'm crazy about you, too."

He gently nipped her bottom lip, then bent his head and went to work kissing her knuckles.

She'd arrived at the Vegas airport on Thursday. She and Lacey had gone to watch Ty compete in bull riding on Friday. As soon as his event had concluded, Lacey had dragged Celia, mortified and protesting, to the arena's back exit. They'd waited there until Ty had emerged. When Lacey had pulled Celia into his path, Ty had shocked her by remembering her immediately.

She'd been too overwhelmed to say much to him during that first conversation. For one thing, she'd just come off the staggering sight of him riding bulls in cowboy garb that included chaps and a hat. For another, her old crush had looked even better at the age of twenty-five than he had at eighteen.

She and Lacey had gone out to dinner that night with him and a buddy. To her astonishment, Ty had taken a swift romantic interest in her.

They'd been inseparable every waking hour since.

Lacey, like a sane person, had returned to her regular life on Sunday night as scheduled. Celia, like a crazy person, had let Ty sweet-talk her into staying in Vegas for a few extra days. She'd charged additional room nights on her credit card, let her flight home depart without her, and called her boss at the restaurant to beg for more vacation days. Her boss had given her three. Which meant she had to arrive back at work on Thursday or lose her job.

It was already late on Tuesday—nope, early on Wednesday. Her time with Ty had slipped away much too quickly.

The taxi pulled to a stop, and Ty reached for his wallet. Celia let herself onto the sidewalk. A white picket fence surrounded a complex that included a pink A-frame building in the center, a gazebo, and a rusting fairy-tale carriage harnessed to a horse statue. Sprays of plastic white roses tied with royal blue ribbon had been wired to the chapel's front door, around the horse's neck, and at the gazebo's entrance. A billboard flooded with light read *Luv Shack. Everyone's favorite 24 hour wedding chapel!*

Ty took her hand and drew her onto the Astroturf yard. A dimple dug into his cheek as he surveyed their surroundings. "Our driver knew his stuff. This is corny."

"Extremely."

"And perfect."

"You could say that."

"You're perfect. Can I say that?"

She flushed and nodded.

A bell over the front door jingled as they entered the A-frame. More pink paint, more fake roses. Deep within the building the bridal march played.

A woman of approximately one hundred and fifteen years sat behind the counter. She looked up from an issue of *Cosmopolitan* and said in a flat voice without inflection, "Welcome to the Luv Shack, home of the ninety-nine-dollar vow renewal, where all your romantic dreams come true."

"That sounds promising," Ty said.

"I'm Doris, your love event coordinator and fairy godmother. I'll be making sure that—"

"All our romantic dreams come true?" Ty smiled.

Celia bit her lip to keep from giggling. Coming here had been a fun idea after all.

"So," Doris said, gesturing to the sign behind her like

a *Price Is Right* model, "which of these enticing wishes can I grant for you tonight?"

Ty seemed to be taking it all in stride. "What do you have to offer in the way of weddings?"

Doris nodded toward the middle section of the sign. "The Luv Shack Special, the Elvis, the Country and Western, and the Deluxe."

"What's the Country and Western involve?"

"A candle-lit ceremony in our 'Don't Mess With Texas' chapel—"

"Now you're speaking my language."

"—a bouquet of five yellow roses for the bride, a yellow rose boutonniere for the groom, the minister's fee, two country songs of your choice, a keepsake frame, and a CD containing eight photographs. All for just $149.99."

"You read my mind, Doris. How'd you know that's just what I wanted?"

Doris looked back at him, deadpan. Celia knew Doris wouldn't be able to remain immune to Ty for long, and sure enough, after a few seconds her eyes crinkled and she released a dry laugh. "You're a handsome devil. I'll give you that."

"Thank you. You're easy on the eyes yourself." Ty set two hundred-dollar bills on the counter. "One Country and Western, please."

Celia recovered from her shock in time to swipe the cash off the counter before Doris could get her antique arm moving. "Excuse us for a moment?" she asked the older woman.

Doris nodded, and Celia pulled Ty to the room's corner. "Okay, Mr. Country and Western. The visit here has been entertaining. Goodness knows, I can tell you're enjoying yourself. But we've gone far enough. I don't want you to waste any money."

"Waste money? A wedding only costs $149.99, sweet one. Didn't you hear the lady? That includes a keepsake frame."

He was more than a head taller, so Celia had to reach up to place her palms on his cheeks. "Can you be serious for one second? You don't actually want to marry me here at the Luv Shack tonight."

"Yes I do."

"No you don't!"

"Yes." He took her hands in his and cradled them against his chest. His gaze, serious now, searched down to the deepest depths of her hopes. "I do. I want to marry you, Celia. Right now. Here at the Luv Shack. No joke."

All the air sailed from her lungs with a soft *oof*.

"Do you want to marry me?"

"Oh my goodness," she breathed.

"Do you?"

Yes. He was offering her a chance to make him hers forever. It was too heady to bear. Too sweet to turn down. And yet she knew she *should* turn him down for the sake of sanity and prudence. They'd been dating four days. . . .

Her thoughts lost themselves in the blue of his eyes. Time pulled.

"C'mon," he coaxed. "Let's do it. Let's do something crazy for love."

She knew for certain that she would love him forever, that she could never love anyone else the way that she loved him.

"Will you marry me, Celia?"

"Well . . ." she said, her voice tremulous. "I did, after all, roll a seven."

He laughed. "Is that a yes?"

"I . . ." She swallowed.

"Is it?"

"Yes."

He whooped, then crushed her to him in a hug.

For the next twenty minutes, Ty handled paper work and made the necessary selections. Celia stood next to him with her hand wrapped around his elbow, smiling like a jack-o'-lantern.

Right before the ceremony, Celia stepped into the restroom and confronted her reflection. Her curly hair was typically a problem for her. The dry desert air had become her ally, however, and her hair looked better than expected. She finger-combed the big brown curls that fell to her collarbones in layers only someone with a PhD in hairstyling could manage. Leaning in, she applied peach lip gloss.

I'm getting married, she thought. The excitable and daring woman in the mirror looked nothing like her. *Right now. I'm marrying Ty Porter tonight.*

She arranged the folds of the silvery dress she'd charged to her credit card that afternoon. A cross between a toga and a scarf, it tied behind her neck and draped over her body down to her shiny T-strap sandals. Like the extra hotel nights, the dress was something she couldn't technically afford.

Minutes later, she found herself walking toward Ty down the aisle of the "Don't Mess With Texas" chapel. Light from two standing candelabras at the front lit the space dimly, perhaps a blessing. Stereotypical cowboy junk hung on the walls next to decades-old portraits of country singers. Celia recognized June and Johnny Cash and Dolly Parton, but none of the others. A twangy song flowed from the speakers. The edges of her yellow roses were browning.

Celia could not believe this was happening.

If she'd had days or weeks to prepare for this wedding, she'd have changed a lot of things. But as her gaze locked on Ty, she knew wholeheartedly that she wouldn't have changed a single thing about her groom.

When she reached him, he winked at her and took hold of her hands. Tears pooled in her eyes. She loved him with every ounce of the passion she'd harbored for him at fourteen and then some.

The officiate had donned a sheriff's badge and a ten-gallon hat for the occasion. It took him no time at all to lead them through their vows.

One they'd spoken them, Celia's heart began to pound with expectation.

"I now pronounce you little lady and young buck—or, as the city slickers like to say, husband and wife."

That was it? They were married?

Ty kissed her thoroughly.

The fake sheriff picked up a camera and led them through a series of poses, each cheesier than the last. Ty down on his knee pretending a marriage proposal. Ty in the background with his chin on his fist, staring wistfully at Celia in the foreground. Ty lassoing Celia around the waist.

At some point Celia burst into hysterical laughter and couldn't locate her composure for the rest of the session. Suddenly, she could see the whole situation as

Ty did. It was brash and ridiculous, their surroundings kitschy, and all of that only made it sweeter. They were doing something wildly spontaneous. On their fiftieth wedding anniversary, they'd be able to tell their grandkids one heck of a wedding story.

The fake sheriff steered them to the gazebo outside and took some photos of Ty removing Celia's garter—challenging, since she wasn't wearing one. Then a few shots in the fairy-tale carriage, where they were encouraged to wave like royals.

When it was over, Doris presented them with their keepsake frame, a bronze plastic number with a cartoon cowboy and cowgirl smooching in one corner.

That officially concluded their nuptials.

Ty took her to his hotel and asked for an upgrade to something bridal. Then he carried her over the threshold of their room and kicked the door closed behind them.

CHAPTER
TWO

Celia's first conscious sensation upon waking the next morning: warmth. Then softness, then the faint and delicious scent of pine. That smell, Ty's smell, unrolled a movie reel of memories in her mind. The casino, the chapel, the wedding night that had followed.

Oh, the night they'd had. The pleasure of it. She murmured and smiled, drowsily reaching out for him in her half sleep.

Her arm met empty bedding. Slowly, she wedged open her eyelids.

Ty stood at the room's window, his back to her. He'd parted the heavy drapes a few feet and was peering through the gauzy under-curtains that remained. He'd pulled on his jeans. His bare feet sank into the carpet, and the skin of his chiseled upper body gleamed smooth.

All in all, an excellent view for any woman to wake up to. Celia would have been thrilled with it, except that something about Ty's stance communicated tension. Possibly his stillness. Maybe the stiffness of his shoulders.

They'd shared a night that had been earth-shattering. Magnificent. Surely, after that, he couldn't be the least bit troubled.

Could he?

There were good reasons why most people didn't tie the knot at a Las Vegas wedding chapel after four days of romance. Was it possible that those reasons were weighing heavily on him this morning? That he regretted what they'd done—

Everything's fine, Celia. Last night had been the first of thousands of nights she'd spend married to Ty. She just needed clothes. And coffee.

She eased to the side of the bed while holding the white down comforter up to her chin.

Ty turned.

"Good morning." She pushed her feet over the edge.

"Morning." His eyes were kind, but his expression remained tight. Not wholly reassuring.

She pasted on a smile. "A very good morning!" It wasn't easy to drag the comforter off the bed and use it as a shield, but she managed it with a grunt of effort. "Yes, indeed." She sidestepped to where her dress and underwear lay puddled on the floor. Once she'd retrieved them, she backed into the bathroom. "Excuse me for a moment." The comforter got caught in the door. She had to yank it inside before she could shut herself in.

She shimmied into her silver dress, then lathered her hands with hotel soap and went to work washing her face.

Ty couldn't be having second thoughts. *Not possible.* Couldn't be! So how come worry continued to rise within her?

She brushed her teeth with the provided travel toothbrush and toothpaste. Ineffectually, she batted at her curls with a brush. They'd passed the point of redemption.

When she reentered the bedroom, she found Ty standing near the foot of the bed waiting for her. He'd turned on the lamps and parted the curtains fully. Late-morning sunlight streamed into the room.

"Come here." He opened his arms.

She went into them in half a heartbeat.

His strength and heat banded around her, comforting. The scent of the soap he'd used in the shower filled her senses.

He pressed a kiss into the place where her neck met her shoulder.

See? It's fine. Thanks to their hasty wedding, she wasn't feeling as secure as most morning-after brides, that's all. "Hungry?" she asked.

"Yes."

"We can call and order breakfast from room service. I'll bet they have croissants or muffins." She knew all about his sweet tooth for breakfast pastries. "When I've saved up enough money and I have a bakery of my own, I'm going to serve you the most amazing cinnamon rolls you've ever eaten."

Over the past days they'd talked at length about her dream of owning a coffee shop and his goal of winning a world championship in bull riding. This past weekend, he'd won her heart but not the title.

He moved a lock of hair off her forehead, his eyes grave.

Anxiety rekindled within her, but Celia powered past

it. She called room service and chattered to Ty until the food came. When it arrived, she took great care arranging everything on the circular table in the room's corner. Thick linen napkins and heavy silverware. An organic vegetable omelet for her. A basket of breakfast pastries. Coffee and ice water.

After they'd settled into chairs, Ty poured the coffee while Celia tried to think of how to fill the unusual silence between them. "So . . . Doris was funny last night, wasn't she?"

"Very."

"How long do you think she's been working as a 'love event coordinator'?"

"And fairy godmother, don't forget."

"And fairy godmother."

"I don't know. A century?"

Celia held up more than her share of the conversation, reminiscing about each humorous aspect of their wedding. As they talked, she took dainty bites of her omelet. Ty set a blueberry muffin on his plate and peeled off the wrapper, but didn't eat any. Nor did he try the coffee that sat in his cup, its steam dying.

Little by little Celia's dread increased. She kept trying to make him laugh, kept waiting for him to cheer up and start acting like himself. She was used to his charm and teasing, but unaccustomed to his seriousness.

He fiddled with the muffin, breaking it into pieces, then going back through the pieces a second time, breaking and rebreaking them again.

When nothing but a mound of fine crumbs remained, Celia reached her tipping point. "Ty."

"Hmm?"

She set down her silverware and scooted her chair back a few inches. "What's the matter?"

"What do you mean?"

"I mean that something's obviously the matter with you this morning. What is it?"

He rubbed the side of his thumb against his cheek.

She waited for his answer, surrounded by the quiet sounds of traffic on the strip several stories below and a maid knocking on a door down the hall.

His aquamarine gaze bored into hers.

Celia could feel her heart laboring. Dragging in blood. Using all its strength to push blood out.

"I'm sorry, Celia."

"For?" When he didn't answer, she almost had a brain aneurism. *"For?"*

"For pressuring you into marrying me."

That sounded . . . bearable, like maybe he was upset because he believed he'd forced her into a marriage she didn't want.

"I've talked people into doing crazy things before, but never anything like this." He surged to his feet and returned to his spot at the window, his back to her. His hands raked through his hair, leaving furrows in the golden-brown strands. "This beats all."

Stories of Ty's reckless exploits had become legend at Plano East High School. He'd leapt off a cliff a hundred feet above the Brazos, because his brother said he couldn't. He'd made Ashley Sutton promise to go to the prom with him if he could jump his motorcycle over a parked car and land successfully on the other side. He'd competed in street races. He'd bungee-jumped above a canyon to raise money for the booster club. He'd lost bets and ended up having to skydive, streak across the football field in his boxer briefs, and set off a stink bomb on the principal's doorstep.

As an adult he rode bulls, for goodness' sake, a profession that could kill him any night of the week. He was daring. It was just one facet of him that she—who was ordinarily smart, safe, and not given to spur-of-the-moment weddings—appreciated.

"It's okay, Ty." Celia stood. "You didn't pressure me into marrying you last night."

"Yes I did." A pause. He swore under his breath, a sound as soft as it was vicious.

She flinched. Something was terribly wrong. Her stomach wrung like a sponge. Everything was *not* fine.

He pushed his hands through his hair again, then shook his head with what looked like self-disgust.

"Ty?" She hated the fearful tone of her voice.

He turned and faced her, his brows low over his eyes. "I wasn't thinking straight last night, which is no excuse." He flicked a hand toward the bed that loomed beside them. "I never meant for things to go this far."

"You . . . you didn't force me into marrying you, if that what's upsetting you. I made my own decision."

"Without all the facts."

"What do you mean—"

"I'm in love with someone else."

Those words. Six words. They crashed into Celia, knocking the air and life and dreams from her, stopping her heart. Silence detonated like a grenade between them.

"What?" she asked, the word little more than air.

"There's someone else."

Pain cut into her, sinking through layers of skin,

muscle, organs. She stepped back, her hands falling dumbly to her sides. Her knees had turned to liquid. They gave way, lowering her to a seated position on the end of the bed.

He loved someone else.

A few hours ago, she'd fallen asleep in his arms, filled with joy, his exhales against her temple. She'd woken up to this. The man she'd have sacrificed anything for, the man she'd *married*, telling her there was another woman. She wanted to rewind time. A sickening wave of dizziness broke within her. She pressed her hands against her stomach and stared up at him.

He did not come near. "I have a girlfriend at home in Holley. We've been dating for two years."

Her pulse raced frantically, like it was trying to escape.

"Before I came on this trip, we talked about marriage. I've been wanting to marry her for a while now, but she told me she wasn't ready. We fought."

"And broke up?"

He set his jaw.

"No?" She could hear her own hysteria rising. "You didn't break up? You're still . . . dating her?"

"No. During our fight we did break up, but it was a heat-of-the-moment thing. I don't think either of us thought it would last."

She wanted to slap him, shake him, but the agony inside held her motionless. "Why didn't you tell me about her that first night outside the arena?"

He made no reply.

"Because she hurt you. Is that it?"

"She hurt me."

"She injured your pride when she told you she wasn't

ready to marry you. Then you came to Vegas and found me waiting here, eager to boost your ego, more than willing to marry you." She saw the situation with new and horrifying clarity. The end of his relationship had sent Ty on an emotional bender, and she'd been his— his *rebound girl*. Anger began to grind within her like two rusty gears, turning slowly at first, then picking up speed. "A relationship with me must have seemed like a convenient way to hurt her back."

"I wanted to forget about her for a few days."

"Do you make a habit of forgetting about her in every city you visit?"

"I've been faithful to Tawny the whole time we've been dating. I haven't wanted to be with anyone but her. Until you."

"I find that stunningly hard to believe."

"It's true."

"True?" Since their romance had begun, she'd been nothing but fawning and sweet tempered to him. That was over. Fury sent strength through her limbs, and she stormed to her feet. "*True?!* How am I supposed to believe that anything you say is true? You've been lying to me this whole time."

"No. I never lied to you about my feelings for you."

"What are your feelings for me, exactly?"

"I like you."

He *liked* her, which was such a far cry from love that the word lashed her like an insult. "You can't possibly like me, Ty. You've used me. You've treated me worse than most people would treat their enemies."

He made a slashing motion with his hand. "We had a good time. Both of us."

"If you hadn't been in love with someone else and if we'd parted on friendly terms, then yes. I'd have been able to chalk this weekend up to a 'good time.' But you convinced me to stay in Vegas extra days, and then you took me to a wedding chapel *and slept with me*!" Her chest billowed in and out.

Ty remained stock-still, his color high, his forehead creased.

"Last night you said you wanted to marry me, Ty. You said, 'Let's do something crazy for love.' And the whole time your heart belonged to another woman."

"I was drunk, and I was into you, and I was stupid. What happened is my fault."

She pressed the heels of her hands into her forehead. Could a person die from heartbreak? It felt like it. She'd sensed from the start that their relationship was too good to be true. He was gorgeous and successful and illegally charming. He could have chosen any woman in Vegas. Yet she'd convinced herself, even though he'd never told her outright that he loved her, that what he felt for her was real and unique. It wasn't. *He* wasn't the same person she'd fallen for in the ninth grade. He was as untrustworthy as a bridge built on sand.

She dropped her hands. "What are you going to do now?" It shamed her, but she wanted to hear him say that he'd decided to leave Tawny in his past and give their relationship a chance.

"I'm going to go home to Texas and tell Tawny what I've done. I'm going to try to make things right with her."

Devastated, angry tears rushed to Celia's eyes. She didn't know Tawny, but instinctively she hated her because she possessed Ty's love. "Will she forgive you?"

"Probably not. But I'm going to ask for her forgiveness anyway. We have a lot of history between us. I've known her since we were kids."

Celia grabbed up her sandals, then went in search of her purse. She struggled to hold back her tears but couldn't manage it. They tumbled over her lashes and raced in hot streaks down her face.

She would be returning to her life in Oregon, and Ty would be returning to his life in Texas, because he did not love her. Despite the vows they'd spoken and the things they'd done in the king-sized bed, he didn't want to be married to her. He wanted to marry Tawny, a person he'd known since childhood and had been dating for two years. Two years!

Celia had been living at such a high level of euphoria for the past few days, the fall back to reality was steep and the impact crushing.

Where was her purse? He'd said so many beautiful things to her! His kisses . . . What was she going to do? The way he'd made her feel. She couldn't stand to lose him—yes she could. And would. He was a cheater! *Where's my purse?* The tender way he'd looked at her. The laughter. It had all been a lie. And even so, she loved him. She'd put herself and her feelings out there, and he'd chosen someone else.

She spotted her purse and pushed its strap over her shoulder. After shoving the tears from her cheeks, she looked back at Ty one last time.

He hadn't moved. He still stood framed by the window, beautiful in his masculinity.

She'd been dating him four days, and he'd managed to betray her worse than anyone had over the whole course of her life. "Do you want a divorce, Ty? Because I believe an annulment is out of the question."

"I'm not thinking that far ahead yet."

"Just so you know?"

"Yes?"

"I'll never forgive you for this."

His expression remained uncompromising. He nodded once, a taut motion. She could tell that he hadn't expected her to forgive him. He just wanted her gone.

She couldn't breathe. Desperate to get away from him, from this room, from her own disgrace, she moved to the door. Yanked it open.

Celia did not look back as she strode down the hallway toward the elevators. She never wanted to see Ty Porter's face again.

Not for as long as she lived.

CHAPTER

THREE

THE PRESENT

The limo Ty had rented smelled like cologne and puffed-up expectations. He leaned back against the leather seat at the rear of the car, his arms outstretched along the top of the black leather upholstery, one boot resting on the opposite knee.

Four of his high school buddies rode inside the car with him. One was about to get married, so the rest had traveled to Vegas for a bachelor party. The guys were amped about the night to come. The sights and sounds. The drinking and gambling.

Their excitement did nothing for Ty except make him feel years older than the others. It took a lot to stir his adrenaline these days. He rode bulls. An evening in Vegas, a city he'd visited so many times he'd grown bored with it, left him with a chest full of emptiness.

He angled his attention out one of the limo's tinted side windows and watched without really seeing as the city passed by. The days were long in Nevada in May. Even though they were on their way to dinner, the sun had only dropped halfway to the horizon.

An ugly pink color caught his eye. His body tensed. Sitting forward, he squinted at the view. A pink building with a white picket fence. A ridiculous carriage hooked to a fake horse.

"Can you stop?" he called to the driver. "Would you mind pulling over for a second?"

The driver eased the car to the side so that the traffic behind them could pass.

"What's up, man?"

Ty glanced at his friends, who were looking at him with curiosity. "Nothing." He focused back on the chapel. "I just remember seeing this place once. Years ago." Astroturf still covered the yard. The tacky gazebo-thing stood. Even the Luv Shack billboard remained, though it had faded.

"Doesn't look like much."

"No." Through their eyes, it probably looked like the least interesting building in Vegas. And yet, what Vegas could not do, what little could do for him these days, this chapel had just done. It had jolted his cynical body and sent his heart beating with hard, fierce strokes.

He hadn't seen the Luv Shack since that long-ago night. He hadn't done anything special to avoid the place during his trips to Vegas, he just hadn't had a reason to search it out. Why bother to visit a place sure to bring up bad memories?

The memories aren't all bad, his conscience reminded him. *Are they?*

Celia.

He could still picture her exactly. The mellow green eyes with the long lashes. Delicate nose. Perfect skin even without makeup. Short slim body, with just the right amount of curve. Curly brown hair that had a hint of red in it when the sun hit it right.

Way back when he'd first met her his sophomore year in high school, he'd thought she looked like a little forest fairy that had stumbled into Plano East.

His vision took in every detail of the chapel. It surprised him, how much coming here meant.

"Ready to head on?" a buddy asked.

"Not yet." Pieces of the days he and Celia had spent together that December came back to him. The night they'd come to the Luv Shack together, she'd looked as hot as anything in that silver handkerchief she'd called a dress. She'd smelled like lemons. She'd looked at him with tenderness while they said their vows. They'd laughed all the way through their lame wedding photography session.

What had happened between them the next morning . . .

His muscles tightened. "Okay, we can head on. I'm good." Although he wasn't.

The car moved forward, and Ty ignored the urge to crane his head so that he could keep the chapel in sight. He let it go.

His friends stared at him.

He lifted a shoulder, as if his interest in the Luv Shack had been nothing but an impulse. "Thanks for stopping."

"Sure."

"Now let's get to the restaurant so I can buy you boys a round."

That got them back talking, trading insults, chuckling. He joined in with his voice, but inside of him a wind had begun to howl.

Celia sat at her kitchen table and considered sobbing. The benefit of sobbing was that it felt good in the short term. The drawback was that it left you with nothing but an ache in the lungs in the long term.

Her old laptop rested on the surface of the kitchen table, her bank's website open and displaying a list of her checking account withdrawals. A stack of bills sat beside the computer, alongside a calculator and note pad with frantic numbers in columns. The matte darkness of an eleven o'clock mid-May night filled the rectangles of her kitchen windows.

She didn't have enough in her account. Again. With a shuddering breath, she knuckled her eye sockets.

The stress of owing money she didn't have and couldn't pay back had been fraying her more and more over the past six months. She'd been pressing through because that's what she did. In fact, that pretty much summed up her identity: Celia, a woman who put one foot in front of the other and pressed through no matter how drained or overwhelmed.

This, though. This money thing truly had her worried. Her "press through" strategy was burning like a piece of paper held too close to the flame.

This past month she'd carefully watched the spending of every single dollar. She'd cut coupons and avoided extras, thinking that if she slashed spending, she could perhaps begin to pay off her credit card.

Then today her car's transmission had gone out, effectively jamming her scorched piece of paper straight into the fire.

Her car's age had begun to show four years back, but she'd been sticking Band-Aids on it because it was paid for and she couldn't afford a new-to-her car or a lease. The mechanic had told her today that a new transmission would cost fifteen hundred dollars.

Fifteen hundred!

Misery burned her throat from the inside. She couldn't put any more money on the credit card. She'd hit her limit already. And she refused to get another card. The interest on the one she had was already killing her, not to mention the mental weight of carrying around debt.

What was she going to do? She couldn't stand to ask Uncle Danny or her parents or older brother for money. Her parents were currently living in Scotland, her brother in Boston. They all viewed her as independent and admirable.

She'd have to make do without a car. Lots of people got around by bike or bus. Right? Her mind wheeled, trying to imagine how she could make it work.

She shut down her computer and stared without seeing at the wall opposite her. Self-doubt reared up and turned on her with biting teeth, just as it always did at her lowest moments.

Maybe she shouldn't have rented this apartment. Five years ago, when she'd decided on this little place, it had seemed so affordable, so perfect with its central pool and fenced yard the size of a cereal box. She surveyed the happy paint colors that surrounded her, the bright patterns, the vintage flea market finds—each choice made lovingly over time.

Maybe she shouldn't have taken the job at the university, working in cafeteria administration. She'd simply wanted something with good hours and health insurance, but perhaps longer hours and a higher income would have been the better course. That route would have allowed her to provide better financially—

"Mommy?"

Celia swiveled toward the sound. "Sweetheart?"

Her daughter, Addie, stood in the doorway that led from the living room to the hallway, wearing her Rapunzel pajamas and holding the small ivory blanket she'd had since she was a baby.

"What are you doing awake?"

"Couldn't sleep." Addie held one eye closed and one eye slitted against the light. Her dark blond hair, straight as a board and cut in a long bob, stood up in a matted section near her crown.

"Come give me a hug." Celia stretched out her arms and, when Addie reached her, pulled her onto her lap. Addie nestled against her exactly the way she'd been nestling against Celia since birth: one side of Addie's face flat against Celia's upper chest, Celia's chin resting on the top of Addie's head, Addie's hands holding her blanket, Celia's arms holding Addie's slender weight. Celia inhaled the strawberries-and-cream scent of Addie's shampoo. "Is your stomach hurting?"

"Yeah. I think I need my tea."

"Chamomile?"

"Mmm hmm."

"Okay, I'll get you some." Celia deposited Addie on the chair and got the teakettle going. Addie's acid reflux occasionally flared up late at night. Had it not been for

the reflux, her child would be sleeping soundly and her
bank account would be in order. The cost of the tests
Addie's gastroenterologist had ordered, including one
where they admitted Addie to the hospital, put her under
anesthesia, and then looked around her esophagus and
stomach with a scope, had more than wiped out Celia's
savings.

Addie surveyed the items on the kitchen table. "What're
these?" She fingered the stack of bills.

Celia never dealt with financial matters around Addie.
"Just letters."

"Letters about money?"

"Um," Celia hedged. Even though she did her best to
insulate her daughter, Addie always proved so intuitively,
frighteningly smart . . . a soon-to-be kindergartener
who could just as easily be polishing off a doctorate
in psychology.

Addie's brows stitched together in the center. "What're
we going to do about our car?"

Their breakdown on the way to day care this morning had classified in Addie's mind as a very big event. "I
haven't decided yet."

"Can we fix it?"

"It can be fixed, yes." *By anyone who has fifteen hundred dollars to spare.*

"If we need help, Uncle Danny will let us borrow
his car."

"Of course he will." Celia plopped a tea bag into
a teacup from her mis-matched collection. After she'd
poured hot-but-not-too-hot water over it, she gave it a
drizzle of honey and placed it in front of Addie.

Addie looked at her in her solemn way.

Celia took the chair next to Addie's. "Aren't you going to drink your tea?"

"It's too hot."

"No it isn't. Here. Let me try." Celia took a test sip.

Still, Addie regarded her. She blinked, pushed a strand of hair off her forehead, and set her small pink lips. "I'm going to buy you a new car, Mommy."

"No, no, Punkie." Her nickname for Addie had started out as Lil' Pumpkin Pie then abbreviated into Pumkin' Pie. Then Punkie Pie or merely Punkie. "Mommy's going to handle it—"

"I can do a lemonade stand. 'Member last time? I made lots of money."

"Yes, you did."

"Or I can sell some of my princesses. I have lots. Maybe—" she chewed her lip—"maybe Tiana? Or, no—I have two Ariels. I could sell one of my Ariels."

Addie adored her Disney princesses. That she'd suggest parting with even one pricked Celia's heart painfully. "That's so sweet of you, but you don't need to raise money to buy me a car. In fact, you don't need to worry about the car or anything else, okay? We're perfectly fine."

"I'm going to buy you a fur-ar."

"A fur-ar?"

"Yes. I'm going to buy you a fur-ar. In red."

"A Ferrari?"

"That's what I said."

Celia chuckled and kissed Addie on the temple, in the exact spot where she'd kissed her one million times before. "I don't need a Ferrari. I have you."

"'Course you need a fur-ar. Our other car is stinky. I'm going to get you a red fur-ar."

"Well, I'm going to get *you* a pink fur-ar. So take that!"

At last, Addie smiled. Celia grinned back, then watched Addie bend her head to take a cautious sip of tea.

This child was her world, her soul, her all. Celia's whole life revolved around this small and serious girl, who was given to worry, who wore glasses, and who had a heart of purest gold.

Since Addie's birth, Celia had only had one goal in life. No matter what sacrifice it demanded of her, no matter how hard she had to work or how tired she became—her goal was to provide Addie with the best childhood she possibly could, a childhood of security and love.

She'd done her all-out best, and her all-out best had still landed them in this situation—unable to pay their bills and as of today, without a car.

When Addie finished her tea, Celia escorted her to her room and cozied up alongside her in Addie's narrow twin bed. The glow of the night-light washed the room in a shade three times warmer than darkness.

"Tell me a story?" Addie closed her eyes and drew her blanket close.

"Which princess?"

"Sleeping Beauty, please."

Celia herself wasn't a huge fan of the princess stories. She worried that they set an unrealistic standard of female beauty and that they communicated the ridiculous idea that girls were in need of princes to rescue them. Addie, however, loved them, and Celia understood that sometimes the heart adored what the heart adored. So her strategy had been to put limits on Addie's princess watching, to compliment the princesses' internal qualities, and to assure Addie that the princesses could have saved themselves if the princes had been smitten by bad guys.

She pitched her voice to its calming go-to-sleep tone. "A few years after Aurora married Prince Phillip, she decided to hold a special ball."

"Oooh."

"The ball would benefit the soup kitchens all across the kingdom. The soup kitchens, of course, fed anyone who was hungry, because Aurora cared very much about taking care of others less fortunate. She decided that the ball would be for all the four-year-old girls in the land—"

"I'm almost five."

"—for all the four-year-old girls *who're about to turn five* in the land. Aurora invited the girls to come to the castle, dress in gowns and wear high heels, and have their hair done up with jewels or sparkly butterfly clasps or tiaras."

Addie relaxed down into her covers.

"Or, if the girls preferred jeans and sweatshirts, then that was fine, too. Aurora respects individuality. All the girls were allowed to go into the fabulous castle gardens and pick flowers and make themselves bouquets."

"Servants," Addie murmured.

"Quite right. The girls picked the flowers and then the servants, who were all treated very well and paid excellent salaries and given medical insurance, made them into the most beautiful bouquets you've ever seen. Aurora, being as gracious and generous as we know her to be, also invited the boys of the kingdom to the ball so the small princesses would have partners to dance with."

Celia could sense sleep overtaking Addie by degrees. "When the boys and girls arrived at the ball, they couldn't believe their eyes. They drank hot chocolate from fountains and punch from wishing wells. A banquet table held the most delicious food they'd ever tasted. Blackberry scones, shortbread cookies." Celia sighed. "Orange muffins. Chocolate chip croissants. Pecan bars. Pumpkin walnut bread . . ." Oops. Somewhere along the line her storytelling had morphed into her own fantasy.

She peeked at Addie, whose chest rose and fell smoothly. Addie's lips were parted, fingers still. Trusting.

Well. To heck with the ache in her lungs she was going to have later. Because as Celia stared down at her child, her great love, her eyes insisted on filling with tears.

She was only one person, fallible. Not good enough or wise enough to be this child's mother. Yet that's exactly the sacred honor she'd been given. This role of hers humbled her every day, because even though she wasn't good enough or wise enough, she dearly wanted to be.

She was the only parent Addie had.

Ty spent half the night lying on his side thinking about Celia, the other half dreaming about her.

As soon as he woke, he made his way to the hotel gym and ran on the treadmill. No matter how fast he pounded the track, his thoughts remained fixed on Celia—exactly as they had been since the moment he'd caught sight of that dumb pink chapel.

Frustrated, he returned to his hotel room. Since his buddies were still sleeping off the partying they'd done the night before, he took his computer to the first coffee shop the lobby offered, grabbed a breakfast sandwich and orange juice, and settled into a corner booth.

After a minute or two of searching the Internet, he found a website that claimed it could locate people. Ty typed in *Celia Park* and his last known address for her, *Corvallis, Oregon*, then hit Enter.

Her information came right up.

Ty stared at the screen. Had it really been that easy to find her? She still lived in Corvallis, which didn't surprise him. What did surprise him was that the website listed her name as Celia Park Porter.

She used his last name? He furrowed his brow. He'd have expected her to toss the Porter name on the dirt, grind her heel into it, and spit on it over and over.

Maybe the fact that she'd kept his name meant that she didn't completely hate his guts. . . .

No. She definitely did hate his guts. The simplest answer was that she'd kept his name because, technically, the two of them were still married. It probably made things easier for her from a legal standpoint.

For long moments he studied her name and the ten digits of her phone number. No street address.

He added her contact information to his phone.

The memory of what he'd done to her still had the power to turn his heart to cold steel. Since the moment he'd woken up in bed with her that morning, he'd bitterly regretted his actions in Vegas. Yet he'd never contacted her to tell her so, and she'd certainly never contacted him.

He had a few days of vacation in front of him. He'd planned to go home to Holley, Texas. Instead, he'd travel to Oregon and meet with Celia. He needed to settle things between them, because after all this time, he was finally ready to move on with his life. More than that, he *wanted* to move on. Wanted it with the same forceful determination that had taken him to the top of the world of bull riding.

Those who knew him—who'd watched him ride a string of champion bulls, who'd read his book or seen the documentary about him—understood one thing: Ty Porter went after what he wanted.

He was going to Corvallis, Oregon.

CHAPTER
FOUR

The phone rang, startling Celia. She'd been deep in her own head, plotting schemes that might pluck her and Addie from financial ruin while watering her backyard primroses. She angled the spray from the hose toward her daisies as she stepped onto her tiny brick patio. Grabbing the phone off the table, she punched the Answer button. "Hello?"

"Celia?" A male voice.

"Yes?"

"It's Ty Porter."

Her heart faltered, then started to race.

"Celia?"

Patter patter patter. The sound of the spray hitting the flowers drew her attention. *Patter patter patter.* She was drowning her daisies.

"Celia?"

"I'm here." She forced the words past her lips. "One moment." Frenzied, she pressed the phone to her chest, dropped the hose, and bent to twist off the spigot. She raced the few steps to the back sliding door, which she'd left open to the living room. Leaning inside, she tried to look and listen over the deafening sounds of her body's panic. She could neither see nor hear Addie, which meant she must still be playing in her room exactly as she liked to do when they returned home on Friday afternoons.

Celia stepped back onto the patio, slid the door fully closed, then retreated to the furthest corner of her backyard in hopes of giving herself added secrecy.

Ty. Calling her. *Why?* The reality of him on the other end of the line stirred up countless images, angers, and an ocean of resentment. She shoved all that away, because the only thing she could afford to think about at the moment was how to make him go away. She brought the phone to her ear. "I'm here."

"It's been a long time."

She didn't know if he meant the time that had passed since she'd answered the phone or the years that had come and gone since Vegas. "Yes."

A pause.

Celia swallowed painfully.

"I'm in Corvallis," he said.

Her stomach dropped like an elevator whose cable had been cut.

"I'd like to speak to you," he continued. "I hoped . . . well, I was hoping I could take you out to lunch so that we could talk."

That voice. Calm and assured with a Texas accent. She'd forgotten the sound of it long ago, but hearing it again . . . hearing it caused her to remember the details of it forcefully.

"Celia? Do you think that would be okay? For us to meet?"

She tried to decide how best to convince him to leave.

"I know it's a shock to hear from me. I'm sorry about that. I could call back later."

"No." Goodness, she didn't want that.

"All right," he answered. "So. Lunch?"

"No. I have nothing to say to you."

"Maybe not, but I have several things I'd like to say to you."

"Look . . ." She pressed her teeth into her bottom lip. "If you've come because you want a divorce, you should have saved yourself the trip. Are you on your cell phone?" She twisted her wrist and confirmed that her phone had captured his number.

"Yes."

"I'll text my attorney's name and number to you. You can have the documents sent there, and I'll sign them."

This time, it was Ty who waited a few beats to speak. "Are you planning to divorce me without ever seeing me again?"

"Yes." She'd expected him to contact her about a divorce in the weeks and months after Vegas. He hadn't—which had always struck her as an odd mystery. She'd allowed herself to check his Wikipedia profile only twice during the years of silence. Both times the details published there had confirmed what her lack of divorce papers inferred. He had not married anyone else. Nor had he linked himself—at least not publically—to a girlfriend.

"I came here to talk with you, Celia. In person."

"That's not necessary."

"It is to me."

"No. I'm not going to meet with you. There's no reason for us to see each other or even stand in the same room together ever again."

"Hey, Celia, think you can speak more plainly?" She could hear the smile in his lazy, teasing tone. "Tell it to me straight?"

A vein near the base of her neck throbbed.

A tapping sound brought Celia's attention up and to the side. Addie peered at her through her bedroom window. She knocked her knuckles against the window again, making more of the tapping sound, then waved.

Celia waved back as fear poured down her spine like ice water.

"I've driven a long way to see you," Ty was saying.

Addie held up a Snow White doll and pointed to the outfit she'd dressed her in.

Celia gave her a thumbs-up and a demented trying-to-look-normal smile.

"If you need time to get used to the idea of seeing me, I get it. I can wait. I'm in no rush . . ."

Celia turned away from Addie, pretending that her attention had been caught by the pear tree.

". . . but I'm not leaving until I speak with you."

"Anything we need to say to each other can be said through our lawyers."

"I disagree."

At any moment Addie might pull open the sliding door and rush into the backyard. Celia's gaze darted to Addie's window. Empty.

If she couldn't convince Ty to go away over the phone—and it appeared she couldn't—then she'd be better off not drawing this out. She'd simply do what she had to do to get him gone. "I'll meet you tomorrow at noon." Behind her, she heard the familiar whoosh of the screen door moving along its track.

"Where?" he asked.

"A restaurant called Jana's. Downtown." Before he could say another word or hear another word, especially one called out by a child, she disconnected the call.

"What's up, ladies?"

Looking over her shoulder, Celia watched Uncle Danny let himself into her apartment using his own key. "Hi, Uncle Danny."

"How is everybody?"

"I'm cool," Addie answered, in their customary way. "You cool?"

Danny went to where Addie sat on the floor beside the coffee table, coloring. He gave her a fist bump. "I'm cool, Addie Potaddie. Can't complain." He looked to Celia. "What about you, C? You're looking a little tense there, sister."

"What, me?" She'd worked herself into a *serious* state of agitation since Ty's phone call the night before. "Nope. I'm fine."

"All right then." He winked at her. "Doing laundry?"

"Yep." She'd been watching TV, folding clothes, and keeping up a conversation with Addie. In fact, ever since yesterday evening she'd been maniacally multitasking. It was a coping mechanism motivated by the desire to cover thoughts that went something like, *Ty Porter has reentered my life—What am I going to do about this?— How can I get rid of him?* over and over again.

Uncle Danny assumed a cross-legged position on the floor next to Addie. He asked her about her coloring book, then picked up a crayon and went to work on the page opposite hers.

Sweet, sweet man. When she'd told him that some friends had invited her out to lunch today—though Ty wasn't a friend and she didn't expect to eat a bite—he'd immediately volunteered to watch Addie for her.

She folded two of Addie's shirts and laid them on top of Addie's clean clothes pile, then reached into the laundry basket for more.

Danny looked just the way one would expect the owner of an online surf shop to look. He wore his graying blond hair in long wavy layers. He had on a faded blue, white, and red Baja hoodie, a shark-tooth necklace made from a leather thong, board shorts, and well-worn brown Reef flip-flops.

He was not, however, an ordinary fifty-six-year-old bachelor surfer dude. He was *her* fifty-six-year-old bachelor surfer dude.

As soon as she'd moved to Oregon for college, her parents had followed her father's work overseas. They hadn't lived in America since. When Uncle Danny, her mother's younger brother, had learned that Celia was expecting a baby, he'd been overtaken by a sudden urge to live in Oregon. He'd purchased a small mid-century modern house in Corvallis and settled into it with his antique surfboard collection and Beach Boys records.

Before his relocation to Corvallis, he'd been Celia's favorite relative. But over the past years he'd become much more: her friend, the only person she trusted to baby-sit Addie, the one who tended to her flowers and collected her mail when she left town, the person whose mellow personality always reassured her that things would turn out fine.

"How did the Party Of Eight group go last night?" She added folded clothes to her pile.

Danny was constantly testing new dating methods and singles' websites. Privately, Celia blamed his lack of success on his predilection for well-coiffed Eastern European women. What hope did he have of finding that breed in Corvallis, much less getting one to the altar?

"The women were so old, C. Which would have been cool if they'd had a good vibe, you know? But they were really square. And American."

"We do, you realize, live in America."

"They were into stuff like cross-stitch and reading. Not one of them would have wanted to go mountain biking or rock climbing with me."

A fault Celia knew he'd have overlooked if they'd been highly made-up or from a place like Belarus. "That's a shame."

"I'm chatting with a woman, though, on one of the sites who seems pretty interested. Might be promising."

"What is her name and where is she from?"

"Olga from the Ukraine." He smiled and lifted his eyebrows a few times. "You good on time?"

She was slated to meet Ty in half an hour. "I'm good." Since Uncle Danny didn't typically heed anything as pedestrian as the Pacific Time Zone, Celia always asked him to arrive for baby-sitting gigs, family dinners, and Addie's school programs thirty minutes prior to when she actually needed him there. He'd arrive about twenty-five minutes past her requested time, and they'd all end up happy.

"I'm glad you're going out to lunch with friends," Danny said. "You should do it more often."

She dug the final pieces of clothing from the hamper, folded them, and stacked them. "It should be fun."

"Go ahead and take my car." He knew about her toasted transmission.

"You sure?"

"Sure, I'm sure. I wanted to take Addie on a bike ride, anyway. I already got my bike out of the trunk." Danny hitched a third-wheel attachment to the back of his bike whenever he and Addie went on rides. "I thought we'd head to Woodland Meadow Park."

The route to Woodland Meadow would take them in a direction opposite the downtown location of Jana's restaurant. "Sounds good."

Celia went to the kitchen and double-checked her preparations. "Everything's here for your lunch when you're ready."

"Great. Thanks."

Celia would have liked to peek at her appearance again before heading out, but she squashed the compulsion. She ordinarily took no more than fifteen minutes to shower, dress, and do her hair and makeup. Today she'd returned to her bathroom repeatedly and ended up spending most of the morning in front of the mirror fussing over herself.

It went against all that was holy, but she *knew* Ty would look handsome. As much as she wished she were above the petty need to look attractive in front of the man who'd dumped her—she wasn't. Perhaps that particular need was unavoidable, hardwired into the female heart.

She swooped up Danny's keys, then kissed Addie on the head. "'Bye, Punkie."

"'Bye, Mom."

Danny gave her a salute, and she let herself out of her apartment. On the way to the car, she rifled through her purse. Wallet, sunglasses, lip gloss, cell phone. Knife with which to stab Ty in the chest? She had all but the last, unfortunately.

During the five-minute drive to the restaurant, she considered the fact that she didn't want to stab Ty in the chest, exactly. But close. Long and brutal near-death torture might fit the bill.

She found a parking space without trouble and reached Jana's at 11:45, just as she'd planned. With so little within her control, she wanted to select the table.

Jana's provided indoor seating, but Celia chose the sidewalk café. When the hostess invited Celia to take her pick, she moved to a table smack in the middle of all the others and against the front of the restaurant so she'd be sure to see Ty before he saw her.

She slid on her sunglasses and hunkered into her chair like a soldier staking out a position for battle. Above, an awning striped with three shades of yellow jutted outward from the building, casting shade. The flap that ran along the end of it ruffled with the breeze. Celia tried and failed to soak in the calm of the seventy-five-degree day, with patches of blue sky visible through breaks in the clouds.

She checked her watch, then made herself take sips of the ice water the hostess brought. A couple selected a nearby table. A few singles drifted indoors. A trio of girlfriends arrived, chattering to one another.

Celia still couldn't make herself accept that Ty was here, in Corvallis. The man she'd once made the disastrous mistake of trusting. Arriving any minute.

This was taking forever. He must be late. She consulted her watch again. Only 11:58.

People walking dogs and shopping drifted by on the sidewalk. Celia searched every face. Repeatedly, memories of Ty pushed their way into her mind, and repeatedly she blocked them. Remembering Ty was a painful exercise she hadn't allowed herself in years.

You simply have to make it through this one meeting, Celia, and then he'll go away. With stern concentration, she tried to relax muscles that insisted on growing more and more rigid with dread—

There he was.

She forgot how to breathe.

He was striding down the sidewalk toward her, looking up, probably searching for the sign that said *Jana's*.

She'd anticipated that he'd look handsome. But "handsome" was something you might say about a male model in a magazine ad; it was too stiff and flat an adjective for Ty Porter.

He had the kind of appeal that pulled your gaze to him, then wouldn't let you look away. She sensed women's jaws dropping, cars narrowly missing head-on collisions, pictures being taken without his permission and texted to girlfriends.

Anger gathered in her throat.

Brown-tinted aviator sunglasses shaded his eyes. A ray of sun caught and shimmered in his hair, which had been expertly cut just like always. He wore a soft-looking, not-too-tight-but-not-too-loose beige T-shirt

that advertised a custom motorcycle shop in brown letters. The square-tipped alligator cowboy boots pounding the sidewalk must be a newer cousin to the pair she
remembered.

He stopped at Jana's entrance and scanned the tables.
She knew the moment he spotted her because she could
literally *hear* it, like a bell ringing.

He threaded his way over, looked down at her, and
smiled. It was a subdued smile, but it had the same
thousand-volt impact of the smiles he'd once given her
in a high school ceramics classroom and then years later
in Las Vegas.

Celia realized that long and brutal near-death torture
would never do. She wished she *did* have a knife in her
purse so she could stab it through his heart.

"Hi," he said.

She gave a half nod.

He settled into the second chair at their table for two,
bringing with him the scent of pine, so subtle it toyed
with a person's ability to detect it at all. He continued
to study her, seemingly unmotivated to say more.

In her recollections, she'd made him small and wea-
selly. But he wasn't small at all. He was big. And by the
looks of it, he hadn't added an ounce of fat to his hard,
lean body in the years since she'd seen him last. He sat,
across from her, completely comfortable in his own skin,
with a kind of offhand grace.

Nearly five years of single motherhood had aged
Celia. But those same years had kissed and coddled Ty,
faintly sharpening his facial features. Small scars now
marked a cheekbone and the skin beneath his bottom

lip, giving him a rugged air that rendered him even more attractive than he had been.

"It's good to see you."

She raised an eyebrow. Did he expect her to respond in kind? If so, he could wait all day.

"You look great."

She blew out a frustrated breath.

He hefted a shoulder. "You do."

She glared at him through her sunglasses, trying to wither him with disdain.

Their waitress came over, her face lighting with recognition when she saw Celia. "Hey!"

"Hi." The young woman looked vaguely familiar, but Celia couldn't place her.

"How are you doing?" the waitress asked.

"I'm well. You?"

"Just fine." She handed them both menus, her movement stuttering when she got her first full look at Ty. "Can . . . can I get you something to drink?"

When Ty ordered iced tea she grinned widely at him, as if he'd said something funny.

After she moved off, Ty flicked open his menu. "What type of restaurant is this?"

"Health food."

"Do they serve burgers?"

"Veggie burgers." A tiny shaft of pleasure twanged within her.

"BLTs?"

"FBLTs."

He glanced at her. "Which is?"

"Fakin' bacon, lettuce, and tomato."

"And fakin' bacon is made from?"

"Organic tempeh. It's vegan."

"Well, that's good to hear. I'm a big fan of tempeh." He set the menu on the edge of the table. "What're you having?"

"Nothing." The ball of nerves formerly known as her stomach wasn't useful for actual eating. Also, she hadn't sunk a dollar into expensive restaurant food in months.

"No appetite?"

"No."

"Not sure how you can resist an FBLT." His crooked half smile sent his dimple into his cheek. "Is this a kid table?" He indicated his wooden seat, which did look miniature with him on it, and their tiny round table. "Why's it so small?"

"It's not small."

"Did you choose this place for the small tables or the lack of privacy or because you knew I'd hate the food?"

"The lack of privacy and because I knew you'd hate the food. The small tables have come as a surprising perk."

Another flash of dimple.

Celia didn't mention that the outdoor seating also permitted her to wear her sunglasses as a shield.

The waitress delivered Ty's tea, then took his FBLT order while giving him a free helping of eye contact with a side of flirting.

Celia glanced around and caught several women studying him surreptitiously. Foolish, misguided women.

When their waitress moved off, Ty added sweetener to his tea and stirred it as if he had all the time in the world. "I was just in Vegas. I saw the Luv Shack while I was there. Do you remember it?"

"No." Or at least she tried not to.

"Seeing it made me want to finish the unfinished business between us."

"The business between us is finished, Ty. Completely, totally finished."

"Then how come we're still legally married?"

She frowned. "I could ask you the same thing."

"I asked you first."

She fiddled with her fork, positioning it perfectly. "I haven't done anything about the marriage because I assumed you'd file for divorce and I'd simply sign the paper." Also, she'd had a baby to worry about and an ongoing lack of funds. She slid her hands into her lap. "Why haven't you filed?"

A shadow passed over his face. "I've never had a reason."

"What about Tawny?" It cost Celia to say the other woman's name out loud, but since he was putting her through this meeting, she figured he owed her some answers.

"When I went back to Holley and told her about you, she made our breakup permanent." He raised a brow. "What? Does it surprise you that she wouldn't forgive me?"

"A little."

He leaned back in his chair. "After the story of our wedding spread through Holley, I was an outlaw to my own family for weeks. They came around slowly. The town started to forgive me when I turned pro and began winning events on the circuit. But Tawny wouldn't even speak to me for more than a year. It took me another two to earn back her friendship."

"Did she marry someone else?" Celia vehemently hoped she had.

"She's had one boyfriend after another, but she hasn't married any of them. Despite everything that's happened, Tawny and I are still meant for each other, and she knows it. The next time she kicks a boyfriend to the curb, I'm going to make my move."

His words hurt Celia more than anticipated. She squared her shoulders. "In that case, let's go ahead and complete the paper work and make our divorce official."

He slipped his phone from his pocket and held a finger over it. "What's your address?"

"There's no need for you to have my address." That he knew her phone number and home city already scared the stuffing out of her.

"So I can send you the divorce papers?"

She pulled her attorney's business card from her purse and pushed it halfway across the table. Thankfully Uncle Danny's best friend from childhood was willing to represent her for a dramatically reduced fee. "You can send the papers to my lawyer."

He put the business card and his phone into his pocket without comment.

Celia lifted her purse from the ground. "Since it seems we've said everything there is to say, I'll be heading out—"

"Nope. I'm not done yet."

She stilled, frowning. "Is the remainder of this discussion required or optional?"

"Required. If you want me to leave town, that is." His lips curled up a little on one side, self-deprecating. "Which I can tell that you do."

She set her purse back on the ground.

He slid off his sunglasses and set them on the table. The blue of his eyes—such a clear, bright, startling color—struck her like a cuff to the head. Just as he was about to speak, a waiter stopped at their table to refill his iced tea.

Celia angled her face toward the street to avoid Ty's scrutiny. *You can make it through this one meeting, Celia.* Her hands were trembling slightly and her blood pressure had climbed to a level that had to be unsafe. *Just this one meeting. Then he'll go.*

Ty studied her profile.

Celia in the flesh, right here in front of him after all this time. Angry and beautiful. Familiar and different.

She had on a stretchy circle of a headband, the size of a shoe-string, that kept her hair out of her face. Her curls fell to her shoulders, an inch or two shorter than he remembered. She'd set her chin at a stubborn angle. Slim nose. Pale pink lips. He wished he could get a look at her eyes, but she'd hidden them behind a pair of sunglasses.

She wore what looked like a pirate shirt as long as a dress, white except for some light blue stitching on the front. A tiny round charm with a C on it dangled from her thin gold necklace.

He didn't like her brown leggings, and he hoped she hadn't paid much for her sandals because they were nothing but soles and a couple strips of leather. Even back in high school, she'd dressed sort of hippie. "Did you get the bakery you wanted?" he asked.

She fiddled with the clasp on one of the bracelets she

wore. "No, I didn't." The bracelet must be magnetic, because after she pulled the two ends apart, they snapped back together.

"Why not?"

"It was impractical."

"Impractical?"

"It would have required a small-business loan and all my time. It might have failed. I didn't want to take the risk."

"Really? You seemed so determined."

She looked at him for a long moment. "I had to grow up."

He scowled, remembering that her dream of owning her own bakery had been important to her once. She'd wanted to brew gourmet coffee, serve tea to people in silly little china cups, and bake muffins. Since she'd gotten such a raw deal from him, he'd hoped that she'd gotten what she wanted career-wise. "What are you doing now?"

"I work at the university in cafeteria administration."

She was a cafeteria lady? Man, how depressing. "Have you lived in Corvallis all this time?"

"Yes."

Celia had been one of those kids who'd moved every few years during childhood. He understood why she'd chosen a hometown and settled down. And he understood why she'd chosen Oregon. It suited her. It was natural and green and granola.

His food arrived, and he took a bite of his FBLT. He didn't like sissy health food. Not a bit. He believed in normal food, exercise, and hard work to stay in shape. "Since you asked, I still live in the greatest state in the country."

"Oh? You live in Oregon also?"

He chuckled, then popped a few baked chips into his mouth. They tasted like stale paper. "Texas. You'll never convince me that it's not the greatest state, sweet one."

She stiffened at his use of the old nickname.

He hadn't meant to say it. It had just come out. He chewed, watching her. Long before he'd liked Celia romantically, he'd simply liked her. Back in high school she'd been a sweet, spunky, quick-witted girl. In Vegas, she'd been those things plus grown up and sexy as all get-out.

Neither the high school Celia nor the Vegas Celia was sitting across from him now. This Celia hated him and to have any woman hate him went against Ty's grain. Especially Celia. There was something about her . . . something that got under his skin and made his chest hurt, even after all these years. "How come you use my last name?"

Her face blanked.

"When I found you on the Internet," he explained, "it listed you as Celia Park Porter."

He couldn't see her hands because she held them beneath the table, but he could hear her fussing with her bracelet again. *Click. Unclick. Click. Unclick.* "I was married, so I used my married name." She shrugged uncomfortably.

He still remembered every detail of waking up in that hotel room bed with her against him. Her head had rested on his shoulder, her palm on his chest. As he'd looked down at her in the dim light, the realization of what he'd done had settled over him like a thousand-pound weight. He'd slid out of bed, showered, and stood at that blasted hotel window, watching cars crawl along the strip for what seemed like hours, freaking out inside his mind while Celia slept.

He'd never been a saint. Of the Porter brothers, Bo and Jake had been the good ones, and he'd been the hell-raiser. Even so, Ty had always viewed himself as mostly honorable. Not the same gold and shiny level of honor that his grandfathers and father had earned, but *mostly* honorable.

When he'd stood at the window that morning in Vegas, he'd known that he'd betrayed the trust of two women and turned whatever honor he'd had to darkest black.

He pushed his plate of food to the side, no longer hungry. Slowly, so he wouldn't frighten her, he reached across the table for Celia's sunglasses. She moved to stop him, then stilled, apparently deciding it wasn't worth a wrestling match. He slipped them off and set them aside. She met his gaze, her expression troubled.

Those eyes. Pretty and almond shaped, green, surrounded by thick brown lashes.

"I'm sorry about what happened in Vegas, Celia."

"Is that why you came all this way?"

He nodded. "Before our divorce is final, I needed to say that to you in person."

"Okay. I've heard you." Celia made a show of checking the time. "Now I'd really better go. I have an appointment."

Fresh regret sank into him like a sharp-tipped dart.

She rose to her feet.

He rose to his. "Good-bye."

She dipped her chin, then turned and walked away from him, her slim legs moving quickly.

He lowered to his chair and watched her climb into an old woodie car, the kind surfers drove in California. She reversed and took off.

"Excuse me." A female voice.

He looked toward the three friends sitting at the next table. College girls? None could have been older than twenty.

"If that woman wants to divorce you, then she's crazy," the tallest one said, her eyes round.

"Nuts," the shortest one agreed.

"You can come out with us tonight," the third offered. "Have some fun."

"I'd like that," Ty answered, "but I'm just visiting. I'm leaving soon."

Their faces fell.

He smiled at them. "Thank you, though."

"You're welcome," they replied simultaneously.

"Oh, shoot." Their waitress walked up to the table. "Has she left already?"

"Yeah."

"I wanted to invite her to the Memorial Day barbecue we're having at River Run." She placed a hand on her chest. "I'm the social coordinator for the apartment complex where we both live."

"I see."

She looked him up and down. "You're welcome to come to the barbecue if you'd like."

He'd been asked out twice in twenty seconds. "Thanks, but I won't be in town that long."

"Oh, okay. Sure."

He asked for the check. She pulled it from her apron and moved away.

Ty stared without seeing at the place where Celia's car had disappeared, remembering how furious he'd been with Tawny when he'd made that doomed trip to Vegas. Later, he'd realized that some part of him must have wanted to ruin his relationship with Tawny. And that's why he had. As soon as he'd ruined it, though, he'd been sorry. Sorry, too, that he'd used Celia to do it.

He'd never intended to marry or sleep with Celia or for her to find out about Tawny. He'd just intended for them to have fun together in Vegas for a few days, then go their separate ways. End of story. But that's the thing about bad decisions—they had the power to take you farther than you'd planned to go. The chemistry between him and Celia had been way more powerful than he'd banked on, he'd acted like an idiot, and Celia had ended up married to a no-good man in love with someone else.

Pieces of conversations from the tables around him and the sound of plates being stacked filled the air.

He'd told Celia earlier that he hadn't filed for divorce because he hadn't had a reason. The truth? He'd had a reason not to file. He'd rather be shot, though, than admit his reason out loud—

Something on the ground caught his eye. He squinted and leaned over. A gold bracelet. Celia's bracelet with the magnetic clasp. In all that toying with it, she must have undone it.

He picked it up and sat for a good while. Gradually, a smile overtook his mouth. Celia hadn't intended to—and would probably be mad if she knew—but she'd just given him an opportunity to do her a small favor.

She'd given him a chance to return her bracelet.

And to see her one last time.

FIVE

The River Run Apartments didn't look like much.

Ty sat in his truck the morning after his lunch with Celia, eying the place. The whole complex was made up of connected one-story units. Gray siding and blue doors. The property didn't look run-down or dirty, just boring. Its best feature was its nearness to the river, which cut through the land a hundred or so yards behind the complex. Green space and trees surrounded River Run's other three sides. To get here, he'd turned off what passed for a main street in Corvallis, then taken a long driveway to the visitors' parking lot.

Celia's woodie car was nowhere in sight, so he figured she was away. He'd decided to wait for her return.

He leaned back in the driver's seat and extended his arm against the door, letting his wrist drop out the open window. His fingertips tapped against the truck's exterior. It had rained earlier, and now everything was damp and cool, with just enough sunlight to turn the puddles shiny. He'd seen lots of cars, birds, dog walkers, and bike riders this Sunday morning—

Wait. Was that Celia? He leaned forward, squinting. The woman walking toward him on the sidewalk was wearing a loose pink sweater over a white tank top and jeans, something Celia would wear. Brown curls. The right build. He'd expected her to drive onto the property, but here she came on foot. Strange. Where was her car? And why did she have a child with her?

Celia was holding hands with a little girl. They had on matching pairs of purple rain boots with pink polka dots on them.

Ty exited his truck and made his way in their direction. Was the kid a friend's child? A niece? Maybe Celia's "little sister" in one of those charity programs?

When Ty was about ten steps away, Celia glanced in his direction. She immediately pulled the girl to a stop.

"Good morning." He crossed the remaining distance.

"Good morning," the girl answered. When Celia said nothing, the girl looked up at her with confusion.

Celia stared at him, her face going completely white.

"What's the matter?" Ty asked. "You all right?"

"I'm fine. I . . ." She leaned toward the girl. "I just realized that I left . . . my umbrella behind. Would you mind running back and getting it? I'll be right behind you."

"The door's locked."

"Here." Celia pulled a ring of keys from her pocket and pressed them into the girl's hand.

The kid shook her head.

"It's okay." Celia faced the girl in the direction of the apartments and gave her a gentle push.

The kid turned back toward her. "You don't let me unlock the door by myself."

"This time I will."

"I don't want to go." She stuffed the keys into Celia's jeans and wrapped her arms around Celia's thigh. She had on a pair of light blue glasses. Colors striped her long-sleeved dress and her pants.

Celia's attention remained on the child for a few long seconds, then slowly lifted to his face. She looked like someone who wanted to beat the daylights out of him but felt the need to pretend politeness in front of the kid. "I'm surprised to see you here, Ty. I thought we'd said good-bye yesterday."

"We did." He pulled the bracelet from his pocket and extended it to her. "But you dropped this and left it behind. I wanted to return it to you."

The little girl's eyebrows rose.

Celia took the bracelet from him and snapped it onto her wrist. "Thank you." She gave him the tightest smile he'd ever seen. "That was nice of you. Well. 'Bye."

The child tapped on Celia's arm.

Celia gave her a "not now" look.

The girl tugged Celia downward, then cupped a hand around Celia's ear. "It's just like in Cinderella," she whispered loudly. "'Member how Cinderella left the glass sipper at the ball and Prince Charming had to find her to give it back? He found you to give your bracelet back."

Celia might hate his guts, but the kid was comparing him to a prince. "I don't think I've met you yet." He smiled at the girl. "I'm Ty. What's your name?"

"Addie Porter."

A white void opened inside his head. A car drove

by, its wheels creating short fans of water. The trees rustled with wind. He took in the sight of her, this girl in bright clothes and glasses. Cute and small. Straight, dark blond hair. Green eyes. He'd no idea how old she was or why she called herself by his last name. "I'm sorry. What was that?"

"Addie Porter," she answered. "This is my mom."

My God, Ty thought.

He glanced at Celia in time to see her eyelids sink closed with despair. A pulse went through him then, painful and ice-cold, as if he'd touched a live electrical wire. This girl, this Addie, could not be *his* child. Surely.

Celia was still married to him. But that didn't mean she hadn't had a child with someone else. He knew nothing about her life in the years since he'd seen her.

Through the roaring vacuum of his thoughts, he noticed Addie watching him, waiting for him to say something normal. "Nice to meet you, Addie."

"You too." She looked back and forth between the two adults, finally settling on Celia. "Mom?"

"It's all right, Addie. I know Ty from years ago."

"He brought you your bracelet," she insisted, still trying to talk Celia into liking him.

"I know he did." Celia tugged her cell phone from her back pocket and quickly typed a text with an unsteady hand. "Addie, I'm going to need to talk to Ty for a little bit. And I just remembered that Uncle Danny wanted to take you on another bike ride today. Doesn't that sound like fun?" Fake excitement filled her voice.

Addie's expression said she wasn't buying it.

Ty walked alongside them as they headed back to their apartment. Two adults with a tornado of tension between them and one kid. Ty had never once imagined that Celia had had a child. Especially one that reminded him a little of his sister, Dru, at that age.

The icy pulse slashed through him again.

Celia started asking Addie pretend-happy questions about her upcoming bike ride with her uncle. Ty remained silent, his gut churning, his temper rising. They took a path around one corner of the complex to an apartment that faced trees and tenant parking spaces.

Celia let them into an undersized living room. Hallway on one side. Kitchen and kitchen table on the other. At the back, sliding doors emptied into a miniature backyard full of color and plants.

Celia, her brows drawn together, watched Addie. Addie, her brows drawn together, watched him. "This is our house," Addie said.

"It's nice." In fact, there were so many colors and patterns going on that it looked like a circus. His mom—yikes, he couldn't bear to think about his mom right now—had raised him in a house packed full of stuff. Maybe that's why he'd gone the opposite way. He liked his rooms plain so he could think.

"Would you like to see my artwork?"

"Sure."

Addie led him to the kitchen and pointed at the fridge. "I did this one at my school—well, my preschool. I'm going to start kindergarten soon. It's a princess, see? She's wearing a tiara and a purple ball dress. . . ."

She continued. Not with chatter, but with a kind of shy seriousness. Ty found it hard to hear her, to focus. The refrigerator door was covered with all kinds of things. Pictures of Addie as a baby, as a toddler.

Pictures of Celia and Addie together. Invitations. Certificates.

Over Addie's voice, he registered the front door opening and closing. Murmured talking. A few moments later, Celia brought over a man who looked like Crocodile Dundee.

"Ty, this is my uncle, Danny Sullivan."

Ty extended his hand and they shook. Danny, who didn't appear to be the type to worry about anything, had worry in his eyes. "How are you, Addie Potaddie?"

Addie gave him a fist bump. "I'm cool. Are we leaving now?"

"Sure are." Danny rubbed his hands together as if he couldn't wait for the bike ride that had been shoved at him. "You ready?"

Danny and Celia guided Addie to the door while talking about helmets, where the two were headed, and when they'd be back.

At the last second, Addie paused on the threshold to look back at Ty. "'Bye."

"'Bye."

Then she and Danny were gone.

Celia closed the door, shutting the two of them into a house gone deadly still and quiet.

"Whose child is that?" Ty asked, his emotions and confusion barely controlled.

Celia sank onto the nearest chair. She looked at the rug and covered the lower half of her face with her hands. Her chest rose and fell unevenly.

Ty gave her all the time he could spare. "Whose child is that, Celia?"

Slowly, as if everything inside of her ached, she pushed

herself to standing. She looked him right in the eyes. "Mine."

"Who is her father?"

She didn't speak, but the trace of guilt in her expression gave him her answer.

His stomach pitched. "I'm not that child's father, am I? If I were, you'd have told me about her a long time ago. Right? You wouldn't have let me live my life without knowing something so important."

Her sigh broke.

He pushed his hands through his hair. Dropped his arms. "Am I Addie's father?"

"Yes."

She'd replied to him with a single word, but that one word changed everything. Who he'd thought he was. His life. His future. "We were only together one night."

"Apparently one night was all it took."

How was that possible? He had buddies who'd been trying for years to have a baby with their wives. "I'm supposed to believe that?"

"No. You don't have to believe it."

"What—what proof do you have that she's mine?"

"None."

"When was she born?"

"Eight and a half months after our wedding night and a couple weeks before her due date."

He thought back over all the years, one on top of another, that had passed since then. All those pictures on the fridge. A baby with hair that stood straight up. A little girl riding a trike. A bigger girl in a princess costume. He wanted to yell. "If this is true . . . if she's mine, then why didn't you tell me about her?"

"Because I didn't want you to be a part of our lives."

"Didn't you think I had a right to know?" His voice climbed in volume.

"No."

"I could have helped you," he accused. "Have you followed my career at all?"

"No."

Shortly after Vegas he'd joined the Bull Riders Professional Circuit. He'd been good to the BRPC, and the BRPC had been good to him. "If you had followed it, you'd have known that I could have provided more for her than this." He gestured to the apartment.

Celia bristled. "More isn't necessarily better."

"What about growing up without a father? Do you view that as better?"

"Until recently, Addie was too young to realize that other kids had fathers. She's never lacked for anything."

He tilted his head. Fury pushed against him from the inside.

"You had your freedom, Ty, and I had Addie. It seemed fair to me."

"You talked with me on the phone a couple days ago. You sat down at a table across from me yesterday. Both times you didn't say anything about Addie. You were going to let me leave without ever telling me."

She didn't deny it.

"I hurt you," he said, "and so you kept my daughter from me."

"Yes, I did." She glared at him. "I did. I didn't trust you to be good to her." The air snapped, anger a tangible thing in the room with them. "Go ahead and leave, Ty. You can keep on traveling and riding bulls and whatever else it is that you do. Addie doesn't know anything about you yet. We'll divorce, and you'll marry Tawny and have a family of your own. I promise you that I'll never contact you or ask you for anything."

Muscles knotted down his neck. "If you think I'd *ever* walk away from a child of mine, then you don't know me at all."

"I'm offering you an easy way out."

"And I'm not taking it," he said flatly. "I want a paternity test."

She drew back, her face defensive.

"If I have to bring in a whole firm of attorneys to make it happen, I will. Am I going to need to do that?"

"No."

He could tell that the threat of lawyers had scared her. "If the paternity test proves that I'm her father, I'll let you tell her. But she *is* going to be told, and she's going to be told right away."

Celia's hand lifted to her neck, her fingertips bending into the skin.

"Then we'll work out custody." He strode through the front door, banging it behind him.

Ty didn't know what to do with himself.

He ended up returning to his hotel. He pulled on work-out clothes and headed for the treadmill in his hotel's gym.

He ran. His head filled with one enraged thought after another. His chest burned with emptiness. He kept upping the speed. Still didn't help. His feet pounded the belt. Sweat rained off him. He had no way of comprehending the turn his life had taken today. He had no skills for dealing with the discovery of a daughter he didn't know.

After an hour, he showered. Still feeling murderous, he climbed into his truck and started driving. He took aimless turns until he stumbled onto a highway. When the highway brought him to the Pacific coast, he pointed the truck north.

Once, he stopped for gas, but he couldn't stomach lunch. Or dinner, either, as the hours crept by.

His brother Bo had gotten married almost two years ago, but he and his wife, Meg, hadn't started a family yet. At the rate his brother Jake was going, he'd never marry. The idea of his sister, Dru, as anyone's wife or mother was laughable. Like him and his brothers, Dru had joined the Marines. She'd been shipped overseas, and there was no telling the amount of damage she was bringing down on America's enemies.

All of that made Addie the Porter family's first grand-child. Ty knew his mom and dad well enough to know they'd have sold everything they had to love and care for a granddaughter. They'd have wanted to rock her when she was a baby, spoil her, and show pictures of her to all their friends. That's what grandparents did, right? Instead, they'd gotten this handed to them, same as he had.

Worse, he was largely to blame.

The sky darkened. A storm rolled over the ocean, each lightning flash brightened the gray water and the white tips of the waves.

For five and a half years, he'd known himself to be the guilty party in his short relationship with Celia. But now it turned out that she'd done something to him, too. She'd hidden his child from him.

He remembered how hoarse her voice had sounded that morning in Las Vegas when she'd said *"I'll never forgive you for this."* The fact that she hadn't told him about Addie proved that she'd meant every word.

He understood now why she'd taken the Porter surname. She'd come back from Vegas pregnant. She'd known her child would one day grow old enough to understand about illegitimacy, and she'd wanted that child to know she'd been conceived within marriage.

It suddenly made sense to him, too, why Celia worked for the university's cafeteria. She hadn't been able to risk starting her own bakery, because she'd had a child to take care of. She'd needed a steady paycheck and health insurance.

The miles passed beneath his truck's tires, silence thick inside the cab. Why hadn't he searched for Celia years ago? Why had she let her bitterness toward him steal Addie's chance at having a father? Why hadn't either one of them taken care of birth control in Vegas? Why hadn't he ended the relationship more gently?

He pulled the truck onto the shoulder of the highway. The dark and lonely view spread outward for miles without a single sign of human life. Full of anger, his spirit swept empty by wind, he began to pray. It was not a pretty prayer. Rugged, unfinished sentences dead-ended into half-formed thoughts. He tried to ask God for help, to make something good out of a lousy situation, to calm him down, to forgive him and Celia.

Ty had grown up going to church. Even though he hadn't attended a single worship service since the night he'd married Celia, he still believed in God. Still prayed.

This particular prayer, though? He sensed that it did nothing. It made him feel no better.

Frowning, he U-turned the truck and headed back toward Corvallis.

Whenever he'd imagined the kids he might one day have, he'd imagined boys. He and his brothers had all been tall, strong kids, and that's the kind of kid he'd expected to have.

Addie was nothing like the picture in his mind. She was small and delicate, colorful. She didn't look like him. She looked a little like his sister, yes. But more than anyone, she looked like Celia.

At Addie's age, he'd been daring, bent on finding trouble, and willing to do any dumb thing to make people laugh. Addie had struck him as the opposite: polite, calm, serious.

It could be that she wasn't his. Before going hog-wild inside his head, he should have waited for the paternity test to come back.

Except, no. He rubbed his thumb against the steering wheel. Addie might not look like him or act like him, but his gut told him what the paternity test would reveal. His gut told him he'd had a good reason for spending the whole day on the rough side of crazy.

She needed to tell Addie.

Celia stood in the shower late that night, her head bowed, hot water pouring over her. She felt like she'd been crying for hours—that spent, fragile, exhausted feeling. But she hadn't been crying. What had happened was too terrible for tears.

After Ty had left, Celia had sat on her sofa in her familiar spot, the spot where she watched TV at night after Addie went to bed. She'd clenched a pillow to her abdomen, bent her legs up, and stayed that way, frozen with dread, shaking.

When anxiety would no longer let her sit, she'd bolted into the kitchen and made brownies from scratch. Full sugar. Full butter. Baking had always been her therapy. In some mysterious way, the creative activity of her hands usually helped Celia order her thoughts. As soon as the brownies had come out of the oven, she'd told herself she'd just eat one of the crimped-looking edge pieces that nobody else would want. She'd ended up eating five of them.

After Addie had returned home, she and Uncle Danny had entertained her at a frantic pace, overcompensating and helpless to stop themselves. Let's go to a movie! Uncle Danny had treated them. Feed the ducks! Walk around the pond! Go eat pizza followed by ice cream! Uncle Danny again treated them. The stress and the food had made Celia's chocolate-stuffed stomach roil.

Three times during the afternoon and evening, Addie had asked about Ty, who'd clearly dazzled her with his handsomeness and similarities to Prince Charming. Celia had employed her usual evasive tactics. She'd finally gotten Addie to bed forty-five minutes later than usual. Then she'd spent thirty minutes explaining to Uncle Danny about Ty and their past.

She turned in the shower, feeling the water pressure shift to her other side. Her arms crossed and wrapped around herself.

That stupid bracelet! Why had she even worn it to lunch? She couldn't believe she'd been so careless, dropping it without noticing. She didn't understand why Ty had bothered to return it or how he'd found her address.

The bracelet was a little thing she'd purchased years ago, one of many inexpensive bracelets in her jewelry drawer, worth nothing. And yet dropping it and leaving it behind—that small mistake—had been the key that had unlocked a predicament that might cost her everything: Addie, her baby, her greatest love.

If that happened, what would her life be worth?

It's not right, a voice inside seemed to whisper, *for you to base your identity on your child*. It wasn't the first time this idea had occurred to her. Building her life on the foundation of her daughter might not, in the end, be the healthiest thing for Addie or for herself. And yet, was it really so bad? To love a child so much?

She groaned, lifting her face and using her hands to slick away water and wet hair. She should have told Ty about Addie from the beginning. If she'd been braver, better, and more noble, he could have been a part of Addie's life from the start.

Because she'd excluded him, he'd thrown the threat of lawyers and a custody battle at her—two things that sent fear down to the bottom of her soul.

She needed to tell Addie. In fact, she needed to tell Addie *tomorrow* that Ty was her father. That way, Addie would have a few days to get used to the idea before she'd need to face Ty again.

Nothing within Celia wanted to share Addie. Nothing. And yet she needed to tell her little girl, because she knew with one hundred percent certainty what the paternity test would prove.

CHAPTER

SIX

"Wasn't it nice of that man to bring you your bracelet?" Addie asked the next morning.

Celia's mood sank. She'd vowed to herself that she'd tell Addie about Ty the very next time Addie asked about him. Instead, ten reasons why she should procrastinate sprang to Celia's mind. First and foremost, she didn't have much time. Riding the bus to day care and then to her job took ages. She'd planned to arrive at the bus stop on the road in fifteen minutes, and the walk there would take ten.

Tonight would be better . . .

No. She'd vowed to herself. *Vowed* that she'd tell Addie when Addie asked. Carefully, she set her spoon in her bowl.

"How did you used to know him years ago?" Addie took a bite of cereal, milk dribbling off her spoon into her bowl. She wore her teal glasses, and Celia had already combed her hair and clipped it back on one side with a barrette. She had on a pink-and-green-striped

Hanna Andersson play dress that Celia'd found at the secondhand clothing shop in town.

Without warning, emotion tightened Celia's throat. Her baby. *Her* baby. She scooted her chair closer to Addie's and held out her hands palms up.

Addie turned to face Celia so that the tips of their knees touched. She placed her little girl hands into Celia's adult hands.

Celia looked down, remembering how she'd held those hands when they'd belonged to a newborn. They'd been the size of walnuts then, the fingers curled in tightly. She could still feel the way those baby fingers had clutched her index finger, with fierce need, as if Addie had understood just how much she depended on Celia's care.

Celia remembered when those hands had belonged to a big-eyed, angel-faced toddler with two inch-long pigtails. Addie's hands had been stubby and soft at that age, with dents for knuckles and nails that Celia had carefully clipped and sometimes painted pale pink with sparkles.

Over the years, Celia had held Addie's hand whenever she'd needed shots. She'd held Addie's hand each time she'd graduated to a new class at day care and they'd walked into the new room together, both of them uncertain about trusting the new teacher. She held Addie's hand when they watched a movie together, when they went on nature walks, whenever Addie needed silent reassurance.

She'd held Addie's hand every single day of Addie's life, because she'd been here.

Every day. Keeping Addie safe from harm.

Where had Ty been?

He's been exactly where you banished him, Celia.

And now that he'd come back, she found herself powerless to protect Addie from him. She could only hope that he would never do or say anything to damage her child.

When she met Addie's gaze, a sheen of tears fuzzed her vision. "I love you."

"I love you, too, Mommy." Addie, ever intuitive, stared back at her somberly, a twist of worry in her expression.

"You asked how I knew Ty years ago."

Addie nodded.

Briefly, Celia told her how they'd met in high school and then again a few years after college. "We . . ." She sought to breathe in air and courage. "We fell in love"—she had, anyway—"and we got married."

Addie's green eyes, the same color as Celia's, went wide.

"Ty's last name is Porter. The same as yours and mine. Ty Porter."

She waited, giving Addie time to process. She didn't know if Addie would be able to connect the dots with only that information or not.

"He's my daddy."

Smart Addie. Celia released a quivering exhale. "Yes."

"I thought so."

"You did? Why?"

"Because he's what I dreamed my daddy would look like."

Tenderness pierced Celia. She wanted to say, *You can't trust his looks, Addie. Unlike in fairy tales, handsome men aren't always heroes.*

"And," Addie continued, "you lost your bracelet and he found you so he could give it back, Mom. Just like—"

"Prince Charming and Cinderella."

"Yes."

Again, the things Celia wanted to say jammed up inside her. *He's not Prince Charming! Don't be foolish like I was and fall for his dumb grin and his sparkling eyes and his stupidly perfect body.* Instead, she asked, "Do you have any questions for me?"

Addie thought it over while the smell of coffee hung in the air. Outside, a car engine started as someone prepared to leave for work.

"Where does he live?" Addie asked.

"He lives in a town called Holley in Texas. But he travels a lot. He's a bull rider."

"A what?"

"A bull rider, which means he rides on bulls . . . you know, big cows? With horns? He rides them in rodeos." This was another thing that would mean nothing to Addie since she'd never been to a rodeo. "And he competes against other men to see, um, who can stay on the longest and who rides them the best." Her words sounded ridiculous to her, which was Ty's fault for having such a ridiculous career. He was a grown man who regularly climbed on top of huge unbroken animals. No one should be able to earn a living doing something so farfetched.

"And he doesn't live here with us because you didn't get along good?"

Within the last year, Addie had asked a few times about her father. Celia reiterated now what she'd tried to articulate then. "Right. We didn't get along very well . . . after our wedding. That's why I live here, and he lives other places."

"Why didn't he ever come see me?"

Celia swallowed. "He would have, except he . . . he didn't know that you were his daughter until yesterday."

Addie's forehead furrowed with concern.

Celia would never want Addie to think that Ty hadn't been involved in her life because he didn't care about her, so even if Addie got angry with her, she needed to try to get this part right. "This is hard to explain, but after you were born, I loved you so much that I wanted to take care of you all by myself. You know how it's hard to share sometimes?"

"Yes."

"Well, it was hard for me to share you with Ty."

"But you always tell me to share."

"Right. That's why I think I made a mistake. I should have told Ty about you. He wanted to be here for you. He wanted to know you."

Addie weighed Celia's words.

"I'm sorry," Celia said softly and with painful honesty. She'd taught Addie to say she was sorry, and Celia tried to practice what she preached. "Can you forgive me?"

Addie regarded her with all the goodness contained in her young heart. "Yes, Mommy."

"Thank you." Celia pulled her into a hug and pressed a kiss onto the top of her head.

"Does he want to see me now?" Addie asked quietly.

"Yes."

"When?"

"Very soon."

"Is he mad at you?"

"He's a little bit mad."

"Do you think he'll forgive you?"

"Yes, I think he will." Truthfully, though, she had no such expectation.

Two hours later, Celia received a text from Ty while at work.

I've arranged the paternity testing. It only involves a cheek swab. Can you take Addie in and have it done today?

She didn't have a car. But she did have several sweet co-workers who'd probably let her borrow their car during her lunch break. *Yes,* she wrote back. *I think so.*

He replied with the address of a medical office in town.

Celia couldn't tell Addie that her father required a DNA test to prove his paternity because he didn't trust her mother. Instead, she decided she'd use words like *routine test, formality,* and *required by our health insurance company* to explain the cheek swab to Addie. So long as needles weren't involved, she fully expected Addie to shrug and go along with the test, none the wiser. Kids were accustomed to not understanding things.

Three days after the cheek swab, Celia received another text from Ty.

Test results came back. Addie is my daughter. May I pick her up tomorrow morning?

Celia had zero intention of allowing Ty to take off with her child. For a full minute, she tapped her heel against the floor beneath her desk and tried to decide how to reply.

She finally settled on the truth, phrased politely in hopes that he wouldn't threaten lawyers again. *I think Addie will feel more comfortable if the two of you spend time together at our house with me present.*

Tonight? he texted back.

Celia grimaced. *How about tomorrow evening?*

Tomorrow won't work for me. How about tonight at seven?

Fine. Addie, at least, would be happy. She'd been asking Celia questions about Ty nonstop all week.

Do you want to tell Addie the news? he asked.

Already have, she replied.

Ty stood on Celia's doorstep that night, certain he looked like an idiot. He was a first-time father to a child he didn't know, holding a box wrapped in shiny pink paper.

He knocked twice, then glanced down at the package. He'd decided to buy Addie a gift a few days ago, just in case the test results came out the way Celia had told him they would. Since he hadn't trusted the local stores to carry what he wanted in the right brand, he'd called Cavender's and asked the lady on the phone what size to buy. He'd had the present shipped overnight to his hotel and paid the girl at the gift shop to wrap it for him. She'd put a really curly silly-looking purple bow on top.

Celia answered the door wearing one of her stretchy headbands, cut-off jean shorts, a loose top falling off one shoulder, lots of bracelets, one anklet, and bare feet. "Come on in."

The apartment smelled like baked chicken tonight

and glowed with bright color and light. Every lamp had been turned on, even though sunset was still more than an hour away.

Addie stood next to the end of the sofa, her hands behind her back. Her attention bounced off his face and down to her feet, which were stuck into a pair of pink slippers. She had on a green dress and tights.

"Hi," Ty said.

"Hello," she said to her toes.

"How've you been?"

She mumbled something.

"Addie." Celia spoke in the tone used by all mothers. "Ty has asked you a question. Can you look up and answer him?"

Obediently, Addie raised her face. She focused on empty space near his elbow. "I've been fine."

"Good."

Celia was watching Addie intently, biting her lip. It made Ty uncomfortable. "It's nice out." He spotted their backyard. "Would you like to sit outside with me, Addie?"

A pause. She nodded.

She'd been less shy around him the day they'd met, but he understood. It was one thing for a kid to talk with a stranger. Another to talk with a stranger who was also, suddenly, her father.

He led the way toward the backyard. Celia hurried over and opened the sliding glass door for them. Ty motioned for Addie to go before him. When Celia attempted to follow them out, he gave her a warning look.

She scowled and set her chin.

He jerked his head toward where he wanted her to go,

back inside the house. What'd she think he was going to do? Throw Addie over his shoulder, climb the fence, and kidnap her?

Celia didn't budge.

Ty met Celia's gaze, full force, letting her read his determination.

After a brief staring contest, Celia moved indoors. Instead of closing the glass slider, however, she simply closed the screen before walking into the kitchen.

Ty had spent the last few days examining his emotions about this whole thing. He was upset with Celia. But over the years he'd learned to treat even the angriest and most annoying women in a friendly manner. From Sacramento to New York City and back, year after year, he'd perfected the art of getting along well with women. He'd assumed he'd be able to handle Celia tonight.

Wrong. He'd been around her for sixty seconds, and he already wanted to throttle her. And also provoke her. And also, for some reason, kiss the side of her neck . . . which was a problem.

He sat on the step next to Addie. Not too close; didn't want to freak her out. "This is for you." He passed over the box.

"Thank you." She looked unsure what to do with it.

"You can open it."

Carefully, slowly, she tore off the paper and set it aside, then lifted the lid. "Oooh."

"Do you like them?"

"Yes. Should I, um, save them or put them on?"

She spoke so quietly, she tested his hearing. "Whichever you want."

Addie tugged off her slippers. Thanks to the tights,

her feet slid right into the pair of pink cowgirl boots he'd bought her. The boots had black soles, pointed toes, and three flowers stitched onto their sides with red thread.

He motioned toward them. "They're supposed to light up."

Sure enough, as soon as she rocked some of her weight forward onto them, the star in the center of the middle flower flashed.

Seeing her in pink cowgirl boots caused something inside Ty to soften almost painfully. His own boots were planted on the ground just inches from her much smaller ones.

She looked up at him sideways. "Thank you."

"You're welcome." He smiled.

She smiled back, her mouth curving gently.

There were two things in life he knew. Bull riding and females. Addie was, although miniature, a female. Good Lord willing, he hoped that in time he could win her heart. "If you decide later you don't like them or want another style or something, you can return them, okay? It won't hurt my feelings."

"No." Her green eyes were earnest behind her glasses. "I like them."

"Where I'm from, in Texas, a lot of us wear boots. Even kids. I grew up wearing them."

"You did?"

"Yeah. They're pretty comfortable. And they're good for walking through a field or riding horses."

"I'd like to ride horses."

"Now that you've got boots, you're all set. Back home in Holley, I have some horses you can ride."

"Really?"

"Yes."

"Maybe . . . maybe my mom and I can move to Holley? And then I could ride your horses all the time."

"I'd like that." He found it was true. "I'll talk to your mom about it."

"She'd love to live in Holley."

He almost laughed because he knew Celia would be dead set against the idea.

"Mommy's nice. And she's real, real pretty." She searched his face hopefully. "Don't you think?"

Ah. A matchmaker. "Yep."

"She said you ride bulls."

"Yeah. Funny job, isn't it?"

She studied him with curiosity, nodded.

"I'm going to be riding tomorrow night in Colorado. It'll be on TV if you want to watch it."

"Okay." Her eyebrows lowered. "Does that mean you're leaving?"

"I wish I could stay longer, but months ago I told the people I work for that I'd be in Colorado. And after that, Idaho. And after that, Montana. But if you don't mind, I'll call you on the phone every night while I'm gone."

"I don't mind."

"They have this thing on the computer that lets you look at the person you're talking to on the screen. We could talk like that sometimes."

"'Kay."

He took her in from head to toe, trying to believe that the child sitting beside him was his daughter. Scientific lab tests had proven it beyond a shadow of a doubt. One night in Vegas had done it. "Did your mom tell you about me? Who I am?"

She dipped her chin.

"I'm real glad that I'm your dad."

Her attention darted to the space next to his elbow again.

"I'm sorry I didn't know about you sooner, Addie."

"Mommy told me that she didn't tell you 'cause it was hard to share. She's sorry about that now. She thinks she made a big mistake."

Interesting. He didn't know if Celia had actually said those things or if, like Addie's statement that Celia would love to live in Holley, Addie had just invented the reality she wanted. "I wish I'd known you when you were a baby," he said. "When you were littler."

She shrugged. "I couldn't do much then anyway."

"Well, I'm here now, and I'd like to get to know you."

"Uh-huh."

"And I'd also like to help you if I can. Is there anything I can do for you? Anything you need?" He wasn't above buying her toys, and lots of them. Like maybe one of those kid-size electric jeeps? Except where was she going to ride it? Celia's backyard was flowery—it reminded him of a field trip he'd taken as a kid to the Dallas Arboretum—but it was no bigger than a sneeze. Sitting here was like sitting inside a green fuzzy closet.

"There is one thing," Addie said, "that I kind of need."

"Yes?"

"A car. Ours broke down."

He'd been thinking of a child's car just now, but he suspected Addie was talking about the real thing. "I saw your mom driving a car with wood paneling on the side last weekend."

"That's Uncle Danny's car. Our car was white and"—
she wrinkled her nose— "really old."

"I see."

"When it broke, Uncle Danny told Mommy that we
could drive his car. I told her we should, but she said
no because it wouldn't be nice to take Uncle Danny's
car away."

"Is your white car in the shop getting fixed?"

"I don't think so. I think it costs too much money to
fix it, so now we have to take the bus."

He frowned. Even though he had some issues with
Celia, it brought him no pleasure to learn that she
couldn't afford to fix her car. And one thing was as certain as the grave: He did not want his child or his child's
mother having to take the bus. "You need a car."

Her gaze asked him to prove that she could trust him.
"Yes."

He'd just learned two important things about Addie.
One, the way to her heart was through her mother. Two,
it looked like the kid had inherited something from him
after all. Like him, she wasn't afraid to go after what
she wanted. "I'll have a car here for you and your mom
by tomorrow afternoon."

Hope lifted her expression.

"I promise you." He extended a hand. "Shake on it?"

She put her hand in his, and they shook. Ty grinned at
her, and Addie grinned back, a dimple in one of her cheeks.

As if a heavy weight had been lifted from her, Addie
popped to her feet and motioned for him to follow. Slowly,
she took him around the garden, introducing him to one
flower after another as if they were people. He listened,
asked a few questions, cracked a few jokes.

Just like when he'd thought about his future kids and pictured boys, when he'd thought about himself as a future dad, he'd imagined that he'd be like his own father. Practical, patient, stern when the situation called for it. Instead, it looked like he was going to be a real pushover. He'd just agreed to buy Addie a car. If she turned that sunray of a smile on him again and asked him to buy her a boat or a pony or a swimming pool, he'd probably buy those, too.

Celia might not like it.

Once Addie had finished the garden tour, she led him on a tour of the apartment. Celia watched them like a grumpy hawk from her post at the kitchen counter.

Addie saved her own room for last. It was tidy: the twin bed made, the majority of the kid stuff organized in a tall bookshelf. Celia had decorated the room in baby colors: pale yellow walls, light blue curtains, and a watery scene of a nursery rhyme he couldn't remember the name of on the bedspread. But judging by the dolls and doll clothes that Addie had been playing with on the floor, the girl herself liked hot pink.

She lowered onto the carpet in the middle of the dolls and crossed her legs. Ty sat nearby, his back against her plastic toy kitchen, one leg stretched long, the other knee bent up. Addie picked out a doll, and in her serious way, started talking. For the next hour straight, she hardly stopped. It turned out that the dolls were princesses. She told him each princess's story, what they liked to wear, and how they did their hair.

Celia came in and out a couple of times. Clearly, she wanted him to leave. He ignored her hints.

Ty didn't know squat about the Disney princesses.

He'd never even heard the names of most of them. Jasmine? Belle? Tiana? Fairy tales weren't his thing, and he sure as shootin' didn't care how the princesses dressed or did their hair.

But the man who'd grown jaded couldn't remember when he'd spent a better evening. Addie fascinated him. Enchanted him. Wrapped him around her pinkie. It entertained him just to listen to her voice.

He expected that it would take him a good while to win her heart. But it hadn't taken her long at all to win his.

This father-daughter bonding session was taking forever. Celia checked the time and decided to put an end to it. She'd already attempted to get Ty to leave twice via subtle comments, but he was either too obtuse or too ornery to react to subtlety. She neared Addie's bedroom.

". . . and Rapunzel had long magical hair." Addie held up her Rapunzel doll for Ty's examination. "When her mom—the evil one not the good one—would comb it and sing, then it would glow."

"That's cool," Ty said.

Celia made her way into the room. "Addie, it's time to start getting ready for bed."

"Already?"

"Yep."

"Well, crud." Ty glanced at Celia. "I haven't finished learning about Rapunzel."

"Mommy, I haven't even gotten to the part where Flynn—"

"Addie," Celia warned.

Addie gave a long-suffering sigh. Both she and Ty pushed to their feet.

"I'd like to talk to you for a minute before I leave, Celia, if you don't mind."

"Um. . . ." She did mind. "Sure. Let me get Addie in the bath, and I'll be right back."

It only took Celia a minute to start the water running, add a squirt of liquid bath soap, and oversee Addie's entry into the water. She returned to where Ty waited and gestured for him to follow her into her bedroom—a space she loved and had filled with twenty shades of blue, ten shades of white, five patterns, and too many throw pillows to count. She shut the door, closing them in.

Ty looked to the bed, then slowly back to her. He lifted one eyebrow. "Isn't this a little forward?"

She narrowed her eyes.

"I mean, we're married and all, but I'm not exactly ready for romance."

"As I'm sure you know, I brought you in here for *privacy's* sake. I don't want Addie to overhear."

"Overhear . . . what?"

A blush burned her cheeks and forehead. She planted her fists on her hips. "Did you have something you wanted to talk to me about?"

He had the bad taste to laugh.

"Well?" she demanded, livid.

He laughed harder. "You really don't like me, do you, Celia?"

"What was your first clue, Ty?"

"You used to like me."

"That was before I married you."

He gave her an unrepentant grin. He wore his usual uniform—a well-fitting T-shirt and jeans. He looked like living, breathing temptation, like a red-blooded male who drove a truck, had a strong appreciation for women, and drank testosterone for breakfast.

Her apartment had minimal privacy options. Even so, Celia realized she'd been wrong to invite him here. As he'd been crass enough to note, standing inside her bedroom with him brought to mind the personal things that happened on beds. She hadn't anticipated this truth because she hadn't had a man in here before.

"What don't you like about me?" he asked.

"You know what."

"Is it my personality?"

"Flaky."

"My career?"

"Preposterous."

"My looks?"

She pondered him for a moment. "Slightly effeminate."

"What?" He glanced down at himself. Humor and challenge glowed in his eyes. "Now that's just mean, not to mention untrue."

Mean? Yes. Untrue? A *hundred times* yes. Ty Porter was the antonym of effeminate. "I'm surprised to learn that you know what effeminate means. I didn't think you understood words longer than two syllables."

"Well, I do. I'm many things—"

"—that's for sure—"

"But I am *not* effeminate." A glint of purpose in the set of his jaw, he extended his fingers toward her forehead.

She hissed and swatted his hand away. "No touching."

"I was just going to put a curl back in place."

"No."

"Shoot, Celia." He stuffed his hands into his back pockets and regarded her with amusement. "What fun is this relationship going to be if there's no touching?"

"This relationship isn't going to be any fun. It's going to be torturous."

His dimple made an appearance. She hadn't expected anything about Ty to resemble Addie. But that dimple, just on the one side, matched Addie's precisely. And Addie's hair was just a few shades lighter than his. "Is this why you needed to speak to me?" she asked. "To hear all the reasons why I dislike you?"

"Just for the record, I dislike you, too."

"Fine. Is that why you wanted to speak to me? To tell me that?"

"Nah, I actually wanted to say thanks for letting me come over tonight. I think it went well between Addie and me."

It had certainly looked that way to Celia. While she was glad that Addie seemed to be taking the situation in stride, it had also chafed to see admiration in Addie's eyes when she'd looked at Ty. Celia had no reason to believe that Ty would prove himself worthy of Addie's admiration. Her daughter's feelings for him may well end in heartbreak.

"As soon as Addie found out that I have horses in Holley, she suggested that the two of you move there."

His words hit her like a bucket of ice water. "Not a chance."

"I told her I'd speak to you about it."

"We're absolutely not moving. Corvallis is our home."

He considered her, taking his time. Right when she was about to launch into a tirade and list all the reasons why she'd never leave Corvallis, he lifted a shoulder in an easy shrug. "Okay."

His capitulation made her suspicious.

"I'm leaving town. I have to be in Colorado tomorrow night for an event."

She'd known it! Unreliable wretch—

"Don't give me that look," he said.

"What look?"

"That look that says you knew I'd disappear the first chance I got."

"Are you providing evidence to the contrary?"

He whistled under his breath. "Man, you're sassy."

"With everyone else I'm perfectly agreeable."

"I told Addie why I had to leave, and I told her I'd call her every night while I'm gone. Is that all right with you?"

"From now on, I'd like you to ask me first before you tell Addie you'll do something."

"I'll try to remember that."

"That doesn't sound promising."

"It's the best I've got. Can I call and talk to Addie?"

She sighed. "Yes, but you're going to have to call between six and eight. Any later and she might be asleep for the night."

"Got it." Before she could blink, he swiped out a hand and moved the curl he'd tried to reposition earlier. There and gone, quick as a flash.

She yelped. "No touching!"

He chuckled and strode down the hallway as if he hadn't a care in the world. "A man's got to have some perks in a relationship, sweet one."

"And *don't call me that*!"

"I'll try to remember that, too."

CHAPTER
SEVEN

Celia had given Christianity a try. More than once. Her parents had taken her to church occasionally when she was young. As she'd gotten older, extracurricular activities had squeezed out the majority of Sunday services, but even so, she'd gone to church camp with Lacey two different summers and shown up at high school Bible studies whenever her friends invited her. Those influences had motivated her to recommit herself to her faith several times across her teenage years. Each time, she'd determined to read her Bible and pray daily like she knew she was supposed to. Each and every time she'd failed. The whole thing had left her with plenty of guilt and very little peace.

Midway through her college years, she'd set aside religion like a coat she'd outgrown. She'd clicked along, happy and secure in her own capabilities. She'd graduated with honors. She'd gotten a job as a sous chef, rented an apartment, enjoyed her network of friends.

And then Las Vegas had happened.

"What is it, Mommy?" Addie asked from the bus seat next to Celia.

Celia looked down at her and raised her eyebrows.

"You just made this sound." Addie did a mad face and mimicked an angry sigh.

"Oh, sorry." Ty's fault! His return and his visit with Addie last night had stirred up thoughts that had been lying dormant at the bottom of the pond of Celia's brain for years. "It's just been a long day, Punkie. That's all."

Addie patted Celia's forearm consolingly.

Celia adjusted the sack of groceries on her lap, covered Addie's hand with her own, and returned her attention to the view out the bus windows.

When she'd come home to Corvallis after having her sliced-up heart handed to her on a platter by Ty in Vegas, she'd spent a month wallowing in depression and devastation and fury. It had been an awful, *awful* month. So bad, she hadn't thought things could get any worse.

Until she'd begun to suspect that she might be pregnant. The possibility of a pregnancy had struck her, a then twenty-four-year-old without a husband, as a whole new level of *worse*.

In desperation, she'd turned back to the God she'd left behind. She'd prayed on her knees each morning and night for a week straight before finally screwing up the courage to take an at-home pregnancy test. While the test had been processing, she'd knelt on her bathroom floor and prayed with everything she'd had. She'd wept and shivered with abject fear. She'd *begged* God not to be pregnant.

When the timer had gone off, and she'd stood looking down at the positive result on the test stick, she'd known that God had heard her prayer. Heard it and refused to have pity on her. She'd not been a good Christian, and He'd held her mistakes against her.

Celia, in turn, had held His unforgiveness against Him. Some people were DIY with home renovation. Since the day that test had confirmed her pregnancy, Celia had been DIY with life, work, and motherhood.

Truthfully, she hadn't missed Christianity's rules or the sense that she wasn't—and never would be—worthy enough to satisfy God. Religion's departure from her life had left nothing behind but a small and benign emptiness. Most of the time the hole within her existed in such a quiet state that it didn't even bother her.

Ty's return had upset her mental equilibrium, though. Having to deal with him had placed a new and heavy layer of stress on her, causing the space within her that God had once occupied to grow large. Noticeable.

Times like these made her wish God was someone she could rely on. Even for a week. Goodness! Even a day.

The bus arrived at their stop with a shrieking of brakes and a prolonged shudder. Celia ushered Addie out. In unison, the trek to River Run and Addie's familiar complaints about the trek began.

"Mommy, I'm tired."

"I know. We'll be home soon."

A few minutes later. "My feet hurt."

"Uh-huh." *Try wearing shoes other than cowgirl boots.*

Later: "Do you have a drink? I'm really thirsty." Addie took a few weaving steps. "I need a snack."

Later still, a tortured groan. "I can't walk *so far.*"

"If I can do it carrying groceries, Addie, you can make it the rest of the way."

As usual, Celia had to take Addie's hand and tow her, tugboat style, across the final stretch to their apartment. Celia lowered the sack and was rummaging in her purse for her keys when she spotted a small box hanging from her doorknob. Its pink paper and purple ribbon matched the wrapping on the gift that Ty had given Addie the night before.

Celia paused. A surprise gift for Addie from anyone else would have been wonderful to receive. But a gift from Ty made Celia's stomach knot. What was he doing? Trying to buy Addie's affection with presents?

Addie had seen the box, too. She turned excited eyes up to Celia.

"Looks like someone left you a present." Celia tried to sound less resentful and worn out than she was.

"That's not my name." Addie moved aside a section of ribbon to reveal that *Celia* had been written on the tag attached to the package.

For her? She couldn't imagine Ty wanting to give her anything except a lecture. Celia freed the box. As she removed its wrapping paper she noticed that Addie was bobbing up and down on the balls of her boots, pressing her hands together and smiling. "Do you know anything about this?" Celia asked.

"No, Mommy." Her tone held such solemn honesty that Celia knew she was lying.

The paper gave way to a plain, unmarked white box. She removed the lid and uncovered a key ring. The silver charm attached to it formed the shape of a peace sign and had been stamped with the words *Give Peace a Chance*. Hilarious. The ring held just one other item. An electronic . . . smart key? It reminded her of the kind of gadget people used to activate alarms remotely or to start new-model cars—

Oh no. *No*.

Addie hadn't told Ty about their broken-down car, had she? Mortifying thought. Even if Addie *had* grossly humiliated her by spilling the beans, Ty wouldn't have, couldn't have, done anything about their car situation. Surely.

Celia pointed the smart key in the direction of the parking lot and pressed the Unlock button. A car parked just a few spots away beeped and flashed its lights.

She could not believe it. Could. Not.

Her eyes bugging out and mouth ajar, she moved toward the car.

Addie dashed ahead of her. More bouncing. "It's this one, Mom!"

Celia stopped directly in front of a brand-new light teal Toyota Prius. Teal was exactly Celia's bright and happy kind of color. And though she'd never told this to a single soul, the Prius was the make of car that she'd have chosen for herself if money had not been a concern. Oh, the safety ratings, the outstanding fuel efficiency.

How could Ty Porter, of all people, know her so well? It bowled her over, this gesture. Was it generosity or foolishness or a bribe or lavish craziness? What? It must be a mash-up between craziness and a bribe.

"Mommy, let's get in it. Let's drive it."

"Let's maybe just get in it for now."

As the two of them slid inside, the new-car smell welcomed them. Celia couldn't spot a speck of dust on anything, not the dash, the console, the seats. She'd never had a new car in her life. She had no frame of reference for such a flawless and shiny interior.

"Do you like it?" Addie beamed at her expectantly.

Celia couldn't recall when her even-tempered girl had ever looked so elated. "I do."

"Now we won't have to take the bus."

Celia remembered all of sudden what Addie had said the night their old car kicked the bucket. *"I'm going to buy you a new car, Mommy."* At the time Addie had planned on raising money through a lemonade stand. It appeared she'd found something a lot more lucrative.

So many misgivings crowded into Celia's brain, she couldn't begin to unravel them all.

"Isn't this car awesome? I think it's brand-new!"

"I think so, too."

"Wasn't it nice of Ty to get this for you?"

"Yes, it was. But, Punkie . . . it's not good manners to go around asking people to buy you things."

"I didn't, Mommy. *He* asked *me* what he could do."

"He did?"

"Yes. You're going to record his show tonight, right? I really, really want to watch it." Addie had voiced this sentiment no fewer than ten times today.

"Yes, I'm going to record it."

"And I can watch it in the morning?"

"Yes." She'd refused to let Addie watch Ty's bull riding live. For one thing, it would air past her bedtime. For another, Ty might be gored by a bull at any moment, and she didn't want her child to see that and be traumatized for life. She planned to screen the rodeo herself this evening and make sure it was fit for a pre-kindergartener's consumption.

They sat inside the car for ten minutes, examining everything, talking about each detail. Afterward, as Celia went through the evening routine of making dinner, cleaning up after dinner, and giving Addie a bath, her brain kept trying to grasp the fact that Ty had given—*given?*—her a car. She didn't know what to do with this information. It didn't fit inside the compartment marked *Bad Guy* that she'd stuffed Ty into.

The phone rang as Celia was brushing the tangles from Addie's wet hair. Addie rushed to answer it, her Ariel nightgown billowing behind her.

"If it's Ty, I'd like to speak to him when you're done," Celia called after her.

It was Ty. And from what Celia heard, most of their long conversation revolved around the Prius and the boy at day care who'd gotten into trouble for biting his friends.

"Mommy wants to talk to you," Addie said to him at last. ". . . Okay, 'bye. Thank you for the car. 'Bye." She extended the phone to Celia.

Celia took it and pressed it against her chest. "Go brush your teeth and start picking out books. I'll be right behind you."

Addie headed off, and Celia let herself outside and retreated to the far corner of the garden. A misting rain fell, dampening her hair, the bridge of her nose, her shoulders. She moved under a tree limb. "Ty?"

"Hey."

"I came home from work tonight and found a key on my doorknob."

"Oh yeah?"

"The key came with a car."

"Huh."

Based on the background noise, Celia guessed he was already at the arena in Denver. "Am I right in thinking that you've given us a *car*?"

"I asked Addie yesterday if there was anything she needed. She seemed pretty sure about the answer."

Celia's shoulders sagged. "Well, children can be dramatic. I think we've . . . we've been doing fine without a car."

"The bus working out for you?"

"Um," she said faintly, finding it hard to drum up enthusiasm, "the public transportation in Corvallis is perfectly adequate."

He snorted. "Really?"

Celia pressed her fingertips into her forehead. "The car was a nice gesture, Ty. But honestly. I can't keep it." She was a single mother used to doing everything for herself. "I don't feel comfortable accepting that kind of a gift." *Least of all, from you.*

"I'm not taking it back," Ty answered. "It's a free country, though, so if you want to walk by the car every day on your way to the bus, then you're welcome to."

She considered taking up her old nervous habit of picking at her cuticles. "If I were—hypothetically, you understand—to accept the car, what would I owe you in return?"

A pause that crackled with static and distant voices filled the line. "Nothing."

"C'mon, Ty. The car has to be a bribe. I need to know the terms."

"No terms. It's a gift, free and clear."

"I can't believe you'd just give us a car."

"Listen, I must owe you a fortune in unpaid child support, right? So if you have to, consider the car a down payment on that."

"How about you cut me a check for the child support?"

"How about you thank me for the car?"

Her tongue and mouth froze.

"Still hate me?" he asked.

"Yes."

He laughed.

Her animosity seemed to provide him with no end of amusement. "Do you still hate me?" she asked.

"Sure do. Nice talking to you, sweet one." *Click.*

"Don't call me that!" she growled into the silence.

It would indulge her vindictive side to scorn the Prius and leave it sitting in the parking lot. It really would. But what would Addie think? The way Addie had looked earlier, when they'd been sitting in the car together! Addie clearly believed that she herself had procured a car for her mother. How could Celia now tell Addie that she'd decided to reject the Prius?

You see, Addie, this is my chance to shove something back in Ty's face the way that he once shoved the love and intimacy I offered him back in my face. Do you understand? No? Well, Addie, your mother is too proud to ever, ever, ever accept anything from anyone.

It figured that Ty wasn't wearing a helmet.

Some of the cowboys had enough sense, at least, to wear head protection while riding seventeen-hundred-pound bulls. Ty wasn't in that group.

Celia had put Addie to sleep an hour ago, caught up on e-mail and household stuff, and now sat in her TV-watching spot on the sofa. She hadn't seen Ty do his thing since Vegas, and she'd intended never to watch him ride bulls again. Yet here she was.

The camera zoomed in on a shot of Ty sitting on a bull inside the chute, trying to get his grip on the rope before the gate opened and the bull lunged free. He wore a black hat and black shirt, a protective vest covered with his sponsors' logos, and leather chaps over his jeans and boots. He'd be attempting to ride a beast named Pummeler. He kept adjusting his glove, testing and retesting his hold while the bull beneath him writhed, head-butted the fence, and generally looked wild.

Very unkindly, Celia found herself rooting for Pummeler. "Buck him off," she muttered, "and dent his arrogance."

At Ty's nod, the gate swung open. Pummeler sprang into the arena, kicking, twisting, launching himself into the air, and spinning all at the same time.

No human should have been able to stay on him. But Ty did, one arm high, his balance and strength jaw-dropping. When the buzzer sounded after eight seconds, he let the bull's momentum vault him into the air and landed easily on his feet. The crowd roared.

Once Pummeler had disappeared down the passage where all the bulls disappeared, Ty lifted his hat, smiled at the crowd, and turned in a circle to acknowledge their support. The down-home commentators with the chicken-fried-steak accents called him a "fan favorite" and a "three-time world champion" and "third in the season's standings."

"Nice try, Pummeler." Celia shook her head and fast-forwarded.

Ty rode again and stayed on again.

Unfortunately, no one would be denting Ty's arrogance tonight.

The next morning—a precious sleep-in Saturday morning—Celia woke to a voice whispering into her ear canal.

"Mommy? Mommy, are you awake? Time to get up, Mom. I'm ready to watch the bull riding."

Celia groaned and covered her head with her pillow. The voice and the child proved persistent.

Ten minutes later, Celia had positioned Addie in the armchair facing the TV while the Bull Riders Professional Circuit played. Celia whipped up some apple-walnut whole-grain pancakes and delivered them to Addie on a tray. Addie ate without ever lifting her gaze from the rodeo. The two times Ty rode, Addie pressed her fists together in front of her chest and held her breath. Each time Ty stayed on, Addie threw her arms into the air in a move that reminded Celia of a football referee signaling a touchdown.

Later, when it came time for them to head to Uncle Danny's, Celia and Addie piled into the Prius instead of walking to the bus stop. At Celia's first attempt to start the car, it came to life, the dashboard illuminating, the hybrid's system purring with remarkable quiet. She cut a look at Addie in her booster seat in the back.

Addie grinned and gave her a thumbs-up.

Celia drew herself tall in the driver's seat and angled

her jaw determinedly. It didn't come naturally to her, the humility required to receive a gift as costly as a car. In order to accept it, she'd had to tell herself Ty owed her the Prius and twenty more like it for the mental and emotional anguish he'd caused her.

She steered them smoothly toward the road without so much as a single mention of pride or of shoving anything into anyone's face.

True to his word, Ty called Addie every night. Each evening between six and eight the phone would ring, Addie would race to answer it, and Addie and Ty would chat. One week of this turned into two, then three, then four.

At Addie's insistence, Celia purchased a map of the United States and tacked it to the wall near the laundry room. Each time Ty traveled to a bull-riding event, mother and daughter would find the place on the map and stick a pin in it.

Celia kept expecting him to forget to call. She was even prepared to send him a text message reminding him of his oversight, but he never gave her the chance. No matter Ty's whereabouts, he faithfully called the little girl who waited so eagerly to talk to him.

Celia herself? The opposite of eager to talk to him. She communicated with him solely through text, and then only if necessary. On Sundays, when Addie and Ty had Skype conversations, Celia went to extreme lengths not to be captured by her computer's camera. She hunkered beneath the table and reached up with her fingertips to move the cursor while Addie gave her weird looks.

Each weekend Celia screened the televised rodeo coverage. An interest in bull riding went against her will, her ideological principles, and her status as someone who'd completed higher education. On top of that, Ty was a bull rider, so she'd have preferred to dislike bull riding. The more of it she watched, however, the more she feared that she, a Pacific Northwest–loving girl, had an intrinsic flaw. In the way that Uncle Danny had a weakness for Eastern European women, Celia had a small and guilty weakness for—for . . .

Cowboys.

Shameful! She could scarcely admit it to herself.

Even more upsetting? Her weakness appeared to center on a particular cowboy with sky blue eyes and a double serving of charm.

As the weeks passed and she saw a few of the riders sustain injuries, she began to root with a little less pep for the bulls Ty rode. Just a little. But still. It was hard to maintain complete loathing for a man who called her daughter every evening.

Partial loathing she managed.

In her more mature moments, Celia understood that she ought to be grateful for the current situation. Ty had gone, which meant she didn't have to see him in person and didn't have to split Addie's custody between them. Even though he wasn't physically present, however, his influence began to permeate everything.

Ty and Holley, Texas, had become Addie's two favorite topics of conversation. Celia would be telling Addie a bedtime story, and Addie would suddenly ask, "Mommy? Did you know that they have a fall parade in Holley?" Then, wistfully, "I sure would like to live there." At the dinner table Celia would ask Addie about her day, and Addie would say, "It was good. Mom? What do you think it would feel like to ride a bull?" They'd be driving to work in the morning and Addie would sigh. "I bet they have good teachers in Texas. It would be really, really fun to go to kindergarten in Holley. The kids there are so lucky."

Addie's talk about Ty, their phone calls, their Skyping, and the map of the USA were more than enough to bear. But Celia was also treated to one other constant reminder of Ty: the cowgirl boots.

Addie refused to wear any other pair of shoes. Since babyhood, Celia had dressed her in Scandinavian style. She'd raked eBay and consignment shops for nubby little knitted hats. Thick patterned tights. Mittens in the winter. Combed cotton dresses with polka dots or stripes or bold colored prints. Sweaters. Mary Janes.

The cowgirl boots ruined Addie's Denmark vibe. But Addie, who'd always been mild, *insisted* on them. And Celia, who'd always purported that children should be free to express their own creative style, pretended to be gracious about the boots when what she really wanted was to have her daughter all to herself again.

Her life and Addie's life had changed. It choked Celia up every time she thought about it—but no matter how it tangled her emotions, how it made her lungs squeeze, how powerless it rendered her—there was no going back to the way it had been before Ty, when their family had been a safe, snug circle of two.

She sensed her control slipping away. The more it slipped, the more the space within—the one which God had once occupied—grew. The more the hole grew, the more she sought to find her everything in Addie. And the more she tried to find her everything in Addie, the more she realized that Addie didn't need her as much as Addie once had.

Celia wanted joy for her child. She did. Without doubt, Ty's involvement in Addie's life appeared to bring Addie joy. It both pleased and hurt Celia to see that joy. Ty already had so much. She'd only ever had Addie. Why, she sometimes wondered, had she been asked to relinquish some of her sole treasure to a man who was already so outrageously blessed?

CHAPTER
EIGHT

One commonplace Wednesday evening in late June, a knock sounded on Celia's door.

She set aside the wooden spoon she'd been using to brown ground turkey for spaghetti sauce and went to answer it. She swung the door open, expecting to see her neighbor returning Addie from the playdate the two moms had arranged for their girls.

Instead, Ty stood on her front step, filling up the space with his impressive height.

Celia's motion stuttered to a stop. The bane of her existence, here unexpectedly and in the flesh.

Ty took in the sight of her, a mix of challenge and enjoyment in his eyes. "Hi."

"Hello." Celia realized she was wearing the tight yellow tank she'd changed into hurriedly after work and wouldn't have worn in public without a peasant shirt over it. The rest of her attire consisted of an old pair of shorts and a dish towel on her shoulder.

"I flew in to surprise Addie. Is she here?"

"Uh . . . she's a few doors down playing with a friend. She should be back soon."

"Can I come in?"

In answer, Celia grudgingly stepped back and let him pass.

"How've you been, sweet one?"

"I've been fine, showboat."

He grinned crookedly. "Showboat?"

"Yep." The sizzle of meat on the stove reminded her of her spaghetti sauce. She returned to the kitchen, Ty trailing. "Since you insist on calling me a nickname, I figured it was only fair to respond in kind." She positioned herself at the stove and went back to work on the ground turkey.

Ty crossed his muscled arms and leaned a hip against the edge of the countertop. "Was showboat the best you could do? I don't like it."

"Good."

"What about Maverick? Adonis?"

She rolled her eyes.

"This might be too obvious, but how about Stud?"

"Believe me. It's not in the least obvious."

"Well, showboat's no good."

She made a scoffing sound. "Tough luck. You don't get to pick." To the turkey, she added the onions, bell pepper, and mushrooms she'd sautéed. Then the tomato sauce. She was doing her best to appear unfazed by him, but in truth it was unsettling and surreal to have spent the past several weeks watching him on TV and now have him standing in her kitchen eyeballing her while she cooked.

"Did you catch any of my bull riding this past month?"

"I did."

"What did you think?"

"I thought it a shame that you couldn't squeeze any more sponsorship logos on your vest no matter how much you'd clearly tried. Have you considered plastering a few across your forehead?"

He released a bark of laughter.

She couldn't fully hide her answering smile. "Or maybe your mouth? As a bonus to the rest of us, it might keep you from speaking."

"Aw," he crooned. "Watching me ride gave you a little thing for me, didn't it, sweet one?"

She turned a withering look on him. "What kind of a thing?"

"A burning-love kind of a thing."

"Hardly."

"Admit it, you missed me while I was gone."

"Not in the least."

"Still hate me?"

"*Yes.*" The child stealer.

As usual, he seemed to find her rancor pleasing. He popped a piece of French bread into his mouth, looking very satisfied with himself while he chewed. Women everywhere would be willing to pay a fortune for his bronze-tipped brown hair. It didn't seem right that God had given it to Ty for free.

"I'm glad I caught you alone, Celia."

"I can't imagine why."

"I've been wanting to talk to you again about moving."

She slanted her attention toward him. "To Holley?" At his nod, she shook her head. "There's no point in discussing it further. I'm not moving."

"Addie's been asking me questions about Holley. She's told me several times that she wants to live there."

His words stung Celia, mostly because she knew they were true. "Have you been pressuring her to move to Holley?"

"No. If I want something, I won't use Addie to get it. I'll come directly to you." He took her measure the way an amused lion might take the measure of a brave prairie dog. "You might be fierce, but you don't exactly scare me."

She stirred the boiling pasta more than it needed to be stirred.

"Addie wants to move to Holley."

"Yes, and next week she might want to move to Japan and the week after that Australia. I don't let Addie's whims determine where we live."

"Holley's my home base. If the two of you lived there, it would make life easier for me."

"My world doesn't revolve around what's easier for you, Ty. I'm all about what's practical. My job is here."

"I'll find you a job there."

"My uncle lives here."

"My family lives in Holley. I have a big family, and they'll all support you."

"Our home, Addie's and mine, is here in Oregon." She indicated the apartment. "This is where we've always lived."

He studied her with eyes of the rarest, brightest blue. Another attribute God had unfairly given him. "What if I made it worth your while to move?"

"Nothing you could offer—"

"A house of your own? The title in your name? Completely paid off?"

She'd had a good head of steam going, but his words released it with a *whoosh*. She regarded him incredulously, and yet she could hardly accuse him of making her an offer he had no intention of fulfilling . . . not when a gleaming teal Prius sat outside in her parking spot. "Do I look like a gold digger to you, Ty?"

"Maybe a really small, pretty one."

"You just offended and complimented me in the same sentence."

"Which takes skill."

She blew out a breath and blotted her hands on the dish towel before swinging it back over her shoulder. "I am not a gold digger."

"Don't get your hackles up, Celia. I know you're not. I was just teasing you."

"Addie's not a gold digger, either. You do know that Addie's love isn't for sale, right?" She assessed him, trying to read his intentions. "You can't buy your way into her life. Becoming her father is going to take years."

"I'm just trying to make up for lost time."

"You can't make up for lost time with your credit card, Ty. That's not what love is."

"Fine, but I want you to know that if you decide to relocate, I'll also pay your moving expenses." He pulled off another piece of bread. "I'll set up the house inside any way you like. I'll handle everything. If you guys move this summer, Addie can start kindergarten at the same time as all the other kids there. It's the perfect time to go."

She placed what remained of the loaf of bread on

the opposite side of the stove, out of his reach. "I may hold Addie back a year. She has a late summer birthday. She'll be the youngest in her whole grade."

He tilted his head, seeming to weigh her words for truth.

Celia wished she had a single reason, other than Addie's summer birthdate, to hold her back. Addie was a quick-minded only child, mature for her years, way ahead academically. She was ready for school.

"You didn't really mean that," Ty said, "about holding Addie back."

"No."

"So move to Holley in time for kindergarten."

"You travel almost all the time. Why would you want us to move to Holley when you yourself are hardly ever there?"

"I'm there more than I'm anywhere. And I want my child to grow up in Texas like I did. I've got land there for her to play on, horses."

Had he seen what had happened to Bonnie Blue Butler in *Gone With the Wind*? "My answer's no. We're not moving."

"Just think about it. The offer's good."

They locked wills—hers fiery, his understated—different, but equally matched.

He broke the moment by moving off to amble around her kitchen, straightening her stack of mail. Studying the photos on the fridge. Thumbing her set of keys. "What happened to the key ring I gave you?"

"Hmm? Oh. It must have fallen off somewhere." She shrugged with fake innocence. "Accidentally." She carried the pot with the pasta to the sink and poured the contents over a colander. "How long are you in town?" Thirty more minutes? Was that too much to hope?

"I fly out tomorrow night. I'd like to spend the day with Addie tomorrow. Would that be okay?"

She bit her lip.

"Just during the time you're at work."

"What do you have in mind?"

He lifted a shoulder. "Normal stuff. A movie. I thought I'd take her to lunch. The park."

She wanted to reject this request as emphatically as she'd rejected the Holley thing. But her mind went back over the past four weeks of phone calls. Technically, asking to spend a few hours with Addie wasn't unreasonable. If she got too territorial, she feared he'd bring in lawyers.

"Celia?" he prompted.

"All right, but I'm going to put together some . . . some rules. And I'll need to be able to reach you at all times on your phone."

"Deal."

A brief knock sounded, followed by girls' voices.

"I'll hide." Ty gestured toward the laundry room.

Celia chatted with her neighbor for a bit, thanked her for having Addie, then waved at the mother-daughter pair as the two headed back toward their own apartment.

"Did you have fun?" she asked Addie.

"Yep."

Tenderly, Celia took Addie's cheeks in her hands, kissed the top of her head, then straightened a few of the dark blond strands that had fallen forward over her barrette. Tempting, oh so tempting, to leave Ty in the laundry room all evening. If only he was timid or compliant enough to stay there. "Interested in a surprise?"

Four words guaranteed to catch the attention of any child. "A surprise? Yes!"

"Let's see if I can come up with three clues. Hmm . . ." Celia pretended to think hard. "One. Map of the United States."

Addie tipped her head.

"Two. Bull rider."

Addie gasped, her thin form straightening tall.

"Three—"

"Doesn't know much about princesses." Ty walked around the corner. "I thought I'd better stop by for another lesson."

Celia watched shyness overcome Addie. Her daughter stayed rooted to the spot, too self-conscious to hug Ty or even look directly at him and at the same time, too ecstatic to contain her delight. She beamed. She blushed. She exhibited all the telltale signs of Ty's legendary effect on females.

Rookie, Celia thought.

"You're wearing your boots," Ty said, pride in his tone.

"I wear them every day."

"You're breaking 'em in, huh? Are they comfortable?"

"Oh yes." Addie peeked up at him, her face sincere. "I love my boots."

Despite the years of etiquette coaching Celia had given Addie, Addie invited Ty to stay for dinner without asking Celia first. Since Celia couldn't veto the idea in front of Ty, he ended up staying and eating spaghetti with them. Afterward, he followed Addie to her room and sat through a long princess-education session.

Celia wasn't sure what else to do with herself while they were back there together, so she sat at her kitchen table with a note pad and pen.

A Few Rules For Your Time With Addie, she wrote at the top of the page.

#1. Please avoid foods with partially hydrogenated oils, high fructose corn syrup, GMOs, trans fats, and red dye.

#2. To ride in a car, Addie needs a booster seat and seat belt at all times. I recommend driving below the speed limit and defensively.

#3. If you're going to bike, or do any other activity where she might fall (roller-skating, skateboarding, etc,) she'll have to wear a helmet and, depending on the activity, knee and elbow pads.

#4. She's not allowed to see anything other than G-rated movies.

#5. If you take her to Mountain View Park, be aware that the metal slide is fast and dangerous. If you take her to Fielding Park, don't go near the swings. The metal bolts are deteriorating. There's a pond at Valley North Park that she could fall into, so I'd stay away from that park altogether.

*** Please pick her up at 7:50 a.m. and bring her back no later than 5:30 p.m. In between, please keep your cell phone charged and nearby.

Celia wanted to jot down at least ten more rules, but she refrained. She didn't want him to think she was a worrier.

Celia was one strange baby momma.

Why hadn't she, Ty wondered as he drove away from River Run, been trying to gouge him for money all these years? Isn't that what baby mommas were known for? He would've been generous. People hit him up for money just about every day of the week—charities, fund-raising committees, friends and distant family members down on their luck, the Society for the Restoration of Holley. He had the funds to answer requests with signed checks. It made him happy to give people money.

Celia, though? His legal wife and the mother of his child? He could hardly *force* the stubborn thing to accept his help. It was downright insulting.

He stopped for a red light and pulled her list of rules for his day with Addie from the front pocket of his jeans. GMOs? He didn't even know what that meant, but he was pretty sure that Celia wouldn't approve of a cheeseburger and fries from McDonald's, something he'd eaten plenty as a kid. What were the chances that he'd even be able to find a G-rated movie in Corvallis? Kneepads? Dangerous slides? C'mon.

When he reached his hotel room, he stripped off his T-shirt, boots, and socks. He found the remote under his reading glasses and an issue of *Investor's Business Daily*. Propped up in bed, he surfed channels, his head filled not with the shows on the screen, but with Celia. Kind of the way he'd been surfing channels with his head full of her for the past month straight. Only worse, because he'd just come from seeing her.

For the first few weeks after he'd found out about Addie, he'd rolled resentment toward Celia around and around in his mouth the way he would a cough drop. She'd kept his child a secret from him, and it had felt good to stay angry about it. In time, though, the cough drop had begun to melt. She'd kept his child from him *because* he'd acted like a rotten jerk to her.

If he could feel a calm sort of kindness toward Celia, that would be good. That's what he'd been going for tonight.

Instead, when she'd opened her door, pleasure had rushed through him at the sight of her. After years on the road, seeing her standing in front of him with a bright, good-smelling house behind her had felt like coming home. The kind of *home* that had nothing to do with her fool apartment.

He couldn't help but like her fighting spirit. She was way smarter and more independent than she had a right to be. And all that cutting humor of hers could make him laugh, really laugh. Which was nothing like the fake chuckles he usually gave women.

He even approved of the nickname she'd given him. He'd have preferred something more masculine, but showboat was pretty funny. He'd pretended to hate it, because he knew anything less would have stolen her fun.

He hadn't wanted to steal her fun, not when the sight of her cooking dinner had been one of the sexiest things he'd seen in years. The whole evening—the cooking, that little yellow shirt, her feistiness, their dinner with

Addie—made him remember why he'd gone so stupid over Celia in Vegas in the first place.

See, this was what living like a monk for five and a half years did to a man. It made him nuts in the head. He was so starved for a girlfriend that he was lying in a hotel room in Oregon, wanting *Celia*. He couldn't have Celia. She didn't even like him. He couldn't trust her. He sure as anything couldn't do anything to hurt her again, ever. Not with Addie in the mix. And the cherry on top? An attraction to Celia could ruin—again—any chance at a future with Tawny, who was the most perfect woman in the world.

He flicked past an educational show about the ocean, then a show about redneck alligator hunters, before stopping on UFC fighting.

Pushing a hand behind his head, he watched two guys beat each other up inside the octagon.

He knew women who were prettier than Celia. Women who wore lower-cut shirts and tight-fitting Western jeans. Women who were, heaven knows, a long shot nicer to him.

He'd do well to remember that Tawny was both sweet *and* a Grade A knockout. With her long brunette hair and athletic body, Tawny could have been a bikini model if she hadn't decided to become a paralegal.

He'd finally earned the right to win Tawny's heart. Which was exactly what he planned to do as soon as she broke up with her pediatrician boyfriend.

Unfortunately, he'd need to finish out the season before he'd have a block of time in Holley that he could use to romance Tawny. Tomorrow night he'd fly to Nashville for an event and after that Billings, San Antonio, and Boise.

His upcoming schedule left him cold. A lot of things had lost their shine for him over the years, but his bull riding never had. He was hard-core committed to it. His intense drive to win at it had shaped his whole adult life.

Until lately. Lately, his mind had begun to wander, and his competitive edge had started to dull. He'd come to care more about talking on the phone to a girl who tracked his travels on a US map that hung on the wall next to Celia's laundry room.

Addie had told him about the map a while back, but seeing it had hit him in a soft spot. Him, whose body had been so hardened over the years, that he hadn't thought it had a soft spot left.

Turned out his child was his soft spot, which he could live with.

But somehow, against all odds, Murphy's Law, and flat-out common sense, Celia had the power to be his soft spot, too. And that, he couldn't allow.

CHAPTER

NINE

Ty arrived the next morning driving a shiny black Escalade. Celia could only imagine what it had cost him to rent a car like that from the airport. Enough to cover groceries for a month plus the new winter clothes Addie would need come fall, probably.

Celia had the booster seat ready. Despite feeling utterly sick to her stomach, she positioned it on one of the Escalade's second-row seats. She helped Addie climb into the car. "Have a great time."

"I will. 'Bye, Mom." Addie looked every bit as excited as she would have if Ty were taking her to Disneyland.

Celia made herself shut Addie's door. She glanced up at Ty, who stood next to her in the parking lot. "Did you read my rules?"

"Every one." He let a few seconds pass. "You good?"

She nodded. "Will you be very careful?"

"Very."

"Okay. Go on."

He got behind the wheel. As the Escalade eased away,

Celia waved at Addie through the tinted glass. In Addie's whole life Celia had only left her at day care or with Uncle Danny. She had no practice trusting her to anyone else. Her lips formed a plastic smile while her mind formed the thought *This might be the last time I ever see my child.*

Her heart shriveled into a small and terrified ball.

An anxious mother was of no worth to her employer.

For the first few hours of her workday, Celia worried that Ty would abduct Addie. She'd seen too many news reports about mothers or fathers who let their child visit the other parent only to have that child stolen away to a foreign country. When she could no longer stand the horrible scenarios filling her imagination, she sent Ty a text. *How's it going?*

Good, he answered right away. His response did not completely mollify her because she had no way of proving his location. He could be texting her from onboard a plane about to depart for Brazil.

Her phone buzzed. *We're watching a really bad Winnie-the-Pooh movie at the dollar theater*, he texted.

For the next few hours, Celia worried about Addie running into the street. Addie hadn't tried to run into the street since she was two, but today might be the day she attempted it, and Celia hadn't expressly warned Ty of that danger in her rules. *Everything okay?* She hit Send on her message.

Yes. Sitting down for lunch. After this, we'll go to the park.

For the next few hours Celia worried that Ty wouldn't

watch Addie closely enough at the park. Parent abduction wasn't the only kind of abduction. A stranger could snatch Addie and . . . and sell her into the slave trade overseas. It happened. Before she could text Ty, he texted her. *We're having fun. I'm being careful.*

For the last few hours, Celia worried that they'd get in a car accident. It might not even be Ty's fault. The most responsible of citizens sometimes got creamed by drunk drivers. *Doing well?*

Yes. We're shopping for toys.

When Addie sees a toy she likes, Celia typed back, *I tell her she can either earn money to pay for it by doing chores or put it on her birthday list.*

I'm letting her buy whatever she wants.

Celia regarded the message with horror. Her fingertips punched at her phone. *You may buy her one thing.*

Five?

One!

Three?

Two. No more.

At the end of the day, Celia took up a position outside her apartment, phone in hand, waiting. When the Escalade turned onto the road leading to River Run, her hunched and knotted shoulders eased for the first time all day. The car appeared to be whole and was bringing Addie back a full ten minutes ahead of schedule.

As soon as the car came to a stop, Celia opened the rear door for Addie, helped her down, and hugged her.

Ty climbed from the driver's seat looking like the definition of calm. "How's it going?"

"Fine."

The knowing light in his eyes told her he'd guessed

at the agonies she'd been putting herself through. He crossed to the back of the SUV, popped the trunk, and took out two boxes. The huge one held a castle-shaped doll house for princesses. The flat, medium-sized one held a tablet computer.

When Celia opened her mouth to protest, Ty winked at her. "We only got two things."

"But—"

He strode off, carrying the boxes. "Stay where you are. I'll set these inside."

"Isn't he awesome, Mom?" Addie whispered. "He's really awesome."

"Did you have fun?"

In reverent tones, Addie updated Celia on her day until Ty rejoined them.

"I've got to take off for the airport, Addie. Can I get a hug?"

Addie moved into his open arms.

Ty embraced her respectfully, not too tight, not lifting her, not too long. "See you later."

"See you later," Addie agreed.

He straightened and faced Celia, a devilish cast to his expression. "Hug?"

He'd put her in a pickle, and he knew it. With Addie watching, she couldn't very well shout, "No!" and bolt indoors. She gave him a stiff side hug, the kind one would offer a relative one didn't like. He was warm. He felt like unforgiving muscle, looked like cowboy, and smelled like pine. "No touching," she whispered into the space near the side of his neck. "Remember?"

"Must have slipped my mind." He released her and crossed to the car. "'Bye, ladies."

Celia and Addie watched the Escalade drive away. Just that fast, like the snap of fingers, Celia and Addie were alone again, returned to their regular, blissfully Ty-free life.

Needing to come down off her day of stress, Celia led Addie through the apartment and into the backyard. The two of them watered flowers, Celia with the hose, Addie with her watering can and with a stream of run-on sentences in praise of the movie, the lunch, the park, the shopping, and Ty's character. "Mom," she concluded, "I sure do like my cowgirl boots."

"I know you do, Punkie."

"I've always wanted a pair of cowgirl boots."

Celia translated, in the way of mothers, exactly what her daughter had really just said. It wasn't a pair of cowgirl boots that Addie had always wanted.

It was a father.

On her way out the door the next morning, Celia scooped up her keys. An unfamiliar weight plunked against her palm. The *Give Peace a Chance* charm had magically reappeared on her key ring.

She released a disbelieving huff. Ty had only been in her apartment last night for about a minute when he'd dropped off Addie's gifts. She couldn't believe he'd had time to attach a new charm or to find and reattach her old one. But clearly, he'd managed one or the other.

Shaking her head, her lips curving into a reluctant smile, she pulled out the kitchen drawer that contained her miscellaneous junk. The old charm lay inside, where she'd tossed it when she'd stripped it off her key ring.

She held the new charm next to it and compared the two. Identical. A matched set of *Give Peace a Chance* key rings.

Peace times two.

"Looks like you also need eggs, more yogurt, meat . . ." Celia jotted the items down, then went back to tapping her pen on her lip and surveying Uncle Danny's open fridge. "You're almost out of butter and also jelly."

"This is amazing." Uncle Danny swallowed a bite of the zucchini bread she'd baked earlier in the day. "This is the best thing I've ever tasted."

Bless him, he praised her cooking every chance he got, and always with heartfelt sincerity. "Thank you."

It was Saturday, and she and Addie had stopped by Uncle Danny's house for their weekly visit. Each time she came by, Celia took stock of his fridge and pantry, crafted a grocery list for him, brought him up to date on his bills, tidied up, and poked around the house looking for things that needed attention (like ferns dying of dehydration, stale sheets, or overflowing trash cans).

Uncle Danny had founded an online surf shop and continued to manage its big-picture issues. But he had no head for details.

"Will you let me sell this zucchini bread online to my customers?" he asked.

"I'm not sure it makes much sense to sell zucchini bread and surf wax side by side."

"Surfers appreciate food, C." He lifted his slice of bread into the air; it was nubby with walnuts and flecks of green. "It's a crime not to make this available to the public."

There had been a time, long ago, when Celia had harbored hopes of making her cooking available to the public. "I'm glad you like it." She closed the fridge door with her foot and set the shopping list and pen on his kitchen counter. "There's that."

"Did I tell you that I'm going on a lunch date tomorrow with Sandy?"

"Sandy?" Sandy's American name didn't bode well for her chances at a happily-ever-after with Uncle Danny.

"She's one of the women from the Party Of Eight group."

"I thought you told me they were all too old."

"What can I say? I'm desperate." He shrugged and took another bite of zucchini bread. His tan and sinewy arms protruded from an In-N-Out Burger T-shirt that dated back fifteen years. "Sandy wheels around an oxygen tank and has a tube that whooshes air up her nose, but I'm thinking, hey, maybe I can be down with that."

Celia laughed. "You might want to schedule a trim before your hot date."

"I need a haircut?"

"Yep." She leaned into the dining room, where Addie sat playing a game on her new computer tablet. "Doing fine, Addie?"

Addie nodded without looking up, so Celia moved back through the kitchen, collected Danny's mail from the basket by the front door, and took it with her to the living-room sofa. She made stacks on the coffee table— junk, letters, bills. Then she went to work opening it all.

Danny stood behind her, his attention snagged by the

TV program that had been playing, a travelogue touting the wonders of Prague. "What time is it?" He patted his pockets, his chest, and even his head before remembering the Ironman Timex strapped to his wrist. "Ty's probably riding right now. One of his rodeo deals is on."

"Not you too, Uncle Danny. You can't possibly like bull riding, can you?"

"Yeah. *Oh yeah*, I like it. It's sweet." He located the remote and flipped channels. Sure enough, the BRPC meet in Nashville appeared on the screen. "Addie told me back when she started following it. I started following it, too, and I've kind of gotten into it. I'm even recording them. Man versus animal, you know? The eternal struggle. Very cool."

Celia couldn't chastise Uncle Danny when she herself had grown into a furtive fan. After weeks of watching it, she'd come to know every rider and bull. She followed the Bull Riders Professional Circuit on Twitter and Facebook. And sometimes during work breaks, she scanned bull-riding-related blogs and read articles online. Her unwilling interest in the sport filled her with about the same level of guilt as did, say, bingeing on homemade desserts.

Celia craned her neck around. She could see Addie across the space, still at the dining table. "I don't let Addie watch the rodeos live," she said, pitching her voice low, "but so long as she's entertained over there, we should be fine to watch it for a minute while we're . . . um, working on bills."

"Sure." He lowered onto the sofa, his eyes focused on the action onscreen.

She handed him his checkbook and a pen, laid the

first bill in front of him, and pointed to the balance. The commentators announced that Ty Porter, veteran and three-time world champion, would be coming up soon. He'd be paired with CrushEm, the most lauded bull of the season, a bull that had only been ridden for the full eight seconds once before in his career.

Uncle Danny whistled. "Ty's finally going to get a chance at CrushEm. He must be amped."

Worry overtook Celia by degrees. A cowboy had injured himself earlier in the season trying to ride CrushEm.

"I think Ty's got a shot at staying on him," Danny said. "What do you think?"

"I don't know."

The show cut to a promo spot of Ty. Dramatic music swelled. Ty, backlit, strode toward the camera through a mist-shrouded barn. He gripped his rope in one gloved hand, his black hat rode low, and the fringe on his chaps swayed with his gait. Tufts of dust launched into the air beneath his boot steps. The hard cast of his expression promised retribution to any bull daring enough to come between him and glory.

Celia groaned inwardly. Insufferable showboat!

While a string of commercials aired, Celia's nervousness continued to climb. She produced more bills for Uncle Danny. He wrote out checks, then she slid them into envelopes and stuck on stamps.

CrushEm was a devil of a bull. That dumb promo spot likely had Nashville's guitar-wearing starlets swooning because it made Ty appear indestructible. He wasn't.

Not for her own sake, but *only* for Addie's sake, she'd begun to hope that Ty would make it through his rides with his head attached. The fear that he wouldn't occasionally made her anxious. Occasionally. And just for Addie's sake.

The rodeo coverage returned, and Celia stilled. Ty sat aboard CrushEm in the chute, gripping and regripping the rope in his now-familiar pattern.

The gate reeled open, and CrushEm exploded into the arena. The bull flung himself up and down while bucking and spinning to one side, twisting with jaw-dropping power, spinning to the other side. Astonishingly, Ty was keeping his seat!

Celia pressed to her feet. "Ride!" Ty continued to fight, to move with the animal, to maintain his balance. "Ride, cowboy, *ride!*"

The buzzer sounded.

Celia whooped.

Ty bounded off the animal, landing and then pitching forward onto his knees and palms. The rodeo clowns distracted CrushEm long enough for Ty to leap to his feet. CrushEm ran at Ty, but Ty vaulted easily onto the nearby gates. After rushing at the clowns a few more times, CrushEm finally conceded to trot off stage.

Celia blew out a relieved breath. Ty dropped to the dirt-covered stadium floor. He lifted his hat, smiled, and turned in a circle in front of the crowd.

Celia became aware that she was standing and brandishing Uncle Danny's stamped bill high in one hand as if it were a pom-pom. Danny was staring at her.

Addie ventured into the living room, her gaze moving slowly from the TV to Celia. "Did Ty just ride?"

Celia lowered her arm. "Yes."

"He stayed on CrushEm," Danny informed Addie. "For the full eight seconds."

"Yes! CrushEm? Really? Can I see it?"

The three of them sat on Danny's sofa. They rewound and watched Ty's amazing ride four times in a row while Celia puzzled over what she'd just done. Had she really jumped to her feet, pushed her fist into the air, and yelled *"Ride, cowboy, ride!"* in front of witnesses? She, who didn't even like Ty . . . except for Addie's sake?

Honestly! Ride, cowboy, ride?

Ty's high-scoring ride on CrushEm propelled him to a blockbuster victory in Nashville. At the close of every rodeo, the event's winning cowboy stood on an elevated platform in the arena's center. Ty planted his boots on Nashville's platform, looking impressive, looking confident, looking like he'd been born to win rodeos. Jets positioned in a circle around him shot steam and confetti high into the air.

Once she'd tucked Addie into bed, Celia attempted to relax while watching a cooking show and snacking on apple slices and organic crackers. The recurring memory of Ty on that platform with the confidence and the confetti wouldn't let her unwind.

In need of baking therapy, she went to work on a batch of snickerdoodles. The moment the cookies came out of the oven, warm and tempting, she transferred the most deformed one onto a napkin. As usual, she felt honor bound to eat the ones no one else would want.

She was saving her fourth homely snickerdoodle from scorn when she received a text from the triumphant cowboy.

Did you know that Holley is called the Color Capital of Texas? he asked. *The town's known for its flowers. Think of all the flowers you could grow in your new garden.*

I have flowers in my current garden, she typed back, the flavors of cinnamon and sugar thick in her mouth. *My flowers and I are happy where we are.*

"Mommy?"

Celia spun to see Addie walking toward her with her white blanket clutched in her hand. "Hey, Punkie." Celia set aside her phone and enclosed Addie in a hug. "Is your stomach bothering you?"

Addie nodded.

"How about some chamomile tea and a snickerdoodle?"

July rolled by, its days warm and sunny. When at home, Celia kept her sliding door open so the breeze and the fresh air could invite themselves in. Addie swam in the River Run pool on the weekends, with Celia acting as lifeguard from a lawn chair nearby.

Celia soaked the heat into her skin, watched her flowers bloom, and wished she could enjoy it all more. Her money woes made enjoyment of anything difficult. She moved her income around in creative ways so she could meet her most urgent bills. But no matter how inventive, she couldn't catch up. Her debt grew heavier. A creditor or two began to call.

To make matters worse, Ty stepped up his campaign to convince her to move to Holley. Several times each week, he insisted on talking to her over the phone. Each time, Celia scolded him and reiterated her request that they communicate through text.

He proved immune to her scolding.

Ty arrived in Boise on a gray and rainy Thursday early in August. He ate dinner with his rider buddies, same as always. Ran on the treadmill the next morning, just like usual. For his first ride of the event, the BRPC randomly paired him with Meteor, a mediocre bull he'd met five times and bested four of those.

Even so, all day on Friday, tension hung over him. He wasn't hungry, but he made himself eat the same thing he always ate for lunch the opening day of an event: a foot-long turkey sub. Just like the rest of the bull riders, he had his superstitions and stuck to his routines.

When he arrived at the arena, he made himself at home in the locker room. He put on his clothing in the same order he always followed, then settled his Resistol black felt hat—the same brand he'd used since he'd started riding—onto his head.

He found a quiet spot in one of the backstage rooms made available for riders and worked his gloved hand up and down his bull rope's length, making it tacky with rosin, preparing it to do its job.

He'd spent the summer traveling around the country, same as always, staying in hotels in all the familiar cities, competing in and winning events. He had more fans than ever. They came out to watch him, sent him messages over the Internet, asked for his autograph, and shook his hand.

He pored through investment magazines each night before bed and worked out in hotel gyms each morning.

He followed NASCAR and UFC. He read the sports pages in order to keep up-to-date with his Cowboys preseason. He had friends on the tour. He had money to burn and freedom and time.

And yet he no longer felt like himself because his passion for bull riding, the one thing he'd always counted on, had left him. He was riding just as well. In fact, he was right at the top in the standings and having one of his best years. What had changed wasn't physical, and it wasn't about performance. It was mental.

He readjusted the rope and went to work on another section of it.

What kind of father would he be to Addie if he only saw her once a month? Celia hadn't pressured him to visit more often. In fact, he got the feeling she wanted him to stay away. But he knew it wasn't right. He hadn't grown up with a missing father. His father, John, had been at the dinner table every night saying grace and scoring the biggest piece of beef.

Since his last visit to Corvallis, a voice within him had started whispering. It told him—occasionally at first and then more often—that he'd had his turn, that it was time for him to step down.

He'd been listening to his own loud and headstrong voice for so long that he hardly recognized that other, softer, voice. And he sure didn't trust it, because it made no sense to him. He'd taken up riding eight years ago, during those aimless months after returning home from the Marines. It had been what gave his life purpose and success. He wouldn't be anything without it.

Besides, he'd made commitments and signed contracts. He *had* to finish this season. At the end of October his schedule would wrap, and he'd have more than two months off back home in Holley. He could see then where his head was at. He'd always planned to buy himself a big plot of land and raise rodeo stock once he retired from bull riding. He'd think seriously about that come October.

It was almost his turn to ride. He'd talked to Addie earlier in the evening, but he hadn't spoken to Celia. His hand paused its motion. He needed to hear her voice.

Looping his bull rope, he walked to his locker. His cell phone notified him that he'd missed a call from his parents. He'd told his family about Addie a month ago. It had taken his mom a few days to recover from her shock. Every day since, she'd called and pestered him because she, and all the rest of the Porters, desperately wanted to meet Addie.

He dialed Celia. While the phone rang, he ground his boot heel into the floor. She didn't answer.

He tried again, knowing she wouldn't pick up. She didn't. And then any time he'd had to spare ran out.

He mounted Meteor inside the chute just the way he'd done hundreds of times. Inside himself, though, something was wrong. His thoughts had gone black. His heart had turned to lead.

The cowboys operating the gate waited for his signal. The huge crowd waited for his signal. No turning back.

He nodded to the gate man and the bull surged free. Ty's body took over, muscle memory kicking in and keeping him seated. The bull moved and he countered correctly. His focus intensified. He was doing fine—

Faster than he could blink, as if giant hands had reached down and jerked him from the bull, he lost his grip and his seat. He went airborne. Sprawling. He landed on his right side with so much force that it knocked the breath from him. Dazed, he looked up to see the bull's hind legs lifting, close. Above him. He tried to pull himself out of the way. Couldn't. Meteor's hooves came crashing toward him.

Again, he tried to move, to roll—

Too late.

CHAPTER
TEN

Celia watched a few of the early riders in the Boise event, got impatient, and started fast forwarding the prerecorded show while scanning images. Her chest lifted on a sigh. She was sitting on her couch for the umpteenth Friday night in a row about to watch Ty Porter—her ex-husband who was only an ex in her heart, the man she'd once loved who'd rejected her outright—ride bulls.

This was not, perhaps, the most emotionally healthy of pastimes. One might suspect that some normal thirty-year-old women were out on dates tonight.

She spotted Ty. Pushed the Play button.

He looked as unforgivingly handsome as ever, she tried not to notice, in his black clothing and hat. He'd been paired with Meteor. Decent level bull, but not wicked difficult.

Meteor burst loose and the ride begin. As usual, Ty moved well and looked firmly in control—

He lost his grip. Just that suddenly, in the space between heartbeats. The bull's upward thrust sent him into the air. Ty, an expert at landings, landed all wrong, dropping hard onto his side without breaking his own fall.

Celia bolted to her feet.

Meteor spun, bringing his hind legs terrifyingly close to Ty.

"No," Celia gasped.

The rodeo clowns ran forward but were too far away to intercede. Meteor's hooves punctured the dirt, then went up again, drawing nearer to Ty with inexorable and deadly precision. "No!"

Ty attempted to pull himself out of the way, but before he could, Meteor's hooves crushed down on one of his legs. Ty's face twisted with pain.

Celia's hands jerked to cover her mouth. Her insides turned to water.

Lightning fast, the bull kicked both hind legs into Ty's chest. The impact slammed Ty backward. His head careened into the ground with sickening force.

The clowns dashed between Ty and the bull, finally herding the animal away.

Ty's body lay in the dirt, unmoving. Celia stared at the screen in horror, frozen except for the tears that rushed to fill her eyes. Several people ran forward and surrounded Ty.

This can't be happening. Celia waited for Ty to come back to consciousness.

He didn't. Medical staff strapped him to a stretcher and lifted him into the back of an ambulance. *Oh my goodness, this can't be happening.*

The telecast replayed the accident a few times in slow

motion, the commentators speaking in somber voices. Celia couldn't stand to see it again and looked away.

How long ago had this happened? She checked to see when the program had begun recording. Boise and Corvallis shared the same time zone. He'd been injured maybe . . . maybe two hours ago?

Why hadn't anyone called her? As soon as she had the thought, she recognized its idiocy. Ty's one-time wife of twelve hours wouldn't be high on anybody's list of contacts.

She ran for her phone. Its screen told her that she'd missed two calls. Her heart sank. From Ty. The calls had come in two and a half hours ago. Her mind traveled back, trying to remember. She'd been giving Addie a bath then. She hadn't heard her phone ring. Though her phone didn't alert her to a waiting voice mail, she double checked her messages just in case. Nothing. He hadn't left a message.

For weeks she'd been giving him a hard time about calling her. Now she'd missed two calls she deeply wished she'd received. She dialed his number and waited while his phone rang, trying not to sob.

He'd been hurt badly, that much she knew based on the visual evidence alone. He might even be critically injured, a possibility that sent her feelings pinwheeling. There was a little girl in this house, sleeping just down the hall, who loved him.

No one answered Ty's cell. She tried again and again, her fingers desperate on the keys of her phone, her heart hammering.

In her memory she kept seeing Meteor's hooves landing on Ty's leg, then striking him in the chest. This was all Ty's fault for doing something so dangerous! And it was her fault for letting him back into their lives. And it was Addie's fault for putting so much stock in Ty. And it was God's fault for letting this happen.

With a furious groan, she tossed her phone on the kitchen counter. She needed to know the status of Ty's condition. She turned up the TV's volume, then powered up Addie's tablet, which operated much faster than her ancient laptop. She went to work checking each website she could think of. No news.

Her thoughts traveled in ten different directions. Her worry rose jaggedly. Finally, overcome, she laced her fingers together and pressed her joined hands to her forehead.

Let him be all right, she prayed. She hadn't prayed for anything in years, but she did so now.

Fervently.

Ty regained consciousness at the hospital on the far side of surgery. The first thing he became aware of was a longing, deep and empty, angry and aching.

For Celia.

Where is Celia?

Gradually, he realized that someone was talking. He slit his eyes open. A nurse, around the same age as his mother.

"How're you feeling, Mr. Porter?"

"Celia." His voice sounded scratchy. "I want to talk to her."

"First we'll get you all fixed up, and then in just a few minutes, we'll bring her back to see you."

"She's not here." He remembered now where she was. In that bright apartment in Oregon that was always so far away. He regretted that she was so far away. Why had he let that happen? "I need to talk to her on the phone."

"Certainly." The nurse's attention moved to the chart she held and then to the machines behind him.

"*Now*," he growled, in no mood to be charming. "I need to talk to her now."

The nurse stilled, looking at him over the top of her glasses. "There are a few things I have to do first. Won't be long." She started back to work, checking stuff, moving around. Clearly, she'd been doing this for decades. Long enough to know that she was the boss of this situation, and he was the sucker strapped to the bed.

It had been this same way when he'd come to in the ambulance earlier. Celia had filled his thoughts. He'd asked to talk to her then, too, but just like now they'd refused.

He groped around in his head, fighting to remember the events that had brought him here. The ambulance ride had been full of light, machines, medics. The sensation of movement. That blaring siren. And pain. Bitter pain. He'd had to set his teeth hard against it to keep from hissing curses.

Once they'd arrived at the hospital, details blurred. There had been doctors and people wheeling him around fast, the fluorescent lights on the ceiling whipping by. The X-ray machine. And then they'd taken him to the operating room.

That was it. That was all he could recall.

It looked like they had him in some lame recovery

area with several other patients, all of them divided by curtains that pulled along tracks in the ceiling. The place sounded of quiet conversations and footsteps. It smelled like artificially warmed sheets.

He glanced down at himself. Most of the pain that had dogged him earlier had been chased away by anesthesia and drugs. A dull headache remained. Also, it hurt to breathe deeply. They'd raised his upper body into a reclining position, and beneath the sheet that covered him, it looked like they'd wrapped his swollen left leg in gauze and immobilized it.

His knee. His knee was wrecked.

The certainty of it cut into him as surely as the surgeon's knife just had. A few hours ago he'd been completely fine and whole. But he already knew that tonight had changed everything. *God, what's happened to me? Help me.* This injury would mean the end of so much—too much to deal with right now.

He needed Celia. When could he talk to her?

The nurse invited him to drink juice or eat crackers. He refused both. She kept her smile in place, asked him questions and summarized his condition, then disappeared. When she came back, she was leading his two closest friends from the BRPC, both fellow riders. The guys wore those pitying expressions people put on around the sick. Reassuring smiles and understanding eyes.

"How're you feeling, man?" one asked.

"I'm going to be fine," Ty answered.

"Just so you know, we've been talking to your mom and dad all evening, keeping them up-to-date."

"Thanks. How long has it been? Since the accident?"

"About five hours."

"Then it's late."

"Close to midnight."

"Do either of you have your phone with you?"

"I do." His buddy pulled a smartphone from his pocket and passed it over.

"I'm going to make a call."

"Sure, man." They nodded, hung around.

"A private call." Ty motioned with his head for them to leave.

Their faces showed surprise, but after a pause they moved toward the waiting room.

It took him a minute of hard thinking to pull Celia's number out of the grogginess in his brain. Once he'd managed it, the phone only rang once before she answered.

"Ty?" she demanded.

At the sound of her voice, he let his eyes sink closed with relief. He relaxed into the support of the bed. "Yes."

"*Thank goodness!* Are you all right?"

"Depends on how you define all right."

"Will you live?"

Blast it all if he didn't smile. "Do you want me to?"

"Yes."

"Were you worried that I wouldn't?"

"Of course I was. I saw what happened on TV."

"Did it look bad?"

"It looked *really* bad. I've been trying to dig up information on your condition for hours, and I've read different reports. What do the doctors say?"

"Mild concussion for starters. That part's no big deal."

"Um . . . your head got slammed into the ground, Ty."

"Maybe, but the dirt on the arena floor is soft and my head's hard."

"Well," she said wryly, "that part I believe."

"I've also got bruised ribs."

"But none are broken?"

"No. I was wearing a protective vest."

"And your leg?"

He paused.

"Your leg?" she prodded.

"An artery got nicked, so they had to fix that first. They told me that the bull came down on my knee and shattered it. Before they put me under they said the ACL and PCL were busted and they'd have to replace the kneecap with an artificial one."

He could hear the slow exhale of her breath.

"I just got out of surgery."

"Are you in a lot of pain?"

"Not anymore. Addie didn't see me fall, did she?"

"No, and she won't see it. But I will have to tell her what happened in the morning because she'll ask to watch you ride the minute she wakes up."

"Yeah." Quiet drifted between them, and Ty held on to it. The only medicine he needed right now was listening to her, even listening to her silence, across the miles. "I miss you, Celia."

A beat passed. "You're high on pain meds."

"Yes," he agreed. "So anything I say now can't be held against me later."

She chuckled ruefully, like he was a lost cause.

Which he might be. *Tawny* was the one for him. His thoughts were swimming, but he was pretty sure he wasn't supposed to feel anything for Celia—except kindly. "There's something about you that gets to me."

"Like mosquitoes get to skin?"

"No. Like alcohol to my head. You're beautiful."

"Ty Porter! If you think I'm going to sit here and listen to you compliment me and sweet-talk me—"

"You have the prettiest green eyes," he said. "They're crazy pretty."

"I'm not some groupie that you can charm—"

"Your hair is sexy. And you have a good heart even though you pretend to be mean. And I like that little necklace you wear with the C on it—"

"Stop it this instant! Getting stomped on by a bull does not give you permission to—"

"You're smart. You make me laugh. I don't know hardly any women who make me laugh. You smell like lemons." He whistled. "I love the way you smell."

"Your concussion has scrambled your brain. We can hope that you won't remember this in the morning and that we'll both be able to return to insulting each other."

He grinned. "Sweet one."

"Showboat!"

He laughed, and in that moment—despite the leg and the hospital and his dark future—everything felt perfectly fine with his world. "I really hate that nickname," he lied.

"Too bad."

"Tell me how glad you are that I survived."

"I'm glad for Addie's sake."

"And for your own?"

"I'm . . . marginally pleased. Now no one will come and repossess my Prius."

"That's not very nice."

"No, I'm not very nice. I'm coldhearted. Vindictive. Anyway, since I'm sure they're about to plump your pillows or shoot you with morphine or let your fans in to dote on you, I'd better go."

He wasn't about to let that happen. "No."

"What do you mean, no?"

"Your day might have been a piece of cake, but my day has been a pain in the butt. I only want one thing, and that's to lie here and listen to you talk for a while longer. So if it's not too much trouble, keep talking."

"Uh . . ."

"Just tell me about your week. What Addie did. Even Uncle Danny. Whatever."

Celia had sass, but she also had compassion.

She talked. And while she talked, Ty drifted on the cocktail of drugs they'd given him. Like a hot air balloon held to earth by a rope, Celia held him to calm with her voice.

Little by little, she steadied him.

"So," Celia said to Addie the next morning, concluding her explanation of Ty's calamity, "that's what happened. He has an injury to his knee, but he's going to be fine." She went for a smile. They sat facing each other on living-room chairs, both still in their pajamas.

Addie's lower lip began to wobble.

Uh-oh. "Addie. He's going to be okay."

"He's hurt." Her eyes glimmered with unshed tears.

"Yes, he is. But he's strong, and he'll get better."

"Will he be able to ride bulls again?"

"I don't know." Which wasn't an outright lie. Celia
had no definitive proof that he'd never ride again. However, after watching Meteor land on his leg and hearing
the tone in his voice last night—then rising early to check
the latest medical updates online—her gut told her that
his accident had been a career-ender.

"But" —Addie pushed a strand of hair off her face—
"he has to be able to ride."

"No, he doesn't. He's been riding for years. Much
longer than most men do. He could go on and do . . . a
lot of other things."

"Like what?"

"He could . . ." She didn't know what handsomeness and charm qualified a person to do. Did Ty have
any other skill set? "He could work with horses like his
brothers do."

Addie appeared doubtful.

Celia waited while Addie sorted through her feelings
and reactions. The night had left Celia no stronger than
a corn husk and about as empty as one, too. After talking to Ty, she'd spent a few hours trying to sleep. A few
hours actually sleeping. And then more hours trying and
failing at sleeping.

Ty shouldn't have said those things to her last night
on the phone. Yes, he'd been battered, operated on, and
drugged. Still! He shouldn't have said that "I miss you"
and "You're beautiful" stuff. Doing so violated all the
rules between them.

Celia had an arsenal of shields and swords that she nor-
mally used against Ty, but those ridiculous compliments
had penetrated like arrows. At the sound of those words,
something within her had turned giddy and fluttery.

Her reaction made her a traitor against herself. She knew better than to *flutter* over Ty Porter. Experience had been such an expensive teacher. Boy oh boy did she know better! That his meaningless flattery, so easily spoken, had had any impact on her at all made her feel like a dupe. He'd likely said "Your hair is sexy" to at least three other women yesterday.

Remember, Celia? Remember when he shared a bed with you and then said "I'm in love with someone else" the next morning?

"Can we go and see him?" Addie asked. "Please?"

Celia considered Addie through eyes almost crossing with tiredness. She didn't know what kind of IV they might be giving Ty this morning, but she could use one that mainlined espresso. "No, Punkie. He's in Boise, Idaho."

"Then let's go there."

"We can't. It's far away, and I have to be at work on Monday."

"You can take a vacation from work."

"I used all my vacation days last April when Grandma and Grandpa came to see us." Her parents had come over from Scotland and treated them to a trip to Olympic National Park.

Addie's features set in angry lines.

"He's not going to be in Boise long, anyway. He told me last night that he wants to go home to Texas as soon as they let him."

"When?"

"I don't know. Maybe tomorrow or the next day? He'll call you later, and you can ask him."

"He needs us, Mommy. We have to go see him."

"We can't, honey."

Addie moved her gaze to the coffee table and stared like she was trying to burn a hole into it using telepathy.

"Do you have any more questions for me?" Celia's patience had worn thin. "Do you want to talk about it some more?"

Addie shook her head, her lower lip pushed out.

Celia turned the TV on to an episode of *Word Girl*. It wasn't bull riding, but it would have to do. "I'm going to take a shower."

Addie ignored her.

Celia padded to the bathroom and stood in a daze beneath the spray. She washed her hair and indulged in a generous portion of lemon verbena body wash. Once she'd stepped out, she listened for Addie the same way she always did when toweling off. Faintly, she could hear the TV playing in the living room. "Addie?"

No answer, which wasn't unusual. "Say, 'Yes, Mom.'"

No "Yes, Mom."

Unease shifted through her. "Addie?" she called louder, and shrugged into her robe. She hurried to the living room, but Addie's chair sat empty.

"Addie?" Celia picked up speed, crossing into the kitchen, looking into the backyard, searching the back hallway, laundry room. All empty. "Say, 'Yes, Mom' right now!"

No reply. She called Addie's name again and again as she raced the length of the hallway to Addie's room. She checked the closet, dropped to search under the bed, then dashed into the bathroom. "Addie!" she screamed.

Silence answered.

Addie was gone.

CHAPTER

ELEVEN

Where is she? Celia's pulse knocked hard in her ears.

Addie must have left the apartment. And gone where? She could have taken off in any direction. She might have been hit by a car or swept away by the river or taken by someone who wanted to hurt her.

Panic pushed darkness into Celia's mind, terror into her heart. How long had she been in the shower? Ten minutes? She should call 9-1-1. No, she should look for Addie herself. She—she should do both.

Celia rushed into the kitchen, swiped up her phone, and sprinted out the front door, leaving it gaping. Frantically, she scoured the view for a glimpse of Addie. Blond hair, pink pajamas.

She couldn't see her anywhere. The surroundings looked all wrong—peaceful and normal and sunny. People were going about their business as if everything were fine. As if the world weren't caving in.

"Addie!" she yelled, hoarse with alarm.

Still no answer. Celia's instincts urged her to go in the direction of the drive that led away from River Run toward the road. She and Addie almost always went that way when they left their apartment. Holding her robe closed with her hand, she ran, her bare feet pounding the grass.

Maybe she should have gone to the river first. Her steps slashed to a halt. She looked behind her. Addie might be washing away in its current while she was dashing in the wrong direction.

No, she'd check the street first. She was doubting herself, didn't know what to do, but she should at least check the street. She cupped her hands around her mouth. "Addie!"

She couldn't see her little girl. Where was she? Where? She couldn't hear her.

Crying now, tears and gasps fighting their way from her, she started forward again. She began to dial her phone. 9-1. A car passed. "Help," she called to the driver, but the word came out as a wheeze. Her imagination barreled forward with nightmare images of police arriving, men and dogs searching, investigators asking her questions. Life without Addie.

Sticks and rocks scored the soles of her feet. Her chest burned with exertion. She tried to dial 1, but hit 2 instead. Just as she groped to backspace, she caught sight of something pink. There, ahead, through the trees and shadows. Her hope rose almost painfully. She craned forward, squinting. She ran toward the road and her view of the sidewalk opened.

Addie, unharmed, sat on the bus stop bench fifty yards away.

Relief poured through her. She'd found her. Addie was fine, thank God. She'd pulled a backpack on over her pajamas. The slippers that hung off the edge of the bench swung slowly. She was looking forward at the two-lane road carrying cars at high speeds just inches in front of her.

Had she been intending to catch the bus? Alone? She sure didn't appear worried about the mother she'd left behind. "Addie Porter!"

Addie's face jerked toward her. She froze for a moment at the sight of Celia bearing down on her. Then slowly she unfolded from the bench.

Celia took hold of Addie's upper arms and sank to her knees on the sidewalk. "You scared me to death!"

Addie's expression went slack and fearful.

"I didn't know where you'd gone. You're not allowed to leave the apartment like that. *Not ever!* You know that. I've told you so many times." Celia became aware of her robe and her dripping hair and tear-wet cheeks. "Wh-why did you leave? What are you doing out here?"

"I'm going to Texas," Addie answered, so quietly that the wind almost took it. "To see my daddy."

Her use of the word *daddy* jolted Celia. She studied her daughter, trying to understand. Before she'd gotten into the shower, she'd refused to take Addie to see Ty. So Addie had . . . stuffed a backpack and decided to set off alone for Texas? *Daddy* was someone that Addie would run away from home for? Since when? But Celia knew the answer. Since the moment Addie had learned of Ty's injury. "You can't go anywhere without me, do you understand? You're four years old."

"Almost five."

"What have I told you about leaving the house by yourself?"

"That I'm not to do it."

"Then why did you?"

She blinked a few times. "I want to live in Holley, Mommy. More than I've ever, ever wanted anything in my *whole life*." She spoke the words without anger or pouting. She simply stated them, stark in their heartfelt honesty. "Daddy's hurt, and he needs us. We have to go to Texas."

Celia opened her mouth, voiceless.

"We have to go, Mommy. Don't you see?"

Celia was *not* going to reward Addie's runaway attempt by agreeing to move to Holley. Yet, kneeling there on the sidewalk with cars blaring by, Celia did see. Her destiny had turned. Despite her own misgivings about Ty and the fact that Addie had only known him a short time—Addie loved him. So much that she'd risked her safety and Celia's anger to go to him.

Was Celia ever going to be able to shower again without her child fleeing for the bus stop? "Leaving the apartment by yourself is not the way to get what you want, Addie."

She expected her sweet child to apologize. Instead, Addie's chin hardened into a mutinous line.

"Can you say you're sorry?" Celia asked. "You really scared me."

Addie hesitated for a long beat, then shook her head.

"Addie?"

Addie frowned, then gave another small, tense shake of her head.

The out-and-out terror she'd just experienced had probably shaved five years off her life. Five years! And

Addie didn't seem to care. Angrily, she took hold of Addie's wrist and led the way back.

Addie's backpack bobbed. "Mommy, if we moved to Holley—"

"I'm trying to get ahold of my temper. I think it would be better if we didn't say anything more right now."

Once they were both back inside the apartment, Addie set down her backpack and went to her room. Celia stood in the foyer, trembling. She wished she had a friend or boyfriend she could rush to, hug, and cry all over. If she had someone like that in her life, then she'd have launched into a tirade against Addie and Ty's screwball notions of living in Holley, Texas. She'd have shaken her fist and vigorously defended her decision to stay in Corvallis. She'd have pointed out that common sense was heavily on her side.

Right? She looked around at her brightly colored, eclectic apartment.

After high school she'd come to Oregon because she loved it. That love, and perhaps the security of the familiar, had kept her here. Their home, her job, Addie's day care, Uncle Danny, their small circle of friends, and the only hairstylist in the country who could layer her curly hair properly—everything was in Corvallis.

Everything except Ty.

Ty's absence shouldn't matter so much to Addie. He hadn't even been a part of their lives three months ago!

She lowered onto a chair, pulled a throw pillow onto her lap, and toyed with its fringe. Should she have considered Holley more seriously? Looking at it impartially, she had to take into account that Ty had offered her a free house, which would be a windfall for her budget. He'd promised to find her a job. In one of their phone conversations he'd assured her that he'd add her and Addie to his health insurance if she quit her job in order to move.

Even so, she hadn't given Holley any real thought. For one thing, Ty traveled most of the year. It had seemed ridiculous to move to a town Ty didn't actually live in. That argument had changed. He'd probably live in Holley year-round now that the bull riding had ended.

So. She was left with just one great objection to a move: She did not want to live in Texas.

Wow, Celia. Selfish much?

For years she'd held herself up in her own mind as unselfish because she was a single working mom whose life revolved around her child. But she had been selfish in some ways, hadn't she? She hadn't told Ty about her pregnancy. She'd kept the baby and toddler versions of Addie to herself. And she'd written off the option of Holley because she liked Corvallis better.

What she liked wasn't the crux of the issue, though. The crux? Whether it was best for Addie to live near both her mother and her father.

It might be, possibly. Which terrified her.

Shoot, she thought. Seriously! This sacrificial stuff bit.

On her way to her bedroom to change out of her robe, she spotted Addie's backpack. Pausing, she lifted it and sifted through the contents.

Addie had packed her favorite dress. A Rapunzel doll. Her ivory blanket. Two crumpled dollars. A handful of change from her piggy bank.

And a matched set of pink cowgirl boots.

Other than the morphine drip, Ty liked nothing about hospitals. He'd pressured his male doctors and charmed his female ones until they'd discharged him. His parents had arrived in Boise yesterday and pushed his wheelchair across three airports in order to catch the flights that had returned them to Texas earlier today.

Thus, just forty-eight hours after his accident, Ty was sitting in his leather desk chair in his own home office, his leg propped on an ottoman. If he kept the leg still, it throbbed with pain. If he moved it, the pain turned so needle-sharp it sucked away his breath.

After the day he'd had, he should be asleep in bed or stretched out on his living room sofa watching NASCAR. Instead, something like obsession had pulled him to his office to search the Internet for details about his accident. He'd read every article he could find and studied photos until his brain had gone dull with exhaustion. Hardest of all to take were the YouTube videos of his ride on Meteor.

When his mom delivered dinner to him, he clicked away from YouTube and switched to ESPN. She and his dad had insisted on staying at his place tonight even though he'd told them he didn't need them to. When she left the room, Ty ignored the plate of food and went back to YouTube.

He stared at the screen in fierce concentration and watched himself go down again and again. He viewed the clips in frame-by-frame slow motion, trying to understand why he'd come off Meteor. Even with all his years of experience, he couldn't see a reason. The people from the BRPC and the commentators and riders who'd been interviewed in the articles all said the same thing. He'd been balanced. His form had been right. And then he'd been in the air, caught between riding well and losing everything.

His life as a bull rider was over. Maybe he could stomach that if he understood what he'd done wrong.

The doorbell rang. Ty eyed the clock on his computer. It was after nine. He felt like dirt and could only hope his mom would follow instructions for once and turn visitors away.

He heard feminine voices, then the sound of footsteps nearing his office. Swearing under his breath, he filled the screen with ESPN again.

His mom knocked quietly, then peeked into his office with a smile. "You have a visitor. I'll be out in the living room if you need anything."

"'Kay."

His mom disappeared, and Tawny stepped into the doorway.

Ty stilled.

Her chocolate syrup–colored hair fell over one shoulder almost to her waist. She had on a pink and green dress and high-heeled sandals. She held a casserole dish in her hands.

Ty saw Tawny regularly when in Holley and communicated with her a fair bit over Facebook and text when away. None of that lessened the effect of her up close and personal. She was homecoming queen pretty with exactly the look he'd always liked best on women: straight hair, shining blue eyes, long legs that made certain he didn't dwarf her the way he did Celia. "Well, well." Ty smiled and leaned back in his chair, making it creak. "Aren't you a sight for sore eyes. I'd get up to greet you, except I can't stand."

"How're you feeling?"

"Better now that you're here. Have you dumped the pediatrician yet?"

"No." Her expression lit with amusement. "Vance and I are doing very well. Here, I brought you this." Gently, she set the dish on top of a low bookcase. "It's that egg and sausage breakfast casserole you like. I thought it might make things easier on you and your parents in the morning."

"You see, Tawny, this is just one more example of how thoughtful you are. You're nice. You've always been nice." It was true. Even when they'd had that big fight when she'd said she wasn't ready to marry him, even when she'd told him they were done for good after he'd confessed what had happened in Vegas, she had not slapped him or screamed or cursed his name. "Thanks for bringing me food."

"You're welcome." She folded her arms lightly. "Are you doing okay? Really?"

"Yep."

"In a lot of pain?"

He shrugged, lied. "No."

"What have they told you about your recovery?"

"Just that I have a lot of physical therapy in my future." He flicked his fingers across the top of the big brace that covered most of his left leg. "I'll have to wear this for several weeks, then they'll switch it to something thinner."

She nodded, full of sympathy. "Will they let you exercise?"

Tawny knew him well enough to know that he needed his running. "The only cardio they'll let me do is swimming. I'm allowed to do upper-body weight lifting."

"What can I do to help you?"

"You can get yourself single. You're really still dating Dr. Amateur?"

"Dr. *Amsteeter* and I are still dating, yes."

"He hasn't bored you silly yet with all that talk about himself?" He'd bored Ty silly with it the two times he'd met the guy.

"Not yet."

"How long have you been together?"

"About a year."

"Huh." Ty scratched his jaw. "You usually stay with your boyfriends between fourteen and eighteen months. The doctor's running out of time."

"Is that so?"

"I've been patient for years, but as soon as you break up with Amateur, I'm going to put a ring on your finger."

She regarded him with such open feminine speculation that he forgot about the pain in his leg.

"Are you divorced yet, Ty?"

"I can be tomorrow if you'd give me a reason."

She held his gaze for the length of a few heartbeats, then broke the moment with an airy laugh. "Go ahead and stay married. Vance and I are happy together."

The pain in his leg returned. "You'll continue to be happy for two to six more months. Then it'll tank."

"I think he might be the one."

"*I'm* the one. As you well know." He tugged at his T-shirt, then spread his hands. "Me."

"I'm glad to see you're feeling like your usual self. I'll

be praying for you, and I'll call your mom tomorrow to
see how you're doing."

"Stay."

"I can't. Vance is baking me peach cobbler for dessert."

"What man does that? Is he even straight?"

She waved and walked out of sight in the direction
of the front door.

"Thanks for coming," he called.

"You're welcome," she called back.

Tawny Bettenfield had been raised on fried okra and
good manners. Her dentist father and stay-at-home
mother had sheltered her and done all the things small-
town southern parents *should* do with their daughters:
take them to church, teach them to ride, encourage them
to be cheerleaders, and pay for sequin dresses so they
could compete for Miss Teen Texas.

Ty had met Tawny in the first grade. Back then she'd
had two perfect brown pigtails and worn ironed dresses.
She'd been sweet and easy to get along with. When he'd
gotten out of the service and they'd started dating, she'd
still been sweet and easy to get along with.

She loved Holley as much as he did and wanted to
live here all her life.

She was a lady.

She was a Texan, for pity's sake.

Ty had known since their very first date that the two
of them were destined for each other.

He swiveled his chair to face his computer and went
back to the videos of his final ride. He watched them
long after his mom's attempt to get him to go to bed.
Watched them past midnight, then one o'clock.

When at last he shut down his computer, he was no

closer to understanding what had caused his fall. He used his arms to push himself to standing, hissing at the pain. *Blasted knee.* He set his crutches under his arms and made his way slowly down the hallway and through his master bedroom. Crutches, foot, crutches, foot, agony knifing up his leg into his hip and ribs.

By the time he reached his bathroom, his hands were shaking. He fumbled through the medicine bottles the hospital had given him as a party favor. Anti-inflammatories. Antibiotics. Cursing, he grabbed a bottle off the counter and squinted at it through the headache pounding the front of his skull.

Vicodin. *Don't mind if I do.*

He couldn't remember and didn't care how long it had been since his last dose. He cared even less about how many pills that pansy doctor in Idaho wanted him to take each time. He drank water from the sink's spout and swallowed two.

If he'd had the strength for a shower, he'd have showered. Turned out it was all he could manage to get himself from the light of his bathroom to the dark of his bed. His knee screamed at him as he lifted it onto the mattress. Once he'd gotten it settled, he peeled off his shirt and rested against a stack of pillows with a groan.

His house echoed with emptiness. His future had turned gray, his purpose grayer.

Where was Celia? That he knew the answer didn't stop the question from coming. Since he'd wrecked his knee, the fact that she and Addie lived in Oregon irritated him constantly. Which must be why he thought about Celia so much. Every time he woke: her. When out of it with drugs: her. When tired. When surrounded by his family. When the pain was worst.

Her. Her. Her.

Tawny had been here a few hours ago, yet as soon as he'd stretched out here on his bed, who had he thought of?

He wanted Celia and Addie to move to Holley more than he wanted pain meds or sleep or even health. It wasn't logical.

He bent an elbow over his eyes. A while back, Celia had lectured him about trying to buy them stuff. He'd heard her. But in his experience, money got things done. He'd never been a patient man. It wasn't in him to sit around politely, doing nothing except hoping that Addie and Celia would move to Holley.

He needed to get them to Texas.

He knew exactly what gift he'd purchase Addie for her birthday.

And tomorrow, he'd buy Celia a house.

We've got to stop meeting like this, Celia thought, staring at her online bank account. *This weekly date of ours depresses me to no end.*

Planting an elbow on the kitchen table, she dropped the side of her head into her hand. She still needed to pay the electric bill, and Addie would need school supplies—

Her cell phone rang, the sudden sound startling her. She flipped the phone face up, confirming two suspicions. It was after ten thirty at night. It was Ty calling.

Since his injury three days prior, he'd called her often. He'd gotten grumpier and become even more blunt. All of which she could deal with far better if this weak, melty feeling would quit coming over her whenever she thought of him. A cowboy had been stampeded by a bull, called her eyes crazy pretty, and—*boom*—she'd gone to mush. Disgusting! She brought her phone to her ear. "Hello?" A purposefully businesslike tone.

"I want you to move to Holley."

"May I ask who's calling?"

"I've been real patient about this whole thing, but now I mean business. I want you to move here."

"Seriously? Huh. You don't say."

"Do you have five hours? I'm about to go over all the reasons, *again*, why you and Addie should move here."

"Thanks, but I don't really want to hear them."

"Well, I'm going to tell them to you anyway—"

"I'm considering it, Ty." She said the words calmly. They held enough power, however, to stretch silence across the line. She could sense the weight of his surprise. "I'm considering moving to Holley."

"I'll have a truck at your door tomorrow."

"I only said I was considering it!"

"Well, consider this. If you don't move here, the house I just bought you will have to sit empty."

Her spine snapped straight, and she frowned at the reflection of herself visible in the sliding glass door. A puff of curly hair on a slim frame. "You bought us a house?"

"I thought about just emailing you a copy of the deed, but I didn't want to be pushy."

"In your case, the not-pushy ship sailed long ago."

"School's starting in three weeks, sweet one. I wanted to have a house ready in case ya'll decide to come to Holley."

"You bought us a house. *Seriously?*"

"You can hang your hat on it."

She assumed that was Texan for *yes*. "When you've mentioned buying us a house in the past, I've advised you against it, Ty."

"It made me happy to buy it, Celia."

"I think you're using the gifts as a shortcut to get what you want."

"Is it working?"

"Absolutely not." She chewed the edge of her lip, curiosity overcoming her desire to remain impervious. "What does the house look like?"

"It looks like a cross between a shoebox and a doll-house. I don't like it a bit, so I figured you'd love it."

She smiled and tapped her pencil on the tabletop. Her gaze ran down the computer's list of her withdrawals. "Here's my concern."

"Yes?"

"Let's just say that we relocate all the way across the country. Maybe Addie and I take a liking to our new house. Maybe it's even possible that you can find me a job—"

"Oh, I can find you a job. I'm like a king down here."

She snorted.

"I'm still waiting," he said, "to hear the concern part."

"I'm concerned that you can't afford to be so generous anymore. It looks to me like your career is kaput."

She could hear him shifting, as if readjusting his position in bed. "I'm embarrassed to have to tell you this, Celia. I really am. I was hoping to keep it a secret, because my image as a dumb hick cowboy is important to me."

"I'm pretty sure nothing will ever threaten your image as a dumb hick cowboy."

"I've had . . . a little bit of luck with the stock market." Celia knitted her forehead.

"The BRPC paid me well, but let's just say the stock market has paid better. Way back in the early days, I invested what I made off riding, and then that made money and then that made money and so on."

"Do you have a financial planner, or do you invest the money yourself?"

"Myself. But if you tell anyone in Holley about this, I'll be mad. I'll have to . . . I don't know, pay you back by taking Addie to a PG movie."

"You're a stock market investment guru?"

"I can easily afford a car that's the size of a Coke can and an itty-bitty house."

"Will you email me some pictures of the house?"

"Yes. Will you move to Holley? Soon? I want to see you so I can argue with you in person."

"Will you email me the pictures tonight? Like, in the next ten minutes?"

"Man, you're bossy. I have a blown-out knee, you know."

"Don't pretend you don't have some sort of computerized device right beside you in bed."

"I know something else I'd rather have right beside me in bed." His voice had a smooth-rough timbre. Like hot, nutty caramel.

Desire coiled in Celia's stomach. She'd have chided him for the comment, except that chiding only encouraged him. "Just email me the pictures, showboat. Your sweet-talking has no effect on me."

"You sure? My sweet-talking is known to work pretty well on most females. No effect on you whatsoever?"

"None," she lied.

"What if I were to tell you how much I like your—"

"Nope. No effect whatsoever."

Once they'd disconnected, she pulled up her email. She hit the button to retrieve mail over and over until at last an email from Ty arrived. Celia downloaded the images of the house.

Oh. She stared, rapt, at a small Victorian. It had been painted French blue, with paler blue trim and lots of old and intricate white gingerbread accents. Instead of rectangular roof shingles, it had small shingles that formed half circles at the bottom. The porch's snowy white fence and posts wrapped around the front and one side of the house.

It looked like the kind of backyard playhouse a millionaire's little girl might have dreamed of. Only bigger.

The next image showed a close-up of the entry. The front door had been crafted from beautiful old mahogany and inset with four square panes of beveled glass.

The final photo pictured what must be the living room—a cheery space full of windows. Sunlight cascaded in, illuminating a fireplace and mouth-watering wooden floors.

Swiftly and uninvited, a deep love for the place clutched at Celia's heart.

Ty—the terrible scoundrel, the bum-legged charmer—didn't play fair.

Over the next few days, Celia and Addie shared some serious conversations about the realities of moving. Celia pointed out the differences in climate. The loss of Uncle Danny, Addie's friends, her favorite parks, their apartment, the pool.

Addie assured Celia that except for Uncle Danny, she'd give the rest up. For them both, Danny was the deal breaker. He'd moved to Oregon specifically for them, to be their family. How could they abandon him? Whenever Celia thought about doing so, her stomach twisted. She relied on him, but he also relied on her.

When Danny dropped by their house a few evenings later, Celia pulled him into her backyard garden, closing the slider behind them. "Has Addie mentioned anything to you about the possibility of us, um, moving to Holley, Texas?"

"Yeah, she has. Are you thinking about it?"

Looking at him, Celia's courage faded. Why had she wasted her time and Addie's hope even considering the idea of Holley? They couldn't leave Uncle Danny. "Don't worry, I don't think it's going to happen—"

"Worry? I'd love to move to Polly, Texas."

Celia's attention honed on him.

He shrugged then smiled, the whites of his eyes bright against his tan. "I'm ready for a change, you know? I'm not used to staying in one place too long. It's not good for my adventurous vibe."

"You'd be willing to move with us?"

"Wherever you go, I go. We're a team."

Gratitude and love coursed through her.

"Besides, the dating pool here has run dry, C. In a

bad way. Did I tell you that it didn't work out between Sandy and me?"

"I'm sorry to hear that."

"I could deal with her ventilator's squeaky little wheels and the tube under her nose and all, but when she told me she doesn't like the beach because its *too windy*?"

"You knew right away she wasn't the woman for you."

"I bet they have some fine women down there in the Lone Star State."

In bed that night, Celia's mind was filled with the decision that hung before her. She had her finances to consider. Schools. The packing and unpacking. That gingerbread house. The question of whether she could stand to live so close to Ty. The question of what would be best for Addie.

"Daddy's hurt, and he needs us." She recalled Addie speaking those words at the bus stop the day she'd run away. The breeze had stirred strands of her hair and emotion had glittered in her eyes. *"We have to go to Texas."*

Celia shifted onto her side, then her stomach. Finally, she flipped onto her back and stared at the ceiling. She'd just made her choice, a realization that caused her pulse to pick up speed.

In the end her decision had had little to do with the gingerbread house and everything to do with the thing she cared about most in the world: her daughter's well-being. Addie's contentment was her only goal, and in

Holley, Addie would be able to live near Ty. She wouldn't be split across a country, always missing him.

Celia might come to regret every microfiber of this decision. Probably would, in fact. But there were no guarantees in life. You had to navigate the path the best you could, try to discern what was right, and then hope mightily for the best.

They were going to move to Texas.

CHAPTER
TWELVE

Celia and Addie sat side by side and held hands as their 737 made its final descent into the Dallas–Fort Worth Airport. A bright and cloudless afternoon sky surrounded them. Below, a metropolis waited.

From her middle seat, Celia could see freeways, a cluster of skyscrapers in the distance, tracks of homes, lakes, and brushstrokes of brownish vegetation. No hills or thick swaths of green trees. No bowl-you-over natural beauty. She swallowed a queasy ball of second-guesses and moved her attention to her daughter.

No uncertainty there. A grin stretched Addie's cheeks as she pressed her forehead against the porthole-style window and devoured the view.

The plane turned, righted itself, turned. The landing gear moved into place with a grind and a thump, then at last they landed with a set of bumps. Addie shot Celia a look of breathless delight. "We're here!"

"Yes." Texas. A state famous for barbecue, ranches, the Alamo, and the assassination of JFK.

Addie bounced, buzzed about Ty and Ty's house and Holley, then returned to gazing out the window.

Celia rested her head against the seat back and let her lids sink closed. Everything had happened too fast. She'd decided to relocate just ten days ago, ten days that had passed in a blur and left her with a sentimental burn in her throat.

When she'd turned in her notice at work, her boss had immediately promoted the girl who'd been holding the position under Celia's. Her replacement was so adept that Celia had been asked to stay at her post for only one additional week.

Her boss had assumed she was doing Celia a favor. But in some respects, Celia would have preferred to work longer so that she'd have had more time to say good-bye to the town that had been her home since the age of eighteen.

From halfway across the country and convalescing from a blown-out knee, Ty had organized their relocation at warp speed. He'd had movers at River Run carrying her bed from her apartment before she'd been ready. He'd bought them plane tickets before she'd given final approval to the flight schedule. He'd called and asked Uncle Danny, without her permission, if they could stay with him their last few nights in Corvallis so that the truck with their stuff and the person driving their Prius cross-country would have a head start.

Celia and Addie waited to deplane, then walked through the terminal to a revolving door leading into the baggage claim area. A middle-aged man stood a short distance away. He wore a neat black suit and held a sheet of paper that said *Sweet One*.

Hysterical, Celia thought darkly.

She and Ty had haggled over the issue of who would pick them up from the airport. Ty's doctors had forbid him from driving, and Celia had asked Ty not to send his family. The Porters were a large group, strong-willed, and probably not very kindly disposed toward her. In the end, Celia had agreed to let Ty send a driver to meet them at DFW.

She approached the man and gave him an apologetic smile. "I think you might be here for me."

"Your name, ma'am?"

"Celia Porter."

His eyes crinkled with good-natured humor. "I am indeed here for you." He took their carry-ons and led them toward the automatic doors. When they exited the heavily air-conditioned airport, they walked into greenhouse-humid, furnace-hot outside air. It enveloped Celia with such ghastly power that she cut to a stop and wheezed. Addie looked around, beatific. Their driver continued on.

What *was* this temperature? 115? 150? Hot enough to slow cook a roast, that's for sure.

Addie took her hand and tugged. "C'mon, Mommy!"

They followed their driver into a covered parking area. Celia had been expecting a simple town car, but the man stopped next to a . . . a stretch limo. Its long white body had been covered at all angles with gaudy cartoon-style artwork depicting broncos, spurs, ten-gallon hats, stars, and footballs. The slogan *Everything's bigger in Texas* scrolled across the side in cursive. Texas flags whipped from all four corners and longhorns had been mounted on the car's front, like the masthead of a ship.

Addie giggled.

An embarrassed blush darkened Celia's cheeks. She'd been on Texas soil for less than thirty minutes, and already she wanted to kill Ty.

"I wish Uncle Danny were here, Mom. He'd like this car."

"Yes, he probably would."

"When will he get here?"

"He said he'd be here by your birthday." Danny had opted to hit the open road and spend several days en route between Oregon and Texas, stopping wherever spontaneity led.

The driver held open the limo's rear door for them, and Celia had no choice but to bundle Addie into the yee-haw limo and scoot in after her. Was it safe for a child to ride in this thing? The Texasmobile had space for twelve adults, two flat screens, and a bar. She and Addie took the spots at the rear. In the event of a collision, Addie would be thrown forward twenty feet.

"Isn't this fun? Look at this!" Addie pointed to the carpeted ceiling and the LED lights embedded in it.

Once she'd gotten Addie into her booster and fastened their seat belts, the car started forward. Air vents pounded Celia's face and chest with artificially cold air.

What have I done, moving here?

Addie spent the next hour peppering Celia with questions, sipping ginger ale on the rocks, and flipping TV channels.

Eventually, the city's sprawl fell away. Fields opened around them, and a good while later they passed Holley's city limit sign.

Celia's first impressions: space and flatness. Electrical

poles marched down the road, upright and symmetrical. Open, slatted fences enclosed plots of land—some bare, some dotted with horses or cattle. They passed an old clapboard church with a historical placard out front, a few windmills, and a sign advertising a cowboy church held at the Swingin' S Ranch. Holley's police station, city hall, and volunteer fire department all shared the same parking lot.

Eventually, the limo hung a left onto a street that felt far more country than residential. Ty didn't live in a neighborhood of homes so much as a neighborhood of ranches. As the street carried them further from civilization, Celia spotted occasional houses set back amid the dip and roll of trees and acres.

"Are we almost there?" Addie asked for the twentieth time.

"I think so."

"Is this where Daddy lives?"

"It looks like it. See?" Celia pointed to a mailbox inscribed with *Porter*. They turned onto a paved drive that took them gently uphill. A fenced pasture hugged the road on the right side. The left side had been left to fend for itself. No sign of a house yet.

Inside Celia, nervousness hummed. She'd spoken with Ty often but hadn't laid eyes on him since his last visit to Corvallis.

She glanced down and smoothed her white peasant shirt. The flat-front turquoise shorts and T-strap sandals she'd chosen to wear with it had seemed presentable when she'd picked them. Now she wasn't so sure.

A house came into view—big and expensive, with simple landscaping that could have been managed by sprinklers and a mowing crew alone. Too new, in Celia's opinion, to have much character. Brown brick covered a majority of the exterior, smooth stucco a minority. Other than the dark wooden posts and buttresses that framed the front entry, there wasn't much decorative detail about the place and certainly no feminine touches.

Celia and Addie unfolded from the limo into the fist-punching heat. Addie's hand whispered upward and found Celia's. Her girl, who'd been so confident, looked to have been stricken by a sudden case of self-consciousness.

The front door opened, and a couple hurried out. Ty's parents, maybe? They were about the right age. A hearty-looking brunette wearing beige capris, a melon-colored cotton top, and sensible sandals led the charge. A slim cowboy, neat as a pin, followed her.

Celia and Addie walked toward them, tense. These two had reason to dislike her, Celia knew. She only prayed they wouldn't make their dislike obvious in front of Addie.

"Welcome," the woman called, waving. "Oh, have we been looking forward to this! John and I've been waiting there in the front room all afternoon, thinking you might drive up at any moment, and here you are." The couple drew within speaking distance. "I'm Nancy, and this is John. We're Ty's parents."

"I'm Celia." *The person who married your son in a twenty-four-hour Las Vegas wedding chapel, then hid your granddaughter from you.* "Nice to meet you both."

"Good to meet you," John answered, his expression friendly.

The gray streak that ran through the front of Nancy's hair matched the color of her eyes, eyes that shone with what looked like true affection. She reached out and gave Celia's upper arm a squeeze. "I've been nagging Ty for weeks about wanting to meet you. What a pleasure."

Celia had no idea how to react in the face of their undeserved grace.

Nancy and John's attention focused on Addie with fascination, admiration, and tenderness. A shine came into Nancy's eyes. She placed her hands together and lifted them to cover her chin and mouth.

"This is Addie." Celia smoothed a hand over her daughter's hair.

Nancy lowered onto her knees before the girl, bracing her palms on her thighs. She gave Addie a smile of such love-struck joy that the sight of it caused emotion to clutch at Celia's throat.

"I'm glad you're here, Addie," Nancy said. "Thank you for coming."

"You're welcome." Addie pushed her teal glasses higher on her nose.

"It makes us so happy." Nancy reached out for John, twining his hand with hers and bringing him forward. "It makes us both so happy that you and your mom are going to live here."

"It makes me happy, too."

"Oh, sweetie. My, oh my, you're a beautiful girl."

"Thank you."

"Ty says that you like princesses. Will you come inside and tell me about them?"

Addie nodded.

They walked up the pathway parade style: Nancy launching into conversation with Addie, John and the driver insisting on pulling the carry-ons.

Like the exterior, the interior of Ty's house served up the color brown: walnut-hued wood floors, khaki walls, furniture that wasn't modern or traditional but somewhere in between. It reminded Celia of a pared-down furniture showroom, with no personal element to it.

"Oh!" Nancy pressed a hand to her forehead. "I was supposed to tell Ty the minute ya'll pulled in. I got so excited I forgot."

"No problem."

"He's not going to be happy with me. He's been a bear to deal with while he's been waiting for ya'll to get here."

"I'll go tell him we've arrived."

Nancy explained where to find the master bedroom, then she and John ushered Addie into the kitchen with the promise of a drink and a snack.

A Berber-carpeted hallway on the far side of the foyer took Celia past what she assumed to be Ty's home office to a half-opened doorway. Ty's bedroom. Stopping on the threshold, she peered in. He was reclining on his bed, propped up by pillows against the headboard. He had in earbuds, was reading an issue of *Money* magazine, and was wearing reading glasses. Glasses?

Light from the lamp on his bedside table shifted through his hair and glinted off his sterling watch. He wore a gray T-shirt that said *Under Armour* across the front. Since their high school days, she'd never seen him in anything but jeans, but this afternoon he had on a pair of cargo shorts, likely to make room for the bulky brace on his leg that began at some point beneath the hem of his shorts and continued to below his calf.

He'd focused his attention on the magazine, but he didn't appear at peace. A troubled groove etched between his brows, and his profile had an air of pained darkness to it.

A rush of treacherous compassion washed over Celia. Ty had always been healthy, handsome, and a little too devil-may-care daring. But in some mysterious way, that was how Ty Porter was meant to exist in the world.

They had their issues. Even so, they'd managed to establish an odd sort of friendship. She was sorry he'd lost his bull riding, which had meant so much to him. Sorry, too, because by the looks of his expression, the leg hurt him mercilessly.

Toughen up, Celia. She had a lot of tenderness to give to a man some day. She just couldn't afford to give it to this *particular* man.

She pushed his door open.

Instantly, Ty's face turned in her direction. Those blue eyes, eyes that could twist a girl's soul into a knot, focused on her intently. For a long moment he said nothing, and neither did she. The air hung between them, thick, but drawing thinner and thinner.

CHAPTER

THIRTEEN

S he was here.

Celia, standing in his bedroom without warning. Real . . . and here. *Here*, thank God. Finally. Ty took what felt like his first deep breath since his accident.

She was prettier than in his memory, so pretty he drank in the sight of her like water. He'd forgotten that her curls had a touch of red in them and just how much the disarray of her hair contrasted with the natural, clean-lined features of her face. He'd forgotten her exact height, or in this case, her lack of it. What he'd remembered: how perfectly her curves were proportioned to her slender body.

The forest fairy. It sure had taken her long enough to come to him.

With a slow motion, he twisted a finger into his earbud cord and pulled them free. He'd only been wearing them because his mom was more likely to leave him alone when he had them in.

As Celia moved toward his bed, she arched a brow at him and crossed her arms.

His family, friends, Tawny, and Holley's church ladies had been treating him like a cracked piece of glass for the past couple of weeks. But based on the look on her face, Celia wasn't going to go that route. She was about to unload a pile of attitude on him, and all he could think was how glad he was and how powerfully he'd missed her. Celia on the telephone and in his thoughts was nothing compared to her in the flesh.

She stopped a few feet away, took in his brace and then his face. "You went to great lengths to get us here. I'll give you that."

His lips hitched up on one side. "It worked, didn't it? I like to get my way."

"What're you going to do the next time you want your way? Full body cast?"

"If necessary."

"Are the glasses and the magazine a costume?"

"Meaning?"

"You knew I was coming, so I'm guessing you dug up some glasses and bought a *Money* magazine and waited for me to find you like this so you'd look cerebral."

"Interesting theory."

"I feel like Daphne from Scooby-Doo."

"Is it hard to believe I might need glasses for reading, Daphne from Scooby-Doo?"

"It's hard to believe that you can read at all."

Ty tilted back his head and laughed. How long had it been since he'd laughed? Since whenever she'd made him laugh the last time, he guessed. He pulled off his glasses and set them and the magazine aside.

"When I got off the plane," she said, "the chauffeur was holding up a sign that said *Sweet One*."

"Really? I've no idea what you mean."

"Right. And thanks so much for sending a limo that only Conway Twitty and children under the age of ten would love."

"Did Addie like it?"

"Yes. But she's under ten. I, on the other hand, nearly died of embarrassment."

"Good."

He pushed his upper body to a sitting position with one arm and extended his other toward her. "Would you mind helping me up?" He didn't need help. It wasn't like he was uncoordinated. Or like this was the first or even second time in his life he'd had to get around on crutches.

Automatically, she gripped his hand. The moment she did, he leaned back hard onto his pillows, pulling her on top of him. Celia's forearms landed squarely against his chest, her hips across the mattress's edge. Her breath gasped inward.

His impulsive decision to tug her down with him might have surprised her, but it ended up stunning Ty. Because in response to the feel of her body braced against his, intense longing flooded him. His senses registered her softness, the scent of lemons mixed with sweetness, the sight of her face hovering inches above his.

Every shred of humor fell from him. His blood began to beat against his wrists, his neck. The doubt and pain of the past couple weeks disappeared until he could see nothing but her.

"You tricked me," she accused.

"Yes." His gaze moved to her lips. "I'm no good. You knew that already." He pressed a hand up her neck into her hair, drew her to him, and kissed her.

She hesitated and then melted against him, letting him take more of her weight. His streak of five and a half years without kissing a woman—broken.

Groaning, he fisted his free hand into the fabric at the small of her back. He couldn't believe she was letting him do this. His entire body roared with heat and possessiveness. He'd never felt anything like this, nothing half so—

She yanked back and *smack*, slapped him.

Ty's face snapped to the side. He brought it back around in time to watch her take two fast steps away from the bed. A spark caught fire in her eyes and began to blaze.

"Did you just *slap* me?" Ty didn't care all that much about the slap—she was tiny and hit like a girl—but he did care that she'd ended the kiss. He felt like a wolf who'd had its food jerked away.

"Did you just *kiss* me?" she demanded.

"You slapped me," he said slowly, scowling. "I have a blown-out knee!"

"I'll blow out your other one if you ever try to kiss me again. How dare you!"

"You were enjoying it!"

She opened her mouth but said nothing. Her chest rising and falling with outraged breath, she pushed her fists against her hips.

"You enjoyed it, and you can bet your bottom dollar that *I* enjoyed it." With a wince, he pushed both his legs over the side of the bed. "Come back over here so I can kiss you some more."

"Absolutely not."

He glanced down at his shirt, where she'd wrinkled

the fabric in two places by bunching it between her fists during their kiss. "You plumb near ripped my shirt. Are you going to try to tell me you don't want to come back over here and kiss me?"

"In my head, I don't want to kiss you. Not at all." She sniffed, lifted her chin. "But . . . there for a second . . . my body did want to, I admit."

He wished he had the use of both legs so he could go after her, corner her against a wall, any wall, and kiss her cheeks, her shoulders, her hands. As it was, he reached for his crutches and pushed to standing on his good leg. He leaned forward on the crutches, watching her intently. Waiting.

"I'm going to be brutally honest with you, Ty. I do have a sort of . . . a weakness for you. I wish I didn't, but I do."

"I have the same weakness for you. These last weeks since I hurt myself, I've missed you. I've about gone wild waiting for you to get here."

"That doesn't make sense, Ty. I haven't been in your life for years. Why would you start missing me now?"

"I don't know."

She pressed her palms to her temples. "This is crazy!"

He lifted an eyebrow. "Crazy powerful."

Her arms dropped, and she regarded him with extreme caution. "What about Tawny?"

"What about her? She's dating someone else."

"If you want to marry her, don't you think you should hold off on kissing other women until she's free?"

"I did think so. But now I've changed my mind." He hadn't planned on kissing Celia. But once he'd pulled her half on top of him, he hadn't been able to stop himself. Tawny hadn't crossed his mind. And he didn't want Tawny in his mind now, either. Not when kissing Celia again struck him as the best idea he'd had in a decade. "Come over here and kiss me, sweet one. We'll see if we can figure everything out that way."

"Stop saying things like that! We can't kiss. Not ever again. I'm serious, Ty. Don't . . ." He read plain truth in her. "Don't mess around with me. All right?"

"I don't want to mess around with you. I want to talk straight up about the chemistry between us." He gestured between them. "Is it possible there might be something here?"

"There can't be anything here. We're just friends."

"We're married."

"Only because—" her voice faltered a bit, but she squared her shoulders and kept on— "we haven't signed the divorce papers yet."

Since his fall, the thought of Celia had been the only thing that had calmed him during the rotten therapy sessions, the boredom, the regret over his lost career. He felt so many contradictory things for her and didn't understand any of them. He only knew that he'd never expected her to let him kiss her, but she had, and his strongest urge was to keep on kissing her until sunrise.

Maybe going so long without physical contact with women hadn't been the best idea. He'd been *trying* to be honorable. Except he wasn't honorable and couldn't buy honorable. He was dishonorable, and now that long stretch of self-denial may have made him stone-cold insane, too. Brutal pain pounded his leg and the muscles in his neck had gone hard as stone.

"We need to think about Addie," she said.

"You think divorce is the best thing for Addie?"

"At least it would give her closure. You must have noticed that she has hopes for you and me in the romance department."

Every night on the phone Addie went out of her way to tell him how pretty and sweet and basically eligible her mom was.

"If she saw us holding hands or kissing or anything like that, Ty, it would fill her head with all kinds of false ideas. She'd get hurt in the end, and I can't allow that."

"*I* don't want to hurt her."

Some of the starch went out of her. "I know you don't."

Ty didn't need Celia to spell out why Addie was a relationship killer for them. He got it. Frustrated, he frowned at the view beyond one of his bedroom windows. Addie was almost five years old, obsessed with princesses, and innocent enough to put stock in happily ever after. She believed him to be better than he was, so of course she wanted him and Celia to become a true husband and wife. If the two of them started down that path only to have things fall apart again, she'd be crushed.

He pushed a hand through his hair and wished for Vicodin. How long had it been since he'd taken his last dose?

"Ty?"

He turned his attention to her. Beautiful, maddening her. Who somehow, since his accident, had become important to him.

She looked edgy and mistrusting.

He could put her back at ease with charm, he knew. All his life he'd used it to get himself out of scrapes. It was as old and comfortable as one of his custom-made saddles. "Are you going to put that no-touching rule of yours back in place?" He regarded at her with wry humor.

"*Yes.*"

"What about for medicinal reasons? Like, right now, for instance, I could use some support to get to the living room."

"There's no way I'm falling for that a second time."

"What if I touch you real respectfully? Like if I run my fingertip over your wrist or something?"

"No."

"Well, just so we're clear, you can touch me anytime you want."

"Thanks, but no. I'd rather . . . um . . ."

"Drink high-fructose corn syrup?" he supplied.

When she released a huff of unwilling laughter, he knew he'd gotten their relationship back on its usual footing. He started from the room, swinging his brace smoothly, making fast progress on his crutches. Celia followed.

"I'm ready to show you your new house," he said.

"Don't you think Addie and I need to spend some time visiting with your parents first?"

"Ten minutes?"

"At least an hour."

Ty groaned.

Addie must have heard them coming, because when he rounded an archway and spotted her sitting at his kitchen table, her head had already turned in his direction. "Daddy!" she cried.

That one word stopped him in his tracks and stole his voice.

Her face bright with excitement, she ran to him and hugged his good leg. He hugged her back as much as his crutches would allow. Love for her swelled within him. *My little girl*, he thought with fierce pride. He'd missed the first years of her life, but she'd called him daddy anyway because her heart was big and generous enough to make room for him.

He'd liked just about every female he'd ever met, starting with his mother right on up. But no child had ever greeted him with such happiness, and none had ever called him daddy.

She looked up at him.

He smiled at her. "Hi, Addie."

"Hi."

He wanted to be her daddy. It was true, what he'd just been thinking—that Addie believed him to be better than he was. When she looked at him like this, though, he wanted to be the man she thought he was.

He'd accomplished some things in his life, but when it came down to it, none of it amounted to anything compared to this. No matter what, he was dead set on being Addie's protector, provider, and biggest fan. The one who'd be there for every important moment in her life from now on, clapping and believing in her. Her daddy.

"Are you doing okay?" She patted his arm softly.

"Yes. How about you?"

"Doing good."

"I see you've got your boots on."

She beamed.

"If this car were any smaller, it'd be a jelly bean."

"Jelly bean!" Addie giggled from her booster seat in the back of the Prius.

"Ha ha ha ha ha!" Celia pretended hilarity.

"From now on I'm going to call this car the green jellybean." Ty attempted to straighten his good leg. "I think Toyota made this car for those short people from *The Wizard of Oz*."

More laughter from Addie.

"This car is a perfect size." Celia wasn't about to let him cast aspersions on her car, even if it did insult his masculinity to ride in a small hybrid and, worse, to let a woman drive.

Ty and Addie launched into a conversation about *The Wizard of Oz*, a movie Celia hadn't yet deemed Addie old enough to watch.

Celia gripped the steering wheel at ten and two. They were on their way from Ty's house to her new house, and she'd just come off an hour-long visit with Ty's parents. Ty'd spent the whole visit staring at her and failing to keep up his share of the conversation. She'd had to compensate for him even though her own thoughts were in a complete clamor. The whole time she'd been answering Nancy and John's questions, in her mind she'd been pointing a finger at their big, handsome son and shrieking, *He just kissed me! He just kissed me!*

Ty had KISSED her. He wasn't allowed to kiss her.

No, he was a grown man. He was allowed to do whatever he wanted. It was more that *she* wasn't allowed to kiss him back. She had, though. The memory made her cheeks flame.

She'd been so surprised, when he'd tugged her to him, and then so . . . so immersed in the most instantaneous storm of desire, that she'd . . . *shoot*! She'd kissed him back. And not halfheartedly. No, no. Quite passionately. So passionately she'd almost fainted from the bliss of it.

For years her libido had lain dormant except for the occasional wistful twinge over a scholarly looking professor or doctoral candidate. How *could* it have betrayed her by showing up now, and with such force, for him?

"Turn here."

Celia turned onto a street lined with Victorian houses, working to focus on the neighborhood instead of the man sitting so uncomfortably near.

The houses reminded her of perfectly constructed confections made by a master pastry chef. Each one beautiful, fancy, and entirely unique. She spotted delicately crafted small Victorians. Big and imposing ones, exquisitely imagined and set to their best advantage on lots ripe with old trees. All had been frosted with the prettiest palette of colors—pink, blue, eggshell, peach, green—three and four hues on every one. Old-fashioned light posts decorated with hanging baskets of flowers stood at regular intervals along the sidewalk.

"Left," Ty said.

A block and a half later, he pointed. "Here's yours."

Celia pulled into the driveway and leaned forward, taking in the sight of it. *Yours*, he'd said. Her gingerbread house. He'd assured her that he'd given it to her with no strings attached. She hoped so . . . hoped, all at once, that he wouldn't want more kisses in exchange for the mortgage.

It boasted two shades of blue, lots of frilly woodwork, and a wraparound white porch. Thanks to the pictures Ty had emailed to her, she recognized it the way she would have a long lost friend. It was even cuter than it had appeared online, in part because of the charming and historic streets that surrounded it.

The three of them made their way across the lawn. Celia used the new key Ty had given her to unlock the front door, admitting them into an interior that smelled pleasantly like pine-scented cleaner and old wood. A hallway led straight ahead. Addie hooked a left into the living room, so Celia and Ty followed. A fireplace surrounded by gleaming custom woodwork dominated one wall, while windows dominated the others. The previous owners had painted the space a soft dove gray and the thick baseboards and crown moldings cream.

"I left the walls the way they were." Ty lifted a muscular arm to scratch the back of his neck. "I figured you'd want to pick out your own paint colors."

"I do. Thank you." This was so awkward! To pretend normalcy with him when her head brimmed with memories of having been plastered against his chest.

Addie peppered Ty with questions Celia hardly registered as they moved from the living room into a dining room that offered a large built-in china cabinet.

The kitchen filled one back corner of the house. More gray paint. Appliances that had all been purchased in the last decade. Lovely marble countertops. Several rectangular windows, which meant lots of lower cabinets but few uppers.

It was a kitchen to cook in. A kitchen *she* could cook in. She could easily picture herself whipping together her

Thanksgiving sweet potato casserole here, or Christmas cookies, or the egg dish she and Addie always ate on Easter morning. With a direct view to the outside, she could even bake while watching Addie play in the backyard. Assuming, that is, that the weather would eventually cool to something in the vicinity of what human beings could tolerate.

When they moved into the hallway, Ty motioned his head toward a closed door. "This is your room, Addie, but let's come back to it. Best for last, right?"

"Right."

The bathroom floor had been tiled with small octagonal tiles, all white except for a row of black about a half foot from the walls.

They'd almost returned to the entry area.

Ty pointed with a crutch to the airy and spacious room at the front of the house. "I thought you might like this for your room, Celia."

Just the way he said "your room" made her skin flush. Clearly, she'd been deprived of male attention for too long.

"It's beautiful." Age-scarred wooden floors. Views of the front and side yards. The space sat empty except for a single box—a shoebox maybe?—that waited in the center of the room. "What's this?"

"A housewarming gift."

Celia bent and flipped open the lid, uncovering a pair of women's cowgirl boots in the classic style. Pointed toe, mid-sized heel. They'd been fashioned out of gray leather with fancy scrolling and stitching all over them.

"Aren't those cool, Mom?"

"They are."

"I told Daddy to get you pink ones, like mine. But he said you'd like gray boots more than pink, even though you're a little bit of a hippie—"

"A hippie?" She angled a look at Ty.

He shrugged.

She wasn't a cowgirl-boot–wearing type of woman. Plus, she had no intention of accepting any more gifts from him. Once they were out of Addie's earshot, she'd try to convince him to return them and keep the money. "Thanks for the boots."

"You're welcome."

"My room now?" Addie stared at Ty with the stillness of a dog watching a squirrel.

"Your room, Addie," he agreed.

Addie hurried to her doorway, waited for them to join her, then swung the door open. "Oh!" she gasped.

The rest of the house was vacant, but Addie's room had been done up in Royal Princess style. A wash of pale pink covered three of the walls. The fourth wall, at the head of the four post double bed, blazed hot pink. A hand-painted and glittering silver tiara had been painted above the bed.

Ty or his female decorator or someone had bought a matched set of white furniture. A chandelier dripped handfuls of pink crystals. The curtains had been made from pale purple-and-white-plaid fabric, then trimmed in hot pink pom-pom fringe. Lamp bases that looked like sugar-crusted fairy-tale castles rose from the bedside tables. The whole room could have come straight out of the Pottery Barn Kids catalog.

Addie stood frozen, her eyes gawking.

Ty chuckled.

As if the sound of Ty's amusement loosened Addie from a spell, she went into motion, touching everything with wonder. "Thank you, Daddy. Thank you."

"You're welcome."

Ty and Celia watched Addie for long moments. Celia knew within her own heart the bittersweet sting that came from mothering a child who was growing up. This room belonged to an older girl. A big girl. And Celia . . .

Well. Celia had wanted Addie to stay a baby forever.

"Are you mad that I didn't ask you first?" Ty asked under his breath.

"No. It's okay." Though it did miff her a little.

"I wanted to do something for her. I hoped you wouldn't mind."

"It's a great room." She stole a glance at him out of the corners of her eyes, taking in the trademark T-shirt, his masculine profile. She could clearly see in Ty's expression the pleasure it had brought him to give this room to Addie.

Celia's experience with Ty had proven him capable of real generosity. It had also proven him capable of breaking her heart.

You can be Addie's father, Ty. We can have physical chemistry. We can shoot comebacks at each other all day long, and maybe we can even grow our unlikely friendship.

But no matter what, I can't ever let myself love you again.

CHAPTER FOURTEEN

Celia woke the next morning to darkness, closely followed by a wave of disorientation. Where was she? She jerked to sitting, heart pounding.

The glow from a plug-in princess night-light revealed one corner of her surroundings. She was in Addie's I'm-either-a-rich-girl-or-I'm-royalty bed inside the ginger-bread house in Holley.

This was her new normal.

Next to Celia, Addie slept on her side, no doubt dreaming of a brave prince and the sweet and spunky maiden he'd fallen for at first sight. She'd balled her baby blanket against her chest, and her lips had parted with relaxation.

Based on the weak light rimming the curtains, dawn hadn't yet fully arrived. Carefully, Celia eased out of bed. She carried Addie's new desk chair from the room so she'd have something to sit on, and padded to the kitchen. Once she'd gotten the coffee maker going, she stood in front of it in her sleep uniform of boxer shorts and cami. Before it had finished brewing a full cup, she helped herself to some. Then she sat on Addie's chair, feeling her aloneness like a cloak. She took steady sips of coffee as she watched the sun rise over her first morning in Holley, Texas.

This is your new home, she told herself, trying to make herself believe it.

She'd grown used to living in an apartment, to having tenants next to her on either side. This stand-alone house felt airy and unprotected in comparison. It also presented her with a blank slate, empty of both furniture and experiences. So many sweet memories had been tied to her old apartment. Those memories—*I rocked Addie here when she was a newborn, I gave Addie a bath here when she was a toddler, I made up bedtime stories here for a thousand nights*—had caused Celia to shed secret tears in each and every room during her final days at River Run. Already she missed—

Enough, Celia! You live here now. Set some goals. Make a list, get on with life.

She pulled a small note pad from her purse and held a pen poised over it.

#1. Resist romantic overtures from Ty.

She paused, then underlined it twice. She'd found this more difficult than expected yesterday when he'd looked at her with need in his eyes and said things like *"I've missed you. I've about gone wild waiting for you to get here."* She drew an asterisk and added,

No more kissing.

She refused to risk her and Addie's emotional health by placing her trust in Ty a second time. If she ever dated anyone again in this lifetime (which was a big if), she'd need to date someone who was capable of commitment to her. The only woman Ty seemed capable of commitment to was Tawny.

Celia took a sip of now-tepid coffee and tapped her pen against her lips. Was there any chance that she could live in Holley without ever having to see Tawny face to face? She prayed so.

#2. *Get Addie settled in the house.*

The moving truck would arrive soon. She had no chance of getting everything in order before Addie's fifth birthday, coming up quickly. But she'd try her mightiest to have it done by the time Addie started school, on Monday. Monday was less than a week away, but if she worked like crazy, she had a shot.

#3. *Find a job.*

It had been years since she'd gone job hunting. She was rusty at structuring a resumé and lacked contacts in this town. Even so, she dearly wanted, for the sake of her self-respect, to find her own job without Ty's help.

Pushing to her feet, she tucked the note pad back into her purse. She needed baking therapy. Her TV hadn't arrived yet so she didn't have her cooking shows. But thanks to Ty's mom and sister-in-law who'd stocked her pantry for her, she did have shelves filled with flour, sugar, baking soda. . . .

Around ten, the doorbell rang.

Celia answered it to find a couple standing on her front porch. A pretty blonde around her own age held a present wrapped in Williams Sonoma paper. Next to her stood a tall cowboy with closely shaved dark hair and striking gray eyes.

"Celia?" the blonde asked.

"Yes."

She smiled. "Hi, I'm Meg. This is Bo."

"Ty's brother," the cowboy added. He extended his hand, and Celia shook it. "Nice to meet you."

They were one heck of an attractive pair. "Thank you. Nice to meet you both."

"Ty told us that your moving truck is scheduled to arrive soon." Meg tucked a strand of hair behind her ear. "We were hoping we could help you unload."

"Definitely. Come on in." From what Ty had told her, she knew that Bo managed a Thoroughbred racehorse farm and that he'd married Meg two years ago. Meg had inherited a fortune, lucky her, and now ran a charity for single parents and their children.

Once they'd bundled inside, Meg handed Celia the present. "Welcome to Holley. This is just a little house-warming gift from us."

"Wow, thank you."

"We're so pleased that you've moved here."

"Mom?" Addie emerged from her room.

Bo and Meg turned to her, every bit as fascinated by the sight of her as Bo's parents had been. Celia introduced them, then unwrapped her gift while Meg and Bo asked Addie questions.

Celia uncovered a gorgeous set of cooking tools that included a spatula, a pasta fork, and a ladle among others. The gleaming stainless steel canister that held them had been engraved with the letter C.

Bo and Addie were still talking, but Meg caught her eye. "I heard that you like to cook."

"I do. This is a beautiful set. Thank you. I'll use it all the time."

"I'm glad you like it."

Celia gestured to the living room. "If I had furniture I'd invite you to sit down. As it is, the only thing I have to offer is food."

"Lots of food!" Addie interjected. She motioned for the newcomers to follow her. "I'll show you."

In the kitchen one of the marble countertops labored under the weight of banana muffins, shortbread, and a cinnamon coffee cake.

Meg and Bo both paused at the sight of the spread.

"You made all this this morning?" Bo asked.

Celia nodded and refrained from confessing that she had a little bit of a compulsion. She'd rather they think her merely industrious.

Bo placed a slice of coffee cake on a paper plate, and Meg chose a muffin. Addie and Celia both helped themselves to shortbread.

"So, Addie." Meg peeled back her muffin wrapper. "Did you have a fun summer?"

"Yes."

"What did you do?"

In her calm and serious way, Addie relayed a story

about the River Run pool and the boy who'd gotten into trouble for shooting her in the face with his water gun.

Meg and Bo leaned against the counter, side by side. They worked on their food, listening attentively, asking follow-up questions. Meg laced a hand through Bo's elbow. He tucked that elbow near to his body in an answering gesture of protectiveness.

They had magnetism between them, these two. So strong that Celia could feel its buzz. What would it be like to have that sort of bond with a spouse? Amazing, probably.

While Meg wasn't necessarily a beauty, her face and demeanor had a sweetness to them that drew Celia in. Meg wore a pink T-shirt, coordinating Nike shorts, tennis shoes, scant makeup, and her hair in a ponytail. Even so, she managed to look elegant.

Bo resembled Ty a little in build and also in the evenness of their well-molded features. She hadn't met him during her high school years because he'd graduated just before she'd arrived. The Porter boys she'd known back then, Ty and Jake, had been the objects of a thousand infatuations. Looking the way he did, she'd guess that Bo had been the object of a thousand more.

When Addie finally paused to blink at her audience and gather breath, Celia saw her chance. "How did you two meet?"

Meg's eyes sparked with humor. "I tried to fire him. It didn't take."

"Fire him?" Addie asked.

"Yes," Meg said to Addie. "He runs something called Whispering Creek Horses. It's a stable. When I took over my dad's ranch, I didn't think I wanted a stable full of horses." Meg lifted a shoulder. "I was wrong. It turned out that I liked the stable, and I . . ." She glanced up at Bo. He glanced down at her. ". . . really liked the guy who ran it."

Bo smiled at his wife with such devotion that the power of it rolled through the room like a tidal wave. Well, there you had it. Celia's story with Ty—we got married and my husband regretted it in the morning— didn't exactly stack up.

"Did you know," Addie said, "that my daddy brought my mom her bracelet when she lost it?"

"No," Meg answered, "I didn't know that."

"It was like in Cinderella."

Heat climbed up Celia's cheeks. Just what she needed. Her daughter manufacturing a romance between her and Ty in front of a couple who had an actual romance going.

"Remember the glass slipper?" Addie continued. "It was like that, only my daddy brought a bracelet. Not a slipper. He's really, really nice."

Meg and Bo nodded.

"He gave me these boots," Addie stated.

"I love your boots," Meg told her.

Bo polished off the last bite of coffee cake. "That was delicious, Celia."

"So's this." Meg lifted what remained of her muffin. "Thank you."

"I mean, it's *seriously* good," Meg said. "You're really talented—" The rumble of a big engine and the groaning of brakes interrupted her.

The moving truck had arrived.

They all poured onto the front yard to watch as the two men who had come with the truck opened the vehicle's rear doors, positioned a ramp, and rolled down the first piece of furniture. Her sofa.

"Would it be okay with you," Bo asked, "if I invited some people from our Sunday school class to come by and help?"

"Sure." It was a weekday and hotter than Satan's armpit. She couldn't imagine that any of Bo's friends would take him up on his invitation, but it wouldn't hurt to let him ask. In her experience, not even close family members wanted to help a person move.

Bo pulled out a smartphone, hit a few buttons, then walked up the truck's ramp. Meg followed. He stopped halfway. "No way, Countess."

"Bo, I can carry—"

"Not on my watch." He gave her a crooked grin, a grin that admitted to all kinds of weaknesses where she was concerned.

Meg shook her head, lips curving. "You're hopeless."

"Yes," he agreed.

Meg crossed toward Celia. "Is there something I can do inside?"

"Absolutely."

What in the world was going on?

While his brother Jake pulled into a parking spot across the street from Celia's house, Ty sat in the passenger seat, scanning the scene. The moving truck he'd hired stood at the curb and lots of guys around his age were carrying boxes from it into Celia's place.

Ty frowned. Who'd invited strangers?

He let himself out and made his way toward the house

on his crutches. Jake grabbed a case of bottled water from the truck bed and fell into step beside him.

Ty motioned his chin toward the water. "What's that?"

"I wanted to get Celia something. You know, for her housewarming or whatever."

"Bottled water?"

"It's practical."

Ty would have teased Jake if Jake had still been up for teasing. But ever since he'd come home from Iraq, injured and fighting post-traumatic stress, his younger brother had been grim. Jake was no longer the brother Ty'd once known, the brother who'd teased and taken teasing. Nor was he someone who laughed. Or even smiled.

As they neared the front door, Bo walked out, his face red from heat and work. "Hey." He came to a stop in front of them. "How's everything at the farm?" he asked Jake.

"Fine."

"Who are all these people?" Ty indicated the men walking past.

"They're friends of ours from church."

Married friends or single friends? Ty wanted to ask. Genuine irritation shifted through him. He didn't want single guys without busted legs unpacking Celia's stuff.

"We're unloading pretty fast," Bo continued. "I think we'll have the truck empty in another thirty minutes."

"I'll go set this down and help you." Jake walked into the house.

Bo eyed Ty. "I spent some time talking to Celia. She seems nice. And your little girl is great."

"Yeah."

"She looks like you."

"You think so? I think she looks like her mother."

"Mostly. But she has your dimple, just on the one side. It looks dumber than a stump on you but cute on her." Bo smiled, clapped him on the shoulder, and moved past.

Inside the living room, Ty saw that Celia's furniture had been pushed to the center of the space. No doubt she wanted to leave herself room to paint before moving the pieces into their places.

He glanced into the front bedroom as he passed, looking for Celia. His parents were making up her bed, an open cardboard box between them. Inside Addie's room, women were unpacking books and placing them on the bookshelves. "Daddy!" Addie ran to him and hugged him.

"Hi, sweetheart."

"Our stuff came."

"Good."

"I'm going to be in here." She skipped into her pink room. "Helping."

"All right. I'll catch up with you in a little bit."

He found his sister-in-law, Meg, and two other women in the kitchen, taking newspaper off glassware. He had a soft spot a mile wide for his sister-in-law, who'd proven herself to be one of the kindest people alive. "Hi, Meg. Have you decided to leave my brother and run away with me yet?"

"I heard that!" Bo yelled from another part of the house.

"Oops," Ty whispered.

Meg laughed. "I think I'll stick with Bo for the time being. I sorta like him."

"I was afraid of that." He looked questioningly toward

the other two women, a blonde and a redhead. The blonde, Kelsey, had been in his high school youth group. "Either of you want to run away with me?"

"I do!" they replied in unison.

"Well, that's more like it."

"It's good to see you again Ty," the redhead said. "It's been years."

He didn't remember her. Not at all.

"Andria," she supplied.

He drew a blank. "That's right. How are you?"

"I'm doing really well."

"How are *you* lately?" Kelsey asked him, her face full of pity. "The whole town's been real worried about you since your injury."

So much for hoping all these church people were married. These two were as single as they came. "Doing okay." He lifted a shoulder. "It's my own fault. Got what I deserved for falling off a bull."

"Aww," Andria crooned.

Meg rolled her eyes.

"I hope you feel better soon." Kelsey spoke with such syrupy sympathy, he could have poured it on pancakes.

Celia appeared in the kitchen doorway that led to the dining room, looking annoyed. Lord have mercy, she was wearing the yellow tank top again. She'd put on cut-off jean shorts and pulled her hair back with one of her stretchy headbands. No shoes, just an anklet, a handful of Bubble Wrap, and a dusty streak on her forehead. She gave him a slit-eyed glare, then disappeared back into the dining room.

He wanted to laugh.

"Thanks for helping out around here today," he said to the women.

"Our pleasure, Ty."

As he was moving around them to the dining room, he spotted some mostly empty plates of food. "What's this?"

"Celia made it all," Meg answered. "Everything's wonderful."

As if the yellow tank top weren't enough. She'd *baked*? He'd always had a sweet tooth. He'd been on the road for years and had eaten three lifetimes worth of restaurant food, but not nearly enough homemade desserts.

Since it would be rude to do what he wanted to do and take everything that was left, he grabbed a muffin and two of the buttery-looking cookies.

"That's going to be hard for you to carry." Kelsey hurried over and held out a napkin. "Here, let me."

"Thanks." He set the food on her napkin and made his way into the dining room with Kelsey on his heels.

Celia stood next to the built-in china cabinet, pulling Bubble Wrap off plates and stacking them inside. She didn't look in his direction.

"You good?" Kelsey placed his food carefully on the dining room table next to him. Quite the nurse.

"Sure am."

"Let me know if there's anything else I can do."

"Thanks."

She gave him a long moment of eye contact before returning to the kitchen. If he kissed Kelsey, he didn't think he'd get slapped.

Balancing his weight on his crutches, he ripped off a

piece of muffin. As soon as it hit his tongue he got drunk on it. Bananas, walnuts, sugar, cinnamon—all in perfect balance. Nothing like store bought. Fresh and so soft it melted in your mouth. . . . He groaned.

Celia shot him a glance.

"I've got a thing for sweet stuff," he explained.

"I didn't remember."

"They say the way to a man's heart is through his stomach—"

"I didn't bake them for you, showboat."

Instead of all the physical therapy appointments, the laps he'd been swimming daily, and the medicines, his doctors should have recommended he eat Celia's food and listen to her call him names. Those two things made him feel a long shot better than all the rest. "I hate that nickname."

"*Big* showboat. How's that?"

He swallowed, then took another bite and almost sank to his knees in ecstasy. "Isn't it a little ironic that the woman who's against red food dye makes the most sugary desserts in the country?"

"I have a multifaceted personality."

"This is the best thing I've ever eaten in my life."

She pushed a curly strand of hair off her face and studied him. "Exaggerate much?"

"Not about food."

Her attention moved down to his jaw, stayed there, then slid lower and stalled on his chest.

Awareness hammered through him. He stopped chewing.

She wanted him. Maybe not as a boyfriend and certainly not as a husband. But physically, she did. She'd told him as much yesterday when she'd admitted that her body had a weakness for him. Just one look like that from her sent his own body racing.

She returned to stacking dishes.

"Were you just staring at my pecs?" he asked.

"What? No!" She kept her back to him. "As stated in our discussion yesterday, we're just friends."

Celia had put Addie forward as the main reason why the two of them couldn't date. He'd thought about their kiss and their conversation all night and all morning. *"Don't mess around with me,"* Celia had said to him. *"All right?"*

Addie wasn't the only one who needed protecting from his actions. He'd done so much damage to Celia the last time that she'd kept his child from him.

She'd convinced him yesterday that it would be best for all three of them if he kept his hands off her. At home, an hour ago, that truth had been clear in his mind and his plan to marry Tawny had once again made sense to him. But here, with Celia in front of him, he couldn't remember why. For reasons he didn't understand, Celia had the ability to confuse him, to turn his good intentions to dust. She made him lose trust in himself.

Give all your attention to Addie, you dummy. Quit worrying about her mother. Now that he had Celia and Addie in Holley, he simply needed to focus on growing his relationship with his daughter.

Clack. Clack clack clack. Celia set more dishes into the cabinet. "Are you planning on being helpful? Or are you going to stand around eating all day?"

Ty polished off the muffin and half a cookie. "My leg's a mess, remember? Eating is all I'm good for."

"Don't forget flirting."

"Flirting?"

"You're good for that."

He cocked his head. A smile crept across his mouth. "Are you jealous?"

She huffed.

"'Cause I am of you. Have any of these guys been hitting on you?"

"Yes. All."

"And?"

"I haven't decided which one I'll make my boyfriend yet, but the day's still young."

"If I have to whup somebody around here, Celia, I will."

"Then start with Jake. He brought me this." She pointed with her dainty foot toward the gigantic pack of water. "You have to admit, that's a romantic gift."

"If so, I must not understand the definition of romantic." He eased himself onto a chair and bent to unload one of the boxes.

"Everyone in your family brought me something today. Your parents brought me lavender sachets from France. Meg and Bo gave me a set of kitchen tools. It was really nice of them. I didn't expect anything."

"We're hospitable down here in Texas."

Celia sliced open a new cardboard box. "Meg and Bo seem happy together."

"They are." He could hear Meg deep in conversation with the other women in the kitchen. "Bo used to be normal before he fell so crazy in love with her. You should see him whenever one of us suggests doing something even a little bit dangerous."

"Like?"

"Four-wheeling. Water-skiing. Bo, Jake, Dru, and I grew up doing stuff like that. But mention it in front of Meg these days, and Bo hits the ceiling. He's like a caveman over her."

"Overprotective?"

"Kind of like you with Addie."

"I'm not overprotective. I'm just . . . careful."

That little necklace of hers was making him crazy. The small gold circle hung in the hollow between her collarbones, catching the light. Every time she leaned over to unpack something, it dangled. He wanted to push it aside with his nose and press his lips to the spot. He inhaled raggedly and watched the necklace sway with burning eyes.

"Ty?"

"Hmm?"

"You're frowning."

"I'm worried that you're going to paint this dining room a crazy color."

"Well, I won't be painting it brown like over at your house, that's for sure."

"Here." He pulled two credit cards from his back pocket and set them on the table. "I got you a Lowe's card. Charge anything you need for the house. Paint or whatever."

Lines formed across her forehead.

"The other one's a debit card. I set up an account for you at my bank. I figured Addie would have school expenses." He went back to lifting stuff out of his box. He knew it was difficult for Celia to accept help, so he didn't want to make a big deal out of this.

"Thanks, but I can't take the cards."

Figured. "Sure you can. I'm Addie's father, and I owe you for child support—"

"You've added us to your health insurance plan and bought us a car and a house, Ty. I'd say we're even."

His brows crashed down. "No we're not. A judge would want me to give you something every month to help with Addie." He slid the cards down the table in her direction. "This is the least I can do."

She pursed her lips.

"Please," he said.

"I can't."

He had a fear, a very real fear, that she meant exactly what she said. He pushed to his feet, which sent a jolt of pain up through his left hip. He gritted his teeth against it. "I'd have painted this house already, except I wanted you to pick your own colors. If you're not going to take the Lowe's card, then I'm going to go buy brown."

"I'm going to buy my own paint, Ty Porter. And that's final."

"Celia," he growled. He wanted to give her and Addie whatever stupid, girly, bright-colored thing they wanted. If he couldn't do that, then what good was the money he'd made?

The shape of her chin turned stubborn. "I've met you in the middle as much as I'm going to. I've moved here, and I'm driving around in the car you gave me, but that's it. That's as far as I'm going to go. Which reminds me, I appreciate the boots you gave me, but I can't accept them, either. Before you leave I'll give them back to you so that you can return them."

"I am not taking back the boots."

"Yes—"

"No. I'm definitely not." Ty faced off against her, glaring the words *You're a pain in the neck*.

She answered him with a look that said, *So are you, buddy*.

He'd always thought of himself as daring, but this small person with the curly hair and the pretty face might be braver than he was. "You planning to be the death of me, Celia?"

"Not quite. Don't you remember? If you die, they'll repossess my Prius."

"Knock, knock." A masculine voice. Ty glanced at the door that led into the living room. A man stood in the opening behind two boys. "Sorry to interrupt. I just came by to introduce myself. I live next door."

"Oh, hi!" Celia put on the kind of happy face she never wore around Ty and moved to the newcomer to shake his hand. "I'm Celia. My daughter, Addie, and I are moving in today."

"I'm Neill Martin."

Celia had said *my* daughter. She'd most definitely not said *our* daughter.

"This is Ty." Celia gestured to him.

Neill leaned over, and they shook hands.

Stepping back, Neill took hold of his boys' shoulders. "These are my sons Tanner and Tyson." One of them looked about Addie's age, the other a few years older.

"Addie will be excited to meet you." Celia smiled at the boys. "She's in her room around the corner if you want to go say hello."

The boys looked at Neill, who nodded. They took off.

"They're with me every other weekend and on

Wednesday nights," Neill said to Celia. "They're with their mother the rest of the time."

Of all the houses in Holley, Ty had bought Celia the one next to a divorced dad. Awesome.

"We'll have to get the kids together sometime," Neill said, staring at Celia the way a calf stares at its mother.

Ty stopped himself before audibly refusing Neill's request. Crazy guess, but he didn't think Celia would take that well.

"I'd like that," Celia answered.

"Where did you move from?"

As Celia and Neill talked, Ty remained silent, watching the two of them. The cheerful personality Celia had put on to chat with this stranger had little in common with her real personality, the feisty-as-feisty-gets personality she showed Ty.

Ty could tell that Neill was digging Celia, and why wouldn't he? A man would have to be blind not to dig Celia. Especially in that yellow top. Especially with the fake personality she was wearing.

"I'm an attorney," Neill was saying. "I commute to Plano for work."

Neill looked to be about thirty-five. He had shiny black hair, glasses, a polo shirt, topsiders. Neill was about as different from Ty as caviar was different from Cheetos.

Celia couldn't seriously like this putz. Cheetos were better than caviar. Everybody knew that.

As their conversation continued, however, it seemed that Celia might prefer caviar. Yesterday she'd told him that there was no chance of a romance between them and that she wanted to make their divorce official. This

Neill was probably the type of character she'd date as soon as the ink dried on their divorce certificate.

Ty's chest tightened at the thought. He wanted nothing more than to sweep out his arm and push Celia behind him. She was *his* wife.

At the same time, she wasn't his wife. He had no influence over her choices. She lived alone in this house with Addie. Neill lived next door. And Ty lived across town. Celia and Neill would have easy access to each other, and Ty wouldn't be close enough to do a single sorry thing about it.

Even so. The thought that filled his head?

Over my dead body.

CHAPTER
FIFTEEN

Celia painted the interior of her house in colors more commonly found inside a package of tropical-flavored Starbursts. For the living room: pale aqua. The dining room: piña colada yellow. Kitchen: mango. Hallway and bathroom: honeydew melon green. Her bedroom: the light purple of an orchid petal.

For two days she worked ceaselessly on priming and painting. Members of the PFHS (Porter Family Help Squad) showed up frequently to lend a hand.

The easiest company was also the worst painter: Meg.

Celia could count all of her true friends on one hand, and Uncle Danny took up a finger. It was extremely rare for her to meet someone and feel that mysterious *click*. But after spending just an hour painting with Meg, Celia was pretty much ready to rush out and buy the two of them best friend heart pendants divided in half by a jagged line. She didn't even mind that she had to retouch the sections Meg had painted after Meg went home.

The hardest company was also the best painter: Jake.

Just eighteen months younger than Ty, Jake had been in Celia's grade all through high school. Celia's deep infatuation with Ty had made her extra aware of Jake because he was Ty's brother. Her attention had heightened every time she'd seen Jake, spoken with him, or heard others discussing him.

Jake had been flawlessly handsome back then, and also the football team's quarterback. Handsome quarterbacks at big high schools in the football-crazy state of Texas were often conceited, elitist, or downright obnoxious. That's not how Jake had been. She remembered him as smart and laid back and kind, careful with his words.

Her recollections of the high school Jake made it painful for her to interact with the Jake of the present. The scar across his face wasn't puckered or red. It was white, smooth, and blade thin. Despite that, it was impossible to miss. Its path started at his nose and slashed across one side of his face. It did not make him ugly. Nothing could. But it did seem to be outward evidence of much deeper inner scars.

The two times he stopped by to help paint, he did so with a minimum of words. At first Celia had tried to reminisce with him about Plano East High School. He'd responded, but his demeanor had assured her that the canyon between his old and current self wasn't challenging for her alone. At the first opportunity, he'd taken his can of paint and gone to work in another room.

Celia had come to the conclusion that the war had killed something inside Jake Porter. Perhaps he'd seen too much over there, been devastated too deeply. He had a stony outward shell and—from what Ty told her— his work training Thoroughbred race horses. But he no longer had much else. Looking into his eyes was like looking into the eyes of a bitter seventy-year-old man, hard-worn by life.

The most absent company was also the most pervasive: Ty.

Since he couldn't help with the painting because of his knee, he kept Addie at his house for several hours each day so Celia could paint. If only it had been an out-of-sight-out-of-mind thing. Instead, she could *not* get that blasted kiss out of her head. Whenever she dropped off or picked up Addie and had to spend a few moments talking with him, she was glaringly, alarmingly mindful of the attraction twining through the air between them. What went unspoken had become more powerful than what they said.

Celia baked in the early mornings to calm herself, worked on the house all day, then kept on working after Addie went to bed at night.

The empty hole inside of her that refused to be filled seemed to urge her to be still and listen. She'd hoped that a more stable financial situation would fill her sense of incompleteness, but no. It loomed bigger every day. What the voice seemed to suggest was that if she would rest, then it could offer her peace.

Rest? She slept too little, she worried too much, and she churned out more predawn pastries than a Nestle Toll House test kitchen on steroids. It wasn't sustainable, this pace. But *rest*?

Rest made no sense to Celia.

She was a single mother. Single mothers didn't rest.

The day of Addie's fifth birthday dawned in an identical way to every other August morning in Texas: hot, humid, and sunglasses-not-optional bright.

Something that would not be identical to its predecessors? Addie's birthday celebration. For the first time, Addie's father would be hosting her party.

When Ty had asked Celia if he could invite his family over to his place for Addie's birthday dinner, Celia's heart had tweaked because she'd always been the one to organize Addie's parties. Nevertheless, she'd agreed. The gingerbread house, covered in draped furniture and drying paint, was much like her emotional state at the moment—not party ready.

And so it was that Celia found herself standing in Ty's kitchen the evening of the fifth anniversary of Addie's birth. The Porter family surrounded her, talking, joking, and snacking on the Ruffles and onion dip that Nancy had brought as an appetizer.

Celia's mind traveled back to Addie's fourth birthday, just one year prior. She'd had no thought then of ever leaving Corvallis. She'd not known most of these people. And she'd had absolutely no intention of ever crossing paths with Ty again.

But here he was. Chewing on a chip while Addie gazed up at him adoringly and explained to him why Cinderella always wore her hair up and Aurora always wore her hair down.

Since arriving at Ty's house forty-five minutes ago, Celia had been trying not to be so ridiculously attuned to Ty's every word and gesture. So far her efforts were bombing. He was wearing another pair of cargo shorts and a navy UFC T-shirt. He looked like the sort of images that came up on Pinterest when a person ran a search for "hot guys." Not that she'd ever done something so debasing.

"Addie Potaddie?"

Celia and Addie snapped their faces toward one another. Uncle Danny had finally arrived in Texas?

"Yoo-hoo! You here somewhere?" Danny's voice drifted in from the front of the house.

Addie gave a happy yelp. She and Celia hurried in the direction of the front door. The bunches of pink and purple balloons that Nancy and Celia had tied to every available spot in Ty's living and dining room swayed as they passed.

Uncle Danny had told Celia repeatedly that he planned to arrive in Holley in time for Addie's birthday. Privately, though, Celia had begun to have her doubts. Over the past days he'd said things to her on the phone like, "Since I'm close to Wyoming I'm going to check out Grand Teton National Park," and "I think I might stop and do some mountain biking at Moab in Utah. They've got some sweet terrain there."

Celia rounded the corner that led to the foyer in time to watch Danny wrap Addie in a bear hug.

"Happy birthday!" He gave Addie a smacking kiss on her hair. "How are you, girl?"

"I'm cool. You cool?"

"I'm cool. Can't complain." He presented his fist, and Addie bumped it. "This hot weather down here is *awesome*, isn't it? I feel like I'm in a Swedish sauna. Good for my pores." He released Addie and gave Celia a hug. "You hanging in there, sister?"

"I'm hanging in there. I'm so glad you're here."

The Porters had gathered nearby. "What a house, man!" Danny said to Ty as they shook hands.

"Thank you." Ty grinned at her uncle.

"You've got a lot of land around you," Danny said. "Real natural vibe."

"I'm glad you like it."

Danny zeroed in on Nancy. "This can't be your mother can it, Ty?"

"She is."

"Are you single?"

"Uncle Danny!"

But Nancy tossed back her head and laughed. "I haven't been single for thirty-five years. But make me an offer. I'll consider it." More laughter. Even her husband, John, joined in.

"I'm hoping to meet some of Holley's single ladies," Uncle Danny told Nancy. "Maybe you can help me?"

"Sure! I'd be happy to help."

Celia introduced John, Bo, Meg, and Jake to Danny. If any of the Texans were leery about a fifty-something man who'd just hit on their mom and was wearing a shark tooth necklace, a sleeveless shirt, and board shorts, they didn't show it. Except maybe Jake. But then, Jake treated everyone with leeriness.

"Now that Danny's here, let's eat!" Nancy clapped her strong hands. "Anyone hungry?"

Celia, for one, wasn't hungry for hot dogs. But since Ty had let Addie choose the menu, Celia acted the way she imagined an easy-going mom might act and pretended to be cool with Addie's choice. Really, though. Hot dogs?! Did a more processed food exist?

Once the dinner things had been swept away, Celia

fetched the cake. Addie had placed a request for vanilla with pink icing. Celia, deep in sanity-via-baking mode, had made a three layer cake large enough to feed thirty. She'd covered it in mounds, dips, and artful crests of delicately flavored peppermint frosting. The topping of translucent sprinkles caught the light and gleamed. Five candles balanced their flames, and all the Porters sang as Celia crossed from the kitchen into the dining room, carrying the cake.

Addie, sitting at the head of the table on a chair that had been mounded with pillows, closed her eyes and took her time formulating her wish.

The contours of Addie's face were so dear and familiar to Celia. The teal glasses. The straight hair in its neat bob. The downy curve of her cheek.

Today her daughter was five years old. Five. And as happy as Celia had ever seen her, here in Ty's big brown house, celebrating her birthday in a way they'd never celebrated it before.

Her precious one, her Addie, was getting older. Sadness descended through Celia like moss through a lake, slow and twisting. Tears gathered at the backs of her eyes.

Ty, who was standing on Addie's other side, caught Celia's gaze. He quirked a brow questioningly, those magnificent blue eyes gentle with compassion.

Goodness gracious! She could handle his teasing, sparring, and bantering. *Anything* but heart-slaying kindness.

Addie blew out her candles, which sent clapping and hooting ringing through the room.

The instant Addie finished her slice of cake, she cajoled them all into moving into the living room so she could open presents. The adults, who were still finishing off their servings of cake and sipping decaf coffee, watched as Addie calmly and methodically unwrapped each of her gifts.

Early in the day, over a breakfast of homemade waffles, Celia had presented Addie with a beautiful set of princess books she'd found online at a good bargain. She'd been hoping Ty would act like a normal person and give Addie a similar caliber gift. But when the last present had been revealed and none were from Ty, Celia began to worry.

When he winked at Celia and made his way out the back door on his crutches, her worry intensified. What had he gotten for Addie that was so large he couldn't wrap it? A Rolls-Royce? A Learjet? A stack of gold bullion?

A loud knock on the front door caused Addie to lift her head from the set of Polly Pockets she'd been playing with.

"Who could that be?" Nancy asked Addie, rounding her eyes with exaggerated confusion. Nancy had clearly been let in on the secret. "You'd better go see."

Everyone followed Addie to the door.

Celia was going to *kill* Ty if he threw more money at her child—

Addie pulled open the door, revealing Ty standing on the front porch next to a round white pony that looked like a sausage overstuffed into a casing of hide. Pink ribbons dangled from the pony's mane and tail and a huge purple bow circled its neck.

"Happy birthday." Ty gave Addie the same breath-stealing smile that had captured Celia's fourteen-year-old heart.

A live animal? He purchased a PONY without asking my permission?

Addie's lips formed an astonished oval.

"Want to come say hello to her?" Ty asked, looking as pleased as if he'd just been handed a winning lottery ticket.

Addie broke from her bliss-daze and went to the pony. "Oh my gosh," she kept whispering as she wrapped her thin arms around the animal's neck. "Thank you, Daddy. Thank you soooo much."

At this rate, her daughter was going to become irredeemably spoiled.

"Is that an overgrown dog?" Bo asked.

"I think so," Jake answered.

"Now, now, boys," John put in. "It might be a cat."

"A sheep?" Nancy chortled.

"A hamster?" Bo proposed.

"Don't mind them, Celia." Meg squeezed Celia's forearm. "They're all horse people, but I happen to love ponies. I convinced Bo to get a few for Whispering Creek, and they're wonderful."

Wonderful! What if Addie fell off? She wouldn't fall as far off a pony as she would a full-sizer, but still. She could break her neck trying to ride a pony.

"She's mine?" Addie asked Ty, as if she didn't dare believe her good fortune. "Really?"

"All yours. What are you going to name her?"

"I don't know yet."

"You want to go for a ride?"

"Yes!"

No! Celia thought.

Ty caught the end of the pony's rope beneath the right-hand grip on his crutches and set off across the lawn in the direction of the stable. Addie took hold of Danny's hand on one side and Meg's on the other, then followed. Celia slid on her sunglasses and rushed past everyone to catch up with Ty.

Ty shot her a look across his shoulder, challenge in his expression. "Go ahead and start lecturing."

"Don't you think you should have asked me before buying my daughter a pony?"

"Our daughter. And no. Why would I want to ask you when I knew you'd say no?"

"Because I'm her mother!"

"Uh-huh."

"And because riding is dangerous."

"Does this pony here look dangerous to you?"

Mostly, the pony looked chubby and woefully hungry.

"I promise you," Ty said, "I'll keep Addie safe. You're going to have to trust me, Celia."

This wasn't exactly the time or place to tell him that asking her to trust him was asking her to do the one thing MOST impossible. "You're giving lavish gifts again, even though *you know* how I feel about—"

"I'm a father. And for the first time in my life, I have a chance to give my daughter a birthday present. You better believe I'm going to give her something good."

They crossed over the driveway, the pony's hooves clanging against the hard surface. The stable, a building that had been constructed in the same general style of the house, drew nearer. Fenced pasture dropped downhill from its front-facing side. Two brown horses watched their approach.

Ty glanced at her. "You're cute when you're angry."

"Shh! Someone will hear you."

"Really cute."

"You're not allowed to tell me I'm cute. We're parents with separate lives, trying to get along respectfully for the sake of our daughter. That's all."

"Does that have to be all?"

Celia caught herself staring at the tiny sexy scar beneath his lip. "I do not understand you, Ty."

"I don't understand myself half the time. For instance, I keep trying to talk myself out of wanting to kiss you. But it's only making me want to do it more."

The blunt honesty in his gaze made her breath jam in her throat. They'd managed to go days without mentioning The Kiss.

It was only after they'd reached the stable and Ty had put a white blanket and a pink—yes, *pink*—child-sized saddle on the pony that Celia realized how expertly he'd diverted her tirade. One intense look from him, and her mind had flown off in a tizzy to fret about their relationship. He'd distracted her completely from worrying about Addie thundering off on an untried animal.

Ty, Addie, Bo, and Ty's dad, John, entered the pasture. The rest of them took up positions along the fence line, Danny and Nancy on either side of Celia.

Ty placed a black English-style riding hat on Addie's head and clicked the strap beneath her chin. The Porter siblings had likely raced around naked on bareback as kids. Even so, the family took in the sight of the hat with nothing louder than the click of their smartphone cameras.

Celia began to fidget anxiously with her cuticles.

Once John had lifted Addie into the saddle, he took

the rope and drew the horse forward at a very slow pace. Bo walked next to Addie on one side; Ty flanked the other side, managing to maneuver the crutches well over the uneven ground. Celia could hear him talking to Addie, telling her how well she was doing.

"Good job, Addie!" Meg called.

"Looks like we've got ourselves a cowgirl, C," Danny said. "How cute is that?"

"Very cute."

"Sweet as can be."

Addie sat straight and smiling in the saddle. The pony's ribbons danced and sparkled in the sunlight, rippling over Addie's boots.

Despite her concerns, the scene before Celia appeared safer than safe. Safer even than biking with Danny. She could fault nothing. Deliberately, she quit fussing with her fingernails. Perhaps the pony hadn't been the very worst idea in the world.

"Don't tell the others," Nancy said softly to Celia, "but Ty's always been my favorite."

Celia took in her mother-in-law's dark hair with the shock of white, the hoop earrings, the healthy glow. Even Nancy had fallen victim to Ty's power? She, who was technically supposed to be impartial?

"Don't get me wrong—he was a handful when he was young. Every time I turned around, that boy was jumping off something or riding something or shooting something. He was too brave for his own good and not much of a rule follower. But—" she shook her head and whistled a low *whoooeeee*— "he was charming. After he'd done some orneriness or other, he'd look at me with those eyes and smile. Well! Never could stay mad at him."

"I can imagine." Celia understood. Boy, did she.

At the same time, she had every intention of succeeding at the very thing every other woman in Ty's life had failed at.

Staying mad.

At five o'clock the next afternoon, Celia finished watering the flower bed she'd just weeded and stepped back to admire her gingerbread house. Since arriving in Texas, she'd painted every room, arranged furniture and rugs, unpacked all the boxes, and decorated every cranny and corner. She'd made a home.

As she drove to Ty's to pick up Addie, her rubbery muscles complained that she'd used them too hard. Before they'd consider forgiving her, they required a steamy shower, dinner, and perhaps one or three or eight slices of the chocolate chocolate-chip cake she'd made that morning.

An unfamiliar BMW sat in Ty's driveway in the exact place where Celia always parked. Odd. She slid in beside it and made her way along the path to his house.

A beautiful brunette let herself out his front door.

Celia's steps cut to a halt.

The woman saw her, lifted a hand in greeting, and continued toward Celia.

A bad taste, like copper, gathered in Celia's throat.

"Hi." The woman stopped a few feet from Celia. "I'm Tawny."

Celia's heartbeat thudded abnormally loud. Somehow, from reserves deep down inside, she managed to smile. "Nice to meet you. I'm Celia." The misery and jealousy and rejection of that long ago morning in Vegas came back to Celia physically, like a punch. All of it. Back. Everything she'd worked so hard to leave behind.

"I met Addie inside," Tawny said. "She's adorable."

"Thank you."

"I just stopped by to bring Ty dinner. I feel bad for him, with the knee and all."

"Yeah."

"Poor guy." Her face held a level of gravity only appropriate for natural disasters.

"Mmm hmm." Ty loved Tawny.

This was the woman he loved.

This was the woman he wanted to marry.

And wretchedly, Celia could see why. Tawny was tall and slender and obviously perfect for him in her high-heeled espadrilles and her breezy yellow and white trellis-patterned dress.

Celia had on red shorts, a white T-shirt, and flip-flops. She'd been gardening in the Texas heat. Of all the times, all the moments . . . She was meeting Tawny after she'd been *gardening*.

"Here in Holley we bring food when someone has a baby," Tawny was explaining, "or is struggling through the loss of a loved one, or has an injury like Ty, you know. We do our best to take care of our own."

"That's really kind of you. I'm sure Ty appreciates the food."

"Have you settled into your new house okay?"

"I have."

"That's good to hear. Don't hesitate to call me if you need anything at all. I'd love to help." Tawny appeared to be as sweet on the outside as a Linzer cookie, but underneath, in the depths of her eyes, Celia read calculation. Tawny wanted Ty for herself. More, she didn't like Celia. How could she? Celia had once married and slept with Tawny's boyfriend.

"I'll see you around," Tawny called as they moved in opposite directions.

Celia glanced back to see Tawny, flowing hair and long legs, stepping into the BMW. She experienced such a stunning surge of envy that she tucked herself, unseen, into a corner of Ty's porch to recover. Celia couldn't claim Ty as her own, but boy, oh boy, she did *not* want Tawny to claim him, either. Just the thought of the two of them together caused her stomach to turn into a lead ball.

She'd do well to remember that Tawny didn't deserve her animosity. It wasn't Tawny's fault that Ty liked her better. Also, Tawny had refused to take Ty back after Vegas and had then given him the silent treatment for years. Admirable.

But when Celia pictured Tawny and Ty's wedding— the two of them standing at the front of a church, both equally stunning, with their cute names that both started with *T*—she had a hard time finding kindness within her for either of them. The prospect of Tawny becoming Addie's stepmother, of having to see and speak with Tawny at Porter family occasions for the rest of her life, sent utter misery straight through her.

She pressed her hands against her face and tried to tell herself that if Tawny wanted to shackle herself to the devastation-on-a-stick known as Ty Porter, then she could have him. Celia didn't believe that any woman would be able to keep a grip on Ty Porter's love and devotion for an entire lifetime. One could speculate that Celia had come closer than any woman, since she had a marriage certificate. But he'd only been hers for a single reckless night. That's as long as she'd held him.

When she knocked on Ty's door, she was still furious, even though she knew her fury was unreasonable.

Ty answered, leaning on one crutch. "What're you all knotted up about?"

"Nothing."

"Is one of your paint colors too normal looking?"

"Is Addie ready?"

"Latest batch of cookies too salty?"

She edged past him into the foyer, catching a whiff of his pine-scented cologne. Had Tawny caught it, too? "Addie! C'mon, Punkie. We need to head home."

Ty watched her with an amused half smile.

"Addie?" Celia called. "You coming?"

"Yes, Mommy." Addie's voice sailed in from the back of the house.

"Will you stay for dinner tonight, please?" Ty asked. "I'll order pizza."

"No thank you."

He lifted and resettled the ball cap he had on. "You're not going to tell me why you're mad?"

"I'm not mad." She wanted to order him to shut up and strip off his T-shirt. No, she wanted to slap him for making her want to see him shirtless. She was losing her mind. Maybe the paint fumes this past week had done it.

"Ohhhh," he murmured under his breath. "You ran into Tawny out there, didn't you?"

She set her jaw.

"You're upset because you like me." Thoroughly masculine pleasure stamped his expression. "You want me for yourself."

"Absurd!"

"What did you think of Tawny?"

"She was . . . nice."

"She's nice, all right."

"And dating a pediatrician, as I recall."

"For the moment. Sure you won't stay for dinner? Pretty please?"

"We need to get home." If she didn't know better, she'd think the flare she saw in his eyes was hurt.

The patter of kid feet approached, then Addie burst into sight. "'Bye, Daddy. Thank you for having me."

"You're welcome." He propped a shoulder against the door's frame. "Tomorrow's the big day, Addie. The first day of school."

Addie nodded.

"Your mom wants to take you there in the morning, but we'll both come to pick you up when school is finished."

"'Kay."

"You'll do awesome."

Addie regarded Ty with a face full of trust. "Yep," she said. "I will."

"Good night."

"Good night."

He seemed a little lost, the big beautiful cowboy, as they walked away and left him behind.

All the way back to the gingerbread house, Celia's emotions heaved. Anger. Why had she let herself get tangled up with Ty again? Despair. How could she bear to send Addie to school tomorrow? Possessiveness. Was Ty eating Tawny's dinner?

When Addie wasn't looking, she stripped the *Give Peace a Chance* charm from her key ring and threw it—hard—into the trash.

CHAPTER
SIXTEEN

Late that night, Ty hit Replay. The YouTube video filling the computer screen in his office began again.

He'd come to know every second of every video. When he was alone, he could watch the ride from several different angles in his own memory. The bull's motion. His counter motion. He could see the years of experience in his form just as clearly as he could see the bull's faults and strengths. Meteor was a twenty-one-point bull. Nothing special about him. Ty had covered bulls just like him hundreds of times before.

He dug his elbows into the surface of his desk and rested his forehead on the flat of his hands.

He missed Celia. He'd brought her to Holley, and she still wasn't near enough to satisfy him.

Every night he missed her.

She'd hardly been at his house all week. Nothing more than a few minutes in the mornings or afternoons.

When she was with him, she amused him, insulted him, and made him laugh. Everything was fine. When she left, his knee killed him and bitterness fought for control of his thoughts.

He lifted his head and stared at the video. He remembered how his instincts had been warning him not to ride that night in Boise. If he'd had a lick of sense, he wouldn't have. Bull riders were superstitious for a reason.

His gaze followed the blur of color and motion on the screen. After all this time, he still couldn't understand why he'd come off Meteor. It bothered him, the question of why. He watched the videos and tried to find the answer in them. Other times he went back over everything that had been printed about the accident. He always hunted for the one clue that would make him understand.

If it existed—the piece of evidence that would explain why his career had ended—he couldn't find it.

He reached into his pocket and pulled out a bottle of Vicodin. He popped the top and saw that just three pills remained. The dose he'd taken earlier hadn't done the job, so he took a slug from his bottled water and threw down another pill. Tomorrow he'd have to refill the prescription again.

He leaned back in his leather chair and closed his eyes. He'd worked hard in his life, and in return he'd achieved what he'd wanted to achieve in the world of bull riding. He'd faced injuries and setbacks and long odds before. He'd overcome them, but he couldn't overcome this.

He was a bull rider with a broken-down career, a wild side that couldn't be trusted, and a heart that seethed for something it couldn't have. Who was he now? How was he supposed to measure his worth without his job?

He didn't know, and he sure didn't like living with this ruined leg every day and every night.

He'd spent years getting his finances in order. He could retire right now, never earn another paycheck, and still be set for life. The thought of retiring, though, filled him with emptiness. How would he spend his days? Golfing?

No way.

He needed *work* to give him purpose.

Just yesterday his neighbor Jim had called to tell him that he and his wife were thinking about selling their acres. If Ty combined his acreage with Jim's, he'd have a big enough spread to begin raising rodeo stock, just like he'd always planned to do when bull riding ended.

Buying Jim's land would offer Ty a future. But . . . but *what*? It was as if he needed to put away the bull riding and his old life first, before he'd have room in him for anything else.

Maybe that's why he'd become obsessed with that final ride. The old bull rider in him didn't understand what had happened on Meteor that day in Idaho. And until he could understand it, he couldn't get past it.

"Okay . . . well, 'bye." Celia and Addie had arrived at Addie's kindergarten classroom a full ten minutes before school started. Celia had hung Addie's backpack on its hook, helped her select a cat Beanie Baby as her friend for the morning, and taken numerous pictures of Addie both with and without her teacher.

"'Bye, Mom." Addie sat at her assigned seat, very still, her hands mounded on the table. She looked like a portrait whose artist had captured politeness, nervousness, and bravery all at the same time.

Addie had chosen to wear the new outfit that Meg and Bo had given her for her birthday, a red polo and a navy skirt dotted with tiny apples. A plastic box of school supplies labeled with her name waited near her elbow. Her kindergarten classroom was as impeccably organized and cheerful as Celia had hoped for.

Time for Celia to leave. Except . . . maybe she should stay a little longer and keep Addie company until her teacher started class? Another picture?

"See you later," Addie said.

"All right. I'll be here when school ends, waiting right outside the school doors for you like we discussed."

"'Kay, Mom."

Her daughter. Her only child. Where had her baby gone? "Do . . . do you need anything else?"

"No, I'm good. 'Bye."

"'Bye. I . . . Are you positively sure you're okay?"

"I'm sure."

"Your lunch is in your backpack."

"I know."

"Addie?"

"Yeah?"

"I love you."

"I love you, too, Mommy."

Her heart cracking clean in two, Celia smiled at her little girl. Then she walked to her car without looking left or right, without thinking. The school PTA would be hosting a Boo-Hoo Breakfast for parents of kindergarteners once the bell rang. Celia wasn't going. She didn't want to cry in front of strangers, nor did she want to risk coming in contact with any parent who might have the gall to feel happy about the start of kindergarten and all the child-free hours it ensured.

The moment she closed herself into her Prius, grief washed through her. She felt herself beginning to slip. Crying quietly at first and then with wracking breaths, she clutched the steering wheel and drove toward the gingerbread house.

For five years Addie's unswerving dependence on her had given Celia's life meaning. As of today, however, her daughter had become an elementary student. From here on out, she'd grow more and more autonomous. Addie had Ty now and all the other Porters. She didn't need Celia the way she once had.

Celia pulled into her driveway and dashed across the yard, sobbing the whole way. Inside, she tossed her purse and keys, then went to sit on the edge of her bed. Her upper body curled forward, heels hooked on the bed frame, arms crossed defensively over her midsection.

She cried because Addie's baby and toddler years were gone and because she'd loved those years. She didn't expect to ever have another child; she'd always viewed Addie as her one and only. Time had played a dirty trick on her and taken away years that she could never get back and never experience again with another child.

Her lungs gulped air, releasing it in stutters. *You're overreacting, Celia. This is ridiculous!*

She wished she'd been able to be a stay-at-home mom for Addie. Wished she'd had more money to buy her things and take her fabulous places. Instead, she'd done the best she could and now wished her best had been better.

She'd blink one time and Addie would be driving off to college and leaving her alone forever. . . .

Knock knock knock.

Celia jerked upright. Terror at being discovered in her current condition sent her scurrying to the mirror above her dresser. She looked a fright—her curls standing on end, her face wet and red, her eyes puffy. Using the backs of her hands, she smoothed the tears from her cheeks.

Knock knock.

Celia peeked out the window overlooking the front yard. A white Mercedes convertible from the '80s was parked at the curb. Meg's car.

She would have pretended not to be home for anyone else on the planet. But empathetic, comforting Meg? Celia sniffed repeatedly to clear some of her congestion and opened her front door.

"Hey." Meg took Celia in, her expression filling instantly with compassion. "Oh no. Are you okay?"

"You caught me in the middle of a crying fit."

"Sad about Addie's first day of school?"

Celia nodded.

"That's why I came. Here." Meg held two tall cups and handed one to Celia. "Iced lattes. Now give me a hug." They hugged for half a minute straight. Meg patted her back. "Let's go sit down so you can tell me about it."

Celia followed Meg into the living room, taking a long drag through her latte's straw. Gratitude over Meg's kindness tempted her to burst into tears again. *Breathe,* she told herself. *Celia Park Porter, like many women who've come before, you, too, are going to survive your child's first day of kindergarten.*

They sat on chairs nestled before Celia's big front

window. "So." Meg tilted her head. She had on a sage green wrap-around top that tied in a bow at the side, crisp shorts, and silver sandals. "Hard morning?"

Celia described getting Addie ready at home, escorting her to her class. "And then she took her place at the table, and you should have seen her, sitting there like a model student. Really, she was ready. She was fine." Celia slid her fingertips beneath her eyes to clear new tears. "I was the one who came undone after I left."

Meg's own eyes had turned shiny with moisture. "If Bo were here, he'd have tissues. Just a minute." She hurried into the bathroom and returned with toilet paper. She passed some over and resumed her seat.

Celia dabbed at her eyes, then clutched the toilet paper ball in her lap. "I think I depend on Addie too much, Meg. It's not fair to her."

"Listen, I have the same challenge. Growing up, I didn't have a close-knit family, but now I have Bo. And he's . . . he's wonderful." Her face softened at the mention of her husband. "I love him so much that it's tempting for me to make him my everything, you know? It'd be easy for me to hang my happiness and my mood, my confidence—all of it—on him."

"So what do you do?"

"I read my Bible and pray every morning. It centers me. It reminds me that God's the most important thing in my life."

Celia didn't really want to discuss God. Guilt wasn't an emotion she cared to heap on top of all her other current emotions.

"Of course," Meg continued, "your situation is different because Addie's your daughter. I don't know what that's like because I don't have a child." She paused. "I wish I did."

Celia had let Meg see her all splotchy and hysterical. Based on the girlfriends' code of ethics, Celia thought that might qualify her to ask a follow-up question. "Have you guys been trying for a baby?"

"We haven't done anything to prevent a baby for about a year. Nothing's happened yet."

Celia nodded and refrained from mentioning that it had only taken her and Ty one night to conceive Addie. So not helpful.

"Bo and I have time. I don't want to stress about it. It's just that I'd *really* love to have a baby with that man."

"I'm sure it'll happen for you."

"I hope so. God's already given me a lot: Bo, the Porters, my father's inheritance. Sometimes I worry that it's greedy of me to have all that and ask for a baby, too."

"I think it's completely normal for you to ask for a child. Of course you want one with Bo." Celia sipped her icy coffee, savoring its bittersweet milky flavor.

"Ty seems great with Addie," Meg said.

"He is."

"Do you think there's any chance that you and Ty . . . ?" Meg shrugged, sheepish.

"That Ty and I will end up together?"

"Yes."

"It would require a miracle."

"Well." Meg regarded her thoughtfully for several seconds. "Sometimes miracles happen."

"Not to me."

"Everyone in Holley is fascinated to see what happens between you two."

The whole town for an audience? Not a comforting thought.

Meg tucked her feet up under her. "Everybody's known Ty since he was a kid, and they've been following his bull riding since the beginning. They're all really proud of him."

"He was an amazing bull rider."

"Since you and Addie arrived, Ty's become the most popular subject there is. More popular than football even, which is impressive."

"What are people saying about him?"

"They're wondering why he kept Addie a secret. Let's see . . . Whether you and Ty have been faithful to each other all these years. Whether Tawny still has a shot at marrying Ty."

Pain skewered Celia at the mention of Tawny. "As far as I can tell, Tawny has a good shot at marrying him. She brought him dinner last night."

"Hmm." Meg swirled her latte. The ice cubes made a swishing sound, and beads of condensation on the cup shimmered in the light. "According to local legend, Tawny Bettenfield has wanted to marry Ty since they were in the first grade together."

"Then why didn't she marry him when she had the chance?"

Meg lifted her shoulders. "She was young. Wanted to wait a year or two more. You can go to any bar in town and place a bet on whether or not she and Ty will eventually tie the knot."

"No!"

"Yes. Apparently Tawny's odds have gone way down since you moved here."

Perhaps Celia could come to appreciate Holley, Texas, after all. Even without a farmers' market, an organic grocery store, or a hairstylist who understood curls. "Tawny's beautiful."

"But Ty doesn't love her."

"I think he does."

"And maybe *he* even thinks he does. But he doesn't."

"Meg," Celia said, skeptical.

"Bo thinks that Ty's been faithful to you since the day you married."

The statement took Celia by such complete surprise that she gawked for a few moments. "Is this *Ty Porter* we're talking about?"

Meg raised an eyebrow, a faint smile on her lips.

"We were married almost six years ago. He—he adores women and they adore him. I'm sure—I mean, that is . . . I'm certain that he's had dates and girlfriends in every city he's traveled to. That's a lot of . . . cities."

"Bo knows him pretty well. That's all I'm saying."

Since Vegas, Ty hadn't had any girlfriend long enough or public enough to register on his Wikipedia profile, true. But Celia had never imagined, never expected, that he'd remained faithful to her. That just flat-out could not be right. Bo didn't know his brother as well as he thought he did.

Meg glanced at her watch. "I hate to leave, but I have an appointment back at Whispering Creek." She met Celia's gaze squarely. "Will you be all right?"

"I'll be fine."

Meg gathered up her purse, and they made their way to the door.

"Thank you for the latte and for coming, Meg."

"Caffeine and a friend have always done wonders for me."

"It was like you had ESP or something. You came at the exact moment I needed you."

Meg had walked onto the porch. At Celia's words, she turned.

"What is it?" Celia asked.

"God has often used other people to help me through difficult patches. It means a lot to me to think that He might have used me just now to do the same for you."

"Oh."

"Will you come to church with Bo and me on Sunday?"

Celia hadn't attended church in more than a decade. She'd likely be smitten by lightning the second she set foot in the building. However, she was feeling so mushy and appreciative toward Meg that if Meg had asked her to scale Everest, she'd have rushed out to buy hiking gear. "Sure."

"Perfect! I'll text you the details."

Celia stood on the porch, waving as Meg drove away. So far this morning she'd delivered a child to kindergarten, had a breakdown, and been rescued from her breakdown by a girlfriend.

Now the time had come, for better or for worse, to find herself a job.

SEVENTEEN

Celia spent the rest of the week job hunting. And also trying to avoid Ty, a man disinclined to be avoided.

Hard to say which pursuit she enjoyed less.

She continued to rise at dawn and pour her concerns into baking. During Addie's kindergarten hours she combed the newspapers and Internet in search of companies in need of employees with her credentials and experience. She sent out résumés electronically and by mail. Answered listings with phone calls. Communicated with headhunters.

The job openings she'd come across so far either paid too little or were offered by restaurants that expected her to work nights and weekends. Addie went to school during the day. If she worked all night and all weekend, when would she see her child?

Midmorning on Friday, Celia bowed to a self-destructive urge and visited her online checking account. She stared at the numbers on the screen with desolation and no small amount of panic. Eventually her eyes unfocused and the digits went blurry. Her remaining balance had whittled to an amount that terrified her.

Maybe she'd been stupidly prideful to refuse the credit cards Ty had offered her. If it came down to it and she needed money in order to put food in Addie's mouth, Ty would help her, she knew. But the thought of taking anything more from him caused her whole body to cringe. She'd managed to provide for Addie and herself all this time.

Needing air, she shoved her chair away from the dining room table she'd commandeered as a makeshift office. Pushing her keys into the pocket of her shorts, she struck off toward Holley's old town square on foot. No need to drive. The heat could hardly do any more damage to her mood or her curls.

Since moving to Holley, she'd been consumed first with house renovation and then with her job search. She'd yet to visit the historic heart of the town.

She followed the slightly uneven sidewalks past one stately Victorian after another until she found herself standing at one of the square's four corners. The scene reminded her of a set from a Western movie. A beige stone courthouse, dreamt up by an architect who'd possessed both flair and an affection for clock towers, dominated the center. A street paved with bricks framed the courthouse, and storefronts framed the street. Some of the old buildings were tall, some narrow, some flat-fronted, some decorated with scrollwork, some painted gray or green. A wide sidewalk, almost a boardwalk, ran in front of the collection of shops, businesses, and eateries. The people strolling on it were shaded by overhangs, awnings, and porches as varied as the buildings they protruded from. Baskets of flowers hung from each of the light posts, trailing vines of English ivy.

Celia browsed through Carrie's Corner first, a gift shop that smelled like the apple pie candle flickering near the register. Next, she window-shopped at a country-and-western home furnishings store. Long family-style tables covered with red-and-white-checked tablecloths filled the interior of a barbecue restaurant called Taste of Texas.

In no establishment did she spend a single penny, of course. She hadn't even brought her wallet.

Celia skipped over a law office. She walked through Mrs. Tiggy Winkles, a lunch spot doubling as an antique store. She lingered inside the cool of The Bookery, which contained not only shelves lined with books but also leather chairs cozied up next to decorative lamps spilling light. Next came a place where kids could paint pottery. Then—

Celia came to a sudden stop. A large picture window had been set into an off-white storefront and painted with the words *Cream or Sugar* in gold cursive. Through the glass, Celia could make out what looked like a bakery display case.

Like the rest of her generation, Celia had a healthy fondness for coffee shops. Unlike the rest, she didn't often go inside them. For one thing, she couldn't afford the expensive drinks and pastries they served. But there was another, more subtle reason.

It hurt her to go inside.

Somewhere during her middle school years, she'd hit on the idea of owning and running her own bakery one day. It had become her dearest dream.

She'd gotten a degree in Nutrition and Food Service Systems, then nabbed a job as a sous chef after graduation. Her plan had been to work just long enough to save the money she needed in order to cover her bakery's start-up costs. While she'd been putting money aside, she'd researched the industry. Tested recipes. Spoken to men and women who owned their own shops.

She'd done all that, anyway, right up until the day of her positive pregnancy test. She'd set aside her imaginary coffee shop and turned her attention to the realities of life, knowing that nothing about her future would ever be what she'd envisioned.

A deeply buried piece of her hadn't forgotten it, though. Whenever she saw a coffee shop or, more rarely, ventured inside one, her heart would ache. Old pain, familiar and bearable. She had Addie, after all, and Addie was worth a hundred of her own dreams. But she still carried around a sore spot for the coffee shop her younger, more naïve self had once longed for.

Someone had taped a piece of paper to the bottom corner of Cream or Sugar's window. It read *Help Wanted*.

Cars trundled by on the street. People walked past. Celia remained motionless, hope battling against her common sense. The owners might just need a floor sweeper. And even if they didn't, the job likely wouldn't pay enough to support Addie.

She glanced down at herself anyway. Did she look presentable enough to inquire about the position? Yes, but just. She had on her airy white peasant top with the blue stitching around the neck. Tangerine shorts, fitted to above the knee. Her trusty T-strap leather sandals that she preferred to think of as "character filled" rather than just old.

She scooted out of sight and removed her headband, her anklet, and all of her bracelets except one. After stashing everything in her pockets, she finger fluffed her hair.

She let herself into Cream or Sugar's interior: a long, narrow space brimming with the smell of fried dough and coffee. An old-fashioned bar, like the kind a 1950s soda shop might have had, protruded from the wall on the left, ran in front of four swiveling round stools bolted to the floor, then turned and became a display case that continued to the back. The wood floors were fabulous, but the walls were dingy white and decorated with cheaply framed prints of glazed donuts.

A woman who looked to be about sixty stood behind the counter making change for a ruddy-faced man holding a white paper sack. A mother and her two young daughters chatted at a table halfway back. The girls' mouths were mustached with chocolate.

Celia moved deeper into the shop. The display case held four varieties of donuts. Glazed. Glazed with chocolate and sprinkles. Jelly. And cinnamon-sugar cake. Beyond that, just some Texas sheet cake and a tray containing chocolate chip and M&M cookies. Two glass pots of coffee, one with a brown handle and one with an orange sat side by side on a simple hot plate behind the counter. No espresso machine.

Cream or Sugar appeared to be more of a run-in-and-run-out donut shop than the kind of bakery Celia had first supposed. For one thing, there were no scones.

The woman behind the counter and her male customer launched into a conversation about mosquitoes.

Celia laced her hands in front of her and waited, self-
conscious.

More talk of mosquitoes. Speculation that last winter had not been cold enough to kill them all off. Celia
couldn't imagine the weather here becoming chilly
enough to merit a sweater, much less cold enough to
kill mosquitoes.

"Can I help you, honey?" the woman asked, raising
her voice. Both she and her customer turned toward
Celia.

"Yes. I saw the *Help Wanted* sign out front. I came in
to ask about the position."

They studied her for a long and awkward moment.
The man gave Celia a pleasant smile, then murmured
something about getting back to work and left with his
paper sack. The woman continued to size Celia up. In
no hurry, apparently, to fill the air with speech.

Celia approached the stretch of the counter near the
register. "I'm Celia Porter."

The woman's brows rose. "Ty's wife?"

Wow. This town really was small and Ty really was
famous here. "Yes."

"And you're looking for work?"

"I am."

"I'm Donetta Clark. My husband and I own the place."

"Nice to meet you."

"Come and sit down." Donetta gestured to the built-
in stools.

Donetta had dressed her pear-shaped body in beige
clamdiggers and a white T-shirt that had a red capital *T*

outlined by blue on its front. Tiny baseballs hung from her ears, also decorated with the *T*. White pom-pom socks peeked out the heels of her navy Keds.

Celia balanced her rear on one of the round padded seats and tried for good upper-body posture.

"Do you have any experience working in a shop like this?" Donetta asked.

Celia detailed her college degree, her stint as a sous chef, her years in cafeteria administration at the university.

Donetta listened, hazel eyes shrewd. She sported shoulder-length brown hair and bangs with an array of frosted-blond strands feathered about her face. The blond streaks brought to mind store-bought coloring kits, the kind that came complete with a cap punctured with holes.

"Oregon State University did you say?"

"Yes," Celia answered, "I attended there and then—"

"My cousin's son went to college in that part of the country. He turned into a real tree hugger. Lives with his wife and kids now in one of those houses that's powered by the sun. They nearly froze to death last January."

"Oh."

Donetta leaned a generous hip against the display case. "Honey, I think you're overqualified for the job here."

"What kind of help are you looking for?"

"Someone to work from around nine in the morning until closing at four. We had a young man working here, but he up and quit a week ago."

"That's too bad—"

"He ran off to Lampasas after some woman who sells

hair extensions. He will—mark my words—spend the rest of his life sitting at one of those kiosks in the mall trying to interest shoppers in fake ponytails and the like."

Celia nodded, commiserating.

"Anyhow. Jerry and I get here at four every morning to make donuts. We open at six and we like to pull out by ten. We have season tickets to the Rangers, and some of the home games start at one. You better believe we like to be sitting in our seats fifteen minutes before game time with our Ranger dogs, our sodas, and our nachos."

"Sure. I understand." Celia was not a baseball fan. Or really a fan of any sport at all. Except, mayhap, bull riding.

"We've been running this place for twenty years, and we're gettin' real close to retirement. I might not look it, but I'm sixty-two years old."

Celia widened her eyes with faux surprise.

"It's true. Jerry and I have ten grandkids. At this point in our lives, we don't want our work interfering with our baseball."

Two more customers entered, and Celia waited while Donetta served them donuts and Styrofoam cups of coffee. "Ya'll come back now."

The door wheezed shut behind them.

"So, like I said," Donetta said, straightening the handles of the coffee pitchers until they were in line, "we need someone we can trust to mind the shop for us till closing at four. We're open Monday through Friday, plus a half day on Saturdays."

The mother and her two daughters rose from their table and stopped to exchange pleasantries with Donetta.

Celia did the math in her head, adding the hours

the job amounted to. Close to forty per week, in day shifts that lined up well with Addie's school schedule. She didn't particularly want to work on Saturdays, but nothing came without compromise. If she could bring Addie along on Saturdays, then she could roll with it.

Her gaze traveled over the shop, seeing not so much what it was but what it could be with her influence. She already itched to buy paint and donate a Sunday to covering the walls with a new color. She could bake pastries at home and bring them in for customers to sample. If she hunted online, she might be able to find an espresso machine. . . .

Everything hinged on the pay. Below the level of the counter, Celia crossed her fingers.

She'd worked out a bare-bones budget this past week. Taxes, food, utilities, phone, Internet, gas, insurance, credit card payments, clothing for Addie. She knew exactly how much she needed to earn to cover the basics. To have any hope of paying off her debts, she'd need additional income. She'd been toying with the idea of baking and selling custom cakes in her free time.

"Ya'll come back now," Donetta called as the mother shepherded the girls out the door.

"How's the job sound?" Donetta asked Celia.

"So far so good."

"Here's why I said you're overqualified. I paid the hair extension salesman minimum wage. Seeing as how you're Ty's wife and experienced and all, I could up that a little." Donetta named an hourly salary that was just over half of what Celia needed. "Sorry, hon. That's the best I can do."

Celia kept her face impassive. Inside, though, her

hopes crashed. Could she possibly work out a way to support Addie on that amount?

Fruitless. She already knew she couldn't do it.

Her common sense had warned her that the pay would be too little. People who worked behind counters at cash registers did not make a lucrative hourly wage. Hope, though, was a funny thing. She had a practical personality. But sometimes, like years ago in Vegas with Ty, when she wanted something enough, her hope dared to reach too high. Occasionally it still managed to convince her logic that there might be a chance when there was no chance.

"I'd really like to work here," Celia said quietly. "Truly, I would. But I'm afraid that you were right, that maybe I am—"

"Overqualified?"

"Yes." She swallowed against a foolish wad of emotion.

"I figured." Donetta scooted a note pad and pen in her direction. "Write down your number, and I'll let you know if I hear about any jobs around here that would be right for you."

"Thank you."

"You have a little girl, don't you?"

"I do."

"Take some cookies to her. On me." Donetta placed two M&M and two chocolate chip cookies in a bag.

Celia accepted the gift and climbed off the stool. "Thank you again. It was nice meeting you."

"You come back now."

Celia walked into the heat. She moved away from Cream or Sugar keeping her head up and her face genial so that Donetta wouldn't think her heartbroken.

Two storefronts later a tingling sensation of awareness slid down the base of her neck. That particular tingle meant that Ty was nearby. She combed the faces of the people milling on the square's sidewalk and spotted him fifteen yards away, walking in her direction with the help of his crutches, looking right at her and grinning.

Of all the people she might have run into at this low and depressing moment, he was the worst. Ty, King of Confidence, Sir of Wealth, and Duke of Carefree Fame. Confidence had likely gilded him in the womb. His wealth and fame had come to him because he'd been good at sitting on top of bulls. He had no way of relating to mere mortals who had to do actual work in order to survive.

His brown T-shirt had either faded perfectly or been bought to look as though it had. The dimple that caused her heart to catch made an appearance. "I've been looking for you."

"I can't imagine why."

"I went to your house. Your car was there but you weren't, so I figured you'd come to the square."

"Your mental powers rival Einstein's."

He laughed. "You're rude as ever."

"I prefer to think of myself as charmingly feisty. Why were you looking for me?"

"I missed you, sweet one."

Horrible fellow. Whenever he said these sorts of things, he reminded her of the man she'd fallen in love with. Twice.

"You've been avoiding me all week, and I can't take it anymore. I'm sick of seeing you for five minutes when Addie comes over to ride. I'm greedy. I want more."

"Just so you know, I don't believe one word that you just said."

"Then I'm going to have to do a better job of convincing you."

They stared at each other, the air between them sizzling. The memory of the kiss they'd shared came back to her in excruciating detail.

"Can I buy you a snow cone?" he asked.

"No. I—"

"I'm buying you a snow cone, and you're going with me even if I have to toss you over my shoulder." He didn't wait for a response, just used a hand to turn her in the direction she'd come and give her a nudge. "Are you going to make a scene in the middle of Holley's downtown, or are you going to come along nicely?"

"Bully." In truth, a snow cone didn't strike her as a terrible idea. "I'm going to come along, but probably not nicely."

They moved toward one of the square's corner outlets.

As they walked, women either smiled at Ty, greeted him, or peeked at him surreptitiously. None remained immune to him.

Moving with athletic grace on his crutches, he led Celia to a lot just behind the square. A horseshoe-shaped driveway surrounded a building the size of an outhouse. Its owner had painted the tiny structure like a candy cane, in red and white stripes. A rainbow-hued sign read *Sally's Snow Cones* and listed the available flavors beneath. Windows opened out from both sides, one serving drive-through customers, one walk-ups.

"What'll it be?" Ty asked.

Might as well go for gold. "The Supreme." Which

promised watermelon, grape, lemonade, and coconut flavors.

Ty's lips quirked at her choice. If nothing else could ever be said about Ty's feelings for her, at least it could be said that he found her amusing. Tawny he probably found lovable, sexy, and particularly skilled with casseroles.

Which would, of course, trump amusing.

Ty went old school and ordered strawberry. They took their snow cones to one of two wooden picnic tables situated under a tree. Celia sat, settling her bag of cookies next to her. As Ty lowered himself onto the bench across the table, she heard a soft rattle, like the click of pebbles in a jar.

"What's that sound?"

"Nothing."

Quite possible. The noise had been faint.

When she sampled her snow cone, blessedly cold and tart lemonade syrup ran down her tongue.

Ty pulled off his sunglasses, revealing the impossible sheer blue of his gaze.

Celia knew exactly what Ty's woman-attracting superpower was. It was his eye contact. He could look into your eyes and without saying a word assure you that you were the most fascinating woman in the world and call you beautiful in six languages.

She fidgeted in her seat, thirty years old and experiencing a hot flash beneath the power of his eye contact.

"What brought you to the square today?" he asked.

"I just came to look around."

"Let me know when you're ready to find a job. I'll help you." A car pulled up to the drive-through window.

"Not that I want you to be in any hurry about that. Take a break for as long as you want."

She dipped her head and concentrated on her snow cone, wondering how much longer she'd be able to afford the pride that kept her silent. "Weren't you going to see your doctor this morning?"

"Yep."

"And?"

"The knee's healing fine. He doesn't want me to drive for another three weeks, though."

"That's too bad."

"I ignored his advice. As soon as Jake brought me home from the appointment, I got in my truck and came to find you."

"Ty," she said, disapproving.

"I'm not very good at following rules. And the no-driving rule is just stupid." He ate a spoonful of snow cone. "I made it over here fine."

"Did the doctor say anything about your bull riding?"

"Bull riding is over for me."

She studied him, looking for clues that would tell her how devastating the news had been for him. "Without a doubt?"

"Without a doubt."

"I'm sorry." With three world championship titles, he was one of the greatest bull riders of all time. Though he hid it well, the end of his storied career had to be difficult for him to accept. "What are you going to do now?"

"The BRPC has asked me to commentate some of their broadcasts."

"They want to put that face"—Celia pointed at him—"on TV?"

"Believe it or not, some women—just a few and not you, clearly—actually like my face."

"Wonders never cease." Her lips tilted into a smile.

"The other thing I'm thinking about doing is raising rodeo stock. Bulls, sheep, horses. Did I tell you that's what my dad does?"

"You'd mentioned it."

"My neighbor and his wife have decided to sell. If I buy their property, I'll have enough land to get started."

"Are you going to do it?"

"I might try to." His strong fingers toyed with his sunglasses. "Jim's land runs in between my property and a plot that belongs to an old guy named Howard Sanders. I already know Howard's going to want Jim's land, too. It used to be in Howard's family back in his granddad's time. He's been waiting for years to get a shot at it."

"Will Jim sell it to you over Howard?"

"Probably. I've got deeper pockets."

"And let me guess. Jim's wife likes your face."

He smiled crookedly. Something like fate pulled between them. It made her want to throw away reason, place herself in his lap, and hug him with every ounce of strength she had. "I talked with Meg a few days ago."

"Yeah?"

"She told me that Bo thinks that you've been faithful to me ever since our wedding."

He hesitated for a split second, then his face turned chiding. "Do I look like the faithful type to you?"

"No. I told Meg that I thought Bo's theory was ridiculous."

"I'm not to be trusted, Celia."

"I know." She got lost in him for a moment, dumbly wishing he *was* trustworthy. Wishing he'd loved her then. Wishing he loved her now.

Whoa! As usual, his nearness was muddling her brain. She pushed to her feet in a hurry. "I'd better go. Thanks for the snow cone."

———

Ty watched Celia drop her trash in the can, then walk quickly away from him, carrying her white paper sack. He scowled.

He and Bo hardly ever talked about Ty's dating life, yet Bo had guessed the truth. His older brother had always been full of intuition about people and horses that proved right. It sure would be nice, though, if Bo would keep his genius-level intuition to himself.

With a flick of his wrist, Ty tossed what was left of his snow cone into the garbage. He'd needed to see Celia today. It hadn't been optional for him. He'd been unable to sit in his house for another minute without her.

Physical desire he understood. But what drew him to Celia with such power was a lot more complicated. Celia was made up of a thousand traits, like any person. Some of her traits he liked and some he didn't. But the way her traits stacked up, plus the way his traits stacked up, somehow made her into someone that he'd *needed* to find just now.

Thanks to chemistry or stupidity or maybe even God, an invisible bond existed between the two of them.

He'd told her the truth just now when he said he couldn't be trusted. More than he wanted Celia, he wanted what was best for her and Addie. He was *trying* to protect them from himself. He wasn't very good at it. Honorable people resisted temptation, and resisting the temptation of Celia had never been his strong suit.

With effort, he pushed to standing. He made his way back to the square on his crutches, then turned in the direction of the donut shop.

When he'd first spotted Celia, she'd been coming out of the donut shop looking like someone had stolen her puppy. If he had to guess, he'd say her white sack had been filled with cookies. The Celia he knew was too cheap to buy somebody else's cookies. Why would she, when she could make the best cookies in the world inside her own home?

As his hand wrapped around the donut shop's door handle, he spotted a *Help Wanted* sign taped to the front window. Ah. The forest fairy had been in here about the job, it hadn't worked out, and she'd left with cookies as a consolation prize.

Hadn't he told her over and over that he'd get her a job? Instead, she'd ignored him and gone job-searching on her own. As usual, her stubborn independence chapped his hide.

He let himself in.

"Well, who do we have here?" Donetta Clark, who had a daughter about his age, straightened tall behind the counter.

"Trouble. That's who."

She slapped her hands together and laughed. "Ty Porter, you rascal!"

"Donetta, you look gorgeous. Still giving Jerry heart palpitations?"

"Every day. Did you hear about Willie Mickel and the heart attack he had? All that muesli he'd been eating split his heart right down the middle. Ended up face-down dead on top of his cereal back in June. Proves that a body can't take that much health food."

Ty chuckled and spent a few minutes shooting the breeze with her about her family and the Rangers. He eyed the food she had for sale, lined up behind glass. He knew from experience that it didn't taste half as good as the stuff Celia made. "I've been dreaming about your sheet cake for weeks, Donetta. Will you be mad at me if I buy all the sheet cake you have left?"

"I won't be too mad." Her eyes twinkled as she pulled out the tray holding the thin chocolate cake covered with chocolate frosting. "You gonna eat all this yourself?"

"I have a big family." In truth, he knew that buying her sheet cake would sweeten her toward him.

"Speaking of family." She began moving the squares of cake into a flat box. "Did you know that your wife was in here earlier? Cute little thing with those curls and all."

"I noticed the sign out front. Did she come in for the job?"

"Yes, but I couldn't pay her enough. It's a shame, too, because she'd have been good."

"I agree." He rested a forearm on the top of the display case and considered his best strategy. "You're a woman who appreciates some pride in a person, aren't you, Donetta?"

"Oh, you'd better believe it."

"I appreciate pride, too, but between you and me, I've got my work cut out for me with Celia. She doesn't want anyone doing for her what she can do for herself. Not even me."

"Sure," Donetta soothed, "sure." If she could have

craned her ears forward to catch more juicy pieces of gossip, he believed she would have.

"I want to help Celia," he said.

"'Course you do."

"Personally, I think this is a perfect place for her to work. It's close to her house. You and Jerry are great people to work for. Plus, she loves to bake."

"She's certainly the kind of employee I'd want to have."

"In that case, I have an idea."

Donetta shut the lid on the cake box and met his gaze directly. "I'm listening."

He and Donetta, he sensed, were fairly equal in street smarts. They'd both been around the block a few times. "Whatever you can pay Celia, I'll match." He didn't want to make Celia's pay so high that she'd be suspicious. Just high enough so that she could afford to work here.

"Don't you want to know how much I offered to pay her before you go off making that kind of promise?"

He smiled. He'd been raised by parents who knew how to pinch a penny, and he respected people like them. Donetta was frugal. But when it came to Celia, he was not. Whatever this venture cost him, he'd willingly pay. "Sure, if you want to tell me."

She told him.

How was anyone supposed to survive on that? Even twice the amount seemed pitifully small. No wonder Celia had turned down the job. "I'll match it."

Donetta took his measure. "And if I agree, then what? You want me to call Celia and offer her double what I did earlier?"

"Maybe wait until Monday." Again, he had to be

careful, or Celia would be on to him. "And then, yes. I'd like you to call her and offer her double."

"I could tell her that Jerry and I had a long conversation about hiring her and that we took another look at our budget." Donetta, no dummy, caught on fast. "I'll say that Jerry convinced me that we could pay her more, after all."

Ty nodded.

"Without mentioning your involvement."

"Without mentioning my involvement to Celia or anyone."

"Except Jerry."

"Except Jerry," he agreed. "Otherwise, it's our secret."

"So at the end of every week, when I write Celia a check, you're going to write me a check for half the amount?" Donetta's head angled in question.

"Every week. You have my word."

She rolled her tongue around in her mouth, thinking it over.

He'd left Las Vegas after their wedding and gone on to achieve far more than his rightful share of his dreams. Celia had gone on to achieve none of hers.

The time had come to make that right. Celia had always wanted to own a coffee shop. Cream or Sugar didn't belong to Celia and was probably in worse shape than the bakery she'd imagined. But it gave him a place to start.

"Ty?" Donetta extended her hand, and Ty shook it. "You have yourself a deal."

CHAPTER

EIGHTEEN

Celia froze as a sudden epiphany struck.

She shook the bottle of multivitamins she'd been in the process of lifting from her kitchen drawer. Then shook them again for good measure, listening.

All at once she knew exactly what sound had come from Ty's pocket yesterday when they'd been sitting down together at Sally's Snow Cones. It had been the rattle of pills in a medicine bottle. It had *not* been nothing.

It could be he was carrying around something benign, of course. Maybe Tylenol or a container of gum or mints. If she'd heard that telltale rattling coming from anyone else's pocket, she wouldn't have given it a second thought. But knowing Ty's personality and the circumstance of his injured leg and lost career . . . Her instincts warned her that she needed to give it a *long* second thought.

She glanced out the windows. It was fully dark. She'd tucked Addie into bed more than an hour ago.

Were the pills pain meds? If so, was Ty's pain so urgent he needed to keep them in his pocket? Worry twined through her thoughts. Could he be using the pills to medicate more than physical hurt?

She grabbed her phone and dialed. "Uncle Danny?"

"What's up, C?"

"Would you mind coming over to my place for a little bit? Addie's asleep, and I need to run an errand."

"Happy to." He did not ask what kind of errand she needed to run at nine o'clock at night. Yet another reason why she loved him. "Be there in five."

At some point before Celia had arrived in Texas, Ty had added the gingerbread house key and also his house key to her key ring. She hadn't had occasion to use his house key until now. She slotted it into the lock on his front door and turned it smoothly. If she barged in and found him wrapped in a set of foolishly trusting feminine arms, then so be it.

She closed the door behind her and strode purposefully across his foyer in the direction of his bedroom—

"Well, this is a nice surprise."

His voice brought her to a halt. Slowly, she turned. He was sitting in a suede chair in his dark living room, the TV flickering with an image of two men beating each other up inside a ring. He'd propped his bad leg on an ottoman. An investment-type magazine lay on the side table next to him with his reading glasses on top, as if he'd set both aside when he'd switched off the lights. All in all, a pretty lonely-looking Saturday night for Holley's best-loved celebrity.

"If you were on your way to my bedroom, don't let me stop you." His sardonic smile reminded her of a hunter observing prey. "I'll follow you there."

"As if."

"You didn't come by for a slumber party?"

"Of course not."

"When you pulled me into your bedroom back in Corvallis, things seemed a little premature. Believe me, I'm *more* than ready to shut myself into a bedroom with you now."

Her knees went limp like Jell-O at the dangerous timbre in his voice. It struck her how alone they were, the two of them, in the dark and private interior of his house. "Once again I'll remind you that we both agreed to be respectful friends."

"I remember you doing a lot of talking after our kiss. My memory is sketchier on what I agreed to."

She pulled the cord on a nearby lamp. In response, honeyed light fell from it, burnishing one side of his face. Crossing halfway to him, she hitched up her yellow dolman top, which kept wanting to slide off her shoulder, then set her hands on her hips. "Stand up."

His gaze bore into her with piercing force as he stood, gripping his chair's back to compensate for his ruined leg. He had on a black T-shirt, gray basketball shorts, and an invisible sign across his chest flashing *IRRESIST-IBLE* in neon letters.

"Empty your pockets."

His brows formed a V. "My pockets?"

"Empty them."

"No."

"Remember when I asked you 'what's that sound' yesterday? I think I know. Pills?"

His face lost its humor. "They're for my leg."

"Let me see them."

"My prescriptions are none of your business. We're respectful friends, remember?"

"I leave Addie in your care all the time, Ty. In order for me to trust you with our daughter, I need to know what you're taking." She presented her hand palm up.

He ignored it.

"I'll get the bottle myself if I have to," she threatened.

"I'd enjoy it if you tried."

"Hand it over."

He pushed a hand into a pocket, then flipped a bottle through the air to her.

She caught it and angled it to the light. "Vicodin." Frowning, she considered him. "This is a narcotic and also habit forming."

"Take it up with my doctor if you don't like it. He has something called an MD."

Whenever she spent time with him during the day, he was entirely too quick-witted and sharp-eyed to make her think him anything other than fully lucid. Even so, she sensed danger in the bottle she held in her hand. She could almost feel it against her palm, the peril these small pills represented for Ty.

His career had been ripped from him by injury. And goodness knows he could be too daring. Disappointment plus pain plus a careless nature? Not a good combination, especially because Ty had no one to keep close tabs on him. "Are you careful to take exactly the dose prescribed?"

"Careful enough."

"Wrong answer." She whirled and stalked to his bedroom. It made her mad, the chances he took with himself. The stupid stunts, the bull riding, and all the rest of it. *What's the matter with him?*

His bedroom carpeting muffled her footsteps as she sailed past the bed and into a master bathroom that glistened with polished travertine. She could hear the thud of Ty's crutches moving fast behind her, following.

If this prescription had been given to anyone a shade less self-destructive than Ty, she wouldn't have felt it necessary to take drastic action. She unscrewed the childproof lid and held the bottle above the toilet.

Ty rushed to a stop in the bathroom's doorway. "What the—"

She dumped all the pills in. They made quiet splashing sounds.

"Why did you do that?" he demanded.

The empty bottle had his doctor's contact information on it, so she tucked it into her shorts. "Because Addie loves you."

"And you? How do you feel about me?"

"I . . . care about you."

He jerked his chin toward the toilet. "I need those to sleep."

"Then allow me to recommend warm milk."

"I'd like to see you try to sleep with a shattered knee."

"Warm milk and Advil, then. Do you have any more bottles of Vicodin anywhere else?"

He set his lips in such a way that she knew he did. She slid one bathroom drawer after another open. In the third one she found a second bottle. Unscrew. Dump. Splashy sounds. This time she flushed the toilet and threw the bottle in the trash for good measure.

Ty glared at her, eyes fiery.

"I'm going to call your doctor on Monday and give him a piece of my mind. You injured yourself over a month ago, Ty."

"You don't know anything about recovering from this type of injury."

"That's true. However, I do know something about you. You're a great pretender, but I want you to tell me how you're really doing. Since the accident. Look into my face and tell me the honest truth."

"I'm doing fine."

She searched his features, carefully weighing. "You're struggling."

"I will be tonight, since you've thrown away my medicine." He pushed a hand through his hair, leaving tracks. "You do realize I can get a refill tomorrow."

"I need you to promise me that you won't do that."

He only stared at her. Time ticked by, and her throat turned dry. She wished she could hug him and apologize and assure him that she was only doing this because someone needed to. Someone, anyone—her, even—needed to watch over him and protect him from himself.

Silence pulled for so long that she grew certain he had no intention of promising her anything. She'd go home, regroup, and prepare to fight this battle with him again tomorrow.

He was mostly blocking the doorway, and didn't move to let her pass. She turned to the side to edge by. As she did, his arms extended so that they trapped her, one on each side, his palms planted against the wall near her head. The crutches fell with a clatter.

Celia looked into his face, so close she could see the darker blue icicles cutting into the pale blue of his irises. Need coursed through her, mixing with nervousness and determination. She collected her courage. "Promise me you won't take any more Vicodin."

Their profiles hovered just inches apart. Her breath entangled with his. Still, he didn't speak.

She licked her lips.

His gaze followed the motion. Heat and strength radiated from his body.

"Addie," she whispered—

"And you?"

"Addie *and I* need you to find a healthy way to come to terms with everything that's happened to you. For what it's worth, I have faith in you, Ty." Quaking inside, she looked straight into his eyes. "This is hard, what you're going through. But I believe that you can come through it without Vicodin and without going off the deep end. I need you to believe that, too."

She could tell by the hardening of his jaw that she'd struck a nerve. Her ability to read him had not failed her. "Now. Please promise me that you won't take any more Vicodin."

"Tell me something first."

"Okay."

"You said you cared about me. I want to know how much."

She never let herself think about the depth of her feelings for him. No way could she tell him what she didn't know herself . . . at least not without ending her ramblings by taking hold of his face and kissing him until she had no breath left. He smelled like heaven.

She ducked below his arm, dodging away from the hand that made a grab for her. "I care about you the way respectful friends care about each other," she called over her shoulder as she dashed from the room.

"Celia!" he yelled.

She ran. Ran and ran, perhaps even leaving his front door gaping. Ty didn't scare her, but the dark temptation he made her feel terrified her right down to the center of who she was.

Two a.m. came and went. Then three a.m.

Ty couldn't sleep. He read about trading and walked aimlessly through his deserted house. He watched the YouTube clips of his ride on Meteor.

Finally he dug through a dusty stack of old CDs until he found one with a peeling sticker on its case that read *Ty and Celia Got Hitched at the Luv Shack!* above their wedding date. He hadn't viewed the pictures in years. He fed the disc to his computer and very slowly clicked through the eight photographs.

He and Celia looked like kids—dumb kids. Especially him. They also looked so over-the-top happy together and Celia looked so painfully pretty that after he'd spent long minutes poring over them, he couldn't bear to look at them anymore, to remember. He ejected the CD and returned it to the bottom of the pile.

He'd wrecked everything that morning in Vegas. When he'd woken up and found himself in the middle of the wreckage, his decision to try to salvage his relationship with Tawny had been the best choice left to him. Or at least he'd thought so then and for almost six years. Now he wasn't so sure. He went back to pacing his dark house.

To his surprise, Advil mostly took care of the ache in his leg. If only it worked as well on the emotional junk that wouldn't go away.

He found himself in his big modern kitchen, an empty place no one baked banana muffins in. He opened his pantry and looked at the food on his shelves. He could stick a bag of popcorn in the microwave. But why? It was three a.m. His stomach felt like a stone. His vision had gone blurry with tiredness. He didn't want food.

He wanted a small curly-haired woman and his little girl to live here with him. Since he couldn't have that, he wanted his old life back. But he couldn't have that, either.

He ended up planting his forearms on the granite island, interlocking his fingers, and laying his forehead on his wrists. His chest expanded and contracted. How had Celia looked into him and seen what she'd seen tonight? She'd stripped him bare with her words, held a mirror up to him, and left him no place to hide.

Nobody said things like that to him. Nobody had reason to. His friends and family all thought he was doing well, or well enough, considering. He didn't understand how she'd known about the things going on inside of him. He didn't remember giving her any clues. He must have, though, because she'd come tonight. And she'd known.

"I have faith in you, Ty."

Stupid him, because his eyes glazed with wetness at the memory of her saying those words, looking right at him, into him, even. It had undone him. He'd never imagined how much he'd needed to hear her say that.

He'd given Celia no reason to have faith in him. He found it hard to find enough faith in himself to get through the day most of the time. But he didn't doubt Celia's honesty. She'd meant what she'd said. She had faith in him.

He began to move his lips in almost silent speech. It took a while for him to understand that he was talking to God. He'd doubted and sinned. He'd put himself first. When it had suited him, he'd left his relationship with God by the side of the road.

As usual when he prayed, his past mistakes crippled him with regret. His injury had kicked him down so much, though, that his choices were pretty much pray or check himself into a psych ward. So he kept on praying. He asked God for help and healing. For rescue. For sleep. For Celia to love him even though she shouldn't love him and he shouldn't ask God for something so ridiculous.

At the end, the prayer brought him around to one final request. "God," he asked in words that were below hearing except in his mind, "I don't know who I am anymore. Show me who you are. And show me who I am."

CHAPTER

NINETEEN

Church had changed since back in the day.

It was Sunday, the day after her pill-dumping session at Ty's house, and Celia had followed through on her promise to Meg to attend church. Meg and Bo stood next to her on one side and Addie stood on the other.

Pounding, thumping, frankly *rocking* praise music flowed over them. Printed lyrics scrolled down a screen to the right of the stage, but the voices around Celia were singing with such enthusiasm and confidence that it made her think they hardly needed the lyrics. Leading them was a band that included three guitarists, a keyboardist, a drummer, and two singers.

Where was the choir? The hymnals? The organ? For that matter, where were the pews?

The churches of Celia's childhood had looked like churches, with steeples, stained glass, and boring white hallways holding Sunday school classrooms. When Meg and Bo had fetched her and Addie this morning, that's the kind of place she'd been expecting. Instead, they'd driven to a Christian school in a nearby town, explaining that their church rented out the school's auditorium on Sundays.

The song ended and another immediately began, equally powerful and modern. Celia glanced at Addie, who stood motionless, eyes wide. Celia could only imagine what might be going through her mind. At five, Addie wasn't exactly a veteran of the concert scene. And this worship service, thanks to the darkness bathing the congregation and the illuminated musicians on stage, reminded Celia of a concert.

Plus, the people around them were dressed more like concertgoers than churchgoers. She and Addie had on dresses and their fanciest pairs of shoes, which put them in a more formal category than anyone else in the place.

When the music finished, the audience lowered into the rows of auditorium seats. The band exited and a man wearing jeans, chukka boots, and a plaid shirt with the sleeves rolled up walked onto the stage. He looked to Celia like a technical assistant, so she expected him to grab a microphone and duck offstage.

No. He set his Bible on one of those black music stands, then made a joke about the pro football game scheduled for later in the afternoon.

This was Meg and Bo's pastor? He couldn't have been much past twenty-seven or a pound over a hundred forty-five. Again, Celia had the disorienting feeling of having expected one thing and being served something entirely different. Like ordering oatmeal and receiving an omelet.

Pastors wore dark suits. They had politician type haircuts and slick edges to them. They spoke in dramatic fashion about sin. Didn't they? This pastor had a hip and spiky haircut and probably played Xbox with his buddies on the weekends.

Addie tapped her arm. "Crayons," she whispered.

Celia doled out the crayons and paper she'd brought along to entertain Addie. Then she folded her hands in her lap on top of the church bulletin she'd been given and listened.

Meg and Bo's pastor was not a particularly skilled orator. He had no holy aura about him. No grand hand gestures or great charisma. But as his sermon sank in, discomfort began to gather in Celia's breast. Mild at first, then exerting more pressure with every minute that passed. Because . . .

God was here.

In this auditorium that had no stained glass. Speaking to her through the words of this Doogie Howser preacher. He was here, and Celia, who had not sensed Him in years—not since that day when she'd knelt and begged Him for a negative result on her pregnancy test— sensed Him now. In a way that was so real and close that it felt as if she'd been pursued into an alley that ended in a brick wall. No way out.

Her heart rate kicked into a higher gear.

The pastor did not speak about how Christians should strive to be better than they were. He didn't try to persuade them into having a quiet time every morning or praying more or signing up to be missionaries in Africa. In fact, he talked nothing at all about what the congregation could do for God and talked endlessly about what God had done for the congregation through the death and resurrection of Jesus Christ.

He preached grace.

And then he preached God's love.

And then he preached grace some more. "'To the praise of his glorious grace,'" he read from the Bible, "'which he has freely given us in the One he loves.'"

Celia found it increasingly difficult not to squirm. With her thumbnail, she began to push at her cuticles. She'd thought, sarcastically, that she might be struck by lightning for walking through a church's doors after so many years as a heathen. Well, she felt as if she *had* been struck by lightning—just not in the way she'd supposed. She felt stricken by the possibility that God might actually love her as much as this pastor seemed to believe He did.

She thought back on the emptiness she'd long grappled with. When had it begun, this dissatisfying feeling of seeking and hungering after something she could never quite grasp? She could remember it as far back as her childhood, when she'd been forced to move every few years. It had been with her in high school, when she'd hoped that Ty Porter would like her back and make her feel whole. She'd sought to find her anchor in her college degree, and after that in her goal of owning her own coffee shop. She'd looked to fill it with family, but she hardly saw her brother, and her parents were nothing but occasional houseguests. Even Addie, her dearest treasure, the person she'd poured every drop of her love into, had been unable to fill her up.

The more the pastor spoke, the more her emptiness stirred. It reached out, seeking a love that was unconditional and eternal and big enough to satisfy.

Her version of Christianity had been about avoiding

drinking, lying, curse words, and sex before marriage. Sure, there'd been stories of the cross and the song "Jesus Loves Me." But what had been the result? Her belief that religion meant trying to do—or not do—stuff in order to please God.

After that pregnancy test had come back positive, she'd been certain that God had turned His back on her because she hadn't been good enough. She'd let go of her faith in Him because she'd understood with dull certainty that she'd *never* be good enough. And she'd grown weary of trying and failing.

This pastor was agreeing with her, in a way, freely acknowledging that no one in the room would ever be good enough. But he claimed that was all right because *Jesus* had already been good enough for them all.

Unshed tears burned her eyes. She told herself somewhat frantically to think about something else. Her job search or Addie's kindergarten or anything—

It was as if God's hands held her cheeks, keeping her attention on that long ago day when she'd hit her knees and prayed not to be pregnant.

Think back, He seemed to say.

It wasn't hard to remember her terrified desperation. She'd been a young and heartsick working girl back then. The possibility of becoming pregnant had panicked her. At the time it had been almost impossible to imagine how she'd cope with a baby.

What would you have had me change?

Her mind went blank. Her thoughts spiraled. If God had answered her prayer the way she'd wanted Him to back then, if her pregnancy had never been, she wouldn't have Addie.

Addie's blond head bent in concentration over her coloring. Celia watched as her glasses began to slip down her nose. Addie pushed them back with her index finger and continued to work on a scene depicting a plump white horse with a big bow on top of its head.

Addie was the greatest joy of Celia's life. Not a burden. Not a tragedy.

A gift. A gift that God had perhaps insisted on giving her even when, in her fear, she'd asked for the opposite.

Mercifully, the sermon concluded. Having been granted a reprieve, Celia stood on shaky legs for more songs, then sat for the offering and announcements, then stood again for the final song. The whole time her brain listed like a ship trying to right itself. She needed time and space to think about all this. To process.

Meg, Bo, Celia, and Addie filed into the foyer at the end of the service. People walked past them, talking, greeting friends.

"So," Meg asked, "what did you think?"

"The music was loud," Addie answered.

Meg smiled and affectionately rolled a lock of Addie's hair around her finger.

Meg and Bo moved their gazes to Celia. They struck Celia as two people assured with God, with themselves, and with each other. So much so that they had kindness enough to share with their surprise sister-in-law and niece.

"It was good," Celia said. A mere figment of nothing to describe the earthquake that had just happened inside of her.

Meg gave Celia a hug. "Thank you for coming."

Within an embrace that smelled like blooming roses,

Celia could almost feel God's arms around her, His voice whispering, **I love you, Celia. I've always loved you.**

Through methods known only to him, Uncle Danny had managed to find what might be the only mid-century modern house in all of Holley, Texas.

Danny stepped onto his porch as Celia and Addie made their way up his front walk, Celia carrying a cake. "My favorite girls!" He had on a . . . *a Ty Porter T-shirt?* The man who never wore new clothing had on a black T-shirt so new that it still bore fold marks.

Addie ran to hug him and the two of them went through their usual fist-bumping routine.

"What are you wearing, Uncle Danny?" Celia asked.

"My new shirt. Sweet, isn't it?" He stuck out his arms and turned slowly.

Heinous, more like. A cheesy image of Ty riding a bull plastered the shirt's front. The back read *Ty "The Terminator" Porter* in a flaming red and yellow font and listed the years he'd won his world championships.

"Want me to order you one, C?"

A surprised laugh bubbled from Celia. "No. But thank you."

"I want one!"

"'Course you do," he said to Addie. "If I can get one in your size, I will. Won't we look sharp riding our bike around town in our matching shirts?"

"You haven't been riding in this heat, have you?" Celia asked. The forecasted high for this third day of September: ninety-seven.

"'Course I am. I've taken to this weather like a seal to

water. Every time I'm out in it, I just soak in the vitamin D. Can't get enough."

"Really?" Celia wrinkled her nose. "It doesn't feel like the inside of a furnace to you?"

"Mo-om," Addie protested. "It's perfect here."

"I agree with Potaddie. It's perfect here." Danny looked at her cake. "What'd you bring me?"

"Lemon poppy seed." After the monumental things that had occurred during the church service earlier, Celia had been feeling like a stroke patient struggling to recover normalcy. She'd gone straight to the kitchen when they'd arrived home and started in on her therapy. Neill had brought his boys over, and he and Celia had talked while the cake had baked and the kids had played. Baking hadn't helped her organize her thoughts much today, but it had produced one pretty cake.

Danny lifted the cake from her hands and led them inside. More mid-century modernness everywhere Celia looked.

Within minutes, they'd settled around his kitchen table with slices of cake and glasses of coconut water over ice.

"I know I've said this before." Danny took a moment to close his eyes and chew with a blissed-out expression. "But this is insanely good."

"Thank you."

"You have got to let me sell this online."

"Lemon poppy seed cake alongside wet suits?"

"It'd be awesome!"

Celia took a sip of coconut water and tried not to wince. As health conscious as she was, she'd never been able to bring herself to like coconut water. It might be more hydrating than plain water, but it also tasted yuckier than the original. For Addie's sake, she'd pretend to drink it, then dump it in the sink.

"These Texans sure are mannerly, aren't they, Celia? Everywhere I go they greet me, shake my hand, and offer to help me out. Ty's mom, for one. Nancy? She and I have been talking and scoping out my next dating move."

Another example of the Porter Family Help Squad in action.

"She's a great lady," Danny continued. "If she wasn't taken, I'd snap her up in a minute—"

"But she is. Taken."

"Which is a shame." He forked off another bite of cake. "Now that I'm in a new part of the country, I've decided to revisit the online dating thing. I've found a couple of ladies who live within driving distance of here."

"I don't know, Danny. Online dating hasn't been that productive for you in the past."

"Nah, but hope springs eternal. Waiting on the right wave takes patience. It's the same with this. If I keep trying, keep waiting, then the right woman will eventually come my way."

"Like a bump on the surface of the ocean."

"You and me. We're here." He moved two fingers back and forth through the air between her forehead and his. "There's this one lady that I met online through a site called Flirty and Over Fifty. She lives in Hugo, Oklahoma, which is just two hours from here. I can't really tell from the picture what she's got to offer in the looks department. I know she has diabetes, loss of vision in one eye, and a recurring case of the hiccups—but, hey, she might have some real potential."

"What's her name?"

"Betty."

No potential. Unless she was born and raised in the Czech Republic, then changed her name to Betty upon her arrival on American shores.

When they'd finished their cake, Danny—true to his insistence that he enjoyed the heat—took Addie out on a bike ride. Celia went to work assessing his fridge and attending to Danny's other housekeeping needs. She'd swept half his living room when her phone buzzed to signal an incoming text. The tingling sensation that cascaded through her in response meant only one thing.

She pulled her phone from her purse. *Are you ever going to wear the boots I gave you?*

Nope, she answered. *Are you ready to return them and get your money back?*

Never. Then ten seconds later, *Will you be coming over tonight to flush any more medications down my toilet?*

Not unless provoked.

I'm thinking the plumbing pipes beneath my house are feeling pretty painless and relaxed right about now.

She caught herself smiling. He didn't seem to bear her any ill will. Of course, that may be because she'd fled (in fear of her chastity) before securing his sworn promise not to take more Vicodin.

Bring Addie over this afternoon? Ty asked. *Whitey's lonely.*

Out of all the girly and fanciful names Addie could have chosen for her pony, she'd tossed up an air ball by choosing Whitey. *Whitey doesn't care about anything except her next meal*, she typed back.

Okay, I admit it. Whitey's fine. I'm lonely.

Her fingertips hovered over the phone. She wanted to write *Why don't you call Tawny?* but Ty would be even more insufferable to deal with if she confirmed the envy he already suspected she harbored toward Tawny. *We're spending the day with Uncle Danny*, she typed instead. *He's lonely, too.* The fact was, a part of her wanted to drive to Ty's house. She did, in a way, sort of . . . miss him. Ludicrous. Also worrisome, because she'd definitely not given herself permission to miss Ty.

Danny and Addie, sweaty and red faced, bustled into the house with the bike and third-wheel attachment.

Ty sent her another text. *Come over after you leave Danny's.*

No, she answered. *Don't you have any cowboy things to do? Like spit tobacco? Rope stuff with your lasso? Chew cud?*

It's cows that chew cud, sweet one.

She burst out laughing, only to swallow the sound when she looked up and saw that Addie and Danny were watching her.

"Who's that?" Addie asked.

"No one." Celia slipped the phone back into her purse and returned her attention to sweeping.

"Was it Daddy? You like him, don't you?"

"Hmm?" Ever the rotten actress.

"You like him."

It didn't look like Addie was going to drop the subject, so Celia faced her and took up her mommy face and tone of voice. "Of course I like him. He's your father, and he's a good man."

Danny snickered.

Addie regarded Celia with the heaping and withering scorn that only a five-year-old can muster.

"What?" Celia asked defensively, her spirits starting to slump because she knew what.

"You like Daddy the way that the princesses like the princes in the movies. And in the end, the princesses and the princes always kiss each other, Mommy. *Everybody* knows that."

CHAPTER TWENTY

Monday mornings. A day and time of the week not known for bringing joy.

But as Celia stood in her dining room with her phone clasped to her ear listening to Donetta offer her double the pay to work at Cream or Sugar, she realized that this particular Monday morning brought with it bucket loads of joy.

"So what do you think?" Donetta asked. "Do you want the job?"

"Yes. *Yes!* I definitely want the job." Celia pressed a cool hand to her hot cheek. "Thank you so much. You won't be sorry, Donetta. I'll work really hard for you. Wow. Thank you!"

"You're welcome, honey. Can you start tomorrow?"

"Yes. I can."

"See you at nine." Donetta clicked off.

Celia lowered the phone. For a minute straight she stood unmoving in the silence, grinning from ear to ear. She was going to get to work at a bakery, many years after she'd put that dream away. A bakery!

Oh my goodness! It felt like a gift beyond price. Too sweet to be true . . . and yet it was. She, Celia Park Porter, baker! She'd no longer have to stress over her job search. She could support her daughter. And she'd done it herself, without Ty's help. But with, she suspected, God's.

The timing couldn't be a coincidence, surely. Yesterday she'd been to church and heard God tell her He loved her. Today Donetta had called and miraculously offered her twice as much per hour as she had last week.

Astonishing. Humbling. Thrilling!

With a squeal, Celia broke into a dance. Her bare feet thrummed against the floor. Her hips swayed. Her hands jabbed skyward. It was vaguely tribal and wholly uncoordinated.

I have a job!

Celia wasn't the only person finding a foothold on their career aspirations that morning.

Across town, Ty climbed a hill alongside his neighbor. Jim had been eager to show Ty the land he had for sale, and Ty hadn't asked to tour the property on ATVs like he should have because he hadn't wanted to sound like a wuss. So here he was, hiking up a hill on his crutches. His shoulders and his good leg were in agony and all the movement had caused his bad leg to hurt like a— He cursed inwardly, keeping his face turned from the older man so Jim wouldn't see his pain.

At last they reached the hilltop, and Jim stopped. "Here we are." Jim tilted his straw Stetson to blot sweat from his forehead, then tugged the brim back into position.

A 360-degree view spread out from where they stood. Mostly grassy, with some bunches of trees here and there—a typical north Texas landscape more familiar to Ty than the back of his own hand. He'd grown up on land just like this. He'd built his home on the property next door because this type of acreage made him comfortable.

"What do you think?" Jim asked.

"Well, like I told you, I have a mind to raise rodeo stock. Looks perfect for that."

"It is. See just there?" Jim pointed to a stream that wound across a section of the property below them. Greenery had grown up around the water source, which formed a natural pond at one point, before continuing out of sight. "That's Whispering Creek." In salesman fashion, Jim went on to describe the features of the land and the improvements he'd made to it.

Ty had built his house four years ago. Since then, he'd had reason to come over to Jim's occasionally. Neighbors helped neighbors, and there'd been times when the two men had worked together to clear downed tree limbs after thunderstorms, when Ty had loaned his generator to Jim, when Jim had let him borrow a power tool. This was the first time, though, that Ty had viewed this land with the option of owning it. As it happened, the idea of owning it felt exactly right.

He filled his lungs with air, smelling warm earth and sunbaked grass. For the first time since his fall off Meteor, interest for something beyond bull riding began to awaken inside of him.

He could do this. He could raise stock and spend his energy and time doing something that had meaning. He hadn't left all his worth behind him on the dirt floor of an arena in Boise, Idaho.

Jim finished talking.

"I want to buy it," Ty stated.

A smile dawned across Jim's face. "I'm glad to hear that."

"Would you like cash or a check?"

Jim chuckled. "You know that Howard Sanders wants it, too."

"I do."

"Howard's been calling Marjorie and me for years, reminding us of his interest in buying the place. I can't say he's been the easiest neighbor. He's opinionated about everything under the sun and we've had our run-ins."

"I can imagine."

"I'd rather sell the land to you."

It didn't hurt that Ty could outspend Howard many times over, and that Jim knew it.

"I told Howard, though, that I'd give you both an equal shot at the property."

"Understood. How about you work up a price that's fair and pass it along to us both? If Howard is willing to pay above your asking price, I'd appreciate the chance to make a counter offer."

"Fair enough."

"Will you agree to sell the land to the man who's willing to pay the most?"

"I will."

"That's all I ask." Ty's determination rose. In no time at all, he would own this property.

The next morning Celia drove her Prius to Cream or
Sugar so she wouldn't appear for her first day of work
looking heat-rumpled. She'd chosen a scoop-neck green
top and a lighter-than-air knee-length patterned skirt.
Even though neither piece required ironing, she'd ironed
them both twice in hopes of making a good impression.

She let herself into the bakery and found Donetta
making change for a customer. Donetta tipped her head
toward the door at the rear of the space. "You can go
on back, hon. Jerry's there."

The bakery case ended with a slab of wood that could
function as a counter, but hinged at the wall so that
workers could lift it and walk past. Celia did so, then
made her way into a square room.

A large commercial oven loomed in one corner. Double refrigerators. The appliances appeared old, but not
awfully so. Clinton era, not Reagan. Metal counters,
sinks, fixtures. The short hallway that proceeded out of
the space looked to hold a stairway, a rear exit door, and
likely a bathroom. Numerous open shelves ran horizon-
tally around the kitchen. Some held bowls, pans, trays;
others contained industrial-size bags of supplies like
flour and sugar. Everything appeared rigorously clean.

A man stood with his back to her, stirring what looked
to be cookie dough. As she approached, he turned.

"Jerry?" Celia asked.

"That's me." He spoke with a quiet, unhurried voice.

"I'm Celia. Nice to meet you."

"You too." He gave her a gentle smile. Apparently this
was Celia's champion, the one who'd talked Donetta
into paying her extra. He reminded her of Hulk Hogan,
except ginger-haired and without the muscle definition.

"Thank you for hiring me."

"You're welcome."

She'd have liked to hug him or babble with gratitude. "What can I do to help you?"

"In a minute you can help me get these cookies on the sheet."

"I'd be glad to."

He told her where to find an apron and a box of hairnets. She donned the apron in two seconds. The hairnet—less familiar. In her sous chef days, she'd simply worn her hair pulled into a ponytail. Either Donetta and Jerry were old-school or Donetta had been motivated by the sight of Celia's flyaway curls to make a trip to the nearest culinary supply store.

Celia pulled on the white mesh net and glanced at the mirror that hung in the hall wall near the back door. She resembled a Los Angeles gang member.

After washing her hands, she arrived at Jerry's side. He handed her a tool that looked like a mini ice-cream scooper and the two of them began to place balls of cookie dough on trays.

"Do you like to bake?" he asked.

"Very much."

And with that, Jerry's conversational needs seemed satisfied. He'd brought Hulk Hogan to mind because he sported the kind of mustache that went up one side of his mouth, crossed over the top, and went down the other side.

When they finished, they slid the cookies into the oven.

"Now we'll move on to sheet cake." Jerry riffled through a small rectangular recipe holder and handed

Celia a weathered recipe for Texas sheet cake. She spread it carefully on the counter to study it.

Jerry began collecting the ingredients they'd need.

"What kind of baking schedule do you usually follow?" Celia asked.

"We always make the donuts first thing in the morning before we open. During rush hour, Donetta works out front. I help her when she needs me, and when she doesn't I clean up back here. After that, I take a break for breakfast at McDonald's. Then I come back and make cookies. Every other day I also make sheet cake."

"Got it." Celia started measuring out flour, trying to convince herself of the amazing fact that she worked here now, in Cream or Sugar's peaceful kitchen on Holley's old town square. *They're paying me to do this.* To bake, something she'd do—and regularly did do—for free.

Celia was happily scooping cocoa powder into the bowl when she heard female laughter from the front of the shop followed by the deep rumble of a man's voice.

Her turncoat heart picked up speed as Ty entered the kitchen on his crutches, Donetta following close behind.

"Good to see you, Jerry." Ty nodded at the older man.

"Hi there, Ty."

Ty's attention settled on her, the teasing in his eyes making them an even brighter shade of blue. "Nice hairnet." He wore a weathered navy baseball hat and carried a huge bouquet of amber-colored tulips.

Celia would have said, "Scram!" or "No civilians allowed!" or "I'll shove this hairnet where the sun don't shine!" if Jerry and Donetta hadn't been in the room. "Hello." She tried for a smile that hopefully looked wifely.

"Congratulations on your first day of work."

"Thank you." She'd told him about her new job because she needed him to pick Addie up from kindergarten each weekday afternoon, then take care of her at the gingerbread house until she got off work.

He moved to her, then bent to kiss her cheek.

Celia froze. He was taking advantage of their eyewitnesses to do things she wouldn't let him do in private.

"No touching!" she whispered.

"Hmm?" he breathed near her ear. "I can't hear you." He kissed the sensitive spot where her jaw met her neck, then straightened.

He should be embarrassed to put on a show like this in front of Jerry and Donetta, who were doing a shabby job of pretending not to be fascinated. Instead of embarrassment, Ty seemed highly entertained. Confident as ever. He may not have the DNA for embarrassment.

"These are for you."

She accepted the flowers. "They're beautiful." His impossible sixth sense had once again led him to exactly what she liked best.

Jerry removed a vase from a cupboard and filled it with water for her. "Here you are."

She thanked him and arranged her tulips. It seemed more absurd than ever that this larger-than-life man should be her husband. No wonder Donetta, Jerry, and the rest of Ty's groupies were curious about the oddity of his wife and child. She was too normal for Ty. She'd shown up with Addie out of the blue. And the two of them lived separately from Ty. If she hadn't lived through it, their situation would perplex even her.

"You can put me to work while I'm here if you want to, Donetta." Ty said to the older woman. "I come cheap."

"You're not lifting a finger in my kitchen," Donetta replied, "No, sir. Are you hungry, though, Ty? I've got a cinnamon cake donut with your name on it."

Celia hid an eye roll.

Care to sit down, Ty? Pillow for the small of your back? Footstool? How about we all wave palm fronds at you to keep you cool?

"You know me," Ty answered. "I've never said no to a donut."

Celia arrived home from work that afternoon to find Addie sitting on the edge of her bed and Ty lounging on the rug, his back against her bookcase. Addie was brushing Aurora's hair while rhapsodizing about Grace, her new kindergarten friend. Snow White sat on Ty's leg brace. The rest of the princesses lined the edge of Addie's dresser, like a studio audience.

"Hello, everyone."

"Hi, Mom."

Celia crossed to Addie and hugged her.

"Where's the hairnet?" Ty regarded her with lazy humor. He still wore his baseball cap.

"I left it at work, thank you very much."

"Well, that's no fun."

"May I speak to you for a minute?"

"'Course." He began to lever himself up.

Addie looked back and forth between them with interest.

This time, Celia knew better than to lead Ty into the

dangerous territory of her bedroom. She took him to the back stoop and closed the door behind them. Heat thumped the top of her head like a drumstick might a snare drum.

"Have you taken a look at that Snow White Barbie?" Ty asked. "She's stacked."

Celia didn't let herself smile.

"Can't imagine you approve of Addie playing with dolls that look like that."

No, she didn't. Objectified female body image and all that. "Surprisingly, that's not why I asked to speak to you."

"No? Did you want to speak to me about hiring a painting team to redo your house? 'Cause I'll pay for that in a heartbeat. Whenever I'm in there I feel like I'm standing inside a box of crayons."

It bothered her that in some strange way, Ty's ribbing made her delight in her paint choices much more complete. She drew herself up. "First, thank you for picking Addie up and bringing her home today—"

"Did you just say thank you? To me?"

Despite herself, she did smile then. Raising a hand to shield her eyes from the glare, she squinted up at him. "I guess I did. Believe me, it didn't come naturally."

"I'll just bet it didn't."

They held eye contact across a drawn-out pause. Her attention dropped unbidden to his dimple, then his lips. "Um . . . so it went okay? Picking Addie up? She didn't miss me or feel anxious or anything?" Guilt and second-guessing were constant companions to motherhood.

"Nope, it went fine."

"Good."

He hooked his thumbs into the handholds on his crutches. "You can start in on me now about visiting Cream or Sugar today. That's why you asked me out here, right?"

Freaky mind reader! "Well," she conceded, "yes."

"You might want to start with how the bakery is your place of business. Then you can tell me that you need to concentrate while you're there and my presence distracts you because of your crush on me—"

"I hotly debate that—"

"—and then you can go on to say that I'm part of your personal life, and you don't want your personal life overlapping with your professional life."

"It's true. You *do* belong in my personal life and not my professional."

"Which sounds sort of promising." He tilted his face a fraction, which sent the shade from his brim cutting across his features at a different angle. She could see the faint scar on his cheekbone. "I want to be a bigger part of your personal life." His features turned serious while he stared at her. "I'm crazy about you."

No stammering or apology.

Her mouth went dry.

"I think about you all the time," he said. "I know why I shouldn't want more. But I do."

A terrible and treacherous longing softened her heart. The emotion reminded her just how much she'd loved him once. If she hadn't loved him quite so much, he wouldn't have been able to hurt her as deeply as he had.

She cleared her throat. "Like I was saying. Since Cream or Sugar is my place of employment, I'd appreciate it if you'd keep your distance."

"Whatever you say, sweet one."

"Really?"

"I live to please."

Ty left fifteen minutes later. An hour after that, Celia and Addie readied themselves for a trip to Brookshire's for groceries. When Celia lifted her keys from her purse, a familiar weight clunked against her palm. With disbelief, she peered down at a peace sign key ring. An identical sibling to its predecessors.

Give Peace a Chance III.

On Celia's first day of work, Donetta and Jerry had stayed with her the entire shift. Jerry had explained the kitchen's routines. Donetta had taught her how to operate the cash register and rattled off a string of do's and don'ts.

On Celia's second day of work, the Rangers were playing a one o'clock game at the Ballpark in Arlington. Thus Jerry and Donetta, dressed in matching Rangers T-shirts, pulled out at ten sharp.

Except for the chewing of the trucker putting away jelly donuts at the corner table, quiet settled around Celia. For a few moments, she simply absorbed the details of the bakery. *She* was now in charge of Cream or Sugar.

As customers drifted in, she waited on them with perhaps a little more perkiness and appreciation than necessary. Everyone asked if she was new in town and introduced themselves.

She brewed fresh coffee because the old tasted like swill. She cleaned the shop's front window. She wiped the counter and tabletops. She fantasized about all the things she wanted to bake in the kitchen and all the updates she wanted to make to the front room.

About an hour after she'd taken command of her new domain, Ty sauntered through the door. No crutches. Noticeable limp. He ignored Celia completely, wasting the perfectly good glare she was trying to give him.

Two female friends sat together, sharing a square of sheet cake. "How are you doing?" he asked them as he passed by.

They both startled to attention at the sight of him. "Doing well." Big smiles. "You're Ty Porter, right?"

"Yep."

They gushed over him for five minutes straight. Celia knew, because she timed it.

"Let us know if we can get you anything else," Ty said, finally moving away from the pair.

Let *us* know?

"How about you, ma'am?" he asked the little old lady drinking decaf. "Can I do anything for you?"

Poor thing. She was too frail to handle his lady-killer smile. She tittered, blushed, and thanked him profusely, even though he hadn't done anything.

He walked to the end of the display case, raised the wooden slab, and continued around it like he owned the place. He stopped in front of Celia, tall and lean in a gray NASCAR T-shirt, jeans, and his alligator boots. The lack of crutches and the jeans meant he'd been to the doctor that morning and his bulky brace had been exchanged for something slimmer.

She pitched her voice low. "Do you remember our discussion yesterday?"

"Perfectly."

"Then what happened to staying away from here like you said you would?"

"I didn't say I'd stay away from here. I said 'whatever you say,' which isn't the same thing at all."

He was going to send her to an early grave! She drew in air to let him have it—

"Shh." He motioned with his head. "We have customers."

"*We* don't have anything. You don't work here."

"I'm going to help you. I like this place." He shrugged. "There's donuts."

"No."

"'Course there's donuts." Laugh lines feathered out from his eyes.

"No, you're not going to help me."

"Yes, I am." He smiled like someone who knew they held the winning card. His arms crossed over his broad chest, which pulled the soft cotton tight over his muscled shoulders. "If you have a problem with it, then take it up with Donetta."

Celia ground her teeth.

"Donetta loves me," he said.

If she could have bested him physically, she'd have pushed him out of the shop like a tractor pushing garbage.

"Think for a minute," he continued. "If I'm working out here, then you'll be free to go in the kitchen and bake things."

"I'm not leaving you out here alone! I'm responsible for this place when Donetta and Jerry are gone. I'm going to stay out front and do the job I was hired to do."

"Don't trust me?"

"Nope."

"I'll prove to you that you can."

And with that, he stayed. And stayed. Despite her protests.

He chatted with everyone who came in Cream or Sugar's door. He served up donuts and coffee with his trademark easygoing humor. He went out and brought back lunch for Celia, then insisted she take a break to sit and eat. Fifteen minutes before kindergarten was scheduled to release, he left to go pick up Addie.

Shoot, she thought as she watched him walk away. He exasperated her, but illogically, that did not make her immune to him. Quite the opposite. The bull rider was sexy. Even with the limp. Maybe made sexier *by* the limp.

"You can't fall for him," she murmured. She refused to put herself through that heartbreak again and doubly refused to put Addie through it. Their daughter watched their every move like a teal-glasses-wearing hawk. Besides, as far as Celia knew, Ty was just biding time with her until Tawny became available.

Tawny was far more desirable than she was—any fool could see that. And Ty, despite the good ol' boy shtick he sometimes aimed at people, was no fool.

CHAPTER
TWENTY-ONE

The next day Ty showed up again at Cream or Sugar. And the next. The number of female customers who frequented the bakery between the hours of 11 a.m. and 2:45 p.m. began to skyrocket. Tawny, who'd acquired a sudden love for chocolate chip cookies, was among them.

Without Celia's blessing or permission, a pattern established itself. Ty arrived at Cream or Sugar two or three hours after Celia did, depending on his physical therapy schedule. He left in time to collect Addie from school. During their time together at the shop, he made Celia laugh, he made her want to throw herself into his arms, he made her want to pull her hair out.

Every rare once in a while she'd glance at Ty and catch him staring at her. Staring at her with such hungry intensity that her body would flare with heat. Then she'd blink, and he'd turn away to answer a customer's question, and she'd convince herself—or *almost* convince herself—that she'd imagined it.

He even came to Cream or Sugar on Saturday. Celia
had regretted her need to work on Saturdays for Addie's
sake. As it happened, though, Addie had a ball at the
shop. Ty pulled a stool in front of the cash register for her
to stand on, then taught her how to ring up customers.
Addie peered at everyone in her solemn way, bloomed
under their praise, and somberly smoothed the dollar
bills before placing them carefully in their slots in the
cash register's drawer.

Celia sank into an auditorium seat for her second
Sunday worship at Meg and Bo's church feeling oddly
worried and hopeful at the same time. All week long bits
and pieces of last week's sermon had stitched through
her memory, reminding her of the grace that waited . . .
that refused to go away.

This time around she half expected Doogie Howser
to preach a sermon that would make her feel terrible and
unworthy. It would almost come as a relief, in a way, if that
happened. She could write off last week's message as an
anomaly and go about her life, content that she'd come
to the right conclusion about Christianity the first time.

But no.

Meg and Bo's pastor spoke again of God's love. He
talked about his Savior with such simply spoken passion and gratitude that a lump of emotion formed in
Celia's chest.

"Princess Jasmine is, as we know, very benevolent."
Mother and daughter were curled up in Addie's bed.

Sunday night dimness enfolded them, softened by the pink glow of the princess night-light. "After her marriage to Aladdin, she decided not to sit around on her royal rump."

Predictably, Addie giggled. Five-year-olds could be counted on to laugh at silly words for body parts.

"There's not much career satisfaction in sitting around. A woman can only eat bonbons and shine her jewels so much, right?"

"Right," Addie replied loyally.

"You see, Jasmine had noticed that there wasn't as much access to clean water out in the desert as she would have liked. This bothered the princess, because she wasn't only about beauty and wearing skimpy *I Dream of Jeannie* clothes—"

"Huh?"

"Sorry, over-your-head reference. Jasmine was independent and didn't have to wait around for a man to come and fix the situation with the water. No, indeed. She gathered together a group of like-minded volunteers, and they dug wells so that everyone could stay hydrated."

"After digging wells did Jasmine go to a ball?" Addie looked at Celia hopefully.

"After she'd completed a hundred wells, a sultan from a neighboring province threw a ball in her honor." As Celia detailed the dresses, the tiaras, and the ladies' pointed slippers, Addie's eyelids grew weightier.

At length, Celia's words drifted to silence. Ordinarily she tiptoed out at this point and went to work straightening the house or catching up on email or folding laundry. Tonight, though, she carefully rested her head next to Addie's.

The two of them were safe here in their little house. She still had debts to get out from under, and her relationship—or non-relationship—with Ty constantly unsettled her. So much so that insomnia continued to wake her one or two mornings a week. Neill and her other neighbors had the baked goods to prove it.

Even so, she'd managed to achieve a secure environment for her child. The chamomile tea bags sat on their pantry shelf, unneeded, because Addie's acid reflux hadn't flared up once since arriving in Texas. Celia had assumed the reflux had to do with Addie's physical body. Now it looked as if it might have had more to do with Addie's mental health and the worry she'd lived with back in Corvallis. A shaming thought. Celia had tried so hard to protect Addie from the pressures and financial concerns she'd faced. But kids were smart. They picked up on what went unsaid.

Here in Holley they had Uncle Danny, the entire Porter family, and Ty behind them. She had a job.

"'*Every good and perfect gift*,'" the pastor had read at church today, "'*is from above*.'"

It boggled Celia's mind to think about that kind of love, a love so personal that it had given her all the surprising new blessings she'd just counted.

Celia unstuck a strand of hair from Addie's temple and swept it behind her ear. She couldn't seem to rationalize that kind of love away. Couldn't find fault with it. Couldn't stop longing for it. The girl who'd moved every few years during her childhood wanted a place to belong within the heart of God.

Should we give it one more try, God? You and me?

Padding silently from Addie's room on bare feet, Celia

went to her bedroom and rummaged through her book collection until she found her old Bible. She'd had it since she was a kid and had refused to part with it, despite the fact she hadn't opened it in ages.

She sat cross-legged on her periwinkle-blue rug, wearing her sleep cami and cotton shorts. The curtains blocked out the world beyond. The quiet of her aloneness hovered like a heavy fog.

Gently, she opened the book and paged through. She occasionally stopped to read passages she'd highlighted during her teenage years. Some verses spoke of perseverance. Some hope. All spoke of a faithful God.

After a time, she closed the Bible and simply held it clasped between her hands. She bent her head over it.

She had everything she'd thought she wanted. A healthy, happy daughter. A home, a job at a bakery, the ability to pay her bills. And still, the yawning hole within her remained. The void within her was larger than any mortal person could satisfy.

I . . . I think I misunderstood everything about you all those years ago. I was wrong, and I'm to blame. I've been full, completely full, of mistakes. I'm so sorry. Tears matted her eyelashes and slid slowly down her cheeks. *Thank you for giving me Addie even when I asked you not to. I didn't know then how much I'd love and treasure her.* Raggedly, she begged God for His forgiveness.

The more she basked in the presence of the kind of love that would exchange Jesus' perfect life for the disarray she'd made of her own life—the more the hole within her began to fill.

God loved her. It made no sense that He should. But He did.

He loved her with a pursuing love that she could scarcely comprehend. Her mistakes had been paid for. Miracle of miracles, they'd been paid for. And now she needed only to have faith in Him and accept the waterfall of His grace.

Ty sat in his home office the next morning. He'd pulled down the shades because the room's dimness suited his state of mind.

He knew very well that he couldn't have Celia. He didn't deserve her, and it wouldn't be good for her or for Addie. So, no. He could not have her. The truth of it was like a stew he simmered in all day and all night long.

The person he couldn't charm, kiss, touch, or call cute was the person he was married to, for pity's sake. He wasn't such a dumb jock that he didn't know about irony. His situation was ironic, but not the least bit funny. It put him in a bad mood whenever he was alone, and this morning it had given him a headache, too.

Howard Sanders wasn't helping.

Ty frowned at his ringing phone, which showed Howard as the incoming caller. Irritated, he silenced his phone and returned his attention to the computer. For one week straight, since he and Jim had walked Jim's land together, Howard had been calling him. Twice, Howard had come by Ty's house to complain in person.

Ty clicked to a new website screen and tried to focus. He'd been working on his stocks all morning, killing time before a session of swimming, weight lifting, and physical therapy. It was downright humiliating that he'd been reduced to swimming. Everybody knew that cowboys didn't swim, except what was needed for skinny-dipping or to get from your boat to your water skis. However, his choices were either swim or sit on his butt. And he just couldn't handle any more sitting. Especially in the mornings, when he itched to get to the only part of the day he cared about: the hours with Celia at Cream or Sugar and the time with Addie afterward.

From the corner of his eye, he saw his phone screen go dark. Then immediately relight. Another incoming call from Howard.

So far Howard had made five bids for Jim's land. Each time, Ty had counter-offered for more. They'd gone back and forth like this, driving up the price of Jim's property.

When Jim had contacted Ty an hour ago to say that Howard had raised his offer yet again, Ty had lost patience. He'd offered Jim a hundred grand above the current asking price.

He was pretty certain that amount had shut Howard's wallet for good. Apparently, though, it hadn't shut Howard's mouth. Ty wasn't sure anything could. Jim's land had belonged to the Sanders family since the annexation of Texas right up until Howard's father had been forced to sell it off during the Depression.

Ty understood Howard's drive to reclaim the property. Ties to land and family ran deep for Texans. At the same time, Ty wanted to start some of his own history on Jim's acres. Howard didn't have to like it. Jim was honor bound to sell the land to the man with the most money, and in this bidding war, that was him.

Thirty minutes later, Ty's phone illuminated again. This time Jim's name filled its screen. "Hi, Jim."

"Well, Ty . . ." Pleasure was evident in the man's

voice. "It looks like you finally hit on an amount above Howard's budget."

Ty leaned back in his leather desk chair, gazing at the ceiling. "It took some doing."

"Howard is *angry*."

"I'll just bet."

"But Marjorie and I are very pleased. We'd like to accept your offer."

Ty smiled, satisfaction rising. "Excellent."

Celia arrived at Cream or Sugar bearing gifts. Namely, a platter of pumpkin muffins with streusel topping. She found Jerry in the kitchen, calmly mixing as usual. "Good morning."

His brown eyes warmed and his reddish Hulk mustache pulled up on one side. "Morning, Celia."

"Muffin?"

He rubbed his palms on his apron, selected a muffin, and tried a bite. "Delicious," he pronounced.

"Thank you."

"If you want to serve this sort of thing here in the shop, though, I'm not the one you have to convince." He tipped his head toward the front of the building, sympathy in his expression.

She nodded and straightened her shoulders. "Wish me luck."

"You're going to need it."

She carried the platter to where Donetta sat on her customary stool near the register, reading the sports pages of the *Dallas Morning News*. Donetta's face lifted at Celia's approach.

"Morning! Would you care for a—"

"Muffin?" Donetta finished. The older woman was the worst interrupter Celia had ever met. Eying the muffins critically, Donetta took one and bit into it.

Celia held her breath.

"It's good," Donetta allowed. More chewing, then an arched look. "What's your recipe?"

Celia rattled it off. "And once I have the streusel together, I—"

"Sprinkle it on top and bake. Sure, sure." Donetta ran her fingers through one side of her hair, flipping back the feathered layers. "Were you wanting to serve these here at Cream or Sugar?"

"Only if you like the idea." This shop was Donetta's roost to rule. As much as Celia loved baking, she'd only been working in an actual brick-and-mortar bakery for a week.

"We've had the same menu here for twenty years. Our customers know what to expect, so change makes me nervous." She gestured toward the square with a frown. "There used to be an ice cream shop just there, see? On the opposite corner. Some new owners came in and changed the ice cream from Blue Bell, which everybody likes around here, to gelato. After that you could have heard crickets inside that place. Two months later the new owners left town. Once they'd paid all their debts, you better believe they could fit everything they had into a Winnebago. Drove off in the thing."

Celia had discovered that it was best to nod soberly in response to one of Donetta's cautionary tales.

Donetta finished her muffin and tossed the paper wrapper in the trash.

"I wouldn't want," Celia said, "to change your menu by taking anything away. Your menu is perfect. This location is perfect. You're perfect. Have I told you lately how much I love working here?" She'd learned from Ty that Donetta did not require subtlety. Overt sucking up was preferred. Celia smiled sweetly.

"Taking a page out of Ty's book, are you?" Enjoyment creased Donetta's face. "Trying to charm me?"

"Is it working?"

"It's helping."

"Like I said, I wouldn't dare take anything off the menu. I just thought it might be fun to add a few new things, maybe offer some seasonal items for fall." Assuming fall ever reached north Texas.

"The problem's financial, honey." Brackets formed on either side of Donetta's lips. "Right now I know just what ingredients I need and how much. I know what I'll sell. I can't afford to spend a penny more on anything new or different."

Much like a pie, Donetta's personality had both sweetness and crustiness to it. Celia nodded and tried not to let her shoulders slump. "I understand."

"Let's go ahead and put these out, though." Donetta lifted the plate from Celia and set it where customers could reach it. "We can cut these up and offer them as samples like they do at those city Starbucks. Folks might get a kick out of that."

As Celia returned to the kitchen and the sanctuary of Jerry's company, she narrowed her eyes with determination.

Donetta had won the battle. But Celia had her sights set on the war.

What if Ty had crashed his truck? That would explain his lateness.

It was Thursday, three days after Celia's doomed attempt to ply Donetta with muffins. Ty always arrived at Cream or Sugar between eleven and twelve. It was 12:20. No Ty.

She waited on customers while chewing the edge of her lip. Ty did not technically work here. He just volunteered. Maybe he was playing golf or taking a nap or having a romantic lunch with Tawny. Hadn't Celia tried to convince him that she didn't want him coming to Cream or Sugar at all? So why did his lateness worry her?

It worried her because he'd told her he'd prove to her that she could trust him. Every day since, he'd shown up and worked beside her here at the counter.

He might have crashed his truck. A chill dove through her at the thought. It was possible that he'd crashed it. He wasn't supposed to be driving around with his injured leg, but of course he was so stubborn that he was doing it anyway.

12:25. 12:30.

She began to pray. Since Sunday night, when she'd excavated her Bible and spent time renewing her relationship with God, she had not felt like a brand-new person. She'd felt like the same person, yet changed in important ways. Her nagging emptiness had been filled with a sense of God's nearness.

It took practice to discard all of her old ideas about religion. She'd been working to accept and re-accept His grace, to turn to Him for hope. After depending on no one but herself for so long, it didn't yet come naturally.

Her gaze returned to the window, searching. She did not see Ty.

12:35. Celia picked up her cell phone, then hesitated. What if something had gone wrong and he needed her? What if nothing had gone wrong and he'd think her love-struck for calling?

She peered out the window and—at last!—spotted him. He pulled up in front of the shop on a Harley. He wasn't wearing a helmet. Oy. As she watched, he killed the motorcycle's engine and arched his leg over the seat.

Within moments, he filled the bakery's doorway. The metal watch he sometimes wore flashed as he raised his hand to slide off his sunglasses. He grinned at her. "Hi, beautiful."

A hitch of deep affection caught at Celia's heart. She might be the dumbest girl alive. She knew for sure she was the most relieved. "Hey," she answered, casual.

He made his way around the counter, his hair mussed. "Sorry I'm late."

"I hadn't noticed."

He approached, his gaze too perceptive. "Yes you had."

"Not everyone's life revolves around you, showboat."

"I hate that nickname."

A sense of rightness filled her. Ty was safe. Her world had not come undone.

"I was late because I drove over to Lucas to watch an eighteen-year-old kid bull ride this morning. He'd called and asked if I could look over his form and give him some tips." He pulled a bottled water from the drawer near the register where Donetta kept a supply. After twisting off the top, he drained a third. "The kid's dad has built him a nice setup. He even has a chute."

"Um." Celia drew her brows together suspiciously. "You yourself did not climb on top of any bulls. Right?"

He had the sense to look chagrined.

"You climbed on top of a bull?"

"Just inside the chute. To show the kid something."

"So far this morning you've driven back and forth to the town of Lucas without a helmet on a motorcycle I've never seen before, but I assume you own."

He dipped his chin.

"And you climbed on top of a bull? A bull!" It seemed she'd had good reason to worry about him. "Even inside the chute, they bang around. You could have wrecked your knee again."

His dimple sank into his cheek. "But I didn't."

"It's not safe. If I ever see you on top of a motorcycle without a helmet again or hear about you riding a bull, I'll . . . I'll . . ."

"Go on. I'm dying to hear."

"I'll tell your mother!"

He laughed.

"I will," she insisted.

"I'm terrified," he vowed. He leaned insolently against the counter, measuring her. "I thought nagging was something wives did."

"In case you've forgotten, I am your wife. At least for the moment. So I'm entitled."

"You can nag me all you want. I like it. It means you don't want to see me get hurt." He reached out to re-arrange a curl that kept bobbing close to her right eye.

She dodged out of his reach. "No touching."

"In case you've forgotten, I'm your husband. Aren't *I* entitled?"

"You know you're not. We're—"

"Can I tell you something before you go off on a thirty-minute rant about us being respectful friends?"

She crossed her arms. "I suppose."

"Last night I signed the papers to buy Jim's property."

It took her a moment to adjust to the abrupt subject change. He'd kept her updated on the battle he'd fought to buy his neighbor's land; now his legendary determination had prevailed. "That's great, Ty." Perhaps his new career would keep him off bulls and Harleys. "Really. I'm happy for you. Congratulations."

"Thank you kindly."

"Once the deal closes, I guess you'll be busy birthing animals or galloping around on your horses or whatever it is rodeo stock people do. You won't have time to come into the shop anymore."

"Which should make you happy."

"Very happy," she lied.

He looked at her in that knowing way again, like he could see the truths she'd hidden inside.

She got snared by those dangerously beautiful eyes. This confounded chemistry between them! It had existed in Vegas. And it persisted now. Her hand ached to grab a handful of his shirt and pull—

"How about you go in the kitchen and bake something to celebrate the new land? I can handle it out here."

Humor tugged at her lips. "You can handle an empty shop?"

"Or a full one. My ladies will be coming in soon."

"True."

"I've got this, Celia. Go bake something. Everybody in Holley is talking about those pumpkin muffins you made."

"Donetta won't spend money on anything new. I can't use her ingredients."

"Then use your own. We'll put whatever you make in the display case and sell it. Donetta can't complain about making money on something that cost her nothing."

"I'm nervous! I don't want to overstep and make Donetta angry. Just between you and me, I really like this job."

"I'll protect you from Donetta. Go on."

She wavered. Ty had proven himself more than capable of running Cream or Sugar's front room. The customers loved him more than they loved her, and she loved baking more than she loved working behind the counter.

Ty, who could do no wrong in Donetta's eyes, had said he'd protect her. If he trashed every donut they had and started selling whiskey shots instead, Donetta would applaud and thank him heartily for his good judgment.

"Go." He bumped her arm with his.

Celia drove to the gingerbread house and loaded her baking supplies into her Prius. Thankfully, flour and sugar cost next to nothing, otherwise she wouldn't have been able to afford donating them. When she returned to the shop, she commandeered some empty pantry space, donned a hairnet and apron, and scrubbed her hands.

The scent of a cake baking filled the air, making Ty's stomach growl. Good grief. It smelled like edible sin.

He'd skipped lunch because he'd been running late and he'd wanted to see Celia more than he'd wanted food. "Is it almost finished?"

"Uh-huh" came her reply from the depths of the kitchen.

The mayor stopped by for his daily chocolate glazed donut. Then came a group of four female co-workers.

Most days, Ty found it hard to believe he worked in a donut shop. Thing was, he'd have done a lot worse to spend time with Celia. This job was easier than shooting fish in a barrel, and he liked talking to people. Plus, coming here gave him a reason to escape his empty house. He hated his empty house.

At the sound of footsteps, he turned to see Celia walking toward him holding a yellow one-layer cake. Thanks to the hairnet she'd probably just removed, her curls were messy and made her look like she'd rolled out of bed after a long night in the sack. He caught a whiff of vanilla.

As fierce as Celia was, Ty had learned to read her face. Right now he saw pride and vulnerability both, and the sight caused something within him to burn with tenderness. He cared for Celia way more than he'd planned to care, which was straight-up painful and pointless. He cleared his throat. "What kind of cake is this?"

"Brown butter cake."

He reached for two paper plates and plastic forks. "We get the first two servings, right?"

"Right." She set down the cake and carefully sliced it.

He never wanted her to discover that he was paying part of her salary. Just the thought made him uneasy, because he knew how much stock she put in her belief that she'd succeeded at Cream or Sugar without his help.

"In celebration of your new land." She handed him his plate.

"Our new land."

"*Your* new land—"

"That I'd like to share with you if you'll let me."

"How about we eat?" They stood facing each other, taking their first bites at the same time.

Warm cake melted like a river of sweet butter in Ty's mouth, so good it almost blew his head off. He swallowed. "You're extremely attractive to me in this moment."

"That's the cake talking."

"You're ruthless. You know exactly what you're doing to me, but you don't have any pity."

Even though she shook her head over his nonsense, he could see her delight.

"You're a genius, Celia. Like the Mozart of cake."

"No!"

"You are. You're incredible. Can I have your autograph?" He was trying to decide how to trap her against the bakery display case and make out with her when an elderly couple entered the shop. They approached the counter, moving slower than pond water.

"I'm going to sweet-talk these two," Ty whispered, "into buying this."

"Don't oversell it. They might try it and hate it."

"Not a chance."

It only took him thirty seconds to convince the couple to buy Celia's cake, and that was because he spent the first twenty-five seconds asking them about their day.

In no time, he had them seated at a table with coffees and slices of cake.

He found Celia hiding behind the cookie display. He took hold of her hand, his grip strong and secure. These were the first strangers to ever pay for her cooking, and he knew that she desperately wanted them to like it.

The old folks finally managed to get cake into their mouths. While they chewed, which seemed to take an hour, nervousness crept over Ty, tightening his muscles. He'd ridden bulls for eight years, almost lost his life a dozen times, and *now* he was nervous.

"Well?" Ty asked them. "What do you think? Was I right?"

The husband turned to face them. "You were right. This cake is wonderful. *Wonderful*. Dear?"

His wife nodded, patting her lips with her napkin. "Oh my, yes. This reminds me of a cake my mother made when I was a girl. I never thought to taste anything like it again."

"Glad to hear it." He squeezed Celia's hand to draw her attention. She was so close he could see the spiky ends of her eyelashes. "Looks like this is a good day for both of us. They love your cake."

"Wow," she murmured. "They love my cake."

They loved my cake! Celia thought while cleaning Cream or Sugar's kitchen. She kept replaying the moment when that adorable old couple had called it wonderful. They, and all the customers that had eaten it after them, had loved it. It seemed too good to be true. She'd crafted the recipe herself, poured every drop of knowledge and instinct she had into it.

They loved my cake. The validation sang through her like a cool breeze while she locked up the shop. After all her years of undiverted concentration on Addie, she had something new to call her own. Baking was *her* thing, her great passion.

They loved my cake, she marveled while driving toward the gingerbread house, filled with gratitude. Before Ty's reentry into her life, she'd been a cafeteria administration lady. Now she was a house-owning, Prius-driving pastry chef.

CHAPTER

TWENTY-TWO

Early the next afternoon, Celia's cell phone rang right as she was sliding a batch of apricot muffins into the oven. Same as yesterday, Ty had insisted on watching the front so that she could bake. She bumped the oven door closed with her elbow, wedged her phone against her ear, and went to work wiping down the counter. "Hi, Uncle Danny. How are you?"

"Not very well."

At the listless tone of his voice, she straightened. "What's happened?"

"Remember Betty?"

"The one you met online?"

"Right, right. The one who lives in Hugo, Oklahoma."

"I remember."

"Well, I drove up to see her. We're not a love connection"—it sounded like he was cupping his hand over the phone—"but we were having a nice time anyway. We went to the movies last night and as we were leaving the theater I slipped on a step and fell."

"What? Are you all right?"

"I fractured my pelvis."

Her heart thudded at the news. "Oh no."

"Can you believe it? I was just mountain biking in Moab! And now I've been brought low by a stairstep. A stairstep, C."

"I'm so sorry."

"Surfers are birds that are meant to fly free, you know? We're not meant to be grounded."

"Where are you now?"

"I'm at Betty's house. I couldn't go back to the hotel after they released me from the hospital because I can't walk. All I can do is lie in bed. Betty's been a trooper, but this situation is *so* not cool."

"I'm leaving right now." She folded her towel and stripped off her hairnet. "I'll come and get you and bring you home."

"I'm not sure I'm up for the drive."

"It'll be fine."

"I don't know . . ."

"Can you text me Betty's address?"

"Yes."

"I'm on my way." She peeled off her apron and grabbed her purse. Just as she reached the back door, she remembered that she couldn't leave Cream or Sugar without notifying Ty and asking for his help. She hurried to the front and found him dropping a few quarters into the outstretched hand of Tawny Bettenfield.

Tawny looked over at her. "Hi, Celia."

"Hi."

Tawny wore a pencil skirt, a sleeveless silk top, and a chunky pale blue necklace. Sleek dark hair cascaded down her back. Why, oh why, did Tawny's place of employment have to be located on the square? The proximity made it far too easy for her to visit Ty.

"What's with the purse?" Ty regarded Celia with worry.

"I'll tell you in a minute."

Tawny smiled at Celia, then at Ty. By the looks of it, she'd purchased her usual chocolate chip cookie. Celia suspected that Tawny had never actually eaten a single cookie. The cookies were simply a cheap and dependable way to gain access to Ty.

Tawny tipped a finger back and forth between herself and Ty. "We were just laughing about the time we tried to catch crawfish in fifth grade."

Celia nodded stiffly.

Tawny detailed the crawfish story, then explained to Celia that many people in Holley held crawfish boils in March.

Celia urgently needed to hit the road so that she could rescue Uncle Danny, but she wasn't about to leave Ty alone with this woman. Tawny never treated Celia with anything other than friendliness. Yet Celia *knew*, down low at gut level, that Tawny was not to be trusted and was most definitely not her friend. She waited through the story, fussing with her cuticles.

"Well." Tawny aimed a breezy look of camaraderie at Ty. "I'd better head back to work." She lifted her white paper sack a few inches. "Can't wait for my daily treat."

The moment the door shut behind Tawny, Celia addressed Ty. "Uncle Danny's in Hugo, Oklahoma, and he just called to tell me that he's fractured his pelvis."

His forehead furrowed. "Is he okay?"

"As okay as he can be, I guess."

"Why is he in Hugo?"

"To meet one of his Internet love interests."

Ty whistled under his breath.

"I'm going to drive there and bring him home."

"I'll take you."

"Thank you for offering, but I can't leave unless you're able to cover for me here, then pick Addie up from school and keep her until I get home. Can—I know it's a lot to ask. But can you do that for me?"

"Sure, but—"

"I'll check in with you once I'm on the road." She started toward the back door, Ty limping behind her. "Oh, and when the timer goes off, will you take the muffins out of the oven?"

"Yeah."

"I don't know if Donetta will want us to close the shop early today or if she'll want to come back in and relieve you so you can get Addie from school on time."

"Don't worry about it. I'll speak with Donetta, and we'll take care of it."

She pushed through the back door and hurried down the steps.

He kept pace, propping his hand on the roof of the Prius as she scooted into the driver's seat. "Celia, if you'll slow down, I'll work everything out so that I can come with you. I want to come with you. Let me drive you there."

"No, no, it's fine. It's just two hours away. If you'll take care of the shop and Addie for me, that's more than enough. Thank you. I appreciate the help."

Reluctantly, he stepped back so she could close her door. She reversed from her parking spot. He'd raised a hand to shield his eyes. The motion had caused the hem of his T-shirt to ride up on one side, revealing a glimpse of lean abs. Oh boy. Even frowning, he was illegally sexy.

She put the Prius in drive and pulled onto the road.

A plump woman wearing a Hawaiian muumuu and a brown bowl haircut answered Celia's knock.

"Betty?"

"Yes, and you must be Celia."

"I am."

"Come on in." Betty, who looked to be the same general age as Danny, issued Celia into a musty foyer. "Your poor uncle took a fall."

"I heard."

"He's right over here." Betty led the way into a living room reminiscent of *Hoarders*. Stacks of old magazines lined every wall, some stacks reaching the ceiling, others leaning precariously. Two long-haired cats covered the dark green sofa, collectible knickknacks filled the side table, and a pile of sweaters had buried one of the two chairs. In the middle of it all sat a rollaway twin bed, which had been elevated at the head by more magazines. Uncle Danny lay on it, snoring softly, clothed in nothing more than a shark tooth necklace and a pair of plaid boxers.

"Here he is," Betty pointed out, in case Celia hadn't noticed.

Celia felt her cheeks heat as she took in an eyeful of the nut-brown skin of Danny's chest, arms, and legs. Modesty had never been Uncle Danny's strongest virtue.

"Have a seat." Betty spoke softly, in deference to the sleeping patient. She indicated the one open chair, and Celia sat. Betty took to the sofa alongside the cats, which put nearly naked Danny smack in between them.

"Your uncle's had a hard, hard time since the accident last night."

He didn't appear to be having too hard a time at the moment.

"He fell on a step and *crack*, he fractured his pelvis like a wishbone."

There was only one way to look at Betty—across Danny's bare abdomen. "I'm terribly sorry that this happened." Celia valiantly tried to ignore the abdomen. "Especially while he was here visiting you."

"Do you think he's all right? He's been sleeping a lot."

"I assume he's fine."

"They've heavily dosed him with medications, so maybe that's why. I just don't know." She pressed her lips together, her attention combing Danny's form. "I'm worried. I don't want him slipping into a coma or something."

"I'm pretty sure he's fine." Celia hadn't anticipated arriving here and finding him asleep. What protocol applied when retrieving an injured uncle from an Internet date gone wrong? Did you immediately wake the uncle and usher him to your car? Or did regular rules for napping apply? "Maybe I should wake him? So that the two of us can be on our way."

"You were hoping to leave *today*?" Betty shook her head. "I don't think he'll be able to travel so soon."

"Did the doctors give you instructions when they released him?"

Betty lifted a cat and pulled a few papers from underneath the animal. She handed the stapled sheets across Danny's legs to Celia. While Betty relayed in doomsday tones what the doctors had told her, Celia scanned the information. Danny needed rest and immobility so that the pelvis could knit back together. "Did the doctors say anything about surgery?"

"They said it's not necessary. The pelvis will heal itself in time. He's pretty bad off right at the moment, though. Oh dear." Betty's spine straightened with a joint pop. "Did he stop breathing?"

Alarm spiking, Celia jerked her gaze to Danny. He only gurgled, shifted his face to another angle, and resumed snoring. Both women watched him, Betty with a fretful expression, Celia balancing the hospital papers on her knees. She was afraid to relax any deeper into the chair. It smelled like a mixture of mothball and yogurt.

Betty started hiccuping. "Sorry. I have a recurring case."

"No problem."

They smiled with strained pleasantry at each other.

Danny released a honking, shuddering snore.

"Perhaps . . . perhaps we could cover him with a blanket?" Celia suggested.

"Oh, believe me," Betty answered with feeling. "*I tried.*"

"Well." Celia looked at her watch. "I'd best wake him up so that we can get on the road." Gently she shook his shoulder. "Uncle Danny? Uncle Danny?"

It took some doing, but he came around.

"Hey," he wheezed. He'd been soaking in so much

Texas sun that the whites of his eyes appeared almost neon against his tanned skin. "You're here."

"I'm here."

His hand fumbled for hers, and she grabbed it, squeezing warmly. She hadn't forgotten all the times he'd been there for her when no one else had been.

"I don't think I'm going to be able to go on a ride with Addie today."

She smiled. "No. The only thing you're going to be doing today is driving back to Holley with me."

He winced. "I don't know about that, C. Don't think I can handle the drive today. My pelvis, like, seriously hurts. Bad."

Celia made sympathetic noises. Inwardly, though, his words concerned her. She could not leave him here, yet the two of them couldn't stay here overnight. If she'd had a dust allergy, she'd be dead already. More important, she had a daughter back in Holley. She'd never left Addie for a whole night with anyone. Not once.

Danny rolled his head toward Betty. "Hey there, Betty."

"Hello, Danny."

"Is it time for another dose of painkillers?"

Betty and Celia consulted, checked his prescription, and determined he was due for more pills.

"Just a sip," Celia said as she held a glass of water to his mouth so he could drink down the meds. God help them all if he tanked up on water and needed to use the restroom.

Betty excused herself and went to click computer keys in a nearby room. Celia spent the next twenty minutes doing her best to cajole Danny into driving home. He was woozy and kind, but he was also terrified of moving . . . anywhere. He insisted that he couldn't make the trip. After a time, his eyes grew heavy, and he resumed the snoring, gurgling, and leg twitching thing.

Celia perched on the edge of her chair, watching one TV show after another while Danny slept, wondering how in the world she was going to get Danny home.

Gradually, the sky darkened. Shadows stretched across the living room, elongating with Celia's worries. She turned on a lamp. The cats prowled the house, eying Celia with suspicion.

In all the years she'd known him, Celia had never had to force Uncle Danny to do anything. Was she really going to have to override his pain and his wishes in order to somehow carry him? wheel him? drag him? to her Prius—

A quiet rapping came from the window behind her.

Startled, Celia turned toward the sound.

On the other side of the glass, silhouetted by bands of orange and pink sunset, stood Ty. The slow smile he gave her was just about the most beautiful thing Celia had ever seen.

He wore the same white Dallas Mavericks T-shirt and jeans he'd had on earlier, but he might as well have been wearing a superhero's red cape.

Celia hurried to the door. "Addie?"

"Is doing great. My mom and dad are with her at your house."

"I thought I told you not to come."

"With you I've learned it's best to act first and ask permission second."

"In this case I'll forgive you, because I'm really, really glad to see you."

"Come 'ere." He took her into his arms and hugged her tightly. She placed her cheek against his chest and hugged him back. She was in terrible trouble, because his hug felt to her like what she imagined a *real* husband's hug would feel like. Reassuring, warm, endlessly strong. More achingly tempting to Celia than even The Kiss had been.

CHAPTER

TWENTY-THREE

In the magical way he had, Ty made everything better. He strode into the living room, took in the situation with one sweeping glance, then gave Celia a look that caused her to laugh so hard that tears overran her eyes.

"Rotten luck," he said, when she'd finally gotten herself under control. "Both the men in your life injured in the same summer."

"As if *you're* one of the men in my life. Conceited as ever."

"I feel sorry for Danny. You're not much of a nurse."

"I beg your pardon! I'm a perfectly good nurse."

"You flushed my Vicodin down the toilet."

"Your Vicodin deserved to be flushed down the toilet!"

Betty shuffled into the living room, and Ty broke all land and speed records at winning her undying devotion.

He made a trip to Danny's hotel to pay the bill and bring back Danny's suitcase. Then, when Betty refused to let him buy take-out dinner for them all, Ty set the table, filled their drinks, and transported Betty's tuna casserole into the dining room as if he were carrying Cleopatra on a litter.

Danny didn't feel up to joining them for the meal. Nonetheless, Ty convinced him to don a shirt and settled the older man at the table on a chair they'd padded with a comforter. "How you doing?" Ty's big hand kept a grip on Danny's shoulder, steadying him. "All right?"

"Hanging in there, Ty."

"Can I do anything to make your chair more comfortable?"

Danny shook his head, face bleak with the discomfort Celia knew he must be suffering.

Betty started hiccuping.

Ty placed a paper napkin in Danny's lap. "I'd really like to see you eat something, man. Can you do that for me?"

"I don't know. Stomach's not too steady at the moment."

"Just give it a try."

Then the four of them—the-marriage-in-name-only couple and the reason-why-you-shouldn't-date-online couple—started in on the food.

As grateful as Celia was for the above-and-beyond generosity Betty had shown them all, she had a hard time getting the tuna casserole down. It was not good. Or maybe even edible.

Halfway through dinner Danny began to nod off again, his upper body slumping forward. With his bull rider's fast reflexes, Ty shot a hand out and caught Danny in the chest before he could land facedown in his food. Carefully, he propped Danny up. Danny's breath snicked, then fell into a snoring pattern now familiar to them all.

Ty resumed his own seat. "So, Betty?"

"Yes?"

"How are you feeling about your date with Rip Van Winkle here?" He nodded at Danny. "Best date ever?"

Celia burst out laughing.

Betty giggled into her napkin. "Maybe the most memorable."

"Tell it to me straight," Ty said. "You want to marry Danny, don't you?"

Celia had to hand it to him. He was irredeemable, but in the best possible way.

Another round of giggles from Betty. "No, Ty. I don't want to marry him."

Snore snore snore.

"You sure? Consider the advantages, Betty: He's laid back. Not difficult to entertain."

Betty shook her head, her ample cheeks pink with amusement.

"It seems," Celia said to Ty, "that the old broken pelvis routine has failed to win Betty's heart."

"Poor guy, missing out on a lady as pretty as Betty."

Betty looked back and forth between them. "How did you two say you know each other?"

"We're friends," Celia answered, "from long ago."

"You're not dating one another?"

"No," Celia answered quickly. Ty said nothing.

"Do you have a boyfriend?" Betty asked Celia.

She shifted uneasily. "I don't."

"What about you, Ty? Do you have a girlfriend?"

Blue eyes blazed as he looked across the table at Celia. "I'd like to have one."

In the awkward silence Celia could hear a cat under the table, rhythmically cleaning its fur.

Betty angled herself toward Celia. "I happen to know a few nice young men your age."

Celia set down her fork and placed her hands in her lap. "You do?"

"One's a friend's son. He owns the mechanic shop."

Behind Betty, Ty caught Celia's gaze and shook his head with threatening slowness.

"And then there's the new high school principal. He's divorced with seven kids, but all the kids live in Alabama with their mother."

No, Ty mouthed.

"He sounds . . . interesting."

No! Ty mouthed.

"You're very pretty, and your uncle had nothing but good things to say about you. You'll have no problem finding someone special. If you'd like me to call either of the men I just mentioned, let me know."

"I still don't think Danny will agree to leave," Betty said.

Celia and Ty had helped clean the kitchen. They'd loaded Danny's stuff in the trunk of the Prius and prepared its passenger seat by reclining it to a hospital bed angle and placing borrowed pillows along its length.

"Oh, he'll agree," Ty said. "Celia, do you want to get the car's air conditioner going?"

"Sure." She and Ty spent some time thanking Betty, then Celia walked from the house to the car and cranked the cold air. Peering through the front windshield, she waited.

After a few minutes, Ty emerged from Betty's house carrying Uncle Danny in his arms. She could tell by Ty's face that he was saying something joking to distract Danny, who had his jaw clenched. Ty had shattered his leg this past summer. He still wore a brace beneath his jeans. There was no way he should be carrying something as heavy as Danny. Yet he wasn't even hurrying. He was moving with utter care to make sure he didn't jolt her uncle.

Something inside Celia's chest dropped with a hollow thump as realization expanded within her. Oh, God. Bo had been right about Ty, hadn't he? Ty had never been the villain she'd wanted him to be. He had honor. He was a tarnished knight, yes, but he *was* a knight. He'd come to Hugo to rescue her. He was carrying her uncle. And she suspected that he had been faithful to her all the years of their marriage.

She ran around to open the passenger-side door. Ty laid Danny on the seat and Celia did what she could, repositioning his pillows, buckling his seat belt for him. She sensed that she ought to say something encouraging to Danny, but her revelation had cleaved her in half. All she managed was a pat on his hand.

She and Ty circled to the driver's side. "I'm driving you guys home, sweet one."

She paused. "But you have your truck."

"We have Danny's car, too. It's parked in the hotel lot."

"Oh. Right."

"I'll get my family to come back with me tomorrow. We'll return Betty's pillows and drive the other cars back to Holley."

"That's a lot of trouble."

"Nah, we're Texans. We like driving our trucks on two-lane roads with nothing to look at but fields."

Since she had no better plan, she climbed into the backseat behind Ty and next to Danny's laid-out upper torso.

"Man, this car is small." Ty slid the driver's seat back until it touched her kneecaps. "Is this a Hot Wheel?"

When he flicked on the car's headlights, they illuminated Betty and her breeze-stirred muumuu. She stood on her porch waving, and her two cats frowned at them through the living room window as they pulled away.

Ty glanced across at Danny. "I'm going to drive really carefully. Just relax, and we'll be there in no time."

"'Kay."

"What kind of music would you like?"

"Got any Beach Boys?"

"Yep." Ty pulled a CD case of the Beach Boys' greatest hits from the door pocket.

"Where did that come from?" Celia asked.

Ty slid the CD into the player. "When I was at the hotel earlier to get your stuff, Danny, I checked your car. Figured some music might help the drive go by faster."

The wistful strains of "Surfer Girl" filled the interior.

"Dude," Danny breathed gratefully. "That's righteous of you, brother."

Hugo was so small that before Celia had buckled her seat belt, they were out of it. Ten minutes after that, and right at the tail end of "Kokomo," Danny conked out again.

"What are your plans for Danny once we reach Holley?" Ty asked. "We can't take him to his place. He needs care."

"I was thinking I'd take him to my house."

"And put him where?"

"In Addie's room? Addie can move in with me."

"But you work. You'll be gone most of the day."

Celia swallowed. He had a point.

"I told my mom what happened with Danny. She wants him to stay with them while he's recovering. She and Danny are buddies."

"Ty! They haven't even known each other a month."

"But he's family, and my parents have empty bedrooms at their place. What do you say?"

"It's up to Danny."

"Danny will want to stay with my folks." He raised his phone and hit speed dial. "My mom's a great caregiver. Perfect mix of tough love and sweetness."

Celia tried to protest again, but he was already talking to his mom. His Texas accent filled the car, punctuated by a low laugh at something Nancy had said. When he looked across to check on Danny again, she could see the masculine lines of his profile and the definition in the forearm that held his cell phone.

He clicked off. "It's all set."

"Ty, are you sure? That seems like a lot to ask of your mom."

"I'm sure."

"Okay. Thank you."

Celia sat in the dark of the backseat watching Oklahoma give way to Texas, her mind whirling. A knight, indeed. Things that had always mystified her about Ty began to slide into place.

"You're quiet." Ty met her gaze in the rearview mirror.

"I'm thinking."

"About?"

"You." As his attention returned to the road, she considered him. "I'm going to ask you something, and I want you to be completely honest with me."

He waited, his head angled slightly in question.

"You haven't been with any other women since Las Vegas, have you?"

He said nothing. The heavy quiet said a million things.

"You don't have to confirm it," Celia said. "I can see now that it's true. Which makes me ask myself *why*. Why would you remain faithful to me after a relationship that lasted less than a week and a spur-of-the-moment wedding? I never expected you to be faithful. In fact, I assumed you hadn't been."

"Marriage means something to me, Celia. I made a promise to you in front of God. My parents have been married a long time. My grandparents all stayed married until their deaths."

"All right, but that doesn't fully explain why you were faithful, does it? There's more." The car's engine hummed. Cars going the opposite direction whizzed by, their headlights sending flashes of illumination through the interior of the Prius, there and gone.

"Look," he said. "As much as I love spilling my guts, can we have this conversation another time? Your uncle's lying right beside me."

Celia raised her voice a notch. "Danny?" No response. "He's out, Ty. He can't hear us."

Ty grunted with frustration.

"I never understood why you didn't divorce me. Year after year went by, and you never contacted me."

"I finally did."

"But why so long? You'd decided to steer clear of other

women. So why didn't you suffer through, I don't know, just a year of abstinence? Then you could have divorced me and gone back to living your life. A year would have been long enough to give a respectful nod to the institution of marriage. Instead you waited five and a half."

He exhaled roughly. "I'd rather talk about anything else." He pushed a hand between the back of his head and his seat. His fingers curled into his hair near the cords of his neck.

It was like that game people played—when you drew close to the thing you were searching for and the leader said, *Hotter, you're getting hotter.* Well, Celia believed she was getting very hot. Closer to the truth than she'd ever been. "I think you waited so long because you were punishing yourself. It took you that long to feel that you'd punished yourself enough."

Silence.

"C'mon, Ty. Blunt honesty. It's just you, me, and the Beach Boys."

A long pause. "You're not a hundred percent wrong," he said.

No. She was a hundred percent right. All this time, the guy who'd seemed like the quintessential devil-may-care lady's man had been punishing himself for what he'd done to Tawny and to her in Las Vegas.

She angled herself so she could glimpse more of his face in the mirror. He was scowling out the front windshield with features that may as well have been carved from stone. Shadows pooled beneath his cheekbones.

"What happened in Vegas rocked you, didn't it? Because you were, and are, good-hearted."

"No," he said flatly. "I'm not."

"Yes. You are." *"I'm no good,"* she remembered him saying to her the day she'd arrived in Texas. And the day they had snow cones, *"I'm not to be trusted."* At this point it royally offended her—the girl who'd been trying to assure herself of his mean-heartedness for years—that he'd try to confess mean-heartedness to her now. "The gifts are all part of it, too, aren't they?" She thought back, cataloguing them in her brain. "You brought me my bracelet when I dropped it. Then you jumped at the chance to buy this Prius. You purchased us a house and added us to your insurance. You even tried to convince me to accept credit cards. You felt guilty, and the gifts were all part of your penance."

"Good grief," he growled. "You're making me sound like a wuss."

"You're not a wuss. And you're not a criminal. On the other hand, you're not a saint."

"No."

"You did break my heart in Vegas."

At least a mile went by before he spoke. "I know."

"But until now, I didn't fully understand that you were sorry."

"I told you I was sorry at lunch that day in Corvallis."

"I didn't realize then *how* sorry."

"Can we talk about something else? Anything? My funeral plans? Cancer?" He gestured toward Danny. "Your uncle is literally lying *right here*."

"Okay." She took a breath. "But first I want you to know that I'm sorry, too. I'm sorry that I didn't tell you about Addie when I found out that I was pregnant."

Her words swirled and sank around them. At length, he nodded. "So it's agreed. We're both sorry?"

"Yes."

"Can you ever trust me again?"

Oh my. That was like asking her to jump across a river. A leap too far to dare. "I don't know. It's going to take time."

His steely gaze flicked to the rearview mirror. She read physical desire there, as well as unflinching determination. "I've got time."

CHAPTER

TWENTY-FOUR

The next morning, Saturday, Celia fiddled with Cream or Sugar's display until she'd positioned each donut and cookie to its best advantage. "I think I might go into the kitchen and make something," she said to Addie as she slid shut the door to the case. It was near eleven, and they'd hit a lull in business. Plus, Celia had been craving walnut tea bread. "Will you be fine out here?"

"Yes." Addie stood tall on her stool and settled her palms on either side of her beloved cash register.

"Call me when someone comes in, okay? I'll help you."

"Sure, Mom."

Celia made her way into the kitchen and turned her concentration to achieving just the right blend of flour, baking powder, baking soda, and cream of tartar. Twice, customers arrived. Celia went to assist Addie, then washed her hands and got back to baking.

She stilled when she heard the shop's door open a third time.

"You don't have to come out," Addie called back to her. "It's Daddy."

Sure enough. She recognized both the bass rumble of Ty's voice and the telltale cascade of tingles that started at the top of her neck and swirled like firework sparks all the way down to her pinkie toes.

When they'd arrived at Ty's parents' house last night, Nancy had been waiting to greet them. After transferring Danny to a guest bedroom, they'd gone on to Celia's, where John had been baby-sitting a sleeping Addie. Celia had said good-bye to Ty with his dad standing there, watching. It had been brief and impersonal and part of her had been glad. She'd needed space from him so she could digest all the things she hadn't known about him before. And now did.

She combined her dry and wet ingredients while listening to the muted tones of Addie and Ty's conversation and laughter. Initially, the idea of having to share her child had filled her with selfish worry. Lately, though, the help of Ty and the other Porters had begun to feel like a blessing.

Eventually, Ty strode into Cream or Sugar's kitchen wearing a black T-shirt and weathered jeans. "Good morning, my darling angel."

"I've no idea who you're referring to." Celia didn't pause in her walnut chopping, though his handsomeness affected her like champagne that had gone straight to her head.

"Addie said something about painting the shop tomorrow."

"Yes. I sucked up to Donetta so much this morning that she finally agreed to let me paint. I need to get it done before she changes her mind."

"I'll call my family and see who can help. . . ." He slowed, his attention on her feet. "Wait. Just. A. Minute. What do you have on?"

She set down her knife and modeled by lifting one heel to the side and then the other. "The boots you gave me." It was still hotter than the Sahara, so she'd paired the cowgirl boots with her tangerine shorts and a white V-neck T-shirt.

He lifted his gaze to hers. She watched his eyes darken. "You in those boots?"

"Yes?"

"Is the sexiest thing I've ever seen." He vowed it to her with such seriousness that her heart began to knock against her ribs. "It's about time you started wearing those boots."

She groped for and couldn't find a come back. "H—" she began. Where had her voice gone? Why such a coward? "How'd it go with the cars this morning?"

"It went fine. I sacrificed my pride and drove Danny's surfer car all the way back from Hugo."

"Thank you."

"You're welcome." He moved toward her.

Too nervous to keep looking at him for fear that she— or he—would do something foolish, she pointed to the small wrapped gift and homemade construction paper card sitting on the metal counter. "For you."

"Really?" Carefully, he picked up the card that Addie had made for him.

Among the many things Celia had realized last night? That she and Addie had been remiss in thanking Ty for all he'd done for them. She'd set Addie down with art supplies after breakfast, then the two of them had gone shopping at Carrie's Corner on their way to the bakery.

For long moments Ty stood with his head bent over the card, unmoving. Addie had drawn herself and Ty standing on a hill that looked like an upside-down U. They were holding hands, and Addie was wearing pink boots and a ball gown. Inside she'd wanted to write *To the World's Best Daddy*, so Celia had helped her string the letters together.

Celia could sense something gathering in him. It almost looked as if moisture sheened his eyes.

Her heart *really* began to pound.

Without glancing at her, he set down the card and opened the present. A key chain. The charm attached to it had been made out of an old nickel stamped with the image of a longhorn and covered with glass resin. It was tiny in the palm of his strong hand.

"It's just a little something," Celia said. A key chain had seemed appropriate, since he kept giving her *Give Peace a Chance* key chains. Also, it had been affordable. Far more so than, say, a house and car. "A token of our appreciation for everything you've done."

He continued to look down at it. "Thank you."

"You're welcome. It's nothing, really—"

He pushed the key ring into his pocket and then his head came up, his eyes burning with emotion and heat. He came toward her, reaching for her hairnet. This wasn't the first time he'd tried to snag it from her head. It had become a game.

She sidestepped quickly.

He darted out a hand. She yelped, dodging. He anticipated her reaction, hooking a finger lightning fast

under the net and pulling it free. She stilled as her curls
fell to brush against the top of her shoulders.

With a flick, he sent the hairnet sailing into the room's
corner, where it splatted like a dead balloon.

Again, he moved toward her, intent in his eyes. *Mercy!*
Their relationship had been on a plateau for weeks, but
now one card and key ring had pushed him over the edge.

Her rear came up against a corner where two counters
met, trapping her. He stopped so close she could see the
pulse in his neck. His expression informed her that he'd
been patient as long as he could stand to be. That he
was about to crush their truce. That the consequences
could hang.

"There might be customers out front," she said weakly.

"There's no one there."

"There's Addie."

"She won't leave the cash register. She's like a soldier."
He closed the space between them even more, until there
was hardly a millimeter left. Goodness . . . Her will to
resist him was disintegrating. She could not kiss him
again! He presented a deadly danger to her well-being.
And to Addie's. And . . .

He lifted her hand and turned it palm up.

"No touching." Her breath caught. "Remember?"

"You might not have noticed, but I've never liked rules."
Light as a whisper, he ran a fingertip from the pad of her
thumb to her inner elbow.

"Hate it." But she murmured it like a benediction,
like a plea.

He pressed a kiss to the inside of her wrist.

"Awful," she whispered.

"What about this?" He kissed the side of her neck.

In the tender hollow there she could feel the rasp of his stubble. "Even worse." Her lids drifted closed.

He pulled back. Straightened.

She opened her eyes to find him watching her with fierce concentration. His hand lifted and cupped the side of her face. The rough pad of a finger caressed the skin near her temple. Taut silence wound around them, Ty promising her things with his eyes that he had no right to promise and that Celia had no business believing.

She almost couldn't *bear* the fire inside of her that was such acute ecstasy and need that it felt like pain. Wonder struck, she ran her hands up to his shoulders, memorizing the feel of the ropes of muscle. Then higher, along the sides of his throat, until her fingers finally tunneled into the hair at the back of his neck.

Never had she wanted anything as sharply as she wanted him to kiss her. And still, he waited, staring at her with wolfish intensity. Celia teetered on the cusp of hyperventilating. *Kiss me*, she wanted to scream—

He kissed her. And not lightly.

The feel of his lips! The taste of him. It all came back to her in a rush of memories. The breath-stealing power of it. The wildness of her own reaction.

He deepened the kiss, leaning into her, one hand supporting her upper back, the other raking into her hair. She kissed him back, wishing he could be hers and hers alone.

"Mommy?" Addie called from the front of the shop.

Celia reared back.

Ty's arms, like iron bands around her, didn't budge. He lifted his face just enough so she could see that his features were stark, his color high.

"Yes?" Celia answered Addie with a voice embarrassingly high-pitched.

"No one's coming in."

"Okay. Thanks for letting us know." She should push him away. Instead, she rested her palms on either side of his ruggedly beautiful face, a face a million women loved.

He gripped the fabric across the back of her shirt.

She lifted up onto her tiptoes and kissed him. A string of light kisses, separated only by shimmering glimpses of space and time to drink in the sensations.

"And I need to go to the bathroom!" Addie yelled.

With a groan, Celia angled toward the doorway that linked the front room to the kitchen. "Then come on back."

Footsteps answered.

This time Celia did push Ty away, even though he still seemed inclined to stay right where he was, as if he didn't care who saw him holding her. She extricated herself from him a bare second before Addie burst into the room. Their daughter shot them a look on her way past toward the bathroom. "If anyone comes in, don't use the cash register without me, please." The bathroom door closed behind her.

In the abrupt quiet that followed, Celia could feel the weight of Ty's stare. Um . . . they'd just been kissing each other as if this was their last hour on earth. She couldn't think of anything pithy to say or do in the face of that. Gathering her courage, she looked into his pale blue eyes. The air thickened. Her temperature climbed.

Addie returned from the bathroom. "Did anyone come in?"

"Nope," Celia answered, and Addie rushed from the room.

The pause between them lengthened, full of physical longing and the thousand-pound realization of what they'd just done.

She opened her lips to say . . . something. Then pursed them. Knit her brow.

Unlike after their last kiss, she would not be flying into an offended huff and insisting he could never kiss her again. A few hours from now she might regret what had just happened between them, but she didn't at the moment. Nor could she see an ounce of regret on Ty's face.

"Aren't you going to rip into me?" he asked.

"To be honest, I'm having trouble thinking straight at the moment." She cleared her throat. "Once I can think straight, *then* I might rip into you. I usually have no trouble finding a reason."

He chuckled.

She faced her chopping board and, very inanely, resumed chopping walnuts. Even in her daze, she was aware that there *were* reasons not to launch herself back into his arms. Just because she didn't care about those reasons currently didn't mean they didn't exist.

Celia heard Cream or Sugar's front door open, then the sound of voices. Customers had arrived, which meant Ty needed to go help Addie.

"I'm glad you're taking this so well," Ty said, ignoring the customers.

"Mmm hmm."

"We're adults, after all. And married to each other. We're allowed to kiss."

If the authorities knew how he kissed a woman, she was pretty sure they wouldn't allow it. "Right."

"No harm done."

She laughed out loud. Even to her own ears it sounded a little nutty.

"Uh-oh. *Now* are you going to lose it and rip into me?"

"No, no. As you said. We're adults. We're allowed."

He regarded her with confusion. "I'm not used to you acting so normal."

"Daddy! Come help me, please."

He left. Celia continued to chop. *Chop chop chop.* She felt like a stranger in her own body. Her hands looked like they belonged to someone else. *Chop chop.* As she relived every second of their exchange and the kiss that followed, warmth unrolled within her. She paused to fan herself, then went back to chopping. She had walnut dust now, and still she kept on.

Ty's kiss had incinerated thought. It had stolen from her the responsible mother side of her personality and replaced it with . . . she didn't know what. The infatuated young woman she'd been in Vegas—

Only, no. That was a cop-out. She hadn't reverted back to that girl just now. She'd kissed Ty as a grown woman. As herself. Not Celia the high school freshman, or the besotted fool from Vegas, but the mom, the person who moved money around trying to pay the bills. She'd kissed him as an adult who had a complete understanding of all his faults and all his strengths and who had wanted him anyway.

Did their kiss herald mass disaster? Or was it possible to kiss Ty Porter from time to time without her life falling down around her?

After Celia tucked Addie into bed that night, she walked around her house, unsure what to do with herself. She ended up on her living room sofa. She propped her feet on the coffee table and clicked on the TV to a cooking show. Her brain, however, was so full of Ty that she couldn't concentrate.

She'd had enough time now since The Kiss #2 to remember the reasons why she shouldn't have done it.

On the other hand, no man other than Ty had kissed her since Vegas. She'd forgotten how incredibly—wildly, gloriously—heavenly it was.

Her phone buzzed to alert her to an incoming text. *You're not second-guessing our kiss are you?* Ty asked.

No. Then she added, *You big showboat.*

I'm not second-guessing it either.

She rested her phone against her abdomen and smiled.

A moment later, another buzz. *I can't stop thinking about you,* he wrote.

Good night, she typed.

Good night, sweet one.

It gave her a trembly fearful feeling inside to admit that she hoped he'd kiss her again. If he did, she had every intention of kissing him back.

Kissing, she rationalized, was fairly harmless. Right? She wouldn't place her heart in his hands this time around. And she'd make sure they were very, very careful not to let Addie see.

If she went into it with those things in mind, then it ought to be fine to kiss Ty now and then. No strings attached. Just the pleasure and none of the pain.

Celia carried the paint and supplies she'd purchased into Cream or Sugar on Sunday. She stuck a Norah Jones CD into the boom box Donetta used to listen to baseball coverage, then helped Addie set up the jewelry making kit she'd been given for her birthday. While Addie strung beads, Celia took down the cheap donut prints and moved furniture. It took a while to measure the walls and calculate the width of the wide toffee- and white-colored stripes she envisioned. That done, she began the long job of taping.

She'd chosen to skip church this morning for two reasons. One, she only had today to paint and would need every hour to get the job done. Two, she wasn't sure God would approve of the twist her relationship with Ty had taken. She didn't know what He would disapprove of, exactly. She simply had the sense that she ought to feel badly about some aspect of it.

She'd balanced herself on a step stool and was reaching up to press painter's tape against the wall when Ty walked in.

He looked up at her, eyes sizzling. Oh, the male beauty of him in a baseball cap and his gray Under Armour T-shirt and jeans.

A blush raced up her neck to her face.

"Daddy!"

He turned to Addie, and the two of them talked about her jewelry-making.

Celia returned to taping, her skin positively flaming. *Suave*, she thought. *So subtle, Celia!*

After some self-debate, she'd decided to wear a loose navy top over a cami plus her jean shorts. She wouldn't dare get her new boots near paint, so she'd left them in the kitchen. The ridges of the stool's step pressed against the soles of her bare feet.

"Hey, Celia?"

"Mmm?" A strangled sound.

"Can I talk to you for a sec?" When she glanced over, he shifted his head toward the kitchen. "In there?" The wicked curl at the edge of his lips told her exactly what he had in mind.

She poised on the edge of decision, then clambered down and followed him. "What have you been up to this morning, Ty? I made pancakes and then—"

The second they were out of sight, he pulled her to him and kissed her. The pleasure of it slammed into her.

He walked them both across the kitchen without letting up. He lifted his head just long enough to shove open the pantry door with his boot.

"You're taking me into the pantry?" she stage-whispered, laughter in her voice.

"I'm desperate." He drew her into a room twice the size of a coat closet and filled with the scent of flour.

"My family might show up any minute. I want to get in my chance at this before they get here." He pulled the string attached to the overhead light, clicking it on. As if he'd been doing it all his life, he linked his hands behind the small of her back.

The man really did have towering confidence. There wasn't a shred of awkwardness or hesitation in his manner.

"You smell good," he said.

"So do you." That woodsy aroma got her every time.

He nuzzled his face into her hair, then pressed light kisses to her neck, jaw, and cheek before finally reaching her mouth. Celia arched into him, kissing him. She even stepped on top of his boots in her bare feet, then lifted to her tiptoes.

She let the escalating joy of it continue for a couple of minutes. Five? Within his embrace it was hard to have any sense of time. Who could care about the future when they had *this* between them?

She finally did force herself to end it, because she hadn't forgotten that Addie sat in the next room and that his family was due to arrive momentarily.

She plunked her forehead against his chest, hardly able to believe the masterful way he had of turning her body into liquid heat. "So I guess this means that yesterday's kiss wasn't a one-time thing."

"Not hardly." His voice sounded deep and sexy.

"There's just one thing I ask." She looked him in the eyes. "So long as you're kissing me, I request that you not kiss anyone else."

He quirked a brow. "I haven't kissed anyone since Las Vegas. I'm not going to start now."

"Tawny likes you, Ty."

"Tawny's dating a pediatrician."

"Do we have a deal?"

"We have a deal. Does the same go for you? You're not going to kiss that tool, Neill?"

"No. Ty?"

"Yes?"

She sighed with regret. "I think we'd better leave the pantry."

His fingertips grazed lightly up the back of her neck. "I don't want to."

"Any longer and your parents might be standing in the kitchen when the two of us walk out of here together."

He resettled his baseball cap, his expression ornery, humorous, disgruntled. "Who cares?"

"I care! Listen, we've got to be very careful not to let Addie see us like this or do anything at all that would make her suspect."

"I know."

"Then help me out. Be . . . covert."

As intent as a chess player, he ran a thumb down her neck, then her arm, all the way to her hand. He interlaced their fingers. "I'm not good at pretending."

"Are you kidding me? I've seen you shovel more dung than the people walking behind the elephants at a circus. You pretend with every woman you meet: the heavy-handed compliments, the appreciative banter, the smile. You don't mean any of it."

He appeared ready to break into laughter.

"I've got you figured out," she stated.

"And you still like me?"

"Just this much." She held her thumb and pointer finger half an inch apart.

"I think you like me more than that."

"We need to leave the pantry now." She'd have gladly stayed in the pantry with him all day. It made her happy—foolishly, excitedly, happy—just to have Ty look at her this way, talk to her this way, hold her hand this way. And yet, the real world waited.

Channeling her inner Bond girl, Celia eased open the pantry door and peeked out. The coast was clear.

Within minutes the Porter Family Help Squad began to arrive. First Jake—not a churchgoer, apparently. He and Ty filled nail holes and groove marks with putty, then started painting. Nancy, John, Bo, and Meg came after church. Nancy brought lunch, and once they'd all taken a break to eat the picnic-style food, they worked side by side.

For every second of the day, Celia's attention tracked Ty. She meditated over the timbre of his voice. She noticed the muscles running along his spine, the strength in his wrists. Her tummy lifted with delight each time their eyes locked.

At one point he drew near to her with his paint roller. "You going to run off and hide behind Uncle Danny this afternoon?"

"*Yes,*" she answered sincerely. "He needs us."

"I need you."

"He needs us more."

On Monday, Celia went to work at a freshly painted Cream or Sugar. The interior walls of the bakery fairly glistened with beautiful new stripes. Though Donetta felt honor bound to grouse about the change, Celia could tell that she approved.

After Donetta and Jerry left for the day, Ty arrived. While Celia baked, he found numerous reasons to lean against the wall and watch her make pecan pie. Twice he succeeded at whipping off her hairnet. Both times he proceeded to kiss her senseless.

The next day Celia transported her collection of tea-cups and saucers to the bakery. She'd purchased them one at a time over the years at flea markets. Not one cup and saucer matched any other, yet Celia had always found them charming. It pleased her to give her dine-in customers the option of not only caff or decaf, but also Styrofoam or china.

"Those cups," Ty drawled, "are so girly that no man will ever drink coffee out of them."

"Any man secure in his masculinity will be happy to drink from them."

"How much coffee do they hold? A tablespoon?"

"In my opinion, they hold the perfect amount."

"What do you know? You're tiny. You're so tiny you could take a bath in one of these." He held up a white teacup painted with pink rosebuds. "Go on. Jump in." He tilted it toward her. "Water's warm."

She laughed. "You have an underdeveloped sense of class."

"There's one classy thing I appreciate." He met her gaze and held it until she looked away. "How about you let me buy you your own coffee shop?" he asked. "Instead of working for someone, you'll be the owner."

"That's very sweet. But no. Definitely no. You know how I feel about your compulsion to buy things for me. I want to make my own way and earn my own success."

"Well, that's a bummer."

"Secondly, I love Cream or Sugar. No other coffee shop would have a spot on the square, or these amazing hardwood floors, or this soda counter." Protectively, she settled her hand on the old-fashioned display case. "You may not have noticed, but I like old and kitschy things."

"I noticed."

"This shop is one-of-a-kind. As soon as I convince Donetta to buy an espresso machine it'll have everything I could hope for. I couldn't duplicate it in a strip mall."

During a quiet moment between customers and right after she'd set a batch of macaroons out to cool, he convinced her to visit Cream or Sugar's second story. Donetta and Jerry used most of the upper square footage for storage, the rest for an office.

Ty only needed the hallway. From there, they could hear if customers arrived, but could be seen by no one.

More kissing senseless.

When Holley's mayor interrupted them by stopping in for his daily chocolate glazed, Ty left to wait on him. Celia remained in the hallway, clinging to the wall because her legs had gone woozy.

Mothering Addie had brought Celia enormous joy. But it had always been a joy closely accompanied by responsibilities. Was she doing this mothering thing right? Could she afford to keep a roof over Addie's head? Would Addie get sick this flu season?

The sort of dizzy, soaring joy Ty brought into Celia's life was totally unfamiliar to her. Which might be why she was having a hard time trusting it.

It's fine, she kept telling herself. *Your finances are under control. Addie is flourishing at school. So what if a bone-meltingly handsome man kisses you occasion-ally? It's fine.*

She'd been working hard, after all, to keep Ty in his proper place in her emotions. He was fun and thrill-ing, but he was not to be loved in *that* kind of way, the disastrous kind of way.

Inside Cream or Sugar's pantry, she'd told him that while the two of them were kissing each other, she ex-pected him to kiss her only. Then she'd stated the obvious: that Tawny liked him. He'd answered with, *"Tawny's dating a pediatrician."*

He hadn't said, *"I don't care about Tawny anymore. I only care about you."*

He'd said, *"Tawny's dating a pediatrician."*

Which somewhat implied, didn't it, that if Tawny ever stopped dating her pediatrician, then everything might change? Caution tugged at Celia's shirttail.

It's fine, she assured herself. *Don't worry about it. It's all fine.*

CHAPTER

TWENTY-SIX

Teenaged kids ordinarily hid their boyfriends or girl-friends from their parents. In Ty and Celia's case, the reverse applied. They hid their boyfriend/girlfriend status from their child.

The three of them sat around Celia's dining room table Thursday night eating healthy organic pasta with lots of vegetables in it, laughing and talking.

For Addie's sake, Ty did his best to pretend not to have a crush on her mother. As he looked across the table at Celia, her eyes sparkling, her hair held back by a headband, then looked to Addie, her small face smiling, her calm voice telling them stories about kindergarten, he couldn't remember a dinner he'd enjoyed more. His memory reached back over dinners with his bull-riding buddies, celebration dinners after winning events, fancy romantic dinners with women, holiday dinners with his family.

None held a candle to this.

Once they'd cleaned up the meal, he sat next to Addie

while she showed him how little she needed his help with her math homework. That done, she picked up a book her teacher had sent home to read aloud. The story, about a girl named Jane and her dog, struck him as really lame. But Addie read it perfectly.

Celia took over for Addie's bath, then for the very first time, gave him the honor of putting Addie to bed.

"And that," he said, closing the third of three books he'd read to her, "is the last one you're allowed, right?"

Some kids might have tried to fib, but Addie just looked at him in her serious way and nodded. She wore a nightgown with an orange-haired mermaid on the front. Thanks to all the princess lessons he'd had, he recognized the mermaid as Ariel, wife of Eric.

"You're going to tell me a story, right?" Addie asked.

"Uh . . . is that what happens next with your mom?" Celia had only told him about the books.

"Yes."

"Then I'll do my best."

He adjusted the pillows behind his back and crossed his boots at the ankles. She handed him her glasses. He set them on the nightstand, switched off the lamp, then lifted the covers so that she could scoot underneath and lie with her head on her pillow.

"Didn't Mommy look pretty tonight?"

"She sure did."

"She's really good at cooking, too."

"Yep, she is."

"Did you know that Mom took me over to Mr. Neill's house one time to play with Tanner and Tyson?"

The news caused his breath to still in his lungs. "No, I didn't know that."

"And did you know that they came here one time?"

"No."

"Well, they did." Addie gave him a meaningful look. She pulled a little white blanket close to her chest. "You can start the story now."

He'd never been a jealous person. But a drought usually ends with a flood. And Addie's words had brought down the most powerful flood of possessiveness. It all but turned him mute.

"Go on, Daddy."

"I . . ." He had to work to concentrate his thoughts. "I could tell you the story of the Alamo."

She wrinkled her nose. "Hmm?"

"The story of the Texas revolution. Jim Bowie? Davy Crockett?"

"That sounds nice, Daddy." She placed her hand on his elbow and patted. "But would it be okay if you told me a princess story? I like princess stories at bedtime."

"Oh. Sure." He scratched the side of his head. "There was this princess named . . ."

"Belle?"

"Belle," he agreed. "And she liked being a princess because it was fun to be famous and rich."

Addie looked up at him out of the corners of her eyes, doubtful.

"The prince was, uh, nice, and they had fun doing stuff that was . . . fun." What in the world was he supposed to say? He'd hadn't made up a story since high school English, and he'd been bad at it then.

"You're supposed to tell me about all the princess's good works."

"What kind of good works?"

"Feeding the poor, protecting the environment, helping orphans."

Celia! If he hadn't wanted to strangle her for toying with Neill, he'd have laughed out loud. "How about saving an animal? Is that good with you?"

"Yes."

"So Cowgirl Princess Belle had this ranch called the Lazy B. She realized that the . . . armadillos that lived on the ranch kept getting eaten by mountain lions or run over by Ford trucks."

Addie giggled. "You're not supposed to talk about animals getting run over."

"Our secret?"

"Okay."

"Close your eyes." She did. "So Belle called the prince on her cell phone and told him to take care of the problem—"

"No." Her eyes flashed open. "No, no, no. In the bed-time stories, the princesses always take care of their own problems."

"They do, do they?" Telling.

"Yes."

"Okay, then. Uh . . . Belle strapped on some six-shooters and saddled up her horse."

"What was her horse's name?"

"Whitey?"

Addie gave a soft smile. "I love Whitey."

"I love you," he said.

She studied him for a moment in the dimness. "I love you, too, Daddy."

His chest ached with emotion. "Where were we?"

"She'd saddled up Whitey."

"Right, and then she rode around her ranch until she found the mountain lion. She took out one of her six-shooters and—"

"Used it to scare him into a cage," she cut in. "A safe one."

"Oh."

"So she could give him to a zoo."

"If you say so. And then she put some signs next to the road outside her ranch. One had a picture of an armadillo on it and said *Armadillo Crossing*. The other one told everybody they had to drive at just ten miles an hour. This made the locals mad, but she was really pretty, so they put up with it. She saved the armadillos. The end." Quiet followed. "How'd I do?"

"It was good for your first try."

He stayed with her for the next ten minutes, holding her hand and watching her fall asleep.

He found Celia sitting at the kitchen table, peering at her laptop. He scooped her up with one arm. She screeched. He swung her legs up and hooked them over his other arm as he carried her into the living room.

"Your knee, Ty!"

"I'm carrying you with my arms, not my knee."

"The extra weight!"

"What extra weight? You can't weigh more than five pounds."

"People will see us!"

"Who? Neill?" He jerked the curtains over her living room windows, then lowered onto the sofa with her in his arms. She climbed off his lap but didn't go far. Tucking her feet beneath her, she leaned a shoulder into the sofa back and faced him. He extended an arm along the top of the sofa and toyed with the hem of her shirtsleeve. She wore the gold necklace with the dangling C that always made him want to kiss the spot beneath it.

Had he only thought her pretty before? Now he couldn't take his eyes off of her when they were in a room together. She'd become gorgeous to him. "Addie told me that you've gone over to Neill's house and that he's come here."

She had the nerve to look amused. "And?"

"I'm jealous. Do you like him?"

"As a neighbor and a friend. But who knows? I may come to feel more for him in time."

"Celia," he threatened.

She grinned.

"The only person I want you to feel more for," he said, "is me."

She leaned forward and pressed a quick kiss to his lips.

Their hands met between them, and he played with her fingers while he studied her clear green eyes. Her house made him dizzy with all its crazy colors. Tonight it smelled like tomato sauce. And he'd never felt more at home anywhere in the world. "I could spend all the rest of my nights just like this."

"Looking deeply into my eyes?"

"Looking deeply into your eyes," he confirmed.

He was not a good man, not the man he wanted to be. He didn't view himself as what Celia deserved in a husband. None of that had changed.

A better man wouldn't have kissed Celia that day in Cream or Sugar's kitchen. But a better man hadn't been there that day. He'd been there. And the power of that one kiss had all but changed the course of his life.

Now that he'd kissed her, he planned to keep her. To play every advantage he had. Use every ounce of skill with women he possessed. All of which proved his selfishness and, at times, weighed him with guilt.

As a result, he was determined to make this relationship worth her while. He'd sacrifice much for her. He'd do anything she asked of him. He'd pay any price, except one.

The price of giving her up.

Ty and Jake sat on Jake's sofa, an open bag of Fritos between them. Friday night football filled the jumbo TV screen in HD.

Ty would much rather have spent the evening with Celia and Addie, but Celia only let him come over to her house at night occasionally. Two nights in a row was a no-go.

So here he sat, next to Jake. Which was a whole lot worse than sitting with Celia and a long shot better than sitting in his stupid house by himself.

The Cowboys completed a long pass and both of the brothers clapped. All of the Porter siblings had put in time watching football together over the years. Now Dru was overseas and Bo spent most of his free time staring at his wife like she was made of gold. That left him and Jake. Since Jake never had much to say, watching football was pretty quiet.

A person would never guess, looking at where Jake lived, that its owner had earned a small fortune training racehorses. Jake owned a unit in an industrial building that had been chopped into lofts and renovated a couple of years back. The TV was his only luxury. The rest of the loft reminded Ty of the Marine barracks he'd spent years living in. Bare and plain.

Ty extended his legs onto the leather ottoman, crossing the bad one over the good.

"How's the knee?" Jake asked.

"Getting better."

"You ever figure out why you came off that bull?"

"No. Never could." A while back, Ty had asked Jake to take a look at one of the videos of his ride on Meteor. Jake had a good eye for the details of bull riding. He'd done a little rodeoing himself in high school, and he'd followed Ty's entire career. More than once Jake had been able to tell Ty when bad habits were creeping into his form. The video, though, had stumped Jake just as it had Ty.

That he hadn't discovered the reason for his fall still bothered Ty. He tried not to visit YouTube anymore, but a couple of nights a week, he found himself at the site anyway, watching the clips.

Commercials came on. Jake rattled Fritos in his hand, then tilted his head back to funnel them into his mouth. "You ever think that sometimes there is no logical reason for something?"

"No."

"Then why'd you come off that bull?"

Ty answered with silence.

"It's not always possible—" Jake paused for a long moment—"to make sense of things."

Ty knew that Jake had plenty in his own life he'd probably like to make sense of. He'd lived through an explosion that had killed three of his men in front of his eyes.

"You're saying that my fall off Meteor was just random chance."

"Or karma. Or the universe kicking your butt. Who knows?"

"The universe? I don't believe in *the universe*. Do you?"

Jake shrugged, his jaw hard. "I don't really believe in anything anymore."

"God?" Ty asked.

"No."

Ty drew his brows together. That was troubling.

Jake turned back to the TV.

The Porter kids had grown up in church. They'd racked up summers at VBS. Gone to church camp. Jake had turned grim after his accident, but Ty hadn't realized he'd become so cynical that he no longer believed in God.

Since the night Celia had flushed his Vicodin, Ty had been praying. What's more, it seemed to him that God had been listening and answering.

Jake took up another handful of Fritos. "I don't think we always get to understand the things that happen to us. That's all."

Maybe not. But in his case, Ty refused to accept that the universe or karma had caused his fall. He could believe, maybe, that God had caused it.

He scowled at the football game. Could he? Could he believe that God had caused his fall? The idea hadn't occurred to him until this minute. If he accepted that God might have had a hand in his accident, he'd have to accept that God didn't mind letting his knee get crushed, and that God didn't mind ending the career he'd lived for.

Ty watched the rest of the game with Jake, then headed home to a house that welcomed him like a coffin.

He sat down at his desk and woke his office computer. Something about one of the YouTube videos chewed at the back of his memory, unsettling him. He pulled up the clip.

Right as he was coming off Meteor, he thought he saw something. He paused it and rewound it. Watched it over and over again, seven times in a row.

Technically, there was nothing to see. And yet his subconscious kept picking up on something. A strange play of light. Just enough to make him remember how, right when he'd come unseated, he'd felt as if he'd been pulled off by hands.

God's hands? An angel's hands?

Closing his eyes, he remembered back to the days before his fall. He'd been going through the motions, pushing through the feeling that he should quit.

He concentrated, thinking backward through the calendar. He'd begun feeling like that after he'd found out about Addie. He'd had to say good-bye to her and Celia so that he could travel to his next event. Right afterward, his drive for bull riding had started to run out.

Could it be that *God* had been telling him to retire, and he'd been too much of a knucklehead to listen?

The idea was sort of Looney Tunes.

Yet Ty knew instantly that it was right.

God had been patient with him for a long time. A very long time, now that he thought about it. Longer than a human father would have been patient. But after Ty had been reunited with his wife and then found out about his daughter, God's patience with his traveling and his leaving had ended.

Ty hissed a breath between his teeth. After weeks of searching for an understanding of what had caused his injury, understanding was rolling over him fast.

God wanted husbands to commit and be husbands and fathers to commit and be fathers. So God had pulled him off of a twenty-one-point bull so there could be no blaming the bull. He'd ended Ty's career.

Ty lifted his head and hit Play, watching the video one last time with new eyes. His neck pricked as the images scrolled in front of him. There was no earthly reason why he'd come off that bull.

Bull-riding fans could wonder, people could ask him about it, Jake could blame it on chance. But from now on, for the rest of his life, Ty and God would know exactly what had gone down.

Ty lowered onto his good knee, bowed his head, and prayed for all he was worth.

He'd been an idiot. Blind. Interested only in his own success. He'd gotten exactly what he deserved when God had taken his bull riding from him. A shattered knee, in all honesty, was less than he deserved.

Forgive me, God. Please forgive me.

When Ty had asked if he could join Celia, Addie, Meg, and Bo at church on Sunday, Celia had been delighted. She'd immediately told him that he could. Things had been hunky-dory, in fact, right up until the instant when Celia had comprehended the topic of Doogie's sermon.

Forgiveness.

First the pastor spoke about the unconditional forgiveness they'd received from God. Then he implored them to receive that forgiveness, turn, and forgive others.

By degrees, Celia's body grew more and more rigid. Why couldn't he have preached on *any* other subject today? On tithing, even. Or all the reasons why it was wrong to dance. She found it discomfiting in the extreme to sit next to Ty through a sermon on forgiveness. It felt as though Doogie's words were directed specifically at the two of them.

Ty crossed an alligator boot over a knee. His hand rested on his thigh, right next to her skirt. She'd been very aware of him ever since the quiet part of the service had started. Especially that hand. But as the sermon progressed, she got to where she could practically count his breaths. She trained her gaze ahead with all the terror of a soldier on her first day of boot camp.

She and Ty had come to a good place in their relationship. But full and complete forgiveness? The hurt Ty had caused her in Las Vegas was like a knot in a rope. She'd been pulling the two sides of the rope farther and farther apart for years and the knot had grown tighter and smaller and more impossible to untie.

She loved the thought that God stood ready to forgive her. But forgive Ty? Ty forgive her? As if their wedding and the years of keeping Addie from him had never happened?

It didn't seem realistic or fair or smart. Her resentment over the way Ty had treated her in Vegas protected her from making herself vulnerable to him again. Wasn't it enough that they both knew they were sorry for the things that had happened in their past? It felt like enough.

In the foyer after the service, Ty, the man who shied from nothing, made small talk with Bo and Meg. As Celia watched him throw back his head to laugh at something Bo had said, she realized that the pastor's words had troubled him, too.

During the car ride home, Ty invited them both to his place so Addie could ride Whitey. Celia told him that Addie could go, but that she needed to bake petit fours for a custom baby shower order before heading to his parents' house to visit Danny.

Unlike usual, Ty didn't try to sweet-talk her into changing her mind. Ty and Addie drove off together. Celia stood on the sidewalk outside her gingerbread house, watching his truck's taillights.

"Neighbor!"

Celia turned to see Neill, with his glossy Clark Kent hair. "Hi, Neill."

He finished moving his sprinkler to a new section of lawn, then made his way over to her. He wore the sort of thing she'd once fancied she liked on men: flat-front shorts, a rumpled polo, and horn-rimmed glasses. The glasses made her remember the times she'd caught Ty wearing his reading glasses.

"I haven't seen you in a few days," Neill said. "You faring okay?"

"I am."

"Things going well at Sugar and Cream?"

Not worth correcting. "Yes, they are. Thanks."

They stood with their arms crossed, watching his sprinkler shoot its spray of arcing water. Pleasantly cool breeze sifted through Celia's curls. After weeks of unrelenting heat, the late September weather had begun to turn. The air now held the promise of fall, of clear, crisp days. "It's nice out."

"It's better." Neill conceded. "But still too hot."

Neill had been raised in Washington State. They were Pacific Northwest soul mates. And so it made no sense, none at all, that his comment irked her. She curled her toes inside her cowgirl boots and bit back the urge to defend Holley, which was, by all accounts, unbearably hot in the summertime.

"Would you like to come inside?" he asked. "There's air conditioning."

"Actually, I have an order to fill for a client, so I better get busy baking." Once she'd begun offering her own baked goods in the shop, customers had begun asking if they could place special orders with her. Donetta had given Celia her approval so long as Celia filled her special orders on her own time. Word had quickly spread.

"Let's get the kids together soon."

"Let's."

He tossed back the front of his inky hair. "Whenever you have a spare moment or need anything, don't hesitate to knock on my door."

The thing was—she didn't want to knock on his door. He was a smart, nice, good-looking divorced father of two. But he did not have wicked blue eyes. He did not make her laugh. He did not have the ability to melt her into a puddle with a single look.

CHAPTER
TWENTY-SEVEN

All the next week, Celia and Ty continued with their established routine. When he arrived at Cream or Sugar, she went to the kitchen and baked. Every chance they got (plus several chances they outright stole), they kissed each other in secret. This, despite the fact that an unspoken tension lived between them now. The sermon they'd sat through together had stirred up all their issues, issues they couldn't discuss. They could not mention the M word—marriage. Or the F word—forgiveness. Or, heaven forbid, the L word—love. If they did, they'd risk breaking the fragile bond they had.

Their romantic relationship was superficial. However, its superficiality was what guaranteed its existence. As long as it remained superficial, Celia deemed it harmless. The moment their romance became dangerous was the moment she'd have to walk away. Knowing this, Celia had decided not to rock the boat.

In the end, it didn't matter what Celia had decided. Because Ty rocked the boat.

"Hey," he said to her on Sunday, as they were letting

themselves into the gingerbread house. "Want to sit for a minute?" He gestured toward the matched set of rocking chairs on her porch.

Nancy had brought the rockers over earlier in the week. She'd been purging furniture from her garage and had insisted that Celia would be doing her a favor by accepting the chairs.

"Sure." Celia lowered into a rocker as Ty took the other. Neither of them rocked.

Ty had just driven them home from church—where, for the second week in a row, they'd endured sitting side-by-side for a sermon on forgiveness. *Really, God? Really, Pastor Doogie? Two weeks in a row?*

Addie had already voyaged deep into the house, which left Celia and Ty alone together facing a neighborhood of Victorians and a romance that could easily be shattered by a define-the-relationship talk. Celia began to push at her cuticles.

"Are we going to talk about this forgiveness thing or ignore it for another week?" Ty asked.

"Oh, I can probably ignore it for a lot longer than a week. I think I could go months."

"Huh." He considered her, sympathy and chiding in his face.

Blast him for bringing this up! The day's gentle sunshine and the autumn-tipped leaves on the trees painted a backdrop too serene for this conversation.

And still, he waited.

"I'm not even sure what forgiveness is," Celia confessed. "Is it a decision? A feeling? An act?"

"I think it's a decision. It could involve an act. I guess we can hope the feeling follows."

"I don't know. It gives me a headache when I think about it, it's so abstract."

"Here. I'll look up the definition." He pulled out his smartphone, typed, waited, typed. "'Forgiveness,'" he read. "'To give up resentment or a claim to a justly deserved penalty.'"

Celia winced.

"That's hard for you to accept?"

"My resentments are . . . safe and familiar. I'm okay with them. Maybe it's warped, but I even sort of *like* them."

"They're not good for you."

"I wouldn't know how to let them go."

His expression hardened.

"What was the second part again?"

He checked. "Giving up a claim to a justly deserved penalty."

"I have trouble with that, too. If the penalty was deserved, then why shouldn't the person who's in the wrong pay it? That's justice. Right?"

"Maybe. But at what price?" He leaned forward, setting his elbows on his knees. "I ruined things between us all those years ago, Celia."

She swallowed hard.

"Are you going to be able to forgive me?"

No, came the answer. Celia heard it deep within herself, quiet but adamant.

"I've paid for my stupid mistake. Haven't I?"

She couldn't speak. The turmoil in his blue eyes was snarling her thoughts.

Unbearable silence. For years after their breakup, she'd vengefully imagined this exact scenario. Ty, telling her he'd been wrong and asking for her forgiveness. In a surreal twist, she found herself living the reality. It wasn't satisfying. Maybe because Ty wasn't just the man who'd wounded her any more. He was also the man who worked the counter at a donut shop so she could bake. He was the one who gave Addie riding lessons and picked her up from school every day. He was the one who'd helped her paint Cream or Sugar, who'd carried Uncle Danny to her car. He was the one who didn't seem to hold a grudge for the wrong she'd done him. "Have you forgiven me for not telling you about Addie?"

"Yes."

"Maybe you shouldn't have. What I did was unforgivable."

"It wasn't."

"You're better at forgiveness than I am, then. I wish I could be like you." Her exhale ached. "I admit that the difficulty I'm having with forgiving you is my fault. My problem."

"You've made it my problem, too."

He gave her a long time to say something else, to apologize, or otherwise soften her stance. Her mind raced, trying to decide what to say that would a) put their relationship back on its former footing and b) not be a lie. It took her too long.

He stood, walked to his truck, and drove away.

Pain turned within Celia, dull and smug.

That night, Celia hosted Meg and Bo for dinner. They'd been kind enough to invite her and Addie to their lovely home at Whispering Creek Ranch a few times, and

Celia had wanted to return the favor. She'd been looking forward to cooking for them for more than a week . . . right up until her dead-end conversation with Ty about forgiveness. All day since, her mood had been mired in a wretched shade of gray.

During their meal, Celia pretended to be chatty and happy for Addie, Meg, and Bo's sake. Her false front made her feel all the more joyless on the inside.

She'd put Addie to bed and was spooning homemade chocolate chip bread pudding into bowls for the adults when Meg joined her in the kitchen.

"What can I do to help?" Meg asked.

Celia knew, suddenly, exactly what Meg could do. She turned to face her friend. "I need to go visit Ty."

Meg hesitated. "Ty?"

"I acted like a jerk to him earlier today. I don't think I'll feel right about it until I talk to him."

Meg recovered from her surprise quickly. "Go ahead and go." She waved a hand. "Bo and I will stay here with Addie."

"Are you sure? I'll just run over to Ty's house and bring him some bread pudding as an apology, then run right back."

"Take your time. Bo and I have each other and this dessert to keep us company. We'll be more than fine."

Angel Meg. Celia hugged her and then drove through a darkened Holley to Ty's house. A plastic container of bread pudding rode shotgun. Her dashboard clock read 8:41.

She used her own key on Ty's front door, just as she had on her previous unannounced evening visit. Unlike the last time, she didn't find him sitting in his living room watching TV. Only a few lights had been left on in the front areas of the house.

"Ty?"

Rustling sounds came from the vicinity of his bedroom. "Hello?" He sounded half asleep.

Surely not. Before nine? "I brought you baked goods." She waited in the foyer.

More rustling. Then he pushed open his bedroom door and limped toward her down the hallway. His hair looked a thousand ways toward rumpled. He wore a pair of cargo shorts, which revealed the brace on his left leg. Bare feet. He'd most likely shrugged into his long-sleeved denim shirt seconds ago, because it hung unbuttoned.

Her grip on the bread pudding tightened at the sight of that long slice of bare chest and abs. His upper body was even more defined than her memory had recalled. And her memory had recalled much. "Were you asleep?"

"Sort of." He stopped a few feet from her. After weaving a little, he planted a shoulder against the wall. He smiled. A heartbreaking smile, full of affection for her and self-condemnation for himself.

"What have you been doing all day?"

"Nothing. I've just been here." He said *here* like a bad kind of four-letter word. "What did you bring me?" His words slurred ever so slightly.

"Bread pudding. Um. . . . Have you been drinking?"

"No. I would have, except I didn't have any alcohol in the house."

And then it hit her. "Vicodin." Anger and worry sent her stomach plunging. "Did you take Vicodin again?"

His eyes were vaguely unfocused. "I didn't know you were planning to stop by."

"Ty!"

"My leg hurts. I can't sleep."

"No," she accused, "you took Vicodin because our conversation earlier today upset you. I know exactly why you took it." She set aside the bread pudding and charged into his bedroom. Depressing shadows filled the luxurious space. She flicked on his bathroom light. Sure enough, an open pill bottle sat on the counter.

Tears stung her eyes. *Ty!* What had he done? How many had he taken? She'd demanded he stop taking Vicodin. But she'd failed to secure his promise, and he'd gotten his prescription refilled.

Ty waited for her in his bedroom, standing near the bed, reminding her of the way he'd stood near their hotel room bed in Vegas that devastating morning.

"I'm glad you're here." His dimple tucked into his cheek. "I miss you when you're not here."

"How many of these did you take?" Celia brandished the bottle.

He did not look sorry. Just bemused by her anger. And very sleepy. "Three, I think."

"Are you sure?"

"It might have been four. I'm fine. I've taken more than that before."

"Is this a brand-new bottle? Or have you continued taking Vicodin since I asked you not to?"

"New bottle." He climbed onto his bed, turning when he reached his stack of pillows. He reclined against them. The shirt slid off one side of his chest. "If you don't mind, I think . . . I'll just rest here while you throw a fit or whatever it is you're going to do." He bent his arm over his eyes. His lips hitched upward.

Heartbeat knocking, Celia pulled her cell phone from the pocket of her shorts. Like every zealous mother, she had the number for the national poison hotline embedded in her list of contacts. She hit Call. When a calm-voiced woman answered, Celia detailed the situation, the information listed on the medicine bottle, Ty's approximate weight. Even though she worked to sound competent, her voice trembled.

In order to pinpoint how many pills he'd taken, the woman suggested Celia count the number of pills remaining in the bottle and compare that to the quantity noted on the outside. Celia counted. Ty had taken three, one more than the prescribed dose. The woman told Celia that he should be fine. Hospital intervention wasn't necessary.

Celia thanked the woman, buried the bottle of Vicodin in her pocket, and pulled a chair over to Ty's bedside. She wanted to pummel him with her fists for scaring her so badly. And she'd definitely be placing yet another call to Ty's doctor in the morning to reiterate her warnings about this particular man and this particular prescription.

Ty slid his arm downward, letting it rest on his stomach. Slowly, he turned his head to look at her. "Did you put my bread pudding in the refrigerator?"

"No."

"Will you?"

She glared at him. "The bread pudding is the least of my worries right now."

"Did you come tonight to say you were sorry?"

"Yes."

He regarded her with heavy-lidded turquoise eyes. "You're sorry?"

"I was. But now I'm mad. Really mad. You scared me to death."

"Even though you're mad, can you put my bread pudding in the refrigerator?"

"Fine. I'll do it in a minute."

His eyes sank closed. "You're making me lose my mind. You know that, right?"

"You're making me lose mine, too."

"Will you just shoot me, sweet one? It'd be easier than caring about you as much as I do."

"You're absolutely positive that you didn't take pills from any other bottle today?"

"Positive."

Time ticked. She ran her gaze over his face and form to reassure herself that he was well. Every inch of him looked like it had been created by a master Renaissance sculptor. He was beautiful. He always had been. And to her, he always would be. Until the end of time.

Her call to the hotline hadn't comforted her completely. She couldn't know with a hundred percent certainty that he hadn't polished off an old bottle first before starting in on the new.

She looked up Vicodin on her phone and scrolled through information. Even a prescribed dose could come with scary side effects. What was she going to do? She didn't feel right about leaving him alone all night.

"Celia?"

"I'm still here."

"Will you stay longer?"

"I'll stay a little bit longer."

"Thank you. With you here, I can sleep."

For fifteen straight minutes, she sat at his bedside and

berated herself for getting involved with a man so stubbornly unpredictable, bullheaded, and reckless. How was she supposed to learn to trust him when he did things like this? He knew how she felt about Vicodin, and he'd gone and taken it anyway.

He wasn't the only one at fault, though, was he? She'd all but told him earlier today that she'd never forgive him. Her words had sent him on a Vicodin bender.

Why couldn't she forgive him? *Why?* He'd forgiven her.

Silently, she put his bread pudding in his refrigerator, then slipped from his house. Even though she knew Ty wouldn't like it, she told Meg and Bo about the Vicodin the minute she returned home. Bo volunteered to stay with Ty and keep an eye on him until morning. Reliable Bo.

Late that night, Celia stared at her bedroom ceiling, sleepless and feeling like the Wicked Witch of Unforgiveness. Her memory ran back over everything she could remember from her time with Ty in Las Vegas. Every look, laugh, compliment, kiss. She had not dated him long, but that didn't mean she hadn't loved him. *How* she'd loved him! With every molecule of her body, she'd loved him.

She'd grown up dreaming of a white wedding. Of course she had. A dress and guests and a cake. But she'd loved Ty so much she'd sacrificed all that for the chance to marry him quickly. She'd have given up far more for him, had he asked. As it was, she'd placed her hope, her future, and her body in his hands. And the next morning?

"I'm in love with someone else," he'd said to her. *"I have a girlfriend at home in Holley. We've been dating for two years."*

The old betrayal seeped through her like black liquid. *See?* she demanded of God. She had good, valid reasons not to forgive Ty. Ty had done *that* to her. She still hadn't fully recovered. He'd done *that*!

But *that* wasn't, if she were being completely truthful with herself, why she couldn't forgive him. Underneath her resistance to forgive lay fear, cowering fear, of what might happen to her and Addie if she found a way to forgive Ty fully. She'd already allowed her heart and mind to open to him far more than she'd intended. It flat-out panicked her to consider letting herself care for Ty even one single teardrop more than she already did.

TWENTY-EIGHT

Celia escorted Addie into her kindergarten class the next morning, then drove home, same as always, to get herself ready for work. As she pulled into her driveway, she spotted Ty sitting on her porch steps. Waiting.

Her heart wedged into her throat. She spent longer than necessary pretending to gather her purse so that she could actually gather her composure. She wished she'd taken time to put on something more sightly than a ten-year-old navy sweatshirt and cutoffs.

He tracked her progress as she approached. His hair was damp from a shower, and he wore an army-green USMC T-shirt. Despite that she'd left him sleeping soundly, he appeared the opposite of well rested. His face looked haggard, his eyes bloodshot.

"Hello." She plopped down on the same step he occupied, leaving space between them. "You look like you had an early morning."

"I've been up since four." He took his time surveying her. Quiet elongated. "I'm sorry about last night."

She nodded. "This time, will you promise me that you won't take any more Vicodin?"

"I promise."

The magnetism between them pulled Celia in almost tangibly. What she really wanted was to snake her arms around him and hug him fiercely and maybe cry a little with gratitude over the fact that he was fine. "And I promise that I'm going to work on the forgiveness thing," she said. "I'll spend time thinking about it, praying about it, and reading verses about it." She wedged off her flip-flops and rolled her toes underneath her bare feet. "To be honest, I'm not that great at praying and reading verses. But I'm going to give it my best shot. Faith is new and old for me. I'm trying to get used to it again." Her anklet undulated to a different position, glimmering.

"What do you mean, new and old?"

She explained her childhood of spotty church-going and her adulthood void of belief. "What about you?"

He explained that his parents had taken them to church every Sunday when they were young. He'd been inconsistent about attending through his twenties, but had hung on to prayer.

"Before you went to church with Addie and me, how long had it been since you'd gone?" Celia propped her elbow on her upraised knees and rested her head on her hand to study him.

"Years."

"Five and a half years, by any chance?"

He moved his attention to the street, frowning.

"Ah. More penance." It made perfect sense. He was too blunt to suffer hypocrites. It would have chafed him to sit in a house of God while viewing himself as an irredeemable sinner.

"I'll never get used to that," he said quietly. "How you know things about me that no one knows."

"You know things about me, too. The Prius, this house, the tulips you brought me my first day of work. They're all what I'd have chosen for myself."

He leaned over to pluck some blades of grass from her lawn. He twined them through his masculine fingers.

"It seems like we've both spent a lot of time defining our identity the wrong way," she said. "I tried to view myself as a good person, to find my worth in Addie. It left me unsettled and empty. You've been viewing yourself as a bad person and trying to find your worth in sacrifice and bull riding and in who knows what else."

The grass kept dipping and twisting between his fingers.

"I think we were both wrong," Celia continued. "We were measuring our worth by our perceived goodness or sinfulness. But whether we're good or bad isn't really the main thing, is it? The thing that matters most is that we're *loved*."

His bright gaze flicked to hers.

"I personally might find forgiveness challenging, but I don't think God does. Whatever you've done in the past, I believe He's forgiven you, Ty. It's been paid for. And not by you."

"If He's forgiven me, then He's forgiven you."

A burning sensation pushed against her eyes. Unshed tears.

"He's given us a second chance," he said.

She deliberately shied away from framing that second chance in terms of their relationship. "True. I have a job in a bakery now. You'll soon have a career raising rodeo stock." His new direction meant a lot to him, she knew. It gave the retired bull rider in him purpose. "We're going to do well with our second chances. I know it."

He dropped the grass and took hold of her hand with his stronger one, lacing their fingers together. She scooted close to him and rested her head on the outside of his upper arm and shoulder. They stayed that way for lovely minutes, the simple comfort of his companionship staggering in its power.

"I've got to get to work," she said at last, regretfully.

"If you'd let me buy you your own bakery, then you could show up for work any time you wanted."

"Yes, but any other bakery wouldn't be Cream or Sugar, so I couldn't love it half as much." She sat back enough to look at him.

"Are we good?" he asked. "You and me?"

"Last night you wanted me to shoot you to put you out of your misery."

"And today I want to suffer through another day with you."

She smiled. "As respectful friends?" The definition she'd touted for so long now seemed a paltry description of their status.

"Fine. Respectful friends." He cupped the back of her neck and drew her to him. "Who kiss." Their profiles hovered an inch apart just long enough for her breath to quicken. Then he kissed her, tenderly and firmly, in front of God and Holley.

She scrambled to her feet, scared that if she let it go on she wouldn't want to end it. "We're respectful friends who, might I remind you, kiss in secret."

"Must have slipped my mind." He stood to his full height, tall and imposing, and pushed his hands into his pockets. "How about I come inside so we can kiss in secret?"

Heart arrhythmia. Near death from heat combustion. "I have to go to work!"

"That must have slipped my mind, too."

"Go home and get some sleep." She paused halfway inside her front door. "I mean it. I don't want to see your face at Cream or Sugar today. Take the day off . . . well, until kindergarten gets out, anyway."

"You're bossy, sweet one."

"You're maddening, showboat."

When Celia walked through Cream or Sugar's back door, she found Donetta waiting for her.

"Have you heard the news?" Donetta asked.

"Good morning." Celia hung her purse on its hook in the hallway and looped her apron over her head. "Have I heard what news?"

"That Tawny Bettenfield and Vance Amsteeter broke up."

Celia's spirits took a nose dive. Her motion stalled, and she had to remind herself to tie the apron around her waist.

"Over the weekend," Donetta continued. "They broke up. You know what this means, don't you?"

Celia pulled a hairnet out of the container. From the kitchen, she could hear the rhythmic sound of a wooden spoon against a metal bowl—Jerry stirring cookie dough.

"It means that she's coming after Ty next," Donetta

stated. "That girl's been fishing for Ty harder than a bass fisherman in a televised competition."

What could Celia say? The truth? That Ty might love Tawny back? That the possibility of that turned her blood to ice water?

"Ty has a mighty big soft spot for you, Celia. You better believe that I've seen hundreds of girls throw themselves at him over the years but I've never seen him take a shine to anyone the way he has to you. And I was around during the years he dated Tawny, remember." She paused meaningfully, her Texas Ranger earrings trembling with fervor. "I don't know what's going on inside that oddball marriage of yours except that you and Ty live in different houses. My advice? Make your marriage into the real thing while you still have the chance."

"It's more complicated than that," said the woman wearing the cowgirl boots Ty had given her.

"That's what old Edna Sikes said about Wilbur Thompson when she was a young woman. He proposed to her, but she waited too long to sort out her feelings. He married someone else, and he and his new wife went to live the high life in a palace in Boca Raton. Poor Edna has spent every day since in that rickety old house on the hill eating nothing but rhubarb pie and fried okra."

"I . . . don't want to end up like that."

"Of course you don't! Go claim your man!"

Celia groaned with anguish. "Thanks for you advice, Donetta, but it's a delicate situation—"

"Rhubarb pie and fried okra, honey. That's your other option."

A few hours later Tawny stopped by Cream or Sugar for her chocolate chip cookie. She looked impeccable in a charcoal suit and patent leather heels. She'd parted her dark hair on the side and caught it back in one of those stylishly messy buns—a hairstyle Celia would never be able to achieve with her layered curls, not for as long as she lived.

When Celia informed Tawny that Ty wasn't in, Tawny did an admirable job of masking her disappointment.

All day long after Tawny's visit, Celia felt sick to her stomach. For almost eight years, since the time the two had begun dating, Ty had been planning to marry Tawny. And now Tawny was free. *"Tawny and I are meant for each other and she knows it,"* she remembered him saying. *"The next time she kicks a boyfriend to the curb, I'm planning to make my move."*

The agonizing thing was, Ty and Tawny really might be meant for each other. On paper, they added up perfectly. It could be that God had intended them for each other all this time. Celia tried to wrap her mind around that idea while she finished her shift, while she drove home.

Back at the gingerbread house, she exchanged the usual hug and chitchat with Addie, then caught Ty's eye. "A word, please."

"Sure."

She led the way into her bedroom and closed the door.

He glanced at the bed, then back at her, grinning. "Isn't this a little forward?" he asked, exactly imitating the line he'd given her months ago, when she'd issued him into her bedroom in Corvallis for a private conversation.

So much had changed between then and now. "Very forward," she agreed.

He looked far better rested than he had earlier. "Did I miss anything good at the shop today?"

"Nope." Just the revelation of Tawny's availability. "We were all relieved to have you gone. We didn't have to beat off women with a stick."

Laugh lines delved out from his eyes.

She stepped close to him, looping her hands around his neck and tunneling a few fingers into the hair at his nape. She searched the nuances and masculine angles of his face, trying to fathom whether or not he would choose Tawny over her again. Part of her was positive that he would. Part of her dared hope that he wouldn't. In his eyes, she saw no guarantees either way.

She rose up on her tiptoes and kissed him gently. Then lowered back onto her heels and settled her cheek in the hollow beneath his chin. In answer, he enclosed her tightly in his arms. An overwhelming feeling of heat, of lightning, of crippling affection scorched through her. For right now he was hers. After today? Unknowable.

Closing her eyes, she tried to imprint the moment and tuck it away in her memory.

"What's the matter?" he whispered.

"Nothing."

He closed a hand around the back of her head, protectively. "You said this morning that we were good. Are we good?" She could hear a thread of apprehension in his tone.

"We're good."

Near dusk the next day, Celia sat beside Addie at the kitchen table while Addie worked on homework. Refreshing October air slid through the window screens. Chicken and vegetables baked in the oven. Celia's Bible sat on the table in front of her, unopened.

How was it possible that God had deemed her toddler faith strong enough to face the twin tests of forgiveness and Tawny? It wasn't strong enough. Yet Celia had told Ty she'd study verses and pray, and so she would.

She flipped open her Bible to the concordance. There, she found a tremendous number of scriptures that dealt with forgiveness. She paged to one of them.

Peter came to Jesus and asked, "Lord, how many times shall I forgive my brother or sister who sins against me? Up to seven times?"

Jesus answered, "I tell you, not seven times, but seventy-seven times."

She lifted her head and frowned at the view of her backyard. Seriously? In real life? God expected people to forgive like that? What about the victim? What about all the wrong done to the victim?

What about, she could almost hear God asking, **the wrongs you did to me, Celia?**

I know. But—but what about fairness, God?

Instantly, she comprehended the answer. If God had been fair to her, He'd have consigned her to hell.

Unrest stirred within Celia as His voice became louder and clearer. He was asking her to forgive Ty.

She shut the Bible and dashed into the pantry to alphabetize her spices. She couldn't deal with forgiveness today. Maybe tomorrow.

Turns out, it took six tomorrows before Celia *was* ready to deal with forgiveness. Near midnight, a week after she and Ty had talked about second chances on her front porch step, Celia pulled the little chain on her bedside lamp. Golden light beamed from it, and through gritty eyes she regarded the swirl of sheets and blankets pooling around her waist.

Ty had continued to show up for work all week. Continued to kiss her each day. Which seemed to indicate that he'd not yet eloped with Tawny. He was still—for the moment—Celia's secret boyfriend.

Yet God was not satisfied. Nor was He meek.

She'd kind of been hoping that God would come into her life and fill her with nothing but the sappy pleasure of a Hallmark commercial. Instead, for the past days, He'd been rubbing against her the way a burr that's stuck to your shirt rubs against skin. At this point, the burr had become so insistent that she couldn't sleep.

He wanted her to forgive Ty.

She'd spent time earlier today reading more forgiveness verses. "*You wicked servant,*" she'd read. "*I canceled all that debt of yours because you begged me to. Shouldn't you have had mercy on your fellow servant just as I had on you?*"

Celia bowed her head and let her eyelids drift closed. The forgiveness God had given her had not come cheap. It had come at a great price, and still He'd had the courage to do it. In light of that, what right did she have to withhold forgiveness from Ty? She, who'd been so undeservedly forgiven? Couldn't she cobble together just enough bravery to try?

"I forgive Ty," she said quietly, tentatively, testing the words. They felt rote, with no true feeling to back them up. Maybe, like Ty had suggested, forgiveness was a decision done out of obedience. Maybe later, the feeling would follow?

I forgive Ty. She said the words again and again. *I forgive Ty.* She said them silently at times. At times she whispered them. She opened her hands palms up and did her best to let go.

She wasn't very good at it. Helplessly, desiring to forgive yet lacking the ability, she invited God in. And God, whose character is love, who spoke the world into being, who rescues His people, came.

He came.

And in Him, Celia began to feel her hard heart change.

CHAPTER
TWENTY-NINE

Ty arrived at the shop the next day right as Celia was pulling his favorite dessert out of the oven.

"Do I smell coconut cream pie?" he called from the front room.

"Nope. You must be imagining things."

"I'd know that smell anywhere." He entered the kitchen holding his motorcycle helmet in one hand.

Celia set the first pie on the counter, then reached back for the other two.

"You really must be into me if you're making coconut cream pie."

"It was a slow morning." Not strictly true. She'd simply wanted to bake his favorite.

They let the pie cool to just the right temp, then ate slices of the rich, sweet, milky dessert while standing behind the bakery's display case, as was their habit.

Celia, who'd ditched her hairnet, but still had on her white apron and her boots, listened as Ty praised her pie, her skill with oven mitts, and her attractiveness to the sky and back.

The shop's front door opened, admitting an older gentleman.

Celia sensed Ty stiffen. Odd. Ty liked almost everyone, and almost everyone liked him.

"Hello," Celia called to the gentleman.

"Hello there." He stepped between two bar stools and extended a sun-darkened hand to her. "I don't believe we've met. I'm Howard Sanders."

Ah. The wily neighbor that had fought Ty for ownership of Jim's land. She shook his hand. "I'm Celia."

"A pleasure." He had a closely trimmed white beard and a head full of gorgeously thick snow white hair. His similarities to Santa ended there, however. His face and body were as lean, brown, and gnarled as a strip of beef jerky.

Typically, when she and Ty were behind the counter together, Ty took the lead with customers. This time, he did nothing but toss his empty plate and plastic fork in the trash.

"What can I get you?" Celia asked Howard.

"Is that coconut cream?" He lowered onto a bar stool and gestured toward the pie sitting nearby with two slices missing.

"It is. Would you like some?"

"Yes'm. That and a coffee, please."

"In a Styrofoam cup or china cup?"

"Styrofoam."

Tense quiet fell between the two men as Celia poured coffee and served up pie. Ty slid the caddie that contained cream and sugar near Howard, then crossed his arms over his chest. "What brings you here, Howard?"

"Coffee and pie."

"I've been coming to Cream or Sugar for a while now, and I haven't seen you in here even once before."

"I wasn't hungry for coffee and pie until now." Howard took two sips from his cup while he and Ty glared daggers at each other.

Awkward! Celia was on the verge of charting an escape route into the kitchen when Howard moved his attention to her. "Where are you from, young lady?"

"All over. My family moved around a lot. I lived in Texas during my high school years and attended Plano East."

"Is that right?" He indicated Ty with his coffee. "Did you know Ty there?"

"I did."

A trio of businessmen stopped in for coffees.

While Ty waited on them, Howard asked her about college, places she'd visited in the Pacific Northwest, and what she thought of Holley. As they spoke, he made steady progress on his pie. Once he'd polished it off, he dug some bills from his ancient billfold and placed them under the lip of his plate. "Nice meeting you."

"You too."

He nodded once to Ty, and Ty nodded once back. Then Howard let himself out, leaving Ty and Celia alone in the shop.

Celia took in Ty's inscrutable expression. "That was strange."

"He's strange."

She opened a new package of napkins and went around to the tables, replenishing the dispensers. She'd no idea how much Ty had spent in order to outbid Howard for

MEANT TO BE MINE

Jim's land. She only knew that she didn't want his open wallet policy to end up bankrupting him.

"What in the world are you worrying about now?" he asked, when she reached the table nearest his position behind the counter.

"What makes you think I'm worrying?"

"Seriously, Celia? It's easier than falling off a log to see when you're worrying. What's bothering you?"

She pushed more napkins into a container. "You've had a string of major expenditures lately."

"Yes, but remember? I'm a little bit lucky when it comes to the stock market."

She straightened, her eyes narrowing. "Are you lucky or are you talented?"

"Stupid lucky. That's all."

"No. You're talented at it, aren't you? Really talented."

He ignored her, looking away almost uncomfortably.

Whenever he'd mentioned investing in the past, he'd done so with this same sweep-it-under-the-rug attitude. His success seemed to embarrass the man who was never embarrassed. "You don't like to talk about it because investing isn't the kind of thing a cowboy from Holley, Texas, should excel at." She came around the counter, set her bundle of napkins aside, and confronted him. "Drinking, women, and bull riding. Fine. Making a fortune all by yourself off the stock market? Shameful."

"As usual, you're not making a lick of sense."

"Yes I am, Ty Porter!"

He made a grab behind her and tugged one end of the bow holding her apron secure.

She shrieked and ran. He chased. She put the kitchen's

stainless steel island between them and they circled it a few times.

"Will you bring Addie over to my house tonight?" he asked. "I'll buy dinner."

"Maybe. She might have a playdate at a friend's—"

"I want to kiss you." His lips were smiling but his eyes had gone smoky and determined. "Right now."

"You have to catch me first, which might prove challenging with that bum leg."

"I could catch you even if I only had one leg."

"Isn't that somewhat the case?"

A rumbling sound filled his chest. He made a move.

She pounded up the stairs to the second story, laughing. When he caught her in the hallway, he placed both of his hands on the wall above the sides of her head and took his time lowering his mouth to hers. So long, her heart was drumming by the time he did it.

The moment his doorbell sounded, Ty's mood lifted by a mile. Celia had said she might bring Addie by tonight. He'd pretty much decided she wasn't coming since she usually came earlier, while it was still light out. The sun had just set.

He swung his door open. "I thought you weren't coming. . . ."

Tawny stood on his doorstep. And just like the other times she'd visited him at home since his return to Holley, she held food in her hands. She wore a pink and white Dallas Cowboys jersey, tight jeans, and high-heeled silver sandals that matched her big silver earrings.

"Have you had dinner?" She lifted the two covered dishes she carried.

"Not yet."

"Me either."

He took the dishes from her. She led the way toward his kitchen.

She wanted to stay and eat with him? She hadn't stayed before, but he could guess why she'd decided to stay tonight. He set the containers on the granite island.

She leaned over to peel back the lids. "Chicken-fried steak, mashed potatoes, gravy, and green beans. Your favorite."

"Nice." For the second time today someone had made him his favorite. But only one woman had gotten it right. Chicken-fried steak had been his favorite years ago. His tastes had changed. "I'm surprised you're still bringing me food, Tawny. I injured myself two months ago."

"I guess I'm more doting than most."

"Guess so. Thanks for this."

"You're welcome."

He leaned against his oven and watched her make herself at home in his kitchen.

"I'm wearing my jersey," she said as she worked, "because I brought over the DVD of the '93 Super Bowl. Remember that time you hurt your shoulder and we stayed up all night watching one Cowboys Super Bowl after another, eating popcorn and Red Vines?"

"Yep." They'd been dating then. Mostly he remembered that they'd made out from one end of the sofa to the other while football had played in the background.

"I thought a Super Bowl might be just what you needed to heal your knee."

If so, she'd arrived too late. The knee had already done most of its healing.

Tawny chatted about mutual friends while she set two places for them in front of the tall chairs at the island, poured drinks, warmed up the food.

She'd never looked prettier. She was pretty enough to pose for a NASCAR or motorcycle poster. The kind of pretty that made men take a second look, that made them do and say stupid things. Ty found himself fascinated by her. For the first time in a long time, he was seeing Tawny with new eyes.

"Shall we?" She waved to their filled plates.

They sat. She grabbed his hand, lowered her head, and said grace over their meal. Before letting go, she gave his fingers a squeeze.

As they started eating, she went back to talking, this time about Holley's upcoming fall parade. Ty watched her smooth a section of long dark hair over her shoulder. When she laughed, her blue eyes sparkled.

They had a very long history, the two of them. Dozens of snapshots of her passed through his brain. The neat-as-a-pin elementary school girl. The homecoming queen who'd dated the richest kid at their high school. The first time he'd seen her after returning from the Marines, when she'd been wearing a sorority T-shirt and her hair in a ponytail.

He didn't eat much, though the food tasted good. He talked some. Mostly, he listened. The thoughts filling his head were a lot to wrestle with, to understand.

"Did you hear that Vance and I broke up?"

So. She was finally getting around to her reason for coming. "At least ten people have told me about your breakup. Probably more like twenty." He set down his fork and turned to face her, hooking one boot heel on his chair's rung, planting the other boot squarely against the floor. "I told you that Dr. Amateur's time was running out. He gave it an okay effort, but he didn't even make it as long as most."

"No."

"What happened between you two?"

"We—"

"Actually, let me guess." He scratched his neck, his lips curving up. "He lost his medical license? No? His Range Rover got a flat tire? No? He announced he was gay?"

She chuckled. "None of the above."

"Did he tell you he wanted to marry you, and you told him you weren't ready?"

Both of their smiles faded until only seriousness remained. Ty braced his hands on his thighs.

"I realized," she said, "that I cared about someone else."

"Who?"

She shot him a flirtatious look and rose to clear the dishes. Once she had them all in the sink, she walked into his pantry and came out with a bag of Red Vines. He still ate them and still kept them stocked. She offered him two. He took them but set them aside. She slid her chair out of the way with her hip and stood very close to his bent knee. She took a dainty bite of licorice.

"We've never had very good timing, have we, Tawny?"

"What do you mean?"

"I wanted to marry you before the National Finals Rodeo in Vegas that year, but you turned me down."

"I just needed a little more time."

"Then, for years afterward, I waited for you."

Her face warmed with pleasure.

He lowered his brows—

She leaned into him and pressed her lips to his. She smelled like expensive perfume and lip gloss and his past. He pulled back, then gently, but steadily, set her away from him.

He'd been right about Tawny all along. She was perfect.

What he hadn't understood before? Perfect was a bore. Perfect was like a Red Vine—tight and bright in color. Imperfect was like coconut cream pie, which ran across your plate and made a delicious mess when you ate it warm. He liked coconut cream pie way more than he liked Red Vines.

Tawny was waiting for him to say something, looking at him with sleepy, hungry eyes.

"I'm married," he said.

"For how much longer?"

"Well, that's what I was trying to say earlier about timing. I'm hoping to stay married to Celia for the rest of my life."

Tawny stepped back, her expression sharpening with confusion.

He gave her time to let his words sink in.

"What about us?" she finally asked.

"We'll live in Holley the rest of our lives, and I'll always like you. And I'll compliment you to other people, and we'll be friends."

"I thought we'd end up together, Ty."

"Up until a few months ago, so did I. But now everything's changed."

She frowned down at her shoes, pushed the heel of one

of them into his floor, then looked back up. "It doesn't have to be too late for us."

"It doesn't have to be. But it is. Our timing is so bad, that it almost makes me think we were never meant to marry each other. We had our chances. If we'd been meant for each other, we'd have taken them."

Moisture filled her eyes. She blinked quickly and turned away. "I guess I'll just . . . I'll get my dishes and—"

"Leave the dishes. I'll wash them and leave them on your doorstep tomorrow." He pushed to his feet and handed her a napkin.

She took the napkin and pressed it against the inside corner of each eye.

It had never been in him to feel comfortable about hurting a woman's feelings. He opened his arms. She hesitated, then moved forward to hug him. He hugged her back. It felt bittersweet to say good-bye to someone that, for a big part of your life, you thought you'd marry. They stepped apart.

She straightened her pink jersey. "Why don't you take more time to think about this?"

"I could." He regarded her with kindness. "But my decision won't change."

"Oh, Ty. Just take a little more time." She found her purse and put it over her shoulder. He walked her out. When she glanced back at him on the way to her BMW, he lifted his hand.

Tawny did not make his heart rip open. She didn't turn him on. She didn't frustrate him. She didn't make him the happiest man in the world. She didn't stir his anger to the point that he wanted to swallow Vicodin so he could get through the night. She didn't carry his whole life and future in her hands the way Celia did.

God have mercy on him.

He loved Celia. For him, Celia was perfectly imperfect.

He shook his head. Of course he loved her. Of course he did. This is what love *was*.

Until he'd found Celia again, he hadn't known that he'd spent his adulthood searching for her. But now he could see it plainly. God had been trying to lead him back to her because he'd been too stupid to recognize what she was to him the first time.

He'd married the right woman in Vegas. It had just taken him years to realize it.

CHAPTER
THIRTY

The next morning Celia glanced up from the table she was wiping, spotted Tawny entering Cream or Sugar, and groaned inwardly. This, she did not need. She'd surpassed her limit of pretend-friendly interactions with Tawny Bettenfield.

"Hey, Celia."

"Hi, Tawny." Celia tucked part of her dish towel into her back pocket and approached.

As usual, Tawny had dressed in a silky-looking top, high heels, and cute jewelry. Her hair tumbled down the front of one shoulder. "Is Ty here?"

"He's not coming in until later today. He's with his brothers this morning doing something called a rattlesnake roundup at Whispering Creek."

"Ah." Tawny gave a knowing nod. "Sure."

Tawny, the born-and-bred Holley girl, appeared to be fine with the idea of Ty riding around on horseback and *searching out* rattlesnakes. The Oregon girl was not fine with it. Any sensible person would agree that Ty should leave the rattlesnakes alone in their little hidey holes. The Oregon girl had spent the morning worrying about him.

Most likely if Celia hadn't been worried and Tawny hadn't looked so absurdly beautiful and hadn't broken up with the pediatrician, Celia would have said good-bye. Tawny would have gone about her business. And that would have been the end of the conversation.

Instead, "Would you like a chocolate chip cookie?" Celia asked. Orneriness had made her do it.

"No thanks."

"What about a blueberry scone? I made them this morning."

"That's okay." She moved toward the door. "I'm good. Thanks, though."

Why won't Tawny eat my cooking? "Tawny?"

"Hmm?"

"Can I ask you a question?"

Tawny paused. She raised a manicured eyebrow. "Anything."

Celia stared at her hard. "Do you love Ty?"

Shock slowly separated Tawny's shiny coral lips.

"Because the rumor is that you've wanted to marry him since the first grade. Is that true?"

Tawny said nothing, apparently too polite or too stunned to dignify Celia's question with an answer.

If Tawny had the bravery to admit that she loved Ty, then maybe Celia should have the grace to give Tawny's pursuit of Ty her blessing. A "may the best woman win" sort of agreement. Celia opened her mouth to say something along those lines. What came out was "Ty is my husband."

Tawny's posture stiffened. Her eyes began to narrow.

Celia dropped her hands to her sides and felt her fingers curl in. Weeks of pent-up emotion and confusion over Ty mounted inside her like lava. She couldn't help this ridiculous *compulsion* she had to protect Ty—from himself, from Tawny. "Ty's gorgeous, and he can make your tummy flip with a smile and give you goose bumps with a look. Yes, he can. And so while I understand, very clearly, why you'd love him, I feel compelled to tell you that you can't have him."

"Have you lost your mind?"

"*Have you?* Why else would you chase after a married man?"

"You two are barely married."

"But we *are* married."

"And for your information, I'm not the one chasing after him. Ty's been chasing me. For years."

"Well, not any longer!"

"No? Then how come I was kissing him," Tawny spoke with slow and articulate venom, "just last night?"

A blistering, unbearably painful silence fell. Tawny's words, their meaning, the mental image of Ty and Tawny together, sliced through Celia's brain, her heart. She took two steps backward. *Kissing. Last night.* She set her palm against the cool glass of the bakery display case and groped for balance. Staring at the floor, she willed herself not to pass out or cry or say anything more in front of Tawny.

"Celia?" Tawny asked, tentative. "I'm really sorry I said that."

Celia couldn't respond. With everything she had, she willed Tawny to leave. Right when she sincerely thought she might lose it, she heard the clicking of Tawny's shoes as she walked away. The closing of the door.

The forgiveness Celia had been working to extend to Ty reeled in on itself like a tape measure. And like a tape measure, it snapped closed. She'd known it. She'd known all along that he would do this to her, but like a fool she'd lowered her defenses anyway, and now they were smashed and lying like broken sticks in a circle around her. Worthless.

Oh, Lord. Oh, God. Again. You wanted me to forgive him! And now he's chosen Tawny over me.

Again.

By the time Ty arrived at Cream or Sugar, Celia's stomach had twisted into what felt like a pretzel. Her eyes had gone as moist as Death Valley. Her hands had turned cold and shaky.

If she'd had her way, she'd have locked herself in the pantry and cried buckets after Tawny left. But she was an employee. The bakery's customers didn't know about the devastating information Tawny had handed her. They came in for baked goods and coffee just like they always did.

She was ringing up a line of customers three deep when she saw Ty park his Harley. He pulled off his helmet, exposing rumpled bronze hair. Aviator sunglasses.

When he entered, he greeted the people in line, and they all greeted him back warmly. She could feel his gaze seeking hers, but she studiously focused on counting out change.

"Are you Ty Porter?" a child asked. The red-haired boy looked to be just shy of Addie's age.

"Yeah," Ty answered. "I am."

The boy's face went soft with awe.

"He's a bull-riding fan," his mom said to Ty, settling a hand on the boy's head.

"Good for you." Ty smiled down at the kid. "Who do you root for?"

"You. I mean, I did. Is your leg hurt really bad?"

"Not anymore."

"You going to ride again?"

"No, I'm not."

The boy frowned, his eyes enormous with sadness.

Ty clasped him on the shoulder. "I had a long career. I'm still going to go to some of the events and talk on TV about how the other riders are doing."

The kid nodded. "You were real good. The best I ever seen."

"Thank you."

"Can I have your autograph?"

"If you want it."

"He collects them," his mom added.

Ty set aside his sunglasses and helmet.

One customer left, and Celia served the other and then the boy's mom while Ty handed over his signature and chatted with the boy.

Celia couldn't believe she was about to break up with someone who young children idolized and asked for autographs. She wished Ty wasn't famous, wished he was one of those boring, dependable types who never gave their wives a moment's worry and weren't attractive enough to garner the attention of gorgeous brunettes.

No. She didn't wish all that. She wished Ty was exactly who he was, only trustworthy.

As soon as the mother and son left, Celia went to the

front door and taped the handwritten *Be back in just a minute!* sign she'd prepared to the inset window. Deftly, she turned the lock.

"I'm liking the looks of this," Ty stated.

"Mind coming with me for a minute?"

"I never thought I'd see the day when the rule follower broke a rule and closed the shop during business hours."

"Coming or not?"

"Definitely coming."

She led him up the stairs.

"Now I'm *really* liking the looks of this."

She continued along the hallway to Donetta and Jerry's office, the most private room in the place. With a flick, she turned on the lights. Two metal desks formed an L shape. The space would have been ugly, except for the incongruously exquisite old rectangular windows that framed views of the town square.

Celia crossed her arms.

The sight of Ty's lopsided smile, so full of tenderness, affected her like a dagger. "We can't kiss anymore," she said.

He went still, concern etching a line between his brows.

"And I don't think it's a good idea for you to work here anymore, either."

A few beats went by. "Excuse me?" His voice had gone raspy and dangerous.

Her chest tightened.

"Say whatever it is you need to say to me, Celia. Plainly."

"When we started kissing, I didn't ask where our relationship was going. I didn't ask for a future. I only asked for one thing. I asked you not to kiss anyone else while you were kissing me."

"And?"

"And Tawny came by earlier. She told me that the two of you kissed last night."

Instant fury filled his face. "Is that all she said? That we kissed?"

"Yes."

"She didn't say that *she* was the one that kissed me?"

She'd expected him to have a quick retort, would have been surprised if he hadn't.

"I pulled away after two seconds," he said, "and told her that the chance for a relationship between us was over. Did she tell you that?"

"No."

"That's what happened." The room's stark fluorescent light hid nothing, not a single detail of him. She could see the faint scars on his face, the piercing blue of his eyes, the taut lines of his torso beneath his T-shirt. "Do you believe me?"

Since her confrontation with Tawny, she'd had time to think everything through multiple times. If a friend of hers had come to her with this scenario—a boyfriend who'd kissed someone, then blamed it on the other woman—Celia would have advised her friend to treat the boyfriend with the highest level of distrust. Red flags cropped up during the beginnings of doomed relationships. Celia believed this, believed that women had to heed those flags if they wanted to escape intact.

"Celia?" he asked, tense. "I need for you to believe me."

"Trust is something that takes a long time to rebuild—"

"I would have given you all the time you needed. But this thing with Tawny has happened, and I need for you to believe me *now*."

She still had a dash of intelligence left in her brain. She still had a desire to protect herself. Most important, she had a child. She couldn't afford to be gullible. "Look, I don't even want to know what happened between you and Tawny last night. It doesn't matter—"

"It matters a lot to me."

"This fling between us—"

"Fling?"

"—has been fun, but I can't do it anymore. I'm going to end it before it goes any further or gets more confusing."

"I am not confused." Fierce certainty radiated from him.

"For Addie's sake, we'll return to being friends."

He made a slashing motion with his hand. "I don't want to be your friend. I have plenty of friends. Everyone in this town is my friend." Visibly, he struggled to hang on to his composure. "You can't tell me you want nothing more from me than friendship."

"I want nothing more from you—"

"No," he answered immediately. "That's not true."

She refused to lose her cool, to let emotion overtake her. Even if it killed her, she *could not* show him how much she'd let herself care about him and how much he'd hurt her—again.

They looked at each other with raw and difficult honesty.

"I love you," he said.

Her heartbeat thumped. He'd never said those words to her before.

"I love you." His eyes glittered blue. "And I want our marriage to be a real marriage. I want to be married to you all my life. You. Only you."

She considered running away—out of the building, as far and as fast as she could go, to flee from her razor-sharp longing for him. "You can talk the talk," she said haltingly. "You really can." He'd even talked her into marrying him once. She'd regretted it for years afterward. In her weakness, she'd *wanted* to let him persuade her then, just like she wanted to let him persuade her now. "You say all the right things. And maybe you even mean most of what you say. But think about it. A real marriage between us? Husband and wife? You can't be faithful to me for a lifetime."

"I swear to you that I can."

"I don't—" Her voice broke. She drew herself up. "I don't trust you not to break my heart again, and I can't risk it. I can't risk Addie having to live through that. I'm not the one for you, Ty." It physically pained her to speak the words. "There are so many women who'd jump at the chance to date you—"

"How can you say that to me?" Color rose on his cheekbones.

Now she'd done it. She'd pushed him too far.

"I don't want to date other women."

She tried to swallow. Couldn't. "We can co-parent Addie—"

"I don't want to co-parent! I want to marry you, but I'm an idiot because you won't give me a chance. And you're a coward because you want some kind of guarantee when all I can give you is my word. Life doesn't come with guarantees, Celia. Neither do relationships or marriages. Bad things happen."

"I'd rather avoid the bad things that I can see coming."

"I'm standing right in front of you, and you can't see anything at all."

She felt frozen inside. Stricken. "Ty . . ."

"Sometimes you just have to have faith, Celia. When Tawny kissed me, I stopped it immediately. She's not the one I want. I love you and I want to be married to you. *Trust. Me.*"

"I did," she said. "Once. And once was enough."

He held her gaze for a searing second, then stalked from the room.

Celia remained rooted to the spot, self-righteous in her certainty that she'd done the right thing. And so happy about it that she covered her eyes with her palms and wept.

Ty was not a man given to anger. But Celia had made him angry. Wildly angry.

He drove his truck out of town in search of open space. One turn onto a remote country road that went nowhere led him to another road to another. His pulse beat his veins. A headache pounded his skull.

He couldn't believe that Tawny had screwed him over by telling Celia about that kiss. Why would she have done that? And why hadn't Celia believed him when he'd told her the truth? If Celia would have listened to him and trusted him, he could have rescued the situation.

But no. She'd go to the grave before she'd trust him. She'd rather be unhappy. She'd rather he be unhappy. She'd rather do *anything* than take a chance on trusting him.

He couldn't defend himself against the past because he had made a huge mistake in Vegas. He'd admitted it to her and apologized. He wasn't a perfect man, and he'd even agree that she could do better than him.

On the other hand, he wasn't the same man he'd been in Vegas.

Whenever Celia started acting like he was, it made him crazy. He had no way to prove her wrong. How could he prove her wrong unless she let him prove it?

He raked his hair back with an unsteady hand.

He couldn't have her. She'd told him so in every possible way since the day they'd had lunch in Oregon—

His phone buzzed. A text.

Are you still able to pick up Addie from school today?

He almost threw the phone out the window. Should he curse her every which way to sundown for expecting him to pick Addie up today? Or should he curse her for expecting him not to, like some deadbeat dad too selfish to remember his responsibilities to his child?

He held his body rigid against the rage rising inside him. Drove. Checked the time. Threw the truck into park and typed a message back to her.

I'll pick her up from school like I always do. I'm trustworthy.

Once Ty got Addie back to Celia's house and gave her the food Celia had set out—what kid wanted to eat an organic rice cake and a banana as an after-school snack?—they went into her room just like they always did so she could give him princess lessons.

She started in on a story about Rapunzel.

It took him a while to register it when the room went silent. He'd been staring at the wall, stewing. He looked to Addie and took in the sight of her thin frame and sweet face.

"What's the matter, Daddy?"

"Nothing. I just zoned out for a second. Sorry about that. Go on."

"I'm still hungry," she whined.

"Okay, let's go get you something else to eat." They went to the kitchen, and he gave her at least five food options and three drink options.

She kept wrinkling her nose and shaking her head and saying, "I don't want that. Is there anything else?"

Addie usually behaved like a prize student for Ty. Today she complained nonstop. Nothing would please her. As time passed, Ty's patience stretched tighter and tighter.

When he heard Celia let herself into the house, he pushed to his feet, hiding a wince when pain ran up his injured leg. "Addie, I have a lot of stuff I need to do today. Your mom's here, so I'm going to take off."

"But—"

"I'll see you tomorrow after school." He and Addie walked into the hallway and came face to face with Celia.

She immediately turned her attention to Addie. "Hi!" she said, pretending to be the most cheerful person alive.

"Good day at work?" he asked, making a stab at friendliness in front of Addie.

"Mmm hmm." She avoided looking at him.

Blind, stubborn woman! She was so wrong. And also so beautiful it made his gut churn. He desperately wanted her . . . everything about her and everything she represented.

"What have you all been up to?" Celia asked Addie.

"I ate my snack, but it tasted yucky."

Ty said nothing. An ice cream sundae would have tasted yucky to Addie today.

"Then we played in my room," Addie said.

"Great!"

Addie looked back and forth between the two of them.

"Well. Thanks for bringing Addie home." Celia's gaze stopped on his face for a moment, then crossed by. "I appreciate it."

"Yep." He kissed Addie and left.

"What's the matter with you and Daddy?" he heard Addie ask Celia as he walked away.

He drove straight to a bar called Deep in the Heart. It smelled like beer, peanuts, and cigarettes. Most of the lighting came from the neon signs on the walls. He ordered a shot. After he'd thrown it back, he clunked down his glass. Despair shifted through him. He ordered another.

Music filled the interior of Deep in the Heart, but it couldn't touch the darkness in his head. People spoke to him: the bartender, locals he knew, a stranger or two. He said the expected things. Felt no better. Ordered more shots.

No telling how much time had passed when Bo sat on the bar stool next to him. "I heard you were here."

Ty wanted to tell him off. His older brother. If he'd been more like Bo, Celia would have loved him back. Honorable Bo, who always said and did the right things. Always had, since they were kids. Bo'd been the one helping his father with the horses; Ty had been the one jumping off a cliff into shallow water.

Now Bo had what he deserved: a wife he loved and a home and a career. And Ty had what he deserved: nothing.

He wished Jake had come. Jake was at least as screwed up as he was.

When the room started tilting, Ty swore viciously.

Bo didn't lecture. He just waited until Ty was finally forced to make a choice between the lesser of two evils: leave the bar or vomit. Ty picked leave. Bo helped Ty into his truck, drove him home, and got him settled in his horrible dark house.

Ty lay alone on his bed with his wrist covering his eyes, feeling like he wanted to puke, his head spinning like he was on a carousel.

He hated his house. Why was it so quiet? Why was it so brown?

Why didn't Celia live here with him?

Celia. He squeezed shut his eyes as bitter pain whipped him.

Hours later, Ty slid his eyes open. The only light came from the open doorway to his master bathroom. His ears picked up no sound.

He pushed to sitting and wheezed. It all came back to him, the physical misery of his hangover plus all the things Celia had said to him. The fact that she couldn't trust him.

He hissed every piece of profanity he knew as he limped into the bathroom.

Bo had left a note for him on the counter saying that he and Meg were staying the night in his guest bedroom and to wake them if he needed anything or if they could help him.

No, they could not help him.

Ty pushed the note into the trash and jerked open the drawers one by one, searching. Wait . . . he remembered now. It wasn't in the drawers. He'd tossed it into the cabinet.

He opened the cabinet door. Over on the side, next to his spare change, rested a white paper sack with a receipt stapled to it. It had been there since before the first time Celia had dumped his pills. He tore away the sack and let it fall.

A prescription bottle of Vicodin.

He squinted down at it in his hand. His mouth watered, he wanted the pills so badly. Two or three wouldn't hurt. They'd dull everything he was thinking and feeling.

"I don't trust you not to break my heart again." Celia's words swam through his brain. *"I can't risk it. I can't risk Addie having to live through that."*

Was she wrong? He wanted her to be wrong, wanted to be someone she and Addie could trust. Had he really changed?

Or was he as weak and as faithless as she claimed him to be?

CHAPTER

THIRTY-ONE

Celia woke before dawn the next morning, overcome with the need to bake something fattening. She did her best to squelch the urge and go back to sleep. Gloomy thoughts and depressing feelings prevented that from happening, so she forced herself from bed.

Striving for a healthy emotional outlet that didn't involve sugar, she took herself to her front yard. She stood in the dewy grass in bare feet, watering her plants and pulling weeds while five a.m. darkness sank around her like an anchor. She noted with numb detachment that her caladiums were coming along nicely. Flourishing.

When she finally reentered her house, she faced many productive options. She could catch up with things online. Finalize ideas for an anniversary cake a local couple had ordered. Do laundry. Iron . . .

She marched into her kitchen and stirred together the most wicked oatmeal walnut chocolate-chunk cookies she could muster. As soon as she pulled them from the oven, she stood over the tray and scooped the most deformed one onto a napkin. Since nobody else would want this particular cookie, she'd do it a favor and eat it.

Hot, nutty dough filled her mouth. She chewed—stopped.

It didn't taste right. In fact, it tasted wrong.

She spit the bite back into her napkin, then tossed the napkin in the trash and contemplated her batch. What had she done? As she went back over the steps she'd taken when making her dough, it hit her. She'd left out eggs.

Eggs! A bedrock ingredient. She'd been baking since middle school. Omitting eggs was a novice move. The sort of mistake a ten-year-old might make.

Today was *not* her day. Disgusted and devoid of the mental relief she usually found through baking, she dumped all the cookies in the trash.

After showering, she dressed in a peasant top and canary yellow shorts. She bypassed her boots and donned her trusty leather sandals. Then she sat in her living room watching early morning news coverage of weather, traffic, and DFW homicides while fiercely trying to think of anything except . . .

Him.

She delivered Addie to kindergarten, then parked her Prius back at the gingerbread house and covered the short distance to the square on foot.

American-made trucks passed by her, as did the cars the yuppies owned: SUVs, Volvos, a Lexus. Shade from wide-reaching pecan and elm trees graced both her and the stately Victorians. When she reached the now-familiar square, her gaze took in the hodgepodge of establishments. Each unique in color, brick, or awning, all equally sure of themselves after having survived so long. The courthouse stood in its central location like an elegantly dressed officer ready for duty. The light posts faithfully supported their baskets of blooms.

The word *home* came over her like a *twang* on a guitar string, reverberating physically. The girl who'd moved from state to state all her life had finally found home in a most unusual place. Not in the lushly green northwest. But here. In this funny little Texan town that didn't have a farmers' market and smelled like barbecued brisket.

She made her way toward Cream or Sugar, uncertain whether Holley felt like home because of the place itself or because *he* lived here. If *he* lived in Thailand, she might right at this moment be strolling through downtown Bangkok experiencing the very same mystifying sense of belonging.

She skirted behind Cream or Sugar and let herself in the back. Within minutes, she'd dressed, washed up, and busied herself frosting sheet cake alongside Jerry.

Celia studied him, the man with the Hulk exterior and the marshmallow interior. "What do you like best about being married to Donetta, Jerry?"

He considered the answer for a while. "She's good in bed."

On this particular day, Celia had not expected to smile. But she did smile at Jerry, and it felt like a sentimental gift. "I see."

From the front room, Celia could hear Donetta calling out, "Ya'll come back now!" then launching into a tirade aimed at a customer who'd had the bad judgment to voice the word *Yankees*.

"There's something else," Jerry said. "About Donetta."

"Yes?"

"She interrupts, and she tells tall tales more than her share. But I know her heart. It's a good heart. Donetta's . . . my person. Do you know what I mean?"

"I'm not sure." But deep down, she *did* know.

"We've shared a life, Donetta and me. We've got kids and grandkids. She's the closest friend I have on this earth. I've been married to her for two-thirds of my life. And I only pray that the good Lord takes me first. Because I don't want to live one day without her."

"Oh, Jerry." Emotion lifted within Celia. It was the longest speech she'd ever heard him make.

"I know what folks mean when they say their wife is their better half."

"I think you're the better half."

"No, Celia. It's Donetta. It's always been her."

As she'd requested, Ty did not return to Cream or Sugar. When she arrived at the gingerbread house to relieve him late in the afternoon, he looked hung over and like he hadn't slept. However rotten he'd been feeling, though, he hadn't let it stop him from taking care of Addie.

The same the next day, Friday. He looked like a wreck, but Addie had been able to count on him.

Each evening Celia spent long periods of time in prayer. It hadn't occurred to her to distance herself from God or blame Him the way she'd done in the past. Her decision to renew her relationship with God was the one thing she knew for sure she'd gotten right. Plus, she simply needed Him too much. Her growing faith brought her the only sense of steadiness or peace she had left.

Without God, her life would go back to tasting like the ill-fated oatmeal chocolate-chunk cookies she'd made the other morning. She'd come to understand that God was the most integral ingredient to her life recipe; He was the egg.

Meg began to call and come by to check on Celia more frequently than before. Celia didn't know what to tell her, so she told her nothing. Words seemed superfluous, anyway. She could see in Meg's compassionate face that Meg knew exactly what was going on.

Celia slid the *Give Peace a Chance* charm off her key ring and let it fall from her fingers into the garbage for the final time.

The weekend came. Ty made it easy for her to avoid him. He didn't text. Didn't call. She kept checking her phone, half dreading and half desperate for contact from him. Her brain and her heart continued to face off like bitter enemies.

Addie asked a hundred times on Saturday when she'd next be able to see Daddy and ride Whitey. Celia knew that Ty would be glad to take Addie out riding. In order to set that up, though, Celia would have to communicate with him. The prospect made her turn chicken.

On Sunday Celia and Addie attended church, then spent the afternoon visiting Danny. He'd healed enough to return to his own home, but he still couldn't get around easily. Celia helped him maneuver from his walker to a dining room chair, then placed a slice of cinnamon-swirl coffee cake and a mug of freshly made coffee in front of him. "For you."

He took a sip, his eyes rolling upward toward the ceiling. "It's heaven, C." He tucked into the cake. "And this! You have *got* to let me sell this online at my store. Like seriously." He held a bite of coffee cake aloft on his fork. "If I could feed this to an eligible woman, she'd be putty in my hands."

"The right woman for you will come along one day. I just know it." Celia squeezed his shoulder. "Until then, and always, you'll have Addie and me."

"You're the two best girls in the world."

"Hardly. But at least we're yours, Uncle Danny. And no matter what, we have each other."

The entire time Celia sat across from him, listening to him plan his next dating move, thoughts of Ty suffocated her.

Did Ty truly love her, the way he said that he did? He'd certainly looked earnest when he'd told her he wanted to be her husband. Had he been telling the truth when he'd said that Tawny had been the one to kiss him and that he'd pulled away? Would he start dating Tawny now that Celia had rejected him?

Addie asked Celia a hundred more times when she'd be able to see Daddy and ride Whitey.

That evening, after Celia had tucked Addie into bed, she walked the rooms of the house the same way she'd been walking them since the day she'd ended things with Ty—like a ghost. Aimless and miserable. Missing him.

Before they'd started kissing, she'd at least had him

in her life. He'd been her friend and her supporter. He'd believed in her. She dearly wished she could go back to that. That she couldn't left her with a nagging, unrelenting sense that she'd lost something irreplaceable.

Before he'd stopped coming to Cream or Sugar, she'd thought that the baking had been the best part of the job. Now she realized that it had been him. *He'd* been the best part.

Suddenly, all of it was gone. Not just the kissing, but all of it. She was left with a man whose only role in her life was to collect her daughter from school.

She regretted everything. Everything she'd lost; hurting him, breaking up with him. Yet she continued to stand by her reasons. As agonizing as it was, as much as she cried in the shower each morning and into her pillow each night, as much as she physically yearned for him, she still believed she'd made the right choice. In the end, even if Ty fancied himself in love with her, even if Tawny had been the one to kiss Ty, Celia couldn't make herself believe that he was capable of staying true to her for a lifetime.

She pulled out a dining room chair, and sat at the table where she and Ty had eaten dinner and laughed and given each other heated looks when Addie wasn't paying attention.

God? I feel like the most untrusting, unforgiving woman alive. I broke up with Ty to protect Addie and myself. Do you understand? I think I did the right thing. I think. Did I?

No sense of answer or direction.

You're not really making yourself clear.

She laid her hands in her lap and looked down at them,

listening. The point, she supposed, wasn't whether God answered her question. The point was that *He* was the answer. To every question.

Hard circumstances taught a person valuable lessons. The current circumstance was teaching Celia that even in the center of grief and confusion, God was enough for her.

The burr returned. The one that rubbed against her painfully, convicting. God wanted her to forgive Ty yet again.

She scrunched shut her eyes. "I forgive Ty." She concentrated on working through all the kinks and knots of her unforgiveness. Over and over she repeated it. *I forgive Ty.*

The word *forgiveness* sounded gentle and round-edged. If it had been a drawing, it might have been a sunrise. In Celia's reality, though, achieving that sunrise required dark and dirty work. It meant removing an iron spike of bitterness that had lodged itself in the pit of her soul. The spike was sharp, painful, disinclined to move. With God's help she'd managed to dislodge it once before. But it had come back and may well continue to come back.

One of the forgiveness verses twined through her memory. *"How many times shall I forgive my brother or sister who sins against me? Up to seven times?"*

Jesus answered, "I tell you, not seven times, but seventy-seven times."

For her, forgiveness had not been an easy one-time thing. It was a decision she had to make repeatedly. A process.

More dreary days slipped by.

A new *Give Peace a Chance* key ring did not appear.

Her exchange with Ty went even worse than usual when she arrived home from work on Thursday. She found him and Addie in the front room, playing checkers.

He had on a baseball cap backwards, jeans, his sterling watch. The storm of resentments between them made it difficult to look him in the face.

He said his good-byes to Addie. Celia held the front door open for him. When he passed through, she stepped onto the porch after him. "Ty—"

He stopped.

"I . . ."

The mask he wore around Addie had gone. He gazed at her with undiluted anger and pain. By the looks of it, he was still every bit as furious as he'd been the day she'd broken up with him.

Why had she thought talking to him might be a good idea? "How are you doing?" she asked.

"Not well."

She felt her heart fracturing. *I love you*, she wanted to say. The words filled her. They swirled, pushing against her from the inside, demanding that she give them voice.

At the sound of children's voices, both Ty and Celia looked toward the noise. Neill and his two boys were walking toward the gingerbread house for a playdate.

Ty stiffened at the sight of them, his back muscles tightening. Then he strode toward his truck.

Neill lifted his hand to Celia as he approached. "Hey there!"

"Hey." She tried for a smile.

Her attention cut back to Ty. He swung his head around

and gave Neill a look so terrifying that it would have sent Neill into a dead faint if he'd seen it. He climbed into his truck and started the engine.

She invited Neill and his boys into the house. The kids dove into a new game of checkers. She and Neill watched their antics while Neill told her a story about one of the partners in his law firm.

She loved Ty. *I love him*, she kept thinking. She'd been circumventing it and trying to talk herself out of it in every possible way. All her efforts had done no good. She'd fallen in love with the same man three times in one lifetime.

Maybe she hadn't. Made she'd only truly fallen in love with Ty Porter one time—the day he'd strolled into ceramics class, sat down beside her, and smiled at her for the very first time. When he'd left Texas after graduation and when he hadn't loved her back in Vegas, she'd done her best to pound her love for him into oblivion. But it had proven stronger than the strongest metal ever created.

Neill kept talking.

Celia's gaze rested fondly on Addie's dark blond bob. Her life had been full of her daughter for so long that she hadn't known whether she could love a man again. It came as something of a surprise to her, not just that she could love a man again, but how very, very much she could.

When Neill and the boys left, Celia got down on her knees in Addie's room to help her pick up the toys.

"Mommy?"

"Yes?"

"Daddy's sad."

Celia pushed a curl behind her ear. "I know."

"I gave him some chamomile tea today." She straightened the dress of the Cinderella doll she held. "It didn't make him feel better."

"It didn't?"

She shook her head. "I think he's sad because you're not wearing the boots he gave you anymore."

Addie's feet were still loyally encased by her pink boots, just as they had been since the day Ty had given them to her. "He's nice and funny, Mom. I really like Daddy's house. Whitey's there." Her small fingers smoothed Cinderella's hair. "He has a motorcycle. His bedtime stories are good."

Celia nodded.

"Cinderella's happy now that she married Prince Charming. Daddy will be happy when you put on a white dress and a long"—she indicated a veil with her hands—"sheet on your head and marry him."

Celia didn't have the heart to launch into a talk about how much she and Ty respected each other or the vagaries of adult decisions or why mommies and daddies sometimes chose to live apart. "I love you, Addie," she said simply and truthfully. "Ty loves you, too."

"Oh, Mom. You really need to start wearing his boots."

"Jerry and I have something we'd like to discuss with you," Donetta said to Celia the next day.

"Oh?" Celia continued sweeping the front room of the bakery.

"It's the kind of talk, Celia, that you're going to want to sit down for."

She glanced at Donetta, worry immediately rising. "What's the matter?"

Donetta took the broom from her and indicated the table at the rear of the bakery. "Jerry!" she hollered.

Celia sank into a chair, uneasy.

Jerry emerged from the kitchen and the two of them took the seats across from her. "You know that Jerry and I have been wanting to retire for a while now."

"Yes."

"We were planning to work a few more years, then put the place on the market."

Jerry regarded Celia steadily. The sympathy in his face sent a chill of foreboding through her.

"More than a week ago," Donetta continued, "we got a call from a longtime friend. Out of the blue. He told us he wanted to buy Cream or Sugar."

No, Celia thought. *Please, God, no.*

"It took us by surprise." Donetta shrugged. "We didn't know he had an interest in owning a donut shop. But then, you never can tell about people. He offered us a pretty penny for this place."

A sliding sensation of fear moved through Celia's abdomen. They were going to sell Cream or Sugar to a stranger.

"Our friend offered above what we would have asked for the shop if we'd put it on the market," Donetta said.

"The two of us have spent a lot of time talking about it," Jerry put in.

"We know you depend on this job, and we don't take that lightly. But we also have to think about our retirement." Donetta moved some of the frosted feathers back from her face. "We told our friend that we'd take his offer. Signed the paper work last night."

No! Celia wanted to wail. Why hadn't they told her about this sooner? She'd have offered to buy the shop. She adored this place. She'd painted the walls, baked pastries for it, and cleaned every surface as lovingly as if Cream or Sugar already belonged to her.

Looking into Donetta and Jerry's faces, she could see that they knew all that. They also knew what she didn't want to admit to herself: She'd never be able to get a loan for an amount that would enable her to buy Cream or Sugar.

No. Panic began to tighten around her throat. "What does the new owner plan to do with Cream or Sugar?"

"We're not really sure," Donetta answered.

"Will he keep it a coffee shop?"

"We just don't know," Jerry said.

"We care about you, honey. We'll help you. You're smart, and you're going to be just fine."

She didn't want to be just fine. She wanted to go on working here. It was her dream, this shop. The loss of Cream or Sugar on top of the loss of Ty felt like a staggering weight stacked onto a load already too heavy to bear.

No, she thought again, uselessly. She hovered on the verge of tears as her gaze traveled over the interior of her beloved bakery.

No!

Ty had propped his boots on his living room coffee table. He had the *Wall Street Journal* open and had been trying and retrying to read an article about a hedge fund manager. His concentration was shot. His brain only wanted to think about one destructive thing.

Celia.

He thought about her last thing at night. First thing in the morning. While he showered. As he was getting dressed. Driving.

She'd made his life not worth a nickel to him. She'd made him furious. She'd made him doubt his sanity.

His cell phone rang. He checked caller ID. "Hi, Meg."

"Hi, Ty."

"What's up?"

"I'm just leaving Celia's."

The concerned tone of her voice had him setting aside the newspaper. "And?"

"She's really upset. The people that own Cream or Sugar . . ."

"Donetta and Jerry?"

"Right. They told her today that they sold the shop."

Ty froze, his brain struggling to comprehend. They'd sold Cream or Sugar? Donetta and Jerry had owned it for as long as he could remember. As far as he knew, it wasn't even for sale.

"Ty?"

"I'm here." He rose to his feet in one angry motion, yanked his reading glasses from his face. "Who did they sell it to?"

"Celia doesn't know who. What do you think we can do to help her through this? She absolutely loves that shop—"

"Meg, I'll have to call you back later."

"Sure."

He disconnected and scrolled through his contacts. He hit Donetta's name and paced while the phone rang.

"Hello?"

"Donetta, it's Ty Porter. I heard that you sold Cream or Sugar."

A pause. "It's not common knowledge around town yet, but yes. We did."

His grip on the phone tightened. At this point it wouldn't do any good to rail at her for not telling him about her plans. "To whom?"

"Now, you know I have a deep fondness for you, Ty. But I can't see as how that's any of your business."

"Donetta, God love you, I'm about to have a stroke. Please tell me right this minute who you sold the shop to."

"An old friend of Jerry's and mine. He's lived in Holley forever."

"His name?"

"Howard Sanders."

When Howard Sanders answered his front door in response to Ty's knock, he did nothing but study Ty for a good long while. Gloating lit his old eyes. "Ty."

"Howard."

Like he had all the time in the world, Howard brought a pipe to his mouth and took a long draw.

"Do you know why I'm here?" Ty asked.

"I believe I do."

"Can I come in?"

"Surely."

Ty followed Howard into a dim room that smelled like leather and tobacco. Both men sat. Howard reclined to puff on his pipe. Ty sat upright, intently focused on Howard. "You bought Cream or Sugar."

"I did."

"And not because you want to go into the donut business."

"No."

Ty remembered the day Howard had come into the bakery. The older man had watched him and Celia together. Then and there, Howard must have discovered Ty's weakness.

"You have something I want," Howard said. "You have Jim's land."

"And now you have something I want."

"Yes." Howard extended the hand with the pipe to rest along the arm of his chair. "What should we do about this dilemma?"

"Make me an offer."

Howard's face had so many lines it looked like tree bark. The lines deepened as one edge of his mouth tipped into a smile. "An even trade."

Jim's land was worth far more than the value of Cream or Sugar. Not only that, but Ty needed that land to raise rodeo stock. Without his bull riding, without Celia, his plan to enlarge his farm was all he had left.

"All's fair in love and war." Howard's smile grew.

Ty wanted to snap the older man's neck. Pain flicked along a muscle in his jaw.

"The donut shop for the land," Howard said. "That's my offer."

A sudden chill ran along the back of Ty's neck, his shoulders, and down his upper arms. He sensed God strongly, just like he did every night when he pulled out the bottle of Vicodin. Every night so far, God had stopped him from taking any.

Maybe God was using this situation to test his commitment to Celia—

No, he realized. God already knew the depth of his commitment to Celia. God was using this situation to prove the depth of his commitment to Celia to *him*. He could remember asking God, *Show me who I am.*

His heart drummed as understanding dawned.

God was answering his prayer. All this time, he'd doubted whether he was good enough or trustworthy enough for Celia. His track record stunk. His past actions betrayed him. Celia might never give him another chance to do the right thing. But God . . . God was offering him that chance now.

Almost six years after his greatest regret, God had presented him with a miracle opportunity to do what he should have done in Vegas.

To love her.

"Well?" Howard demanded. "What's your answer?"

"Celia!"

Celia lifted her head. "Donetta?" She was in her bedroom at the gingerbread house in the process of changing out of her church clothes.

"I'm coming up your front walk." The older woman's voice sailed in through the open windows.

Donetta had never once paid Celia a visit at home. Frankly, after the terrible news about Cream or Sugar, Celia didn't know if she could take another meeting with Donetta. "Be right there."

She pulled on a pair of skinny jeans because for the first time since she'd moved to Holley, the day's temperature merited jeans.

"Waiting at your door!" Donetta called.

"Just a sec." She selected a white tank and, over that, a tunic-style purple top.

She peeked in on Addie. After church, Meg and Bo had taken them to lunch before returning them home just ten minutes ago. Addie lay tummy-down on the carpet of her room, engrossed by a game on her tablet computer.

Celia opened her front door. "Hi."

Donetta bustled in wearing her navy Keds, high-waisted pants, and a Rangers T-shirt. The Rangers had made it into the postseason, so Donetta now dressed in Ranger wear every day of the week. "I have news." She waved Celia into the living room.

They settled in front of the picture window in the chairs that faced one another. Drizzle fell over the view of the front lawn, quieting everything, causing Celia's plants to nod beneath the weight of the water.

"News?" Celia asked.

"Two important pieces of news. The first one I promised him I wouldn't tell. . . ."

At the mention of the word *him*, Celia's heart jolted. She knew exactly who Donetta meant.

Donetta blew out a breath. "After we met the first time, remember how I called you back about the job at Cream or Sugar? I told you that Jerry and I had reconsidered and that we'd decided to pay you double?"

Celia nodded.

"Well. I sort of lied about that last part." She tipped her head to the side. "Not sort of. I did lie. Jerry and I didn't increase your salary. Ty did."

Wait. *What what what?*

"He's been paying half your salary since the day you came to work at Cream or Sugar. He wanted to make sure you could afford to take the job there."

She'd run into Ty right after her initial interview with Donetta. He'd taken her to get snow cones. Her mind raced back in time. She hadn't spoken to him or anyone, however, about her desire to work at the bakery. "I never told him about the job offer at Cream or Sug—"

"He came into the shop the same day you did, asking whether you'd been in about the position. He figured it out, honey."

In that mysterious way Ty had of understanding her, he'd found out about the interview and he'd . . . he'd offered to pay half her salary? That amounted to a great deal of money. Money he'd never mentioned to her. Even when she'd been breaking up with him, he hadn't said a word about it. Why hadn't he thrown it in her face? It would have made her feel two inches tall. Instead, even over the past days when he'd been so angry, he'd continued to pay half her income?

She shook her head slowly, dizzily. She'd received the call from Donetta telling her they'd decided to increase her hourly wage the day after she'd first attended church. "I thought . . ."

"You thought what?"

"It seems silly now. I thought at the time, the day you called me, that God had done it. That He'd made it possible for me to work at Cream or Sugar."

"God *did* do it, Celia. He just didn't use Jerry and me. He used Ty."

Celia lifted her hands to her cheeks. She peered at Donetta with round eyes.

"I told Ty I wouldn't tell you. I'm breaking my promise to him, because I think it's for the greater good."

Celia couldn't find words.

"Don't go getting faint on me now," Donetta ordered. "There's more, so take your hands off your face."

Celia dropped her arms.

"Now you're gaping like a catfish."

Celia clicked her lips together.

"That was only the first piece of news. Here's the second. I got a call from Howard Sanders a few minutes ago."

It took Celia a moment to pull up the name. "The man who competed with Ty for Jim's land?"

"Apparently so. I didn't know anything about the land until today."

Celia couldn't fathom what Howard Sanders had to do with anything.

"Howard is the person who bought Cream or Sugar, Celia, and I just learned *why* he bought it. He bought it because he still wants the land."

Celia's ribs constricted around her racing heart. "I don't understand what the bakery has to do with the land. The land is Ty's now, and he'll never sell it. Ever since his bull riding ended, he's been planning to raise rodeo stock. The way he explained it to me, he needs both his land and the new piece of land to do that."

"Howard told me that he visited you and Ty at Cream or Sugar one day."

"Yes."

"Howard must have heard the rumors about the two of you. He came to the shop to see for himself. Howard's observant, honey. He must have recognized that Ty loved you." Donetta's expression gentled. "Howard saw that the person Ty loved, in turn loved the bakery."

A tremor dashed down Celia's spine.

"Howard bought Cream or Sugar so that he could use it as a bargaining chip, Celia. He met with Ty last night and offered him an even exchange. The bakery for the land."

Celia rushed to her feet. "No."

Donetta regarded her levelly.

"And Ty?" Her voice shook. "Ty turned down Howard's offer. Right?"

"No, honey. He didn't. He traded his land for the bakery. For you."

"He couldn't have!"

"He did. That's why Howard called me, to explain that the bakery had already changed ownership."

Celia took off, frantically searching for her purse and her car keys. She dashed through all the rooms once and had to go back through them a second time before locating her purse and keys where they always sat, on the entry table.

Donetta stood in the foyer. "I'll stay here and watch Addie."

"Thank you."

Celia ducked into Addie's room. "I have to leave for a bit, but Donetta's here."

"Uh-huh." Addie hardly even lifted her head.

Halfway across the front porch, Celia realized she wore no shoes. She detoured to her closet, pushed her feet into her cowgirl boots, then rushed past Donetta to her Prius.

"Go get your man, honey!" Donetta called after her, one fist in the air. "Go get your man!"

As she drove to Ty's, the shaking in Celia's hands pervaded to the deepest regions of her. *What had Ty done?*

He'd called her a coward the day of their fight. She'd thought him wrong at the time. She'd viewed her actions as smart. But the brutal truth? Loving him did terrify her.

Being hurt by him again terrified her.

Forgiving him terrified her.

She'd been using her inability to trust him like a breastplate to protect her heart.

She *had* been a coward. But Ty? Ty was not.

In this part of Texas, he was famously brave for his willingness to climb onto the backs of wild bulls. But that didn't cover the half of it. He'd put himself out there that day in the upstairs office by telling her plainly how he felt about her. And now, if Donetta could be believed, he'd gone and proved it by sacrificing his future for her sake.

He needed that land for his own dream. What had he done?

Halfway up the long private drive that led to Ty's house, she met a truck coming the other way. Jake.

They stopped, both rolling down their windows.

He looked at her with his black Stetson low and his scar painfully obvious.

She was so addled, she had no faculty for small talk.

After a tense moment of quiet, his expression relaxed a degree. "He's not in the house. He's repairing a broken section of fence. You'll have to walk to get there."

"I don't mind."

He explained where to find Ty.

"Thank you, Jake."

He tipped his hat to her and she continued on. The Porter Family Help Squad. To the rescue with her house renovations, bakery renovations, Uncle Danny. To the rescue even now.

She parked and headed into the fields. She had no umbrella. The light rain seeped into her hair and steadily wet her top, heavying it. Tromping over grass dried by summer's heat, she cut diagonally toward the faraway fence line. The ground eventually leveled into a wide upper pasture. She could no longer see Ty's house or barn. Trees speckled the land. A cool breeze swept against her, pushed by the low and scudding pewter clouds.

From a distance, she saw him.

He lifted a fallen plank into place, then went to work with a hammer.

He was soaked. His jeans had gone dark with water and his gray T-shirt had plastered to his body, revealing every tendon and muscle beneath.

Her mouth went dry with trepidation, but she did not slow. She kept on, accompanied by the sound of raindrops pattering against the earth.

When she'd neared to within ten paces, Ty's face jerked up.

They both paused, gazes locking. Gradually, Ty straightened to face her, his features hardening with defensiveness.

My God, she called out within her mind. She loved Ty, and she'd injured him. He was mad at her and, what's worse, she deserved his anger. "Why?" she asked him.

He said nothing. Rain trickled down him in rivulets.

"Did you trade your land for the bakery?"

He tossed the hammer aside. "I did."

"Ty," she choked. "Why?"

With both hands, he raked his hair back from a face that had been weathered by grief since their breakup. His water-darkened hair only made the brilliant blue of his eyes more pronounced.

"Maybe it's not too late to get the land back." She planted her boots. "If you go to Howard or the title company right now and say you've changed your mind, maybe—"

"I haven't changed my mind."

"I want you to go right now! And I want you to do whatever you have to do to stop the deal."

"You can't always get what you want, Celia."

She flinched. "I *know* you care about that land—"

"I don't."

"Yes you do."

"I don't," he growled. "Not if having it means you can't have the bakery."

Tears gathered on her lashes. Truly, she couldn't stand that he'd done this for her. "And I don't want the bakery if it means you can't have the land."

"Too bad, because you're going to keep it." He advanced toward her, predatory. "In fact, you're going to run the place because you own it now."

"You mean, *you* own it now."

"You," he insisted, coming even closer.

"Dictator!"

"Forest fairy."

"Showboat."

"I hate that nickname."

"Showboat!"

"Sweet one," he murmured roughly. He stopped only a foot away.

"What are you going to do now, Ty? Without the land?"

"I don't know."

"Why did you make the trade?"

"You know why. Why did you come all the way out here in this weather to find me?"

"You know why," she said faintly.

"I'd like you to spell it out."

Her courage faltered. Did she dare trust him with it

all? Was she really going to put her life and Addie's life in this man's hands?

All at once and very clearly, she understood that, yes. Yes, she was.

"I love you, Ty."

Moments passed, excruciating, while he stared at her—doing and saying nothing.

Perhaps she needed to try again, louder. "I love you—"

He swept her into his arms and kissed her with fiery possession. One of his hands clasped the back of her head. His other bound her against him.

Water. The smell of a storm. Spiraling pleasure.

He pulled back just enough to look down into her face. "I love you," he said. Then they were kissing again, laughing breathlessly, kissing, gasping for air. Just like when Jerry had told her that Donetta was his person—Ty was hers. Her person. He was too handsome, too strong-willed, too wealthy, too daring, and otherwise not ideal. But he was, most definitely, her person.

He lowered her feet fully to the ground.

"I'm sorry about the things I said to you when we fought." She rested her palms against his chest. "It's no excuse, but I was scared."

"I won't let you down."

"If you ever do, I'll hurt you, Ty. I mean, *really* hurt you. Kill you dead. Physically."

"I might be wrong, but weren't you just in the middle of apologizing to me?"

"Yes. I was." After having been so pious about with-holding forgiveness, it was humbling to be the one in need of it. "Will you forgive me?"

His half smile revealed his dimple. *Oh*, that smile. She

hadn't seen it in days and days. It seemed as though she'd had to swim across a hostile ocean to see it again. She'd swim countless more oceans for the glory of that smile.

"I forgive you, Celia. See how easy that was? Try."

"I forgive you, Ty." And all through her, like the clear chime of a bell, the truth of it reverberated. She'd forgiven him, and it felt like freedom.

"I *forgive* you," Ty said.

"*I* forgive you."

"Good, 'cause I forgive *you*."

They said it back and forth, grinning, emphasizing different words in the sentence.

"Not too painful, huh?" He pressed a featherweight kiss against her forehead.

"Oh, it's painful all right. But it's probably good for me to keep on practicing forgiveness if we're going to be a couple."

"Oh, we're *going* to be a couple."

"Addie will be thrilled."

"She'll say she told us so."

He took hold of her hands, his fingers strong and warm, then brought their joined hands up behind his neck.

She saw them then the way that God did. Though neither she nor Ty had viewed their first wedding as something to be valued, God had. He respected marriages—even ones entered into rashly in Las Vegas wedding chapels. She could suddenly grasp that He'd had a plan for rescuing and repairing their marriage all along. When they hadn't cared, He had. When they'd given up, He hadn't. The bracelet she'd dropped back at that restaurant in Corvallis had seemed at the time like an unlucky coincidence. Now that left-behind bracelet didn't seem like a coincidence at all. It seemed like divine intervention.

"Donetta told me that you've been paying half my salary—"

"What? She promised not to tell."

"Even though you *know* how I feel about you buying things for me. You've been paying half my salary, and now you've bought me a bakery without my permission."

"Sue me."

"You're incorrigible!"

"If I knew what that meant, I'd probably agree."

She gave him a light-as-gossamer kiss. "You're also kind, and you're generous."

"In that case, will you marry me?"

"Are you certain you don't want to marry Tawny instead?"

"A hundred percent certain."

"You're choosing me this time?"

"I'm trying to choose you, but first you need to say you'll marry me."

"I'll marry you. When?"

"Tonight?"

She laughed. "I'm not going to be talked into that again."

"Will you spend the night with me?"

"When?"

"Tonight?"

She wanted to say yes more than she wanted a heartbeat.

"Technically," he reminded her, "we're already married."

"Technically, before I spend the night with you, we're going to need to get married again. This time in a church, with Addie, and a wedding dress, and flowers."

"Will you have a baby with me?"

"I already did."

"I want more babies."

"We'll have to debate that. What do you think about moving your office to the rooms on Cream or Sugar's second story? You could help other people invest their money."

"It's not a bad idea."

"You'd be close to donuts."

"I'd be close to you. What do you think about us all living here at my house together after the wedding?"

"Also up for debate. Your house is going to require a lot of redecorating. . . . Why are you smiling?"

"Because you make me smile."

Joy soared through her. Ty loved her. He loved her and he wanted to marry her. "You make me smile."

"My sweet one." His face lowered toward hers. "My calm. My only love. . . ."

"Yes?"

His lips hovered a breath above hers. "You were meant to be mine."

"Be kind and compassionate to one another,
forgiving each other,
just as in Christ God forgave you."

—Ephesians 4:32

QUESTIONS FOR CONVERSATION

1. Have you ever known anyone who was married in Vegas? What type of wedding did they have?

2. The setup of this novel resulted in the classic "secret baby" plotline. Have you read any other books that told the story of a baby kept secret from his/ her father? Why do you think this plotline has had enduring appeal over the years?

3. Ty and Celia talk about whether forgiveness is a decision, a feeling, or an act. What is your opinion?

4. Can you share a time from your life when you struggled to forgive? How did God work in you through that season?

5. Which scenes made you laugh? Which made you angry? Which made you emotional?

6. Were you able to spot any metaphors in the novel? Hint: there were at least three.

7. Over the course of the story, Celia is able to realize

a dream she'd left behind long before. Have you ever had the opportunity to rediscover something you once loved?

8. Do you think Celia is perfect for Ty or vice versa? What made them an ideal match (even though it took them both a very long time to see it)?

9. How are Becky Wade's novels different from other Christian romances?

10. In the end, Ty sacrificed something he wanted for Celia's happiness. Becky Wade likes to portray sacrifice in her novels because she believes it is a hallmark of true love. What's something that someone has sacrificed for you or that you've sacrificed for someone you love?

Becky Wade is a native of California who attended Baylor University, met and married a Texan, and moved to Dallas. She published historical romances for the general market, then put her career on hold for several years to care for her children. When God called her back to writing, Becky knew He meant for her to turn her attention to Christian fiction. Her humorous, heart-pounding contemporary romance novels have won the Carol Award, the INSPY Award, and the Inspirational Reader's Choice Award for Romance. Becky lives in Dallas, Texas, with her husband and three children.

To find out more about Becky and her books,
visit www.beckywade.com.